LAST STAND: VIETNAM

As suddenly as it started, the heavy mortar barrage ceased, only to be replaced by the tearing tarpaper sound of light and medium machine guns using not only the heavier 7.62mm ammunition of the old Type 68 assault weapon but also that of the newer 5.6mm CQ automatic rifle.

Following the blare of a Chinese bugle someone on the west U.S.-Vietnamese side of the gully shouted, "They're coming!" Through the undergrowth they could see Chinese regulars, whose helmets were covered in camouflage netting.

Those first up to the edge were machine-gunned immediately. One Chinese at the middle of a ten-man charge tripped a claymore, and all ten were felled by the ball bearings that exploded toward them in a steel curtain at supersonic speed. But the Chinese kept coming and dying. . . .

WWIII: SOUTH CHINA SEA

Ian Slater

FAWCETT GOLD MEDAL • NEW YORK

A Fawcett Gold Medal Book
Published by Ballantine Books
Copyright © 1996 by Bunyip Enterprises, Inc.

All rights reserved under International and Pan-American Copyright Conventions. Published in the United States by Ballantine Books, a division of Random House, Inc., New York, and simultaneously in Canada by Random House of Canada Limited, Toronto.

http://www.randomhouse.com

Library of Congress Catalog Card Number: 95-96161

ISBN 0-449-14932-3

Manufactured in the United States of America

First Edition: June 1996

10 9 8 7 6 5 4 3 2 1

For Marian, Serena, and Blair

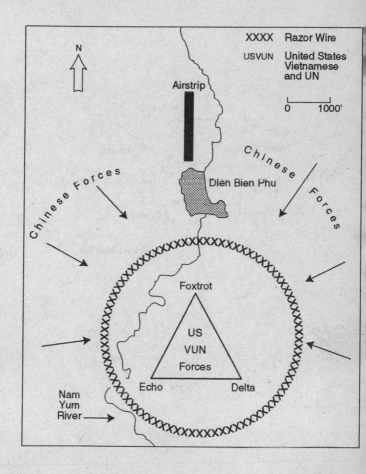

N

XXXX   Razor Wire

USVUN   United States
        Vietnamese
        and UN

0   1000'

Airstrip

Chinese Forces

Chinese Forces

Dien Bien Phu

XXXXXXXXXXXXXXXXX

Foxtrot

US
VUN
Forces

Echo   Delta

Nam
Yum
River

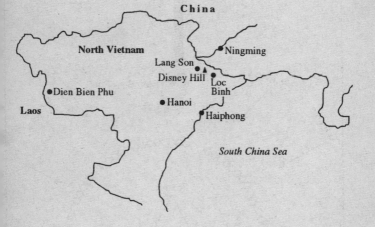

China

North Vietnam

Ningming

Lang Son

Disney Hill

Loc
Binh

Dien Bien Phu

Laos

Hanoi

Haiphong

South China Sea

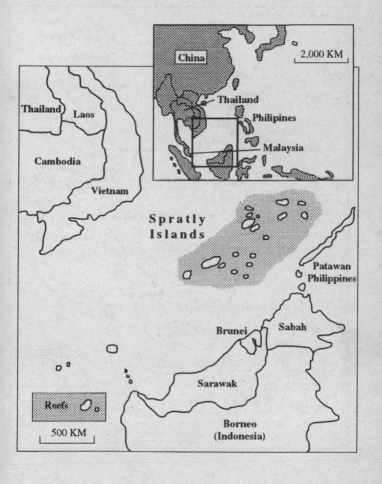

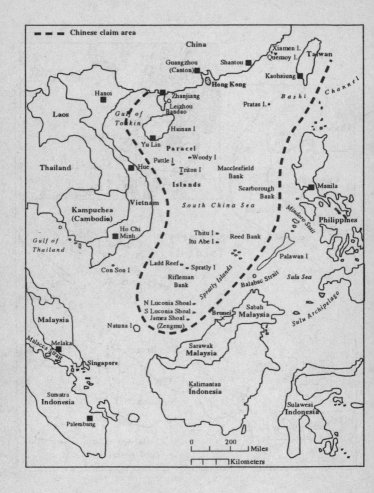

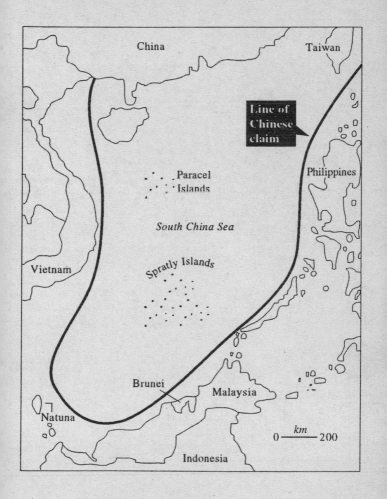

For Vietnam, which fears that China will one day use military power to enforce its claim over the entire South China Sea and its potentially rich oil reserves, the desirability of inviting American forces back into the disputed neighborhood is a form of insurance against what is seen as Chinese hegemonism.

—*The New York Times*, November 1994

WW III: SOUTH CHINA SEA

PROLOGUE

North Carolina

AT THE EMERGENCY Response Force training area at Fort Bragg, one of the recruits was puzzled when told in no uncertain terms that he had to take his dog tags off—put one around his neck, the other in his boot.

"Why my boot?"

"Because," the sergeant said, "if we ever go into combat, you might get decapitated. Then we wouldn't know who you are—correction, *were*."

"That's nice. Thank God we ain't at war."

"Sonny," the sergeant said in his southern drawl, shaking his head, "we could be at war anytime. The new world order is disorder. Since the Berlin Wall came down, since Russia's shake-up, we got more flashpoints poppin' up than you can shake a stick at."

Thousands of miles to the east, in the Pacific, west of the Marianas, the USS *Enterprise* was in its prelaunch mode. High up in the carrier's island in Primary Flight Control, the yellow-jerseyed air boss issued the command for all hands on deck for an FOD, or foreign object damage, walkdown. A dropped pencil or, in the case of the female sailors aboard, something as outwardly insignificant as a bobby pin, could be sucked in and destroy a jet engine or take out the eye of a deck or air crew member.

The FOD walkdown, usually a tedious business with a string of sailors stretched from side to side on the flight deck, heads all down, was fast becoming a more popular duty—with females to walk with and bump into. The air boss didn't like the new Pentagon order assigning women aboard all naval vessels except submarines. Quite frankly, he was afraid a male sailor's downward gaze would soon shift from a deck to a bosom and miss something.

"What are you doing tonight?" a gunner's mate, Stevens, A., head down, asked Able-Bodied Sailor Elizabeth Franks, who was a "grape," a purple jacket, a refueler. They couldn't help but brush up against one another, the line was so tight.

"I think I'll watch a movie," she replied. "You?"

"Ah . . ." said Stevens, a man she'd never seen before. "Think I'll watch a movie too."

"You know what's on?"

"Don't care what's on," he said, shooting her a knowing glance.

"How come?" she asked.

"Oh," he said, "I come pretty much the same as any other guy. Only better."

"Sheesh! Can't you guys ever get your mind out of your shorts?"

"Nope."

"You're married," she said, seeing his wedding band.

"So?"

"Hey, you two!" hollered a bosun. "Less talk, more walk!"

Stevens complained under his breath, "This is gonna be one hell of a cruise. See you later."

Stevens *would* see her later—in the South China Sea— and it would be one hell of a cruise, but for reasons none of the five thousand aboard the mighty carrier could possibly imagine.

Amid the white and gold elegance of the White House's East Room, the President of the United States sat in the center front row, listening to a string quartet playing Vivaldi's "Four Seasons." The music of fall passed into the bleakness of winter, and in that moment he felt the full weight of his office. Politically, the change from the cold war to the new world order had, ironically, meant more disorder than ever before, and with the collapse of the Soviet Union, America alone was the superpower.

But superpower or not, it could not be the world's policeman. It could not be everywhere at the same time. Hard decisions had to be made. Involvement in the Balkans and what used to be Yugoslavia—no; Somalia—yes; Haiti, yes. And every time the President made such a decision, it involved American lives—the world now so volatile in the absence of the

Soviet-U.S. balance that trouble could and did start anywhere. Sometimes a place the President had never heard of before suddenly erupted in violence and was emblazoned across the world's headlines via the vast electronic net of CNN.

In the music there were the stirrings of spring, but winter still held sway, and while the President of the United States listened to promises of spring, thousands of miles west of the East Room, Danny Mellin was still deep in an American winter. . . .

CHAPTER ONE

Oklahoma

ONE GLANCE SOUTHWARD and Danny Mellin knew he was in trouble, the advance winds of the twister coming his way having already dropped the temperature to minus thirty. But he wouldn't stop drilling—couldn't stop. Besides, they'd reached 3,600 feet, and at $11.50 a foot and already in the hole with the bank, Mellin figured he didn't have much choice. His sturdy five-foot-nine-inch frame stood out against the oil rig as he watched the derrick hand fifty feet up the hundred-foot-high rig swing out and help bully a new sixty-foot stand of pipe into position over a massive block, snow-dusted and black around its eye, looking like some enormous predatory head bent on battering the rig to pieces. Beyond, everywhere Mellin looked, the scene was an endless expanse of snow.

Danny, forty-five but looking older, was stamping his feet by the lazy bench, the relief crew warming up in the tin doghouse whose loose roof panel kept flapping in the wind. The bit was going through the Oklahoma rock beneath the barren, snow-flat landscape at just over three feet a minute, and Danny started arguing with himself—the logical, reasonable half of him telling him to pull 'er out and wrap it up, not to tempt the storm, before they got to the four-thousand-foot level. The seismic maps told him he'd probably have another two hundred feet to go before he could hope for a good enough layer that might yield production—*if* there was any oil there at all.

Everyone who wasn't a roughneck, even some of the "worms"—the apprentice roughnecks—thought that all an independent like Danny did was stand around the doghouse worrying the hole, and that when he wasn't at the hole he must be wheeling and dealing in the taverns—that it was all booze and pussy talk. But Danny had spent most of the week on the phone calming down a landowner who said that the mud and drainage pit Danny had drilled last summer hadn't dried properly before being "dozed" over.

Then there was the lease on the equipment. With the Mideast situation as dicey as ever, everyone who had a truck and rusty pipe was trying to make a buck Stateside, sending the rentals cost sky-high. Price of crude had shot right through the roof, and it meant drilling for wells in country that would have been ignored a year before because of cheaper oil. And it had brought out cowboys, along with the roughnecks, guys who were dreaming of a repeat of the big boom of the early eighties and who didn't think about the bust that could follow. Already half a dozen guys, all of them over fifty—most repatriated from the Clinton cutbacks in the armed services after the Iraqi War—had lost a hand or a finger in the quick chain wrap as they'd tried to put on another thirty-foot pipe.

This hole was Rummer Number 6, Rummer being the name of the landowner. The first five holes had been dusters, as dry as an Oakie's throat, so the crew had dubbed this one "Bummer Number Six."

"What's the mud doctor say?" the foreman shouted in the rising wind.

"Same dose as yesterday," Danny answered. The truth was, he hadn't had the rock fragments from yesterday analyzed by a geologist for the best cooling mud, figuring from his own observation that the rock layer they were going through was the same as yesterday's. He could be wrong, but the geologist had been held up by the snow and Danny wasn't going to wait. Every hour with a payroll of fourteen put him further in the damn hole. Besides, you never knew when the next sucker could be your opener for a million-barrel well; then it'd be Hawaii and cold cans of Coors from daylight to dark.

"The shit it would be," his foreman said. "You'd start drilling Waikiki, Danny."

"Yeah, I reckon," Danny admitted. He cupped his hands and shouted across the ice-crusted platform, "What are we now?"

"Thirty-six twenty," the foreman shouted back.

"When we get to 'fifty, better start doing a drill stem." Glancing at his watch, then at the vast, bruised sky, Danny added, "Wiley said he'd be here 'round ten."

The foreman raised his thumb to show he'd heard. Wiley was a "kiosk" geologist with a fold-down, fold-up portable lab, but analysts aside, Danny believed it was as much a matter of sheer luck. You had to be in the right place—a few feet either way and you could miss the pocket, rock reservoirs of oil formed in the waves of sedimentary layers.

Danny wasn't looking for hundred-foot jets of black gold shooting up in the air—that was all Clark Gable and Gary Cooper crap. All he wanted was enough pressure to tap the sucker. And Rummer was no dummy dirt farmer. With his computer, he knew the market almost as quickly as the hustlers on Wall Street, and had insisted on one in six barrels before he'd signed to give Danny drilling rights. Everybody was upping the ante. And some of the cowboys, the Johnny-come-latelies, were rushing in to make their fortune, urged by the government with new tax breaks to drill fast and deep. In Kansas they were even unzipping some of the "stripper" holes— marginal wells of 110 barrels a day that they'd previously plugged. Danny had been in the game for twenty years after 'Nam, and claimed he could smell oil-impregnated rock even before it was separated from the coolant. Anyway, the cowboys'd be sorted out in the first month or so. When they didn't hear anyone yelling "Eureka!" they'd fold with the overdraft. That's when you had to have balls, Danny told himself. In hard times you dig deeper. All the easy oil was gone. Didn't mean there wasn't a million-barrel field around, but you had to hang tough.

There was a hoarse-throated roar from the diesel engine, coughing dirty, coal-brown smoke into the virginal white of wind-driven snow, and everything started to rattle and shake, tiny ice splinters falling down and hitting his hard hat like rock candy as the crew began hauling up pipe for the drill-stem test. Danny put another stick of gum in his mouth, the gum so stiff with the cold it broke like a board. It would be hours before the test results came in. "For cryin' out loud," he said, rolling the gum's silver foil wrapper between his grease-stained gloves, his eyes squinting in the direction of a battered

Cherokee pickup, snow blowing off the back of it like icing sugar. It was Rummer, the farmer who owned the land. He had every right to "visit" under the terms of the contract, but in Danny's twenty years, a well had never come in whenever the landowner showed up. They were plain bad luck.

"Danny!" the foreman called out.

"Yeah?"

"Mud bags are frozen up."

Danny was already holding Rummer responsible for the lack of oil. "Well, unfreeze the fuckers!" he yelled back at the foreman, adding that if Rummer 6 didn't come in today, he'd pack it in, the whole shebang.

"Listen," the foreman said encouragingly. "Maybe old Rummer's different from the rest. Maybe he'll bring us luck, Danny."

Danny walked down from the platform, smacked his boots together, knocking off sticky mud-colored snow, and asked the drill tester, "What's it look like?"

The tester made a face like his mother had just died.

"Shit," Danny mumbled, then seeing Rummer walking over from the pickup, the wind and freezing rain sounding stronger by the minute, he put out his hand, smiling broadly. "Hi, Mr. Rummer. How ya doin'?"

"Fine. Yourself?"

"Terrific," Danny lied. "We could need hulls here any time." He meant the sacks of cotton wool used to soak up the oil if it came up and slopped out over the derrick's deck. One of the roughnecks, warming his hands in the doghouse, shook his head, looking over at one of the two "worms" on the crew. "We could have fuck-all here, that's what we could have."

Danny had lost a worm once when a tornado, screaming out of Missouri, had hit one of the derricks, sucking the sixty-foot pipe stands up high, as if they were straw. He'd told the kid's parents their boy'd been killed while changing pipe. Danny had found that when you told parents that their son had died on a rig, they didn't feel as bad if they heard he was actually working at the time rather than just standing around. Having been a Special Forces type in 'Nam, Danny knew how he, his parents, and his wife Maureen had felt when the Army told him that Angela, one of his two sisters in 'Nam, a nurse, was missing. The other sister had been killed off duty in a Medevac unit by so-called "friendly fire." Danny wished they'd lied and said the Viet Cong had killed both. "Missing" meant a ninety-nine percent certainty that Angela was dead, but there was always that one percent that made some nights hell for him and his family.

There was nothing unusual about the hurricane. It came in as most do, off Cuba, northwest up through the gulf, laden with evaporated seawater, slamming into the Texas coast then pivoting halfway between Corpus Christi and Galveston, gusting at over two hundred miles per hour. It immediately lost some speed and heat energy—enough to generate Houston's electric supply for years—and though it hit the mainland, there was still enough fury left for the Midwest.

As the hurricane tore into the southeastern corner of Oklahoma, gusting to 140-plus miles per hour, long, bruised spirals of tornadoes peeled off from the hurricane's eye wall, a darker vortex already swirling purplish-black with rain and dust and debris about the calm core. The spiral heading toward the rig was one of a dozen stalks of tornadoes formed in the same way, howling with the bloodcurdling wail that mixed with the thunder and the rattle of an express train roaring out of control. Swirling tunnels of wind and rain preceded it, smashing into the tin-roofed doghouse, tearing it apart, sending the roof spinning high into the vortex and casting it down again, a section of roof whirling faster now, slicing off one of the roughnecks' arms, the bloodied limb sucked up and lost in the maelstrom into which several sixty-foot-high barrels from the pipe stand had also vanished—to come down a quarter hour later, strewn over southwestern Arkansas.

The roughneck bled to death. Most of the other dead the tornado left in its wake—fourteen—died when the hurricane's surge, a towering wall of water over twenty-one feet in height, slammed into the Texas coast east of Corpus Christi. Danny Mellin and the rest of his remaining five-man rig crew barely escaped with their lives.

It was the closest he'd come to losing his life since his days in Vietnam, where he was taken prisoner and spent a year in the "Hanoi Hilton." So right then and there, throwing up as he saw the mangled body of what had been one of his workers writhing in the snow, Danny Mellin decided he'd had enough of Oklahoma. He'd work for someone else for a change, somewhere he'd be paid a lot for his experience, somewhere someone else had the responsibility for the crew, somewhere he wouldn't have to worry about a crew or making payroll, or freezing in the bone-chilling winds of a midwestern winter.

He decided he'd work for one of the joint U.S.-Chinese oil exploration companies operating in the Spratly Islands. Big pay and warmth. His wife wasn't happy, but he promised her he'd stick with it for only a year.

And so it was, that like the American in the 1930s who had decided to escape a depression-racked America for a more simple, peaceful life on a South Sea island called Guadalcanal, Danny Mellin chose to work in the tropics on a drill ship in the South China Sea. No heavy gear to wear over there. "Hell," he told friends, "all you'd need is your hard hat, a pair of swim shorts, and suntan lotion. Paradise."

CHAPTER TWO

South China Sea

BENEATH A TROPICAL copper sky, day was ending, a current of heavy swells coming down south from Palawan Island in the southern Philippines, curving westward through the Spratly Islands and on over 1,800 kilometers across the South China Sea, toward the lush green coast of Vietnam.

The drill ship, a half-Chinese, half-Californian oil venture, the MV *Chical 1*, known to its crew as simply *Chical*, rose and fell with the swells. Her antiroll tanks minimized the pitch and yaw of the ship so that her drill rig would remain as perpendicular to the sea's surface as possible, the drill column going straight down through the moon pool where the *Chical*'s interior midships was open to the sea like a huge, bright, floodlit swimming pool.

Down below there was the mystery of the coral reef and sedimentary layers as yet unexplored by the drill. They might hold treasure, if the profile gained by seismic shots was promising. Explosions of sound sent down to penetrate the subsurface layers reverberated back from folds or fault lines along which oil may have pooled or natural gas been enclosed. If the drill ship, as opposed to a drill platform, didn't find oil over one reef, it could sail on to the next site amid the archipelago's more than two hundred reefs, cays, and tiny islands. What the *Chical* lost in the stability of a fixed platform, it gained in more seabed covered.

It was purely by chance that one of the Chinese roughnecks working on the weather deck amid the forward port-quarter pipe rack saw the junk, the *Ling Chow*, in the fading copper sea. But he couldn't claim credit for seeing its flag— Vietnamese, a yellow star on a blood-red background—which was flying upside down, the universal distress signal, which meant its radio must be down, or perhaps it had none. The man who first recognized that the flag was upside down—two of the star's five points on the bottom instead of at the top— was Danny Mellin, working a hundred feet high from a monkey board and safety harness up by the derrick man's console and upper racking arm and carriage.

Danny pulled out his walkie-talkie, its aerial snagged for a moment in a strap of his Mae West, and told the pilothouse where *Chical*'s Chinese captain could get a fix on the damaged junk. The *Chical*'s captain, seeing the junk's minisail shredded, ordered several Chinese and American roustabouts to go starboard amidship to lend a hand bringing the junk alongside. Of course, there was always a risk involved in the South China Sea, infested by modern-day pirates who, among other outrages, had preyed so mercilessly on the Vietnamese boat people trying to escape. While the *Chical* helped the *Ling Chow*, drilling would have to be suspended for a while as the extra pitch and roll of the disabled junk, its bamboo sail battens or stiffeners creaking in the wind, would only add to the swells, sloshing against *Chical*'s starboard side.

The sick man they brought aboard the MV *Chical* was strapped down but nevertheless thrashing about in great pain, his face drenched in sweat. He jabbered incomprehensibly in a Vietnamese-Chinese border dialect, and the first aid man aboard the drill ship, a roughneck called Perowitz from New Jersey, was sent to have a look-see to calm him down. Apart from possible fever—Perowitz pressed the automatic thermometer's green button and stuck it in the crewman's mouth—there seemed to be no serious internal problems. Perowitz asked the man what he'd eaten, and his fellow seaman said some rice and fish. Had the rest of the junk's crew eaten the same?

"Yes," a man who seemed to understand a bit of English replied.

And had they all had something to drink? "I mean, drinking the same stuff?" Perowitz pressed.

One of the men who set the stretcher on the drill ship's deck nodded urgently. "Yes, yes, Tsing Tao." It was the Chinese beer that everyone drank on the *Chical* as well.

So the best Perowitz could suggest, seeing how much pain the man was in—the man indicating a lot of gas, his hands arcing over his belly in the shape of a huge balloon—was perhaps a good shot of Pepto-Bismol. A couple of minutes after he had given the man the dose, it looked as if it was working.

"Ah, you've got a bellyful of gas—that's all."

Unknowing brown faces looked at him in the twilight.

"You know," Perowitz said, now in a pantomime mode. "Gas!"

"You drill for?" one of the junk crew said.

"What?" Perowitz laughed. "No, no—not gas like we drill for. You know—uh, fart!"

They were still looking blankly at him when he bent forward and made a fart noise with his mouth. Their immediate recognition was hailed with raucous laughter and a splash off the stern. Mellin could hear the splash from high up near the derrick man's console, since they had stopped drilling. He radioed down to the well deck foreman. "Hey, Randy?"

"Yeah?"

"Somebody threw something over. You tell those junk boys not to dump any of their garbage. Could get caught up in our gear under the moon pool."

"You got it," the deckhand said, and made his way over to the *Chical*'s starboard side.

Only one or two of the dim figures he called out to understood what he meant, and the captain of the junk said it wouldn't happen again. "Sorry." And that impressed several of the Caucasian crew aboard *Chical*, because they'd always believed Asians usually couldn't handle the *r* sound. At that moment oil began rushing up, spilling out like a fine spray as if it was a signal—when in fact it was pure coincidence. The rickety bamboo gangway leading to the *Chical* was suddenly covered in crew from the junk, and Perowitz fell—shot through the head—the crew from the junk running past his body, the twilight spiked by the barrels of their AK-74s.

The first stutter heard by Mellin came from the radio shack just aft of the wheelhouse. The operator, another American, was dead even before his bullet-riddled body hit the deck. His blood made the decking slippery for those who quickly ran to the pilothouse, spraying its glass. Then he finished off the three men on watch once inside. One of the junk men's AK-74s jammed as the *Chical*'s captain, revolver in hand, emerged from his cabin aft of the port side of the wheelhouse. He got one shot away, hitting an attacker, who fell while another brought a short broadsword down hard and fast in a sweep, disemboweling the captain.

Even with all the noise going on, the engine room crew of the *Chical* didn't hear a thing, the chief engineer checking the generating room gauges and making sure the tension on the stabilizer anchor chains wasn't excessive, the chains helping to hold the ship as near one spot as possible. The first engine room man to know anything was wrong was a Virginian, Gary Sales. Having just emerged from a forward hatch onto the well deck, he was struck on the head by a short broadsword, as the captain had been. It split his skull, his grayish brain oozing out beneath the bright deck lights as his body slumped and fell back down to the generating room with a sickening thud.

Danny Mellin was already on his two-way radio yelling a warning. Hearing it, several men working on the aft well deck around the pipe rack dropped what they'd been doing and retreated toward the galley. But they were slaughtered en masse by a dozen of the junk's crew who had climbed up the stern ladder and then, taking over the heliport, raced down the gangway to the living quarters to butcher over twenty more Americans and Chinese asleep or resting off watch.

Now, in the darkness, Mellin understood the splash he'd heard: one of the junk's crewmen had probably jumped off into the water prior to boarding the *Chical* aft of the living quarters and galley. But then why hadn't he heard more splashes? And it suddenly occurred to him, as he heard the zing and whack of 5.45mm rounds spitting up from the deck, that they were climbing up the rig, toward him.

He had only one way to go: not up higher into the rig— they'd keep climbing or firing until they got him—and he couldn't go down. He'd have to jump the hundred feet into the sea instead. But it had to be timed right, when the *Chical* rose and shifted from port to starboard on a long swell; otherwise, if he didn't get enough angle, he wouldn't clear the ship's deck. He heard another burst of AK-74, a sound which, along with that of the older AK-47s, he'd never forgotten from his days in 'Nam, and he heard the perspex in the derrick man's console splitting apart as it was raked by automatic fire. Then the deck lights went out. Red tongues of fire spat up into the derrick, ricocheting, zinging, and whining about.

As the *Chical* rolled to port, Danny clicked the safety harness release button and, as hard as he could, pushed himself off, jumping out into the darkness that smelled now of cordite and salt air. He hit feet first but at an angle, his lower back slapping the water like hard rubber on concrete. He thought he'd broken his spine. Sighting the spray of phosphorescence as he splashed into the water, the junk crew members fired into the general area, a hail of hot, sizzling 7.6mm and 5.45mm splattering about him.

Mellin began a slow breaststroke away from the ship, refusing the temptation to pull the CO_2 cartridge on his Mae West. An inflated vest would keep him afloat but would prevent him from swimming, leaving him totally at the mercy of the current, which was flowing away from the coast of Brunei beyond the rig, back farther west toward more of the Spratlys. He'd wait and dog-paddle as long as he could, until the junk had cast off, then maybe he could swim against the current and back toward the drill ship.

It was hopeless and he knew it. The current was too strong to swim against, and he was swept slowly but inexorably out to sea away from *Chical*. His only hope now was to be picked up by one of the *Chical*'s weatherproof life rafts, which could hold up to sixteen men.

This too was a vain hope, for back aboard the *Chical* the junk's crew was systematically destroying every Beaufort life raft canister and lifeboat on the drill ship, mainly with grenades. Out of the sixty-four men, from geologists to cooks and drillers, roughnecks and roustabouts, crane operators and mud loggers, welders and motormen, fifty-three were dead, leaving only eleven—including Mellin—who had made it off the drill ship before the junk crew could get to them. And now only six of these were still alive, the other five already taken by sharks. The predators, attracted by the turbulence of ship bumping against ship and the smell of blood in the water, killed the five—all Americans—in a feeding frenzy around *Chical*'s stern.

Now almost a quarter mile away, Mellin could hear the heavy-throated chugging of the junk under way, and nearer him he could dimly make out the jagged outline of oil-smeared planks.

In the North Sea he would have been dead already from hypothermia, but in the warmer waters of the South China Sea his death would be a lingering one, dying of dehydration in a world of water, unless he were taken by sharks.

Then he saw a high cone of roiling fire, its orange tongue curling hundreds of feet high, immediately followed by the thunderclap of an explosion. The wellhead had been blown, just as Saddam Insane had blown the wells in the Middle East. It didn't make sense. What did they want?

Now he heard popping sounds, the junk crew using the madly dancing reflections of the wellhead fire on the water to take potshots at the Chinese and American bodies floating about the *Chical*, the junk men making sure that all were dead. And in the strange penumbra of firelight, Mellin could see the black scimitars of shark fins cruising just below the surface.

Danny thought of his wife Maureen and promised God that if he were saved, he'd go back home and never leave the United States again. He hadn't been this scared since 'Nam, and he began to pray again, "Our Father . . ." for if nothing else, that would keep him awake, something in his gut telling him that if his fatigue passed into sleep, it would be the sleep of the dead.

Now the Mae West light went on, the salt having activated it, doing what it was supposed to. Immediately Danny cupped his hand over the bulb, cutting himself somehow on a nail in the loose raft of planks, leaving blood in the water. He jerked the CO_2 cord and the Mae West inflated, but he kept his right hand over the bulb lest the junk crew spot the pinpoint of light in the vastness of the sea and come to kill him. He remembered a prayer he'd always said with his two daughters when they were children:

> . . . tender shepherd, hear me . . .
> Through the darkness be Thou near me,
> Keep me safe till morning's light.

Beneath his hand, held over the light as if he was taking the oath of allegiance, he could feel the pulsing of his heart. It was so faint that for a moment he thought it had stopped.

The sound of the wellhead explosion—traveling at least four times faster in water than in air—raced up east of the Palawan Trough over the two thousand fathoms on the eastern edge of the South China Basin, through Luzon Strait past Taiwan and west of the Ryukyu Islands Trench, where it was heard by a Sound Surveillance System listening post on Taiwan's east coast and another on the southernmost tip of Japan's southern island of Kyushu. From the SOSUS listening post on Kyushu the message passed through the chain of command from the Seventh Fleet's command ship, *Blue Ridge*, the message marked IMMEDIATE TO CINCPAC—Commander in Chief Pacific—copy to Pentagon, Secretary of Navy, Secretary of Defense, and on to the President as Commander-in-Chief.

1662 HOURS RECEIVED SUBSTANTIAL SONAR BLIP STOP ESTIMATE SOURCE SPRATLY ISLANDS STOP LATITUDE APPROXIMATELY 9 DEGREES NORTH LONGITUDE 115 DEGREES 10 MINUTES EAST STOP SONAR TRACE INDICATES MAN-MADE EXPLOSION NOT VOLCANIC STOP MESSAGE ENDS

CHAPTER THREE

The White House

THE MESSAGE HAD merely mentioned an explosion, and they'd have to wait till morning Brunei time to find out exactly what was involved, but the mention of the Spratlys had Admiral Reese, Chief of Naval Operations, already off and running. The suspected explosion, if it was man-made, could be sabotage on one of the oil rigs or drill ships. If so, it opened a hornet's nest of geopolitical significance.

"Mr. President," CNO Reese said, "there are two consequences that directly resulted from the earlier administration's defense cuts and lack of strategic overview in East Asia. Number one, they cut the budget first, as usual, then tried to figure out strategy. Back to front."

"Stern to bow, Admiral," the President joshed.

Reese allowed himself a brief smile in return, but his mood was too braced for relaxing this day. "The second point, Mr. President, is that because of our cutbacks and our loss of Subic Bay and Clark Field in the Philippines, we are perceived by the East and Southeast Asian countries no longer as 'stayers.' I mean by this that our loss of a solid base from which to move into the South China Sea, despite the Seventh Fleet's berthing facilities in Singapore, creates the perception in these Third World countries—and not only in them—that this is not a United States determined to stay for the long haul. And in that mode of uncertainty, we have individual countries starting an arms race in the region. They figure if the U.S. doesn't have a firm foreign policy—or rather, a policy determined primarily by strategic responsibilities instead of budget deficit considerations—then they have to look after themselves. Can't say I blame 'em."

The admiral turned to a wall chart on naval growth in the Pacific. "China makes no bones about the fact that she wants blue water capability. She's been hankering for it for a long time. She hasn't got it yet, but in our perceived absence she means to have it as quickly as possible. SIGINT tells us that the Chinese plan to be ready with carriers, the new Luhu guided missile destroyers, and the new Russian Kilo derivative submarines by 2007. That's not far away, Mr. President. We had hoped we might continue to cut the U.S. deficit by selling them some of our used carriers and other warships. Problem is, Russia is offering bargain-basement prices in China and Southeast Asia. Most importantly, potential buyers know the Russians can establish 'through-life' support and maintenance, because the Russians, ironically, keep building them while we're cutting back and are unable to promise any kind of 'through-life' warranty."

The admiral's assistant flicked over the China chart to one of Japan. "A further measure of these Asian countries' independence is the fact that the Japanese Defense Force, for example, now has the best ship-carrying air defense system."

"In Southeast Asia?" the President interjected.

"No, sir," the CNO replied. Maybe he was getting through at last, he thought. "The best in the *world*."

"Could I cut in here?" asked David Noyer, director of the CIA.

"Please," the President invited.

"Mr. President, in addition to what the admiral says, the agency is convinced that Japan has a three- to four-month capability to develop nuclear bombs."

The President tried not to show any surprise, but his assistant, Bruce Ellman, spotted the telltale push of the leather-bound blotter atop the desk, where he was glancing at the cable from the SOSUS posts.

"In twelve to sixteen weeks," the President said, "you're telling me Japan could field nuclear bombs?"

"Yes," Noyer replied. "In November 'ninety-three they began importing over twenty tons of plutonium for their fast breeder reactors. At least that's what they told us it was for. They already had over five hundred pounds of the stuff by the late eighties."

"That shipment from France?" Admiral Reese put in.

"Correct," Noyer confirmed.

Reese shook his head disgustedly. "Those damn Frenchmen'd sell arsenic to their mothers if they could."

The President ignored George Reese's well-known Francophobia, which stemmed from France's refusal to let the U.S. Air Force fly through French airspace en route to bomb Khadafy in Libya years before.

"And," Reese added, "more to the point, I'll warrant that our intelligence agency isn't the only one that knows of the Japanese capabilities." He looked at Noyer. "No offense to the CIA, David."

"None taken, Admiral," Noyer assured him. "You've hit the proverbial nail on the head. Ever since Shinseito—the conservative New Life party in Japan—gained power over the socialists, they've helped push the Liberal Democratic party majority in support of a more active role for the Japanese Defense Force."

"The Japanese *offense* force," the President posited.

"Well, whatever they want to call it, Mr. President, I don't think you can fault them, with that maniac North Korean within nuclear- and Scud-hitting distance of Tokyo."

"No," the President agreed, "you can't, but if I get your drift, gentlemen, you're telling me that because of our lack of a firm foreign policy—compliments of the previous administration—Japan as well as the Southeast Asian countries we've mentioned in the area feel more vulnerable because of our withdrawal from the Philippine bases. So they're seeking the capacity to defend themselves should North Korea or anyone else start a war. They also see Japan rearming in the face of increased Russian presence in the East China Sea, and know North Korea probably has nuclear weapons. In any case, I seriously doubt that their Southeast Asian neighbors' intelligence agencies don't know about Japan's nuclear ability too—and that alone would frighten the bejaysus out of any of Japan's neighbors."

Noyer and Reese nodded in unison, with Reese turning to the next info chart. "Exactly. Malaysia, Indonesia, Philippines, Vietnam, China were all attacked by Japan in World War Two when her oil and raw materials ran out after FDR's embargo. And if this Spratly Islands issue blows up and there's a shooting gallery in and around the trade routes from the Middle East that pass through there, then Japan couldn't last very long without acquiring new oil and raw materials that come through to her via the South China Sea."

"So now," the President said, "we have North Korea, South Korea, Japan, Taiwan, Thailand, Malaysia, Singapore, and Indonesia all rearming as fast as they can."

"Yes, sir. Even the Aussies and New Zealanders are upgrading."

"Why?"

"They've got a defense pact with Malaysia, Singapore, and Brunei, but Indonesia's presence in West Irian, or what used to be called West New Guinea, is the Australians' big worry. You think we have human rights problems with China vis-à-vis our trade and most-favored-nation clause. You should look at Australia's Joint Intelligence Bureau report on what the Indonesians are up to in West Irian and Timor. It's take the villagers out and shoot them on the spot. Besides, Indonesia's population is 175 million, Australia's is barely fifteen, and it's only a half-hour hop from New Guinea to Australia. All the Aussies have up there in the north are crocodiles and Darwin. Most Australians are crammed into the far southeast corner.

"We've got some damned important defense radar and communications sites up there," Reese concluded.

"They wouldn't last long," Noyer said, "if the Indonesians really wanted to get them. But I'm not concerned about the

Aussies for the moment. It's all this strutting in the Southeast Asian states over the Spratlys that's got me worried."

"Yes," the President said, cutting in. "We've got to run this Spratly incident to ground—if you'll pardon the mixed metaphor—before the accusations start flying, giving every one of those countries the national justification for rearming. Nothing like a nice little war, gentlemen, to boost the ruling parties' fortunes at home."

"Good point," Noyer conceded. "We've got our finger on the pulse with regards to that one—our military attachés, et cetera—but it's difficult to see the whole picture at any one time. Too many players."

"Too many or not," the President continued, "we've got to get on top of this thing. And I want the American public informed because if, God forbid, I have to send American boys over there, I don't want it done on some damned flimsy bit of evidence."

Noyer sighed. "It'll be difficult. I mean, the American public isn't used to thinking about Southeast Asia. Now, if it was Europe—"

"Well, they'd better start," the President said unequivocally, "because we all know, gentlemen, we're on the threshold of the Pacific century. Europe's only going to constitute six and a half percent of the world's population, and in any case it's going to have to fix its own business. But if we're to look after *our* business—and I don't want to put this thing just in terms of dollars and cents, but the dollars and cents are there nevertheless—we need those Asian trade routes more than most, and we need them open all the time."

"Agreed," Noyer said. "I think we had better start some position papers for selected congressmen."

"Not for selected congressmen, David, for *all* congressmen. That's another thing I don't want going on around here. If it leaks out that we're only giving the information to certain congressmen, it'll look like what it is—selective feeding. I don't want any part of that. Not in this situation. I agree, you're right, the foreign policy of this country's been a basket case due to the previous administration. But now's the time—and I hope to God it isn't too late—that we can send out the message that we do not want, nor will we tolerate, another Yugoslavia in Asia."

"Mr. President," Noyer said, "I wouldn't be honest with you

if I didn't tell you that that's exactly what we might end up with."

"Initially," the President conceded, "we may not be able to prevent that, but my point is that if it starts, we're not going to have a grannies' conference here and take six months to decide what we're going to do. I want the information about what's going on down there confirmed and reconfirmed, and I want a U.S.-led U.N. multilateral strategic and tactical plan on my desk within seventy-two hours. That will tell me what we are in a position to undertake and, perhaps more importantly, what we are *not* in a position to do at the moment."

"We'll do the best we can, Mr. President."

"Another thing, David," the President warned Noyer, "I don't want any CNN reporter scooping me on the 'Larry King Show.' Got that?"

"Yes, sir."

"How did they do that in Iraq? I mean CNN getting all that stuff out of Baghdad?"

"Used what we call a four phone, Mr. President," Noyer explained. "You take a small umbrellalike antenna, beam it up to the satellite, and bounce it off right to home base. Very expensive."

"Well, I don't want any four phones popping up with anything we're not ready for, understand?"

"I understand, sir, but they're a determined lot."

"Then you be more determined."

"Very good, Mr. President."

"And notify the U.N.'s secretary general about this Spratly situation as soon as you have details." The President turned his attention to Admiral Reese. "George, I assume the Navy's already on to this, trying to find out just what happened to that drill ship."

"Yes, Mr. President. I've contacted COMSUBPAC in Hawaii and we have an SSN sub, the USS *Santa Fe*, west of Borneo and the Spratlys in the Sulu Sea. It's part of the *Enterprise* battle group and is being dispatched via Balabac Strait between the Philippines and the Malaysian part of Borneo."

"Surface or submerged?"

"Surface through the shallow straits and submerged once we get into the Spratly area, but we can't get too close to the drill ship position because the bottom is relatively shallow around those coral reefs, et cetera."

"Then how are you going to get anybody in there, at least without advertising the fact?"

"The sub, Mr. President. It wasn't the closest, but it's one with an SDV aboard."

"SDV?"

"Swimmer Delivery Vehicle. Can carry up to half a dozen divers, and they can exit the vehicle quickly. It's a separate container behind the sail of the sub."

"So we're sending in frogmen?"

Reese couldn't hide a smile of amusement. "I haven't heard that term in thirty years, Mr. President. The swimmers will fan out and gather what evidence they can."

"You think they'll find any?"

"They're the best we have, Mr. President. And COMSUB-PAC has notified our British liaison officers with the Royal Brunei Army. British Petroleum naturally wants to know what's going on as well. Apparently the rigs and drill ships are equipped with safety video units in cradles high above the deck. It's designed—the video unit, I mean—to be easily scooped up from a chopper."

"All right. Let me know as soon as you have something."

"Yes, sir."

CHAPTER FOUR

THE REFLECTIONS OF flames danced madly in the blister-shaped cockpit of the Brunei army's BO-105 helicopter as it sped out like a dragonfly across a flickering orange sea in response to the U.S. Seventh Fleet's request. It sped toward the enormous flame shooting high above the drill ship's rig, one man in the chopper safely harnessed and ready to extend his reach down after steadying himself on the starboard strut to extract the videocassette from the high stanchion above the well deck mast by lifting a bamboo hoop attached to the camera unit.

While maintaining forward flight, the pilot lowered his lever, using the stick and pressing his rudder pedal to hover over a spot he'd selected below, on the well deck's forward hatch, the fuselage rotating slowly about the main hub's axis. The bamboo hoop, video camera, and cassette in their all-weather plastic sheath had sensibly been painted phosphorescent red, and showed up clearly in the frenetic shadows cast by the fire whose roar was now so loud that the pilot and his observer in the harness could hear it above the near-deafening sound of the four-bladed rotor engine. Now the cockpit bucked violently and the pilot could feel the increasing torque as he fought to keep the helo steady in the waves of superheated air which, above the sea's cooler, denser air, created savage and short-lived convection currents and wind shears that buffeted the helo.

The Bruneian pilot wrestled for control. Five times the helo rose and fell abreast of the stanchion, each time getting a little closer, until the Bruneian in harness could reach out and grab the "hula hoop" and yank the attached video camera assembly out of its weather-protected cradle.

A sudden gust blew the helo toward the stanchion, and the pilot immediately moved to counteract it. But he was a split second too late, one of the rotors striking the stanchion, the helo dropping like a stone toward an enormous shadow of itself on the ship's deck, sliding the full length of the stanchion and crashing into the well deck. One of the rotor's spars cartwheeled and sparked across the well deck and then into the derrick that was red hot from the roaring flame. The spilled gasoline from the helo instantly became a river of fire that quickly raced back to the helo's fuselage, engulfing the shattered cockpit and the two men. There was an explosion which sounded like no more than a pop beneath the steady roar of the gas fire still flaming unabated hundreds of feet up into the night sky.

Though at a state dinner for the British ambassador, His Royal Highness the Sultan of Brunei was informed immediately of the situation. He was the richest man in the world, and every Bruneian citizen had one of the highest living standards in the world—all because of Brunei's oil, from offshore as well as onshore. His Royal Highness immediately put his tiny but superbly equipped 4,657-man armed forces on high alert, ordering Brunei's three Waspada-class fast patrol boats to sea with two surface-to-surface Exocet missiles per boat, but with express orders from the sultan to search, rescue where possible, and identify but not to engage unless attacked.

Within ten minutes the three Bruneian patrol boats had six radar blips on their screens, indicating anything from four junks to other commercial shipping, including what looked like an empty supertanker off the coast of the Brunei coastline heading south from the Malay state of Sabah in Northern Borneo and past the stricken drill ship's position.

No survivors were found in the surrounding waters, but the patrol boat nearest the drill ship was close enough to see, in the spill of light created by the fire of escaping oil and gas, bodies, some of them blackened, strewn about the well deck and the stern near the galley. Aboard the patrol boat a British army observer, Captain Owen, from one of the thousand-man Gurkha infantry battalions—one of three British battalions stationed in Brunei to help protect British petroleum interests—volunteered to go aboard the drill ship. He and two of the patrol boat's crew were shortly on the well deck, but the heat was so intense that they could feel it through their Vibram soles, paint on the well deck already blistering and flaking.

"We'll have to go back!" Owen shouted. "Hose it down first!"

For the next ten minutes, while the two other boats headed farther out to sea, the patrol vessel with Owen aboard used its fire hose to drench that part of the well deck immediately beyond the drill ship's ladder, the paint blisters now washing off like great gobs of wet newspaper, revealing spots of the red antirust primer below.

"Why do you wish to go aboard?" asked the boat's skipper, a spruce young Bruneian in his late twenties. "There's not much to see. I mean, nothing more than you can see from here."

"I'd still like a closer look," Owen said. "Five minutes is all I ask."

"Very good," the boat's captain said in impeccable English. "We'll keep the hose spraying the well deck."

"Right you are," Owen responded.

Once on the deck, however, he could still feel the heat through his boots. He looked about quickly but could see no weaponry, only the casings of expended 5.45mm and 7.2mm rounds. Owen also saw that to get near the bodies of the dead Americans and others, let alone remove them, was impractical at the moment, many of them so badly burned their flesh had melted into the deck. So he left the drill ship none the wiser.

"Until that cools down, we can't do much here," he told the patrol boat captain.

"Who's going to shut it down?"

Owen shrugged. "One of the companies who stopped the fires in Kuwait, I expect."

"But they weren't at sea."

"No," Owen agreed, "no, they weren't." His expression in the raging firelight was one of mounting anxiety. Even if the fire was extinguished, if they couldn't cap it, it would be the biggest oil spill the world had ever seen—a spill that would make that of the *Exxon Valdez* and Penchara River look tiny, a spill that would spread out and surround all the joint ventures spread over the South China Sea and beyond.

In the cylindrical dry-deck housing riding piggyback on the SSN *Santa Fe*, the swimmer delivery vehicle Mark XV was being checked over by two Navy SEALs. The combat swimmers were making sure that all systems were go aboard the flat SDV, which measured twenty feet long by seven wide. With its horizontal stern stabilizer and two vertical control fins, the Mark XV resembled a big Formula One racing car shell, minus the wheels, that had been squashed into a long rectangular shape. In its nose, a blunted triangular housing, was a state-of-the-art obstacle avoidance sonar.

The SDV was also equipped with a computerized doppler Inertial Navigation Subsystem—which would take it to the *Chical* via its silent-running, nickel/cadmium-battery-powered motor. Its normal external component of two fourteen-hundred-pound torpedoes, a 331-pound warhead on each, that once launched from the SDV could run at twenty knots plus, was removed so as to raise the normal five-knot speed to ten knots.

The two SEALs chosen for the look-see mission were ready to flood the piggyback housing to equalize the inside and outside pressure in preparation for launching their craft. They could have disengaged from *Santa Fe* a half hour before, but they were waiting to take advantage of promised bad weather. Via infrared cameras, satellites had picked up a bank of anvil-shaped thunderhead clouds stretching from Sabah, past Brunei, to Sarawak, a sure sign of thunderstorms building on the west coast of Borneo. And so the SEALs who would man the Mark XV waited, the *Santa Fe* meanwhile trailing her long VLF, or very low frequency, aerial, receiving burst message updates on the weather.

In the *Santa Fe*'s combat information center the captain ordered silent running. Among other measures, sandwiches would be prepared in the galley so as not to run the risk of any noise from the big food mixers that might send out telltale vibrations, no matter how small. Even so, unlike a diesel electric boat, a nuclear sub like the *Santa Fe* could not be absolutely silent, as the pump needed to keep the reactor cool could not be stopped. But the *Santa Fe*'s captain was confident that the sound of his boat would not be detected by any potential "hostile," given the noises of other South China Sea mercantile traffic. Also, once the weather worsened and thunderstorms began, the surface hiss of the torrential downpour would help hide the sound of *Santa Fe*'s water pump, and the heavy, cooling rain would also allow the SEALs to more comfortably board the hot drill ship.

When the torrential rain began, the SDV was only a half mile from the *Chical*, and within forty-five minutes the two SEALs had left the SDV and were climbing up the ladder aft of the drill ship's galley housing. The flames still roared high, but the downpour was now so heavy that the decks, if not cool, were only moderately warm. The derrick's steel, still hot, was turning the rain instantly to steam. In their rubber suits and front-mounted Draeger rebreather systems, the two SEALs moved cautiously through the hot fog as if through a giant sauna, which covered the ship in a ghostly pink light.

One SEAL carefully, and mostly by feel, made his way down the aft galley ladder to the engine room. There, with the help of his waterproof flashlight, which cut the steam in a sharply defined roiling beam, he saw the first body. The dead man's white boiler suit had blended so well in the hot steam now pervading the ship that the SEAL didn't see it until he was almost upon it. He found a half-dozen more bodies strewn about in the engine room and, as he had with the first, carefully searched the dead men's clothing, wrists, ears, mouths, and chest areas.

Up on the forward well deck the other SEAL also found bodies, difficult to locate in the shroud that now covered the ship, though the flame from the fire was still vomiting skyward. As he got closer to the well deck's forward hatch, he found over twenty corpses in and around the paint locker and, like his colleague, searched every one as carefully as time would allow.

The heavy rain-peppered swells looked like great ominous walls closing in until they passed beneath the anchored drill ship, the strain on the four anchors obvious from the crack and splitting sounds of chain and cable.

Once back aboard their SDV, docked aft of the drill ship, the SEALs compared notes. In all, they had searched forty-one bodies, the remainder of the drill ship crew either shot while in the water or, like the two bodies found wedged and floating by the prop, most likely killed from concussion after jumping overboard in panic and striking their heads on some part of the ship during midroll.

The two SEALs immediately sent their findings to the *Santa Fe* via their VLF transmitter:

BROOD ONE TO MOTHER STOP DRILL SHIP'S WELLHEAD AFIRE STOP ALL BODIES EXCEPT THOSE IN WATER DEVOID OF VAL-UABLES STOP AM RETURNING STOP MESSAGE ENDS

This transmission was quickly relayed through the chain of command up from the Seventh Fleet's *Blue Ridge* to CINCPAC to the Pentagon, and finally to 1600 Pennsylvania Avenue.

The implication of the message was clear: everyone aboard *Chical* had been robbed. Only those wedged near the prop, which was difficult to get to, had retained wedding bands, wallets, necklaces, watches, and the like. As with the boat people years before, anyone with gold fillings or gold bridges had had them ruthlessly removed by pliers or whatever else would do the job.

"So you were right," the President told his assistant, Ellman. "It was nothing more than a damn pirate raid."

Ellman nodded. "Set the wellhead aflame to occupy us—to cover their real intent."

"Vicious bastards," the President said. The thought of having gold fillings ripped from your mouth, even if a body was dead, was so barbaric it made his gut turn. Still, better a gang of pirates than a clash of nations, one country's sovereignty breached by another. Ellman's press assistant suggested it could have been both, but Ellman shook his head. "No. I think it's clear that this is the act of a bunch of cutthroats, plain and simple."

That possibility was to become a certainty on *Chical 7*, another joint Chinese-U.S. venture platform already in production in the Paracel Islands, five hundred miles southeast of China's big island of Hainan. The Paracels, lying east of the Gulf of Tonkin, were claimed by both China and Vietnam. The rig was afire and deserted except for the dead bodies picked out by a carrier plane's reconnaissance infrared-sensitive cameras. Again the message originated from the Seventh Fleet—the overflight made by F-18s aboard the U.S. carrier *Enterprise*—and was relayed through *Blue Ridge* up the chain of command to the White House.

"Jesus Christ!" the President blurted. "Would someone tell me what in hell is going on?" His angry surprise became outright alarm when he was told that while *Chical 7* was southeast of Hainan, it was also effectively in the Gulf of Tonkin, two hundred miles off Vietnam.

"Vietnam" and "Tonkin Gulf" were the two places in the world that no U.S. President wanted to hear about ever again, but by now over sixty-five Americans working in the Paracels and Spratlys had been murdered. And CNN—nobody knew how they'd found out so quickly—wanted to know why, and what the President was going to do about it. Already the White House phones were jammed with calls.

"This was a leak!" the President thundered, his clenched fist banging the desk. "A goddamned leak somewhere along the chain of command. And I want to know who—"

He was interrupted by Ellman, who seemed in shock. "Mr. President."

"Yes?"

"Sir, we've just heard via CIA's Hong Kong station that China's moving an additional three PLA divisions—over forty thousand men—to the China-Vietnam border."

"Where on the border?"

"Ah—" Ellman looked quickly at his notes. "—within striking distance of a Vietnamese place called Lang Son."

"Has Beijing made any statement?"

"Yes, sir. Apparently the move is to signal Beijing's displeasure toward, and I quote, 'the warmongering Vietnamese imperialists who are blatantly attacking Chinese possessions in the South China Sea.' "

"Call the Joint Chiefs and whoever has the China desk at State."

"Yes, sir."

Ellman gave the task to his junior while he himself called the Secretary of the Navy. "Mr. Secretary? Bruce Ellman, White House. Sir, we're in damage-control mode re this business in the Spratlys and Paracels, and the media are clamoring. Are you up for the 'Larry King Show'?"

"No."

"It has to be this week, sir. Otherwise it'll look like we don't know what's going on."

"Do we?"

"No, but we're trying to—"

"No."

Ellman knew he was on his own.

CHAPTER FIVE

IN HO CHI MINH CITY—once called Saigon—the night was filled with the sounds and smells of scooters and vendor stalls, for even with galloping inflation, enough of the 4.5 million Vietnamese in the city had been able to buy the three-thousand-dollar, two-stroke-powered motorbikes, no doubt sacrificing much along the way. To own a scooter in Vietnam was like owning a car anywhere else.

Despite familiar odors of gasoline fumes mixed in with the pungent smell of cooking and spices, it was still nothing like Saigon used to be. It lacked the excitement and zest of the old Asian "Paris" nightlife. Still, even though it was more than twenty years since Vietnam's defeat of the Americans in '75, the Socialist Republic of Vietnam had failed to kill the entrepreneurial wiles of beggars and ladies of the night. It was simply more organized. Many of the beggars in good health had been sent to reconstructive labor battalions, a move that U.S. Army captain Ray Baker, assigned to the U.S. legation office, endorsed as he walked through the dimly lit city with a mixture of nostalgia and anger.

It had been difficult enough to accept the defeat. Every American alive at the time—and not only those who had fought in 'Nam—had that picture frozen in their memory: the sight of a lone chopper poised atop the American embassy, a string of frantic people falling from it, trying to board, those already aboard shoving them off—everyone for himself. Americans and South Vietnamese in panic. And then there was the sight of Huey choppers heading out from the delta over the South China Sea like so many angry gnats dotting the sky, fleeing, again in panic, landing atop a Seventh Fleet carrier, and once the human cargo had been disgorged, not going back again but being pushed overboard—three million dollars a pop. And when the carriers couldn't provide any more deck space, the helo pilots cut off the engines, coming down in a semi-controlled crash, pancaking on the sea with about thirty seconds to escape before the doomed chopper began its slow then sudden dive to the bottom, bodies floating up and swimming soundlessly beneath the noise from the six-thousand-man carrier, as many on deck as possible—against orders—just standing there, witnessing the historic humiliation and debacle of the awesome American defeat.

This evening Ray Baker wanted to evict that image from memory, but the more he tried, the more persistent and nagging it became, and for a moment he was glad it was night-time, as if the darkness could somehow hide his private sense of humiliation. But on second thought, what the hell did he have to be ashamed of anyway? He'd done his bit, hadn't he? Or was he unconsciously harboring the secret torment that if he'd done that little bit extra during the war—if enough of them had done more, gone that extra mile—it might have been enough to turn the tide? For some vets who had fought in the Iraqi War, a full measure of self-respect had been reclaimed, but Baker had not been with Schwarzkopf's winning team. While many of his buddies had been racing over the desert destroying Saddam Insane's armor and closing on the Republican Guard—when the most terrifying phrase for the Iraqi combat pilots was "Permission to take off!"—Ray Baker was sweating in the shirt-clinging tropical climate of the Mekong Delta, still trying to find out after twenty years what had happened to all those unaccounted-for MIAs and POWs who some believed were still held prisoner deep in the jungles of the north.

Tonight he was going out to meet yet another "lead," the follow-up to yet another informant's phone call about yet another POW-MIA tip—another 100,000 new dong, ten U.S. dollars—just for the meet. Another ten for whatever his informant told him, even if it was bullshit—otherwise the informant might not come back if he did find something more concrete at a later date.

At the U.S. legation office they told Baker he was wasting his time, and he knew they were probably right, but if after all these years he could bring even one American out, bring one American home, it would be worth something. For himself, yes—for the man's family it would be everything. It was worth doing.

He lit another cigarette and made his way toward the heart of Cholon, the big market district largely populated by Chinese, once a thriving capitalist community but now much less so, after the anti-Chinese purges of the late 1970s. Now and then amid the gasoline fumes of the scooters, Baker could smell the freshly made French bread, croissants, and coffee from the sidewalk kiosks. There were dozens of them, the people of old Saigon refusing to give up the habits and civilities that had once made this vital part of the old city one of the busiest capitalist enclaves in all Asia. The Communists had realized their mistake in ostracizing so many Chinese, and were now letting many of them back to revitalize the ancient city of French Indochina, but many had already escaped through Hong Kong or been killed by pirates who boarded the boat people's sailboats to steal, rape, and murder.

Baker walked down an alley lit by Chinese lanterns, heading for Hung Vuong Boulevard. He passed the electronics market, with radios blaring, turned onto Ngo Gia Tu Boulevard, and passed the Nha Sau Church. Although he was over a quarter mile from the Kinh Tau Hu Canal to the south, he could smell its garbage mixed with gasoline and dust, and the odor of more baking in the hot, sticky air. Still, he would rather meet whoever had made the phone call here than at 28 Vo Van Tan—in the War Crimes Museum—where the last Vietnamese who supposedly had a "hot tip" had insisted on meeting him. Baker had been compelled, then, to see the black and white photographs of atrocities by American "imperialists," specifically the American photo of the My Lai massacre and Lieutenant

Calley, and some fuzzy shots of "China's imperialist aggression" against some of the "Vietnamese islands" in the Paracels and the Spratlys.

"Chao."

It was a softly spoken hello, filled more with apprehension than warmth.

"Chao," Baker replied.

"Toi," the Chinese urged, leading the way. He was a man in his late thirties, Baker guessed, no more than five feet two at the outside, and looking furtively around as they passed one of the sidewalk stalls, its wooden plank shelves bent with glass jars full of pickled cobras, the old woman in the stall busy cooking rice. The Chinese man told Baker that it wasn't far.

"What isn't far?" Baker asked, not bothering to hide the irritation in his voice. "Where are we going?"

"Not far," the other man said, and Baker realized that he was probably just a go-between and would cost him another 100,000 dong.

"If this turns out to be nothing," he told the man as he walked more quickly, now passing stalls smelling of fried rice and spices, "you get nothing. Understand? Zero. Zilch."

"Co, phai," the man assured him. *"Co, phai . . .* yes, yes. I understand."

"Good," Baker said.

They made a sharp right turn onto Nguyen Tri Phuong Boulevard, heading toward the canal. Down by the waterway, the Chinese pointed to a sampan with an old man aboard, among dozens of others, then held out his hand.

"Not so fast," Baker told him in English. "Let's hear what grandpa has to say."

"I go now," the man said urgently, his hand outthrust.

"Well, off you go, buddy," Baker told him. "But you don't get one dong until I hear from Uncle Ho here."

The elderly chin-bearded Chinese on the sampan gave no indication that he knew what was going on. He merely stared out from the boat at the black water.

Baker touched his cap as a sign of respect for the elder and said, *"Chao."*

The old man nodded, the white taper of his beard barely visible for a second as he turned to watch a police boat chugging by, its searchlight darting here and there, momentarily illuminating the scores of sampans and other houseboats.

"Parlez-vous français?" the old man asked.

"No," Baker replied, getting more irritated by the second. Why in the hell was he wasting his time by the fetid canal when he could be enjoying a good drip coffee and croissant back at his office?

The old man raised his head in the direction of a younger Chinese nearby—perhaps his son—indicating that he should go away. The young one didn't like it and said something sharp to the old man, who in turn barked a quick rejoinder and waved him off. The young man walked sullenly along by the canal, and in the habit of the Chinese, paused for a long spit, standing there, letting it dribble down his chin before he moved on, casting a faint shadow on the lanterns' silken reflections as they undulated over the wake of the passing police boat.

"I know a secret," the old man said.

Baker said nothing.

"A bad thing has been done," the old man continued, in no hurry to explain himself.

Baker took out a Gitane and lit it, its pungent odor floating about the sampan, shrouding the old man momentarily in a dark fog. How many times had he waited like this for information, Baker asked himself, for the merest suggestion of some of the 2,434 MIAs who were either buried by now or had been kept as prisoners until they were of no more use to the "Black Pajamas," as the Viet Cong had been known to the Americans? How many times had he waited for one decent lead?

"The gangsters in Beijing are in charge," the old man said. "Li Peng's gang."

"They've always been in charge," Baker said impatiently. He remembered the words of the historian Bo Yang: "With each new dynasty and each new reign throughout Chinese history, the throne has never changed, only the ass that is on it."

"But not so much when Chairman Deng was alive."

"Deng," Baker answered, "was as bad as the rest of them. Who called in the tanks at Tiananmen Square?"

"But Deng understood how far to go."

"Did he? I wouldn't know. You should ask the students who were run over."

"Still," the old man said, "there must be order."

Baker had had enough. "Do you know anything about Americans still being held—POWs, MIAs?"

"Yes."

"What do you know?"

"That Li Peng's gang have done a bad thing."

"You mean some MIAs have been taken across the border into China?"

"Possibly, but I mean this giving money to the pirates."

"Look," Baker said exasperatedly, "do you have something to tell me about our MIAs or not?" With that, the American straightened up, ready to leave, adding, "There have always been pirates. They made a fortune smuggling cigarettes, liquor—plundering the boat people. That's not news."

"But this," the old man said insistently, making the point with his left forefinger bent, crooked down like a fishing hook, the shape of Vietnam, "this is to make Vietnam look like the aggressor."

"What are you talking about? What aggression?"

"Against the disputed islands."

Baker didn't know too much about any disputed islands. China and Vietnam were always arguing about some offshore reef or such, especially now with the promise of big oil and gas deposits beneath the South China Sea and with oil accounting for more than a third of all Vietnam's exports. But though Baker's concern was MIAs, he now sensed there was something bigger at hand. It wasn't the old man's chin wagging about Li Peng's gang, but rather his tone. It was the voice of a man who was too burdened, who had heard something in the sampans or the stalls and had to share it. At first Baker wondered why the old man, a Chinese, would be bad-mouthing China, but if there was something China was doing—or about to do—that might bring down the wrath of the Vietnamese on the Chinese Vietnam community, like the pogrom of 1978–79 here in Ho Chi Minh City from which so many Chinese fled, some taking to the open sea, he could appreciate the old man's concern.

"How will Beijing make Vietnam look like the aggressor?" Baker asked.

"The pirates are to use the Vietnamese flag."

"For what?"

"For attacking disputed islands. The flag is to be upside down."

"Distress signal?"

"Yes. It is to get in close." The old man looked at Baker with a face the color of ancient parchment. "How long have you been here?"

"In Vietnam? Five, going on six—" Then Baker fully understood. It was like looking through a microscope, suddenly seeing a blurred slide jump into focus. "You mean the Chinese pay pirates to use the Vietnamese flag so everyone'll think it's Vietnamese attacking?" But why was the old man telling him this? "Because," Baker continued, answering his own question, "it would cause trouble between China and Vietnam again, and when there's that kind of trouble, the Vietnamese take it out on you." He meant not only the Chinese in Cholon, but all over Vietnam.

The old man nodded. "We are the Jews of Vietnam. But all we want is to live here in peace and harmony."

"You want me to tell someone in Washington that Vietnamese Chinese aren't involved? That it's Beijing behind the attack on the islands?"

"Yes. Beijing will deny it, of course."

"Let me get this straight. You say Beijing is doing this—attacking the oil rigs."

"Yes," the old man said, "to give Beijing an excuse to seize all the islands in the South China Sea."

"You think Beijing's so corrupt," Baker went on, "that it would use pirates to attack two of its own rigs, kill its own—" Baker stopped. It was a foolish question. These were the men who had run over hundreds of their own students. A few dozen oil-rig workers wouldn't faze them. "But wouldn't this put off American investors as well?" he asked.

"Not if Beijing and some American investors know the truth of it."

"But that would mean an American company would have to go along with . . ."

The old man smiled. It wasn't a smile of joy, but rather one of wry amusement at the American's naiveté—to think a U.S. company would not secretly side with Beijing, and to think Beijing would be concerned about a few Chinese workers, was to be in a kind of kindergarten of politics. What were a few lives to Beijing if they could use the attacks to bring the world against Vietnam in Beijing's push to claim *all* the islands as theirs?

All Baker could respond with was to say that Americans would never do such a thing—stage an incident, kill their own to frighten away the competition, in this case, Vietnam.

"You Americans," the old man said confidently. "You hold the individual so sacred. Here we are but grains of sand in the ocean."

"But won't the Vietnamese twig? I mean, won't the Vietnamese suspect the raids were to blame them?"

"Of course," the old man replied. "But for the Vietnamese to retaliate against China would be an act of war. It would be to risk international sanctions against Vietnam, and it has taken Hanoi over twenty years since the Vietnam War, since the American defeat, to build relations up with the U.S. again. It's only a few years since the U.S. embargo on trade with Vietnam has been lifted."

"Then China is free to keep hitting whatever claim they like?" Baker asked. "Be their own agents provocateurs? Frighten everyone off the islands, then say they'll have to garrison them with troops for self-protection?"

"Yes."

Baker shook his head worriedly. "But without proof, I can't go anywhere with this. We'd have to have proof that—"

The old man was astonished. "But you are an American officer," he said, as if that explained everything. "If you tell your government what I have told you, surely—"

"They won't believe it. Or rather, they might believe it but they won't do anything unless there's proof positive."

"But you are an officer. A—"

"I am a grain of sand," Baker said. "Besides, why should I believe you—with respect. This could be a Vietnamese ploy to attack their own islands in the Paracels to make it look as if the Chinese—"

"But I have told you the truth," the old man said, his head rising in indignation.

"And where did *you* get it?" Baker asked.

"From people of my blood—who were offered gold to sail with the pirate junks."

Baker could see he'd deeply offended the old man. "I'm sorry but—I mean, I'd need proof. Otherwise it's just another story in a sea of stories that one hears—"

"Dalat!" the old man said. "Near Dalat." Dalat was a temperate city in the central highlands, and during the Vietnam War there had been an unwritten mutual agreement that it was a no-fire zone. Both sides had used it for R&R in one of the stranger aspects of that long-ago conflict. The weather in Dalat was always good. At the coldest, it would rarely fall below 60 degrees Fahrenheit, and at its hottest, wouldn't rise to much more than 73 degrees. A place of gardens, of tranquillity, it would be pleasant to visit if for no other reason.

"What about Dalat?" Baker pressed.

"To show you I am a man of the truth."

Baker, nonplussed, waited impatiently. It had become cooler, a waist-high mist covering the canal, creeping toward the congestion of sampans and other river craft.

"In Dalat there is an MIA."

Baker felt his heart thumping. "Where in Dalat?"

"I will tell you if you will tell your government what I have told you."

"Yes," Baker said, "I'll send in a report."

"The MIA is in a village near Lang Bian Mountain," the old man said. "North of Dalat. The people of Lat village will help if you give them this." He took a small scrimshawed shark's tooth pendant from around his neck. "When will you leave?"

Baker gave the old man twenty dollars, to be shared with the go-between. "In the morning."

Afterward, Baker sent a message to the Pentagon about what the old man had told him concerning the attacks on the oil rigs, but he cautioned that it was only one old man's story amid so many.

When morning came, Baker did nothing about the MIA— there was nothing he could do until he got special permission from the Vietnamese. Lam Dong province, in which Dalat was situated in the central highlands over 225 kilometers north of Ho Chi Minh City, had been closed again to United States citizens, who were still being charged by the Vietnamese with covertly supporting the FULRO—Front Unifié de Lutte des Races Opprimés—United Front for the Struggle of the Oppressed Races—guerrillas in the highlands. The CIA had long denied any continuation of funneling arms, but now and then FULRO rebels would stage another ambush or shoot up one of the supposedly secret Vietnamese reeducation camps, which, rumor had it, were still run for some U.S. POWs and MIAs.

In the evening, Baker went down to the canal to talk again to the old man, to get more details, but he was gone. Baker found him near midnight in a sampan that was bumping among the bridge pilings, his throat cut. He guessed the old man had been killed for what he'd known either about Dalat or about the pirates' attacks in the Paracels and Spratlys.

What Baker hadn't banked on was the Vietnamese response to the very first attack in the Spratlys, but then again, the Vietnamese had had dealings for a thousand years with the Chinese, and they decided to react immediately rather than let their traditional enemy think he'd gotten a toehold in Vietnamese waters. Hanoi headquarters ordered the Haiphong base to attack, and within the hour, with an efficiency that, after the Vietnam War—or what the Vietnamese had called the Second Indochina War—was among the best response times of any Asian coastal navy, two Soviet-made Osa-class missile craft armed with four surface-to-surface N-2 missiles raced out into the Gulf of Tonkin, ready to attack anything Chinese.

The flag behind each of the missile boats, that of Vietnam, fluttered furiously as the Osas' bows lifted and the brown water boiled in urgency, the Vietnam missile boats picking up speed, heading southeast to the Chinese-occupied islands in the Paracels. The boats' crews, however, were under no illusion, for they knew that they were heading toward the People's Liberation Army's new navy, which Beijing had boasted was nothing less than "a great wall of iron."

Ten miles from the nearest Chinese-claimed island in the Paracels, one of the Vietnamese boats' radar picked up two blips advancing from the east at thirty knots plus: two Chinese Huch'uan-class fast-attack hydrofoil boats. A Vietnamese Osa fired its starboard forward SS-N-2 missile, the Chinese hydrofoil immediately going into a defensive "weave" pattern.

Closer now, the Vietnamese Osa fired a second missile, its backblast on the stern immediately raising the Osa's sharp bow so that she gained a knot or two. The Vietnamese captain saw one of the Huch'uan-class hydrofoils leap into the air and crash down again, its portside foil shattered along with the midships and cockpit—now a crushed pile of smoking metal.

The Chinese hydrofoil had turned hard astarboard as the orders were given by its skipper to abandon ship. The second Chinese hydrofoil fired its starboard twenty-one-inch-diameter torpedo from its large, corrugated housing, and now its 12.7mm machine-gun stations opened up against the fast-turning Vietnamese boats which, suddenly slowing near the site of the injured and sinking Huch'uan hydrofoil, machine-gunned all those Chinese in the water.

"Great wall of iron!" snorted one of the Vietnamese skippers, motioning toward the detritus of wreckage and bodies. The second Chinese hydrofoil had already fired its torpedoes, but they were easily avoided by simply opening the throttle, allowing the Vietnamese Osas to skid in wide thirty-five-plus-knot semicircles. There was some stray machine-gun fire from the Chinese—12.7mm tracer playing about the Osas, hitting the Monkey Island, or clear-weather bridge, on one of the Vietnamese boats, but doing no more damage than that.

Hanoi now broadcast to the world via an accommodating CNN that Vietnam had "punished Chinese aggressors" in Vietnamese waters.

In reply, the Chinese vehemently denied that they had violated Vietnamese waters, but stated that "the peace-loving People's Liberation Navy" had been patrolling, as was its right, within two hundred miles of its coastline, which included the big island of Hainan, and from Hainan it had every right to patrol another two hundred miles, as Hainan was indisputably Chinese territory. Beijing immediately requested a meeting of the U.N. Security Council to impose sanctions and other disciplinary measures against the "imperialist aggressions of the Republic of Vietnam bandits."

Vietnam followed suit and asked for U.N. sanctions against China. The fear on both sides of the dispute—and well-founded fear—was that the issue would be ponderously delayed while no action would be taken. In the meantime, both Beijing and Hanoi were accusing each other of violating the other's zone of ownership. It was a very capitalist argument, as seen by the *Wall Street Journal*:

In New York today, a U.N. meeting of Southeast Asian and East Asian nations called to decide who owns what in the oil-rich archipelagos of the South China Sea ended in uproar as the Chinese and Vietnamese representatives came to blows over ownership of the disputed islands.

As well as being rich in oil and natural gas deposits, the islands, the Paracels to the northwest and the Spratlys in the southeast, are also strategically vital to naval and mercantile routes to and from Japan and the United States.

The U.S. State Department is closely monitoring the talks, which it hopes will resume on Monday. Moscow and Tokyo are also watching the talks closely, as the outcome could have serious and wide-ranging geopolitical implications for all island disputes, particularly the so-called "Northern Territories" islands in contention between Russia and Japan.

CHAPTER SIX

Japan

IT WAS 11:55 P.M.—2355 hours on the clock at the Japanese Intelligence headquarters in Tokyo—and Henry Wray of the U.S. Central Intelligence Agency sat quietly enjoying a cigarette, something he couldn't do in Langley, Virginia, because of the strict no-smoking laws. His two Japanese hosts lit up as well. At 11:57 he watched his Japanese counterpart turn up the volume of the Sanyo shortwave receiver. At 11:58 two officers of the JDF, Japanese Defense Force, entered the cork-lined room, bowed to the civilians—four in all—from Japanese intelligence, and took their seats, the red light of the tape machine signaling it had already begun. At precisely twelve midnight the transmission from somewhere in North Korea began—four-digit numbers until 0020, when the code abruptly finished.

"All we need now," Wray said, "is their onetime pad."

"If that's what they are using," his Japanese host replied.

"Hmm . . . it's what I'd use," Wray told them. "You people are so far ahead in computers, I wouldn't run a network on computer digitization. I'd be afraid you'd descramble it in a couple of weeks."

"We've been trying for months, Mr. Wray."

"Call me Henry." He turned to the two officers from the JDF. "How about infiltration of the Chongryun?" It was a large expatriate pro–North Korean organization in Japan that raised millions of yen for Pyongyang. Nearly ten percent of all North Korea's urgently needed foreign exchange was from Korean workers' remittances abroad.

"It and others," the Japanese said. "Problem is, we have no idea how many North Koreans they are broadcasting to."

Whatever the number of agents listening, the CIA and

Japanese Intelligence knew that by now there must be a large organization of illegals, as well as those who had immigrant or visitor worker status, in the pay of Pyongyang. Should hostilities ever break out, either domestically in Japan or between Japan and North Korea, the Chongryun's association of North Koreans and deep cover agents would come out en masse like ants from a nest to sow confusion aimed particularly at Japanese transport and communication networks.

CHAPTER SEVEN

THE CHINESE INVASION of Vietnam began at 0300 hours, the first crossings made on a four-mile front through a marshy area ten miles north of the Vietnamese town of Lang Son and on the left flank at the border town of Dong Dang. All three divisions used in the attack, about 41,000 PLA ChiCom regulars, had already traveled from Nanning in the Chengdu military region by rail to Pingxiang, near the Chinese-Vietnamese border. In the Vietnam War it had been a favorite staging area for NVA regulars to take possession of Chinese-shipped arms and munitions. Now, in this latest chapter of the long border battle between the two countries, Pingxiang once again became the jump-off point for one country's invasion of the other. The Chinese forces were intent on overrunning the jungle-covered hills before Lang Son and the plains beyond, which ran down to the Red River delta and the Gulf of Tonkin seaport of Haiphong.

The Chinese were asked by the Secretary General of the U.N. "to disengage and withdraw immediately" from the border areas. But China, citing the "pirate actions of the Vietnamese imperialists" against a Chinese-owned oil rig and drill site in the South China Sea, insisted that Vietnam's actions amounted to nothing less than "an act of war."

The U.N. Secretary General's office pointed out to Beijing that in fact both Chinese-U.S. venture sites were not within the two-hundred-mile economic zone of China. China disputed this, replying angrily that several joint Chinese-U.S. ventures in the Paracels were within two hundred miles of the coastline of the big Chinese island of Hainan, and that MV *Chical 7*, while beyond the two-hundred-mile zone, was *historically* owned by China, as Chinese fishermen a century ago had been there first to fish and to use the islands and reefs in the South China Sea for repairs and the like. "Furthermore," a statement from Beijing added, if the "imperialist Vietnamese" did not remove their equipment and men from all the islands in the South China Sea, these would be seized by the PLA, as they "historically belong to the peace-loving Chinese people."

Hanoi retorted that this "is typical of the warmongering imperialists in Beijing—who arrogantly aggrandize the territories by intimidation and threat"—and that if China did not recall its three divisions back to Chengdu, the Republic of Vietnam would have no alternative but to "repulse the Chinese with all available forces."

Suddenly the President of the United States and his advisers, with help from the State Department's China and Vietnam desks, realized an uncomfortable truth—the island dispute was centuries old, "like a fight between neighbors—the Hatfields and McCoys," the President realized. Who had actually attacked whom was, in the final analysis, irrelevant. What *was* relevant was that the Chinese claim to own all the islands in the South China Sea was preposterous by any measure, and with the Chinese and Vietnamese on the brink of all-out war, the only consideration was how to stop it before it became general war in the Asian region. Because of this clear and present danger, and the catastrophic effect it would have on the U.S. trade-driven economy, the U.S. might have to intervene, albeit under the auspices of the U.N.

The Chinese attack south on Dong Dang with two divisions was led by General Wei. The other prong—an attack of one division, thirteen thousand men, on Lang Son—was led by General Wang. The assault on Dong Dang was made up almost exclusively of infantry brigades with one armored division leading the thrust south down the Pingxiang–Dong Dang road and railway. The road ran more or less parallel with the rail tracks, allowing Wei to move twice as many troops as would have been the norm on the road alone. Once Dong Dang fell, it was hoped by Wei that Wang's forces on his left flank coming down east of him from Zhilang in China to Lang Son in Vietnam, a distance of about thirty miles, would be able to quickly sever the rail line running south from Lang Son to Hanoi, eighty miles away, thus cutting off the rail line the Vietnamese Army would need to rush reinforcements to the north.

But the Vietnamese Army, already having explosive charges set at Ban Re, seventy-three miles north of Hanoi, blew both the rail line and the road at Ban Re. This prevented the ChiComs from capitalizing on their sudden attack south of the border and halted General Wang's troops before they could press the attack farther south toward Hanoi.

To the north of Ban Re, at Dong Dang, General Wei had better luck, being able to reach the Na Anh junction, thirteen miles west from Dong Dang. There, Wei's infantry and armored battalion, equipped with T 59s upgunned T-55s—managed to sever two roads, the one leading northwest from Na Anh junction to Quinh Son and Na Nien, the other running south to Phu Lang Thuong, thirty miles northeast of Hanoi, the Chinese-Vietnamese border itself barely a hundred miles from Hanoi.

The two prongs of this 41,000-strong Chinese pincer attack, however, were not so much strategic as tactical in design. The Chinese did not intend to stay, but merely to shell and destroy as much of Lang Son and Dong Dang as they could—as they had in 1979—and then withdraw. It was, in short, meant to be a military punishment for what the Chinese were calling "blatant unprecedented Vietnamese attacks" against the *Chical* drill ships in the Paracels and Spratlys. In any event, neither General Wei nor Wang wanted to penetrate much farther south. As it was, they lost over four hundred casualties to minefields the Vietnamese had laid down after China's 1979 incursions.

Vietnamese forces, despite the fast Chinese attack, reacted swiftly. From the Vietnamese garrison at Na Sam, seven miles northwest of Dong Dang, and from Loc Binh, twelve miles southeast of Lang Son, a two-pronged counterattack was launched by four regular infantry divisions well seeded with "Viet Cong" veterans who as young men had fought in the south against the Americans during the Vietnam War. Wei's and Wang's forces, in danger of encirclement, began to withdraw, but by Day Four after the initial Chinese invasion, the

Vietnamese troops had cut off the Chinese retreat from Na Anh and Lang Son. Only those ChiComs from Dong Dang were able to withdraw with only light casualties.

Beijing had only two options now: to give up those infantry battalions of Wei and Wang that had been surrounded and thus trapped by the Vietnamese regulars, or to send in more Chinese troops to release them, Beijing realizing that the defeat of their incursion would be a singular loss of face in a part of the world where "face," and therefore the nation's standing in Southeast Asia—indeed, throughout all Asia—was at stake. Accordingly, Beijing ordered an all-out invasion, not merely to rescue their embattled infantry divisions, but to widen the war and gain a buffer zone of territory, militarily shortening the distance between Hanoi and the old border from a hundred miles to something much closer. If this was achieved, then in the future any Vietnamese hostility aimed at China could be quickly punished by massive retaliation against what was hoped would be a much closer target, namely Hanoi, which might in turn be ringed by Chinese-planted minefields and surface-to-surface missile batteries.

Meanwhile, the Vietnamese raced to reinforce the border zone between and around Dong Dang and Lang Son.

CHAPTER EIGHT

ELLMAN TOLD EVERYONE in the Oval Office that the last thing they needed was indecision based on a lack of coherent foreign policy "which we inherited from the previous administration. We have to avoid giving mixed signals, a foreign policy that's cut from the cloth of the moment, an ad hoc way of proceeding which will make the U.S. look indecisive and weak—visionless. This would have adverse effects for us all over the world—trade deals suddenly put on hold, et cetera.

And an overseas lack of confidence would have a direct effect on the dollar and so on, so that pretty soon we'd see a domestic downturn in the economy, the direct result of those overseas having lost confidence in a firm American position. You can bet your life that all the major oil companies and the subsidiaries which form their infrastructure, et cetera, are watching what we do over these attacks in the South China Sea."

Noyer cut in. "Ellman is absolutely correct. *Whoever* started this row wouldn't have dared to stir up trouble were it not for our hitherto wishy-washy foreign policy. The Chinese saw what we *didn't* do in Yugoslavia—not what little we did in Haiti—and why shouldn't they risk it? They can always pull back, though I don't think they will unless forced to—loss of face, you see."

"Yet," the President said, "can you *imagine* the response if I were to go on TV and announce that we are unilaterally going in to support the Vietnamese—the *Communist* Vietnamese?"

"You could limit the support, Mr. President," Ellman charged, "by providing what the Vietnamese need most—air support. Limit our action to sending in a carrier battle group to operate from the South China Sea."

"And the Chinese air force?" the President asked.

"Minimum threat to our battle group," Reese said. "I'm not saying it'd be plain sailing, and the Chinese do have some squadrons of Fulcrums. MiG-29s. We'd lose some of our aircraft, but we'd beat them—no question."

The President was looking intently at the CNO as if he wanted more. "What about their submarines?"

"A bit dicey," Reese replied. "They don't have anything like our capacity, but some of their seventy-four diesels—whose props are superanticavitation-treated due to that bastard Walker selling us out—could sit still and it'd be hard to find them."

"Yes, but they'd have to come up sooner or later, Admiral."

"Yes, sir, but almost certainly at night." The admiral could see the lines of consternation on the President's face. "I don't think there'd be any problem in the end, Mr. President," he added. "I just want you to know that the opposition might have a trick or two up their sleeve that we don't know about, that's all."

"So," the President said, leaning forward over the blotter, doodling and summarizing, "you all agree our policy should be as coherent in the South China Sea as it is in the Mideast. If you invade a neighbor, you'll risk having the eagle swoop."

"Especially," Ellman added, "if you risk fouling up the sea routes and oil supply—in this case through the South China Sea."

"Trust me," the President assured them. "I won't dodge the oil issue and dress it up as anything else—I'll say unequivocally that the Western democracies need it, especially Japan and the U.S., and if the flow turns to a trickle, the eagle will more than swoop. At the same time, however, our intervention can't be purely economic. We are, as the leading and most powerful democracy, going to put it on record that we are against the Communist invasion of one country by another. We've got to stabilize the region, goddamn it! We want a new world order, not more disorder."

"Ironic, isn't it," Ellman commented, "that since the Berlin Wall came down, we end up having more wars around the world than ever before. I'm not saying we should go back to the bad old days of the cold war, but at least you knew the rules—this is our side, that's your side, and don't walk on the grass. Can you imagine that butchery in Rwanda in 'ninety-four and 'ninety-five happening if the Soviet Union had still been strong enough to exert its influence?" Ellman paused. "Still, if we put ourselves on record now as opposing the invasion of one country by another, we'll be accused of assuming the role of the world's policeman."

"So be it," the President said. "Besides, as you suggested, we don't have to commit troops. Air and naval interdiction—cruise missiles included—would pack a sufficiently large wallop to disincline any would-be bullies on the block."

"We'll be called the bully," Admiral Reese commented.

"Nevertheless," the President said, "tonight I go on record by saying that we will not stand for any more Yugoslavias or Rwandas, and we can set up air and naval blockades. In any case, we won't be impotent in the face of challenges to world peace."

"A Pax Americana," Noyer said. He, like Reese, wanted to know how far the President would be prepared to go.

"If you want to call it that—yes," the President conceded. "Well, we sure as hell can't leave it up to the Russians. And I don't mean to exclude anyone who wishes to help, Lord knows. Canadian peacekeepers, British troops from Brunei,

Australians perhaps, because of their interest in Southeast Asia."

"I agree. The more the better," Noyer said.

"And," the President said, "if we can't beat China's veto on the Security Council, we could still rally a force of friends in the General Assembly so we're not seen as acting just on our own convictions."

"Where will Taiwan stand in this?" Admiral Reese asked. "It's tended to favor a Beijing-Taipei fifty-one, forty-nine percent split on any oil and gas find in the South China Sea."

"Taiwan's a wild card in my view," Ellman said. "It could go with us, but God help us if it goes with Beijing."

The President was noticeably struck by the danger of this possibility. "Good God, we've equipped the Taiwanese."

"We have," Reese confirmed. "Ever since Truman and Cash My Check."

Suddenly it seemed as if all the steam had gone out of the President's stance of no exceptions to his idea of the rule of geopolitical stability. That is, if the Taiwanese joined China in the island dispute, it might very well bring the United States in against one of its oldest and staunchest allies. The President's hands were clasped tightly, his skin blotching. "This is a decision, gentlemen, that Taipei'll have to make. Is its potential oil split of fifty-one, forty-nine with Mainland China worth wiping out all its good relations with the U.S.?"

"But Mr. President," Ellman began, "that's a risk I wonder—"

"Yes, yes, I know, Bruce. It is something you would like to have an idea about first. All right, we'll sound out the Taipei representative here right now. But the point I'm making is that my job and my intention is to lead this country, not to prevaricate, trying to court every single congressman over to our side. I want their support. I'll ask for it, but in general terms. I'll not plod through this one hoof at a time. If you do that you end up with a mishmash of conflicting policy statements." He paused. "Look—over sixty-five American citizens have been murdered. *Murdered!* If we sit back and talk this one to death, how safe will any American feel anywhere around the world? No, I'll go on TV tonight and tell the country I'm moving the Seventh Fleet into the South China Sea for possible interdiction pending the withdrawal of Chinese troops."

Noyer waited till everyone else but he and the President had left the Oval Office. Then he said, "Mr. President, wouldn't it be much easier for your just-stated policy if China didn't come to the Security Council meeting you'll be calling for in the speech? I mean, they're sure to veto any criticism of themselves, let alone any action that might be taken against them."

"Of course it would be better not having them there, but that's highly unlikely."

Noyer nodded. "Yes, it is. You've asked the Secretary General to call a meeting for nine A.M. tomorrow."

"Yes—what are you suggesting? I change it?"

"Yes, Mr. President."

The President sat back, surprised. "Earlier or later?"

"Later. Around four o'clock in the afternoon."

"What on earth will that do to help us?"

"Probably nothing," the CIA director conceded.

"Why four?" the President asked, intrigued.

"Four is a very unlucky number in Chinese. Nine is a very lucky one. Besides, four tomorrow afternoon instead of nine A.M. will give us more time—" Noyer paused. "—to prepare."

The President eyed Noyer for a few moments before he spoke. "Ah . . . I don't think you and I should say any more, do you?"

Noyer agreed and made for the door. "Good luck with your speech, Mr. President."

CHAPTER NINE

COUGHING RELENTLESSLY ON his raft—or rather, the jagged-edged wood planking that had been part of the oil rig's crew's quarters—Danny Mellin was thanking God for the temperate water of the South China Sea. Perhaps if the plan of attack from the junk had a weak point, he thought, it was that the attackers had chosen dusk to make their move, which meant that if anyone else had survived the attack and the blast, then darkness might have prevented them from being picked off by the junk's crew. Then again, darkness provided the junk with cover also, which was probably why they had decided on a dusk attack in the first place.

He had no doubt that the explosion would have been picked up by one of the microphones in the U.S. underwater sonar system. Hopefully, U.S. ships and/or subs of the Seventh Pacific Fleet had already been dispatched as fast as possible to investigate the massive explosion. Mellin could still see the smoky column that was, or rather had been, the joint *Chical* venture. But now it appeared to him not as a roaring inferno shooting hundreds of feet into the air like the Kuwaiti oil fires, but the size of a candle flame, the currents having moved him away from the coast and any immediate assistance.

After a while, in a wash of moonlight, Danny Mellin saw something in the water that he hoped he'd mistaken for the dorsal fin of a dolphin. Its ominous circling of his ever-weakening raft, however, suggested otherwise. Soon he saw a wave breaking on something that didn't seem to move, and he guessed he was near a reef or one of the lonely islands that rose only a few feet out of the water and began to paddle toward it, the fin keeping up.

The rock was Louisa Reef, known in Chinese as Nantong Jiao. It was all of three feet above the sea. He felt the raft being taken away by the current, and once more paddled hard, until he thought his arms would break. He remembered, as if it was a dream, reading in "The Story of San Michele" by Dr. Alex Munthe, how Guy de Maupassant pressed Munthe to tell him what was the most terrible form of death at sea, and Munthe had replied—to be at sea with a life belt to keep you alive during the hell of dehydration. The next morning de Maupassant threw all his life belts overboard.

His hands bleeding from the coral and barnacles clinging to the rock, Mellin hauled himself and his small, broken plank raft up on the reef and hoped it was already high tide. Exhausted, he could do nothing but pray that by morning someone would find him.

It began to rain. He lay on his back, his legs dangling over the edge of the rock, opening his mouth to let the rainwater revive him. He looked around for the fin, suddenly lifting his foot as he did so, but now he could see nothing but the turbulent gray sea all about him.

CHAPTER TEN

THE PRESIDENT OF the United States began his address to the nation about the situation in the South China Sea by calling for a meeting of the U.N. Security Council at four P.M. He pointed out that regardless of claims over ownership of ocean resources, the United States of America would tolerate neither attacks against Americans nor any closure of or other interference with the vital sea lanes through which Mideast oil traveled to the United States and Japan. And for this reason he had ordered the U.S. Seventh Fleet into the South China Sea.

The violence of the long dispute, he pointed out, had spilled over into border clashes before the current invasion of Vietnam by China. China must recover her troops, he said. Failure to do this within seventy-six hours would leave the United States no alternative but to support the position of the People's Republic of Vietnam, which had once again, without warning—and here he referred to the 1979 and 1982 Chinese incursions—been invaded by its neighbor to the north.

"It is not only in our own economic interest to take this action," the President added, "but in the interest of world peace." It was time to extinguish the spark before, "fanned by the winds of old hatreds and intolerance," it ended up with a brushfire which could engulf all of Southeast and Northeast Asia. By Northeast Asia he meant a possible clash between North Korea, South Korea, Japan, and China, and the Japanese-Russian dispute over the Northern Territories islands.

After the speech, taking off his throat mike, he confided to his wife, "I liked that bit about 'the winds of—' "

"Excuse me, Mr. President . . ."

"Yes?"

It was an aide, very tense, armed with a fax just in from the

National Security Agency. NSA had SIGINT—Signal Intelligence—of transmissions along the Kampuchean border that showed incursions by Khmer Rouge Communists on Vietnam's western flank. The President handed the fax to Ellman.

"Bastards!" Ellman said, then apologized in front of the First Lady, adding, "Beijing is obviously behind this. They've supported the Khmer Rouge for years."

"Whether or not Beijing's behind them," the President commented, "an air strike or two over the area should cause them to think again. The Khmer Rouge . . ." He paused. "You know, Ellman, if someone has to test the mettle of our foreign policy, it might as well be the Khmer Rouge. They're as bad as the Nazis. The genocide they've committed is unspeakable. I've never forgotten those shots of the pyramids of skulls they made . . . and to start the world over, dating their calendar the year One. They're psychopaths. Suck up to the Chinese because of Beijing's support. Beijing sees it as an extra army on the Vietnamese flank. I can't think of a better target than the Khmer Rouge. And remember what the Khmer Rouge and Vietnamese fought about after the Vietnam War with us."

"What? Islands?"

"Islands in the Gulf of Thailand. I tell you, these damned offshore islands have caused no end of trouble."

"It would have to be a carrier strike, Mr. President—against the Khmer Rouge."

"Why not B-52s?"

"Too big, given our lack of runways, and because of our allies, like Japan, who fear upsetting the Chinese. No one'll give us landing or refueling rights in Southeast Asia. They're all scared stiff of the Chinese, not only in China proper, but within their own populations. Singapore has seventy-six percent Chinese. Brunei is too small to take the heat. Malaysia has thirty percent Chinese. Indonesia won't help us. So without airfields, we'd have to use shorter-range fighter-bombers off a carrier."

"How about the airstrips at Okinawa?"

"No. Essentially it'd be the same as launching from the Japanese mainland. Tokyo won't give us the go-ahead. They're probably right, strategically speaking. Beijing would go ape, and like North Korea, Beijing can scud Japan." Ellman paused. "I suppose we could launch Tomahawk cruise missiles from one of our subs."

"Yes," the President responded, "but I'd favor the carrier aircraft option over that. And I don't mean an attack by stealth,

I'd want this on CNN. If we're going to stop a full-scale war started by the Khmer Rouge or China before it gets out of hand, I want the world to see American foreign policy straight and simple in action. No hide-and-seek on this one, and like I said, if it comes to kicking ass, I can't think of a better target than those Khmer sons of bitches."

"If air strikes don't do it?" Admiral Reese asked.

Ellman interjected. "We could alert Second Army's Emergency Response Force at Fort Bragg, Mr. President. Do you want me to write up the—"

"Christ, no!" the President cut in. "For God's sake don't anyone notify that—" The name escaped the President for the moment.

"Douglas Freeman," Ellman put in. "He's a good man, sir. In my opinion our best for—"

"I agree," the Present said. "But damn it, if he gets the bit between his teeth before we're ready to move, it could be a media relations disaster. Haven't met the man, but State tells me you put a microphone anywhere near him, it explodes into controversy. I don't doubt he's one of the most brilliant commanders we have—possibly *the* most brilliant—but they say he's another Patton. Can't keep his mouth shut."

"Yes," Reese said. "He even looks like George C. Scott."

"Anyway," the President continued, "we want to try to contain this with naval and naval air action alone."

At the urging of the United States, the U.N. Secretary General called the special meeting of the Security Council. Problem was, as Ellman reminded everyone, the Chinese, like the other four permanent members—Britain, the U.S., the Russian-led Commonwealth of Independent States, and France—had the power of veto over any Security Council resolution.

"We didn't have it in the case of Korea," Ellman pointed out.

"Then how did you manage to get a U.S.-led U.N. force in there?" Ellman's aide asked. The aide, Ellman realized, would not have been born when the Korean War of the early fifties broke out.

"Well," Ellman explained, "the Soviet representative at the time had stormed out in protest over the failure of the U.N. to grant Communist China a seat and left town in a huff. So when North Korea invaded the South and the emergency meeting of the Security Council was called, the Soviet rep was

unable to make the meeting and the remainder of the Security
Council voted unanimously to send in a U.S.-led police action.
That's how we got to get our troops in to throw back the
Communists."

"If China started this," the President noted, "as the Pentagon
and this Captain Baker in Saigon—I mean in Ho Chi Minh
City—suspect, then it's another Gleiwitz."

"I don't get the analogy," Reese said.

"Gleiwitz," Ellman explained, "was a German radio station
on the German-Polish border. It was attacked in 'thirty-nine by
German political prisoners dressed in Polish uniforms so the
Poles would be seen as the aggressors."

"So that Hitler's invasion of Poland," the President added,
"could be seen as a response to *Polish* aggression."

"Yes," Ellman put in. "The analogy now is China having
used the Vietnamese flag—in distress—to get close to the
rigs."

"Pity China wouldn't walk out of the U.N. now like the
Russians did in 'fifty," Admiral Reese's aide commented, un-
knowingly speaking for all present—from Ellman and the
CNO to CIA director David Noyer.

"Yes," the President concurred, "but that's highly unlikely
unless we said something offensive enough to make him leave
the chamber."

"We could call him a turtle," Noyer said, knowing that "turtle" was an extraordinarily rude thing to call any Chinese.

The President nodded. "Perhaps we could switch place
names at the round table. Instead of 'People's Republic
of China,' we could put up 'PROT—People's Republic of
Turtles.' "

It was a joke that eased the tension, but only temporarily;
the stakes and the danger of general war in the area all around
the South China Sea rim were too pressing, for the rim touched
not only China and Vietnam, but Malaysia, Singapore, Brunei,
Sabah and Sarawak, the Philippines, Indonesia, and Taiwan, and had enormous implications for Japan, now the last
U.S. stronghold in Asia. The joke, however, had given the
CIA's Noyer an added incentive, one he could not present to
the President, with or without the others present, but he immediately made a note to pull the People's Republic of China embassy personnel file when he returned to Langley.

CHAPTER ELEVEN

Fort Bragg, North Carolina

"MASON," GENERAL DOUGLAS Freeman said to his senior meteorological officer, looking down at the map of the "mysterious MV *Chical* incident," as reported by *The New York Times*, "what's the weather like in the South China Sea this time of year?"

"Right now," Mason assured him, "it's calm, General."

"Well, Mason, I have a hunch the political climate around there is not going to stay damn calm. I smell a big fat commissar in Beijing pulling the strings on this one."

"We don't know that for sure yet, sir."

"No, but I'll bet my boots on it. Who the hell would send in an identifiable ship to blow a drill ship sky high? Obvious as the nose on your face that it's the Chinese trying to do the dirty on the Vietnamese."

"Sir, that'd mean killing their own."

"Mason, you're a damned good meteorological officer, but in matters of what the individual means to the Communist state, you don't know squat from a hill of beans. One of our generals in the Vietnam War told us that individual life isn't as highly prized in Asia as in the West. Of course, every fairy and do-gooder liberal from Florida to Montana started squawking about how human life is as valuable to an Asian as it is to us. I tell you it isn't. They'd have a nine-year-old walk into some village with a grenade. Use their women too."

"So you say the Chinese would've easily sacrificed some of their own to . . ."

"To make it look like the Vietnamese did it. Yes. And when I'm proven right—" He turned to his chief aide, Colonel Robert Cline. "—we're gonna have to kick ass. And Second Army's Emergency Response Force is just what we need. Hell, we could be in and out of there and drop a few eggs on Nanning before the bastards knew what hit 'em. So, gentlemen—" He addressed his headquarters staff, or rather, those of his headquarters staff who had been hastily assembled in his office. "—I want contingency plans for a full EMREF ground attack against selected targets in southeastern China, Chengdu province—attack plans from both sides of the border. In China against Guangzhou's Fifteenth Army and Chengdu's Fourteenth—and I want RECs—religious, ethnic, and cultural—profiles of all countries laying claim to the Spratlys and Paracels." He paused. The excitement in his eyes was as clear as his next message. "And anybody in this outfit who talks to the press, I'll have his guts for garters. That clear?" There was silence in the tension-charged air. "Very well. Dismissed. Mason?"

"Yes, General?" the meteorological officer said.

"South China Sea's calm now but it's about to enter the monsoon season, correct?"

"Yes, General."

"All right. I want you to give me the worst possible weather scenario for that area—maximum typhoon wind strength, wave height, et cetera. You got that?"

"Yes, sir."

"Then send it to me."

As Mason left the general's office, Douglas Freeman steered Robert Cline over to the map table to show him what he thought would be the order of battle, and strategic and tactical maps of Guangzhou and Chengdu provinces and the Vietnamese-Chinese border area.

"Yes, sir," Cline said, "but what if it *was* pirates? Could be Vietnamese or Chinese or—"

"Bob, you have to take the long view. It's only old ladies and fairies in State who worry about who threw the first punch. The long view—the overview—what happens, is the main thing we have to worry about. We don't see Israel getting all uptight about who was the first to throw a rock in a damn street brawl. They assume it's the Arabs because the Arabs have been their enemy for centuries. And for us the question is, Who is the biggest danger? And that's China."

His arms swept across the map of the South China Sea and all the countries around its rim. "Look at the Chinese claim. It's not just the Paracel Islands it claims, but everything in the damn South China Sea, hundreds of miles beyond any legal economic zones and right in the path of our sea routes. Can't put up with that bullshit—doesn't matter if we find out it was a damn gorilla started it. The point is, we're the major power in the world, and we've got to contain this brawl before it gets out of hand—for our own sakes if not for anyone else's."

With no call from the Pentagon, and boiling with impatience, Douglas Freeman called his old colleague, General William Lynch, of the Joint Chiefs.

"Bill," Freeman explained, "you've got to let me go in with the EMREF."

"Sorry, Douglas, the White House is handling it."

"They're not handling anything. What's the matter with those jokers? They scared?"

"Of letting you loose, Douglas? Yes," Lynch replied. "They're apprehensive. Ellman suggested you to the President, apparently, but quite frankly, Douglas, there are those here who think you're far too—belligerent."

"Too *what*?"

"Belligerent."

"For Chrissake, General, what you need now is the most belligerent son of a bitch in America—and no offense to the late George Steinbrenner, but that's *me*!"

"We need something bigger than the EMREF," Lynch replied, quickly estimating the Chinese strength, but basing it on the strength of U.S. divisions. "We're talking here about three million strong and tried ChiCom army troops—a hundred and fifty divisions—"

"*Two* hundred and fifty," Freeman corrected him. "ChiCom divisions are only twelve to thirteen thousand tops—but they're all teeth. And I agree with you, Bill, we need something bigger than EMREF. But right now you need a seasoned siege-buster like me to plug the hole—to push the bastards back north where they belong and off those islands, and to hold the line while our Second Army boys mobilize in Japan. The EMREF can leave within—"

"Douglas, you're not listening. The White House is sure that the mere disembarkation of a Japanese-led U.N. team this afternoon and the urging of the General Assembly in the U.N. might be enough to settle the 'dispute' on the islands and—"

"General," Freeman cut in, "the U.N. can do fuck-all unless they agree to go in to fight as they did with Schwarzkopf in Iraq. And you're telling me all they'll do is send in observers.

Congress suggested it after hearing the President's speech. Goddamn it, Bill, observers are no good now. What we need are—"

"Douglas, it's no good reaming me out—it's the White House's call and that's that. It wasn't my idea to send in observers. At least *I* would have sent them in by air to Hanoi, but the President feels that a U.N.-flagged ship to Haiphong will give the Chinese time to ponder and save face. That's important to Orientals."

"How 'bout us? We could lose face." There was a pause at the other end of the line, and Lynch waited for the explosion. It never came.

"Well, thanks for taking my call, Bill," Freeman finally said. "I guess all we can do now is hope that the White House sees reason and can douse this thing before it gets out of control."

"Amen to that," Lynch said.

But "amens" and "seeing reason" were to have no effect, for as in all wars, chance and misunderstanding were at large. Two hundred miles southwest of the Japanese island of Kyushu, and three hundred miles south of Tsushima Strait, between Korea and Japan, its government outraged at the idea of a Japanese-led force, a North Korean Russian-made conventional diesel-electric sub lay quietly waiting in the relatively shallow seas about Tokara-Retto, one of the Ryukyu chain of islands that threaded their way in a gradual south-north crescent between Taiwan and Japan.

The sub's silence was absolute, its five-bladed screws still, the sub on a sandbar off a reef in water deep enough to hide the three-hundred-foot, 3,500-ton Tango, but not too deep for its search periscope, allowing its captain, Commander Kim Yee, to survey the sea's surface for miles about him. As Captain Yee made it abundantly clear that anyone who broke the silence would be severely punished, Lieutenant Commander Jeon maintained his position just beyond the periscope column as officer of the deck. Further safety for the sub lay in the fact that the Tango was such a ubiquitous class, with eighteen having been made and four sold to swell the coffers of a foreign-exchange-hungry CIS. In short, a Tango could belong to any country.

David Noyer's meeting with China's representative to the U.N., Lee Chow, took place at a suitably subdued but crowded reception for the new ambassador from Thailand. Here, a polite nod and a few words to one another on Embassy Row would not have to be accounted for in the way they would have been had Noyer, albeit unofficially, suggested they meet.

Noyer waited until Lee had finished consuming his fourth hors d'oeuvre. "Mr. Lee," Noyer said, smiling, extending his hand, Lee accepting it while still chewing. "We have a few photos of you."

"Yes," Lee said. "So . . ."

"You're in various compromising positions," Noyer said, still smiling, "with a beautiful redhead."

Lee swallowed the last of the shrimp and Ritz cracker. "Boy or girl?"

It caught Noyer by complete surprise. "I didn't know you were bisexual."

"I'm not," Lee replied in impeccable English, "but you Americans can do anything with photography. I particularly enjoyed that 'Forrest Grump' movie."

"Gump," Noyer corrected, vying for time. "It was Forrest *Gump*."

"Yes, well, whatever. The scene of him meeting John F. Kennedy and Lyndon Johnson, though we know both men were dead many years before the film was made . . . Correct?"

"Is that what you think?" Noyer responded in an incredulous tone. "We faked the photos?"

"Why not? If you can do it with a movie, the opportunity of monkeying—" Lee paused, considering whether he had used the correct word. "—yes, monkeying with stills, must be what you Americans call 'a cinch.' "

"Why don't we let Beijing decide?" Noyer offered.

"What is all this in aid of?" Lee Chow asked.

"We were hoping you'd be too busy to attend the U.N. this afternoon," Noyer said.

"In return for the photographs?"

"Yes—including the negatives."

"I'm not interested in your photographs," Lee Chow said.

"We could still release them. The redhead's no fake."

"Release them?" Lee Chow challenged. "To what purpose?"

"You'd be recalled."

"Possibly."

"Definitely."

Lee Chow turned his back on Noyer.

Noyer felt dirty and cheap. The Chinese ambassador had

called his bluff. But would Chow back down at the last moment and not turn up at the U.N. Security Council? Noyer doubted it, but it was possible that the Chinese ambassador might retreat, given a night to think about it and of the effect public knowledge of his extramarital affair would have—if Noyer released the photographs—not only on himself, but on his family, and the utter disgrace of a recall to Beijing.

Protecting the U.N.-flagged U.S. ship—the nearest available for carrying the U.N. team having been a U.S. T-AGOS 1, a Stalwart-class ocean surveillance ship—were two of Japan's ten 250 feet long by thirty feet wide Yushio-class diesel electric submarines. Each was capable of 27,220 short horsepower, their engines able to drive the subs at a submerged speed of 20 knots, one Yushio on each flank, the 14-knot convoy preceded by two U.S. ASW armed sonar dipping Sea King helos. But now all their sonar mikes were picking up was the thundering noise of the U.S. T-AGOS 1 and the quieter engines of the two escorting Japanese Yushio subs.

Aboard the waiting North Korean Tango-class sub, four torpedoes were "warm"—ready, each tube flooded, outer doors opened. The navigation officer plotted the vectors and Captain Yee gave the order to fire. The torpedoes streaked out in a fan pattern toward the American ship.

Just moments after the hiss of air and tubes flooding, the passive sonars of both Japanese Yushio-class submarines had the range and position of the attacking submarine, but aside from the two Yushios knowing one another's position for safety reasons, neither Japanese sub could be sure of the nationality of the enemy sub. Even if the sonar operators aboard the Yushio subs could have ascertained by the noise of the hostile that it was a Tango class, which they could not, they still would not have known whether the sub was Chinese, Taiwanese, Korean, or Russian. Their hesitation to fire was not so much a failure of naval discipline, but a result of an official JDF policy of extreme caution and a lack of combat experience dating back over fifty years, to August 1945 when the Second World War had ended for Japan. A long policy of appeasement followed, including Japan's refusal to be involved in any military action with the U.S.-led coalition against Saddam Insane.

The Yushios' hesitation allowed the Tango to leave its point of attack and on quiet battery power to move a half mile then settle where it once again fell silent. The Yushios could have switched from passive to active sonar, sending probing sound waves out in the hope of rebound from the hostile after it had fired on the U.N.-flagged ship, but this would have immediately betrayed their own position, an invitation for a hostile to fire torpedoes at *them*.

The fact that the T-AGOS 1 was an ocean surveillance ship didn't help, for it was well known, at least among the intelligence community, that the partly civilian-manned twelve ships in the class with their SURTASS, or surveillance-towed array sensor, and their superstructure bristling with communications gear, were in effect spy ships.

The fact was that whether the White House had known this or not, the T-AGOS 1, normally operated by the Military Sealift Command, was clearly sailing under a U.N. and not a U.S. flag. For the first time in many years, an old and hitherto firmly held assumption that the U.S. would at all times know precisely where all non-U.S. submarines were and would know what countries the subs belonged to was proven to be wrong.

Hit amidships, the T-AGOS 1 never stood a chance, the enormous implosion of water sending her down in minutes, with only three of her complement, one Japanese observer and two American seamen, surviving.

Presidential adviser Ellman, the White House's point man on damage control, was now on the "Larry King Show," trying to explain why, if the President knew that a T-AGOS 1 was a spy ship, it was used in the first place. Or was the civilian-manned ship used because its maximum speed—from eleven to thirteen knots—was relatively so slow that the President hoped that by the time it reached Hanoi's port of Haiphong the China-Vietnam clash would be over? In short, King wanted to know, was it a cynical, vote-getting political move on the part of the administration for the White House to *look* decisive while hoping time would cool Vietnamese and Chinese tempers?

"No, certainly not," Ellman replied. "It was a U.S. ship that had the kind of sophisticated communications gear the U.N. would need to monitor the situation and report back to its headquarters. Also, in view of Japan's reluctance to become too involved with the situation, it was the best available vessel."

"You know what I think?" the first phone-in caller began.

"No," King said. "You have a question for Mr. Ellman?"

"Well, I think you people at the White House knew what the hell it was. You just told the President what the Pentagon told you, and the Pentagon—am I still on?"

"Yes," King said. "Hurry it up, ma'am."

"I am hurrying it up. I think the Pentagon didn't tell the President it was a spy ship because the hawks over there want to get us in another fight. Reminds me of the Gulf of Tonkin—"

"Sorry, ma'am," King said, cutting her off. "Time's up." He turned to Ellman. "Well, how about it, Bruce? Did the Pentagon come clean? Do the hawks want a fight?"

Ellman was either shocked or good at affecting it. "I don't know of anyone, hawk or dove, who wants a 'fight,' as the lady put it."

"But you knew it was a spy ship—right?"

It was Ellman's face turning a salmon-pink that gave him away. "We, ah—we were informed that an American communications ship was, er, ah—available."

King and millions of viewers were on to it. "You didn't know it was a spy ship?"

"Not at the time."

"Well, when *did* you know?"

"Ah, I can't recall exactly, but—"

"*After* or *before* the ship was sunk?"

Viewers could see Ellman exhale, almost in relief.

"After. The President certainly didn't. The President didn't—I mean it was the Pentagon—to be more exact, it was, I believe, the job of the MSC—"

"What's that?" King cut in.

"The, ah, Military Sealift Command."

"So you didn't know—"

"Not until later."

"After it was sunk."

"Ah—yes. That's right."

The second caller was irate. "I've been waiting half an hour—"

"Your wait's over, sir," King told him. "What's the question?"

"You guys in the media make me sick. You're tryin' to make it look like the President's fault. How about who started it? First we lose, what, twelve Americans on that oil drill ship, and now we lose a whole crew. How many I don't know. What we should be asking is what are we gonna do about it? Sit on our fannies while some Korean egomaniac—"

"We don't know it was a Korean sub that hit it." King turned to Ellman. "There was some talk of the possibility of a mine."

"Ah, mine, shine," the caller said. "What's the difference? We got Americans dead all over the place, and you guys in Washington are doing nothing but talking. We've got to let these tin-pot dictators—"

"Out of time, sir. Have to move on. Good question, though, Bruce. What's the U.S. response going to be now?"

"Well, the Joint Chiefs'll be meeting with the President this evening."

"Uh-huh. But you know, Bruce, we've had a couple of *good* questions here tonight. Isn't there a larger picture here? I mean, let's see . . ." King picked up a news clipping. "*New York Times* asks, 'What kind of message is our apparent inaction sending worldwide?' And you know the *Times* was one of the papers to advise caution in the first instance—in the, uh, *Chical* business."

Ellman was visibly relieved. "And that's exactly what the administration is doing."

"Yeah, but that was in the first instance. Now it and—well, you just heard from the callers—a lot of people—I should say, a lot of *Americans*—are asking, What are we going to do now that the T-AGOS 1 has been sunk?"

"We'll still move with caution. This administration isn't about to commit the lives of young Americans without duly—"

" 'Scuse me, Bruce, but isn't the point this—that you are now being criticized for precisely the kind of thing you people criticized the previous administration for—"

"No, I don't think we—"

"Sorry," King cut in, "but we didn't clear one point up. How many Americans have now died in this sinking and the attack by whoever it was on the *Chical*—wasn't it *Chical*?"

"Yes . . ."

"Yeah, and on the *Chical* drill ship?"

"Forty-one, I believe. But Larry, let me just say something here. We've already ordered the Seventh Fleet into the general area, but we still don't know who it was that attacked the drill ship or—and I must emphasize this—or the T-AGOS 1."

"I understand, but isn't it a bit late for who started what? I mean, China has invaded Vietnam. And everyone—and by that I mean mainly the other countries—is disputing these oil-rich islands. Who are the others, by the way—besides China and Vietnam?"

"Indonesia, the Philippines, Malaysia, Brunei," Ellman replied.

"Well," King continued, "isn't the danger here that if *we*—the United States—don't make up our minds quickly on that, that all these countries could be at war? The South China Seas trade route to Japan and the U.S. could be a war zone."

"I, ah—possibly. That's why I think it's prudent to be careful."

"Nobody's denying prudence, Bruce, but isn't it true that the longer we wait, the more the danger of it spreading? I mean this war between Vietnam and China."

"I think it's more likely that the other countries will want to see which way the wind blows."

"You mean go with whoever wins the war?"

"Possibly."

"All right—last caller. From Oklahoma."

It was a woman's voice, strangled by sobs. "My husband is one of those missing in the *Chical* attack—I mean, the attack on the *Chical*. . . ."

There was a long pause.

"Take your time, ma'am."

"He's one of those missing. . . . He fought in Vietnam. . . . His sisters served. They were lost. He was decorated twice. I just want to know, is Washington doing anything to—" She couldn't finish.

"Bruce." King's tone was more solemn now. "What do we tell this lady? Is there a possibility that Americans may have to fight again in Vietnam, only this time *with* Vietnamese to repel China?"

"Yes—if that's the way we have to go to stabilize the region as you suggested we should."

"Wait a minute, *I* didn't suggest that. I merely asked what the *administration* is prepared to do." King then returned to the caller. "You still there, ma'am?"

"Yes."

"Ma'am—and I know this is an awfully hard question—but you've seen your two sisters-in-law . . . Were they in combat support roles or—"

"Yes, they were nurses."

"Uh-huh. Now, you said they were killed?"

"One was, the other's been listed as MIA."

"Uh-huh. Ma'am, if we—if the United States had to send troops again into Vietnam—this time to fight with Vietnamese, both North and South, against Communist China—what would be your response after the pain and the suffering you've—"

"I . . . oh, I'm sorry . . ."

"No—take your time, ma'am."

"I think a bully has to be stopped."

"You mean China, right?"

"Yes."

"You're one brave lady. Thanks for calling."

"Whew!" King said. "Some lady. Bruce, thanks for coming at such short notice." King turned to his worldwide audience, which, among dozens of other capitals, included Beijing and Hanoi. "Don't go away. Next—the Mongrels talk about their new album, *Struttin' Stuff.*"

CHAPTER TWELVE

Tokyo

JAE CHONG, CARRYING a brown shopping basket, emerged from Shinjuku Station in west-central Tokyo. He walked a mile south, past the Meiji Shrine in Yoyogi Park, then caught a cab to go a mile east to the National Stadium, where he was part of the huge crowd watching Osaka's Hanshin Tigers beating Tokyo's Seibu Lions. After the game he caught the subway to the Ginza district, where he walked down past ritzy stores and viewed the Western-style mannequins with a mixture of envy and contempt. He wished that he could afford the clothing he saw—to buy something for his wife Mia back in Pyongyang. He could work for a year and still be unable to afford anything in the Ginza.

All the money he earned, less what it cost him to live in the far outskirts of Tokyo, went back as a remittance for his wife and two children. They all had to make sacrifices if North Korea was to become a great nation. Without many products to export to earn vital foreign exchange, the remittances of Chong and all other North Koreans living in Japan were vital to North Korea's economy. But the Great Leaders—first Kim Il Sung and now Kim Jong Il—were correct: everyone had to make sacrifices if North Korea was to take its rightful position as Communist leader of Asia.

The new decadence of Japan was everywhere. The young Japanese particularly were a spoiled race. While their parents, the post–World War II generation, subscribed to *Yamato damashii*, the Japanese determination to succeed against all odds, the young Japanese, despite their commitment to the *shiken jigoku*, or hell of examinations, upon graduation from the universities became part of the *moyashiko*, the bean sprout generation—because, like sprouts, they grew up fast but were in the dark. They had no staying power. More and more they wanted more leisure time, and soon. With such weaklings in power, the great Japanese giant must falter and stumble, and then North Korea would be ready to strike.

Of course, there were those who said the Japanese were too powerful a nation to falter, let alone fall, but Chong believed the great leader Kim Il Sung's prediction that capitalism's decadence, its immorality, would undermine its industrial achievements, and his, Chong's, job was to help expedite this "historical process" by whatever he could do as a member of the North Korean expatriate organization, the Chongryun. What made it easier for Chong to believe in Kim Jong Il's prediction was the way in which the Japanese treated the Koreans as second-rate citizens. The Koreans did all the low, menial, dirty jobs, but were not accepted into Japanese society. How to redress such a situation, how to deal with the humiliation that assailed you like the death of a thousand cuts, one slight at a time? The only way Chong knew was to strike back, and not on their terms but your own, to shatter their Japanese spirit, their sacred and exalted *Yamato damashii*.

Chong stood in front of a store window that sold expensive electronics, and gazed at the mirrorlike reflection to check those who were passing him and anyone who paused at the window. Two schoolgirls in uniform stopped to look at the range of portable compact disc and tape players and to watch one of Sony's latest HDVs, high-definition video screens which, instead of having the normal U.S. standard of just over five hundred horizontal or scanner lines, had more than a thousand, and made for a dramatically sharper picture. Chong also watched the TV screen, for its camera was outside the store, taking pictures of passersby.

He knew what the American agent looked like: five-foot-six, 150 pounds, brown hair, blue eyes, smaller than the general run of American agents. The CIA presumably had started recruiting smaller men. In Asia they would blend much more quickly in a large crowd like that at the ball game. But Chong could see no Caucasian nearby, and if anyone was tracking him, he had not been aware of it in the taxi on his way from National Stadium, and a taxi would have been sure to flush the agent out—unless the American had radioed the taxi's number ahead and a tail had been taken over by some Japanese agent from the JDF.

Chong, feeling fairly confident that he was not being followed, moved on down the Ginza back toward Hibiya Park, nearing the Chiyoda-Ku district and the Imperial Palace. He walked down by the moat, looked up at the eye-pleasing greenery that nestled the palace, and then made his way across to Tokyo Station. He could smell himself, having walked so far—about two miles in all—in an L-shaped route that he broke out of by going into Tokyo Station and catching the subway, now full of raucous revelers from the Lions and Tigers game, north a few miles to Ueno Station. Here he bought an iced tea, doing it without putting down his brown paper shopping bag, and made his way by foot another mile eastward to Asakusa Park, his destination the Buddhist Asakusa Kannon Temple.

He was looking forward to its serenity, though he did not believe in Buddhism, another religion of the weak. He made his way up to one of the incense stalls, bought two sticks, and placed them in the holders by the shrine. It was now 9:36 P.M., dark, and in twenty-four minutes, at ten o'clock or as near to it as he could get, depending on the line for a phone booth, he would ring one of his friends in the Chongryun. He walked around to the other entrance to the shrine and, head bowed, quickly scanned the entrance he'd just been in. He was sure no one had followed him. A small child jostled him to get a better look, banging into the bag. The woman began to bow in apology until she saw he was a Korean.

CHAPTER THIRTEEN

THE USS *Enterprise* at its center, the carrier battle group of the U.S. Seventh Fleet proceeding west from Guam in the Philippine Sea was well protected. There were twelve ships about it: two Aegis-system-equipped antimissile cruisers flanking it within the twenty-mile-diameter circular zone; two more cruisers; three destroyers; five frigates, for antiship protection within a two-hundred-mile-diameter zone; and an SSN nuclear attack submarine at a 230-mile forward position from the carrier.

In addition, the battle group was preceded by an E-2C Hawkeye early warning plane and a Viking antisub plane in the outer zone with two CAPs, or combat air patrols, of two F-18s each in the outer defense perimeter. The defense ceiling of the CAPs extended to sixty thousand feet plus above the battle group. Admiral Rawlings, C in C of the battle group, was sure that nothing would get through the formidable protective screen of ships and aircraft.

Tazuko Komura was a beautiful twenty-six-year-old Korean woman with an hourglass figure who worked in Tokyo and hated it. Ever since she could remember, she'd been aware of the subordination of women in her country, and her childhood resentment of the fact had passed into teenage anger that had culminated in an adult rage she found almost impossible to contain. She loved modern American movies, for in them there was comparatively little of the utter subservience of women. Of course, she knew not all American women were like the ones she'd seen in the films, but for all they might have to put up with in American men, the American women were free birds compared to their Japanese counterparts.

Tazuko had two brothers, and all her parents' attention seemed to be taken up by them. She knew her parents loved her too, but in education especially she had seen the two worlds—one for men, the other for women. And at twenty-six, unmarried, she was called a "Christmas cake," something whose value plummets after December 25. Her schooling had stopped after her high school graduation, and all the money the family had was devoted to the education of her two brothers.

She worked for a time in one of Japan's largest clothing stores along the Ginza, where only the very rich shopped. She was one of thirty girls who, dressed exactly alike, every morning received instructions for the day, eyes straight ahead like so many robots, and who then spent the day bowing fifteen degrees and saying, *"Irasshaimase"*—"Welcome"—to thousands of shoppers. A thirty-degree bow would be necessary for introductions, and a forty-five-degree bow for an apology. Unlike her coworkers, every time she bowed she resented it, and could only get through the day by cursing inwardly. She had made the mistake of confiding once to one of the girls, a *paato*, or part-timer, about how much she loathed bowing and scraping to everyone who passed through the department store's doors.

"Why don't you quit?" had been her coworker's response.

"Because jobs aren't easy to come by, that's why."

Her coworker had called her *wagamama*—selfish.

"Yes," Tazuko had replied, shocking her coworker even more. "I want more than a husband, two children, and a lifetime of drudgery."

"You should not talk like that."

"No, I shouldn't," Tazuko agreed with an overtone of sarcasm.

After that incident she had not complained anymore. She had decided to act. In time she became an agent for North Korean Intelligence. Whatever else the Communists might be, Tazuko had become obsessed with their promise of equality for women. At times her inner voice told her that the Communist world was no utopia. But whatever its faults, Tazuko believed that at least its women were treated differently—more like men. Pyongyang told her to keep her job as a greeter—it was perfect cover. Who on earth would suspect someone so subservient, bowing low to the holy customers who passed her as if she were a stick of furniture?

* * *

Aboard the Nimitz-class carrier USS *Enterprise*, two FA-18 Hornets were readying to take off to relieve the two F-18s now on combat air patrol over two hundred miles in advance of the battle group. The fighters were armed with four heat-seeking, Sidewinder air-to-air missiles, two radar-guided Sparrow air-to-air missiles on the wingtips, and a six-thousand-round-per-minute 20mm cannon. In addition, each plane, capable of acceleration from 850 to 1705 kmh in less than two minutes, carried 375 extra gallons of fuel.

The flight deck at first sight seemed a confusion of terrible noise, astringent fuel smells, steam bleeding from the starboard catapult, and groups of men in different colored jackets: red for firefighters and ordnance, green for maintenance, red crosses on white for the medics, white for safety supervisors, blue for aircraft handlers, brown for each plane's deck captain, green for catapult and arrestor gear crews, grape-vested for refuelers, and yellow for aircraft directors. In front of the water-cooled blast deflectors, a Hawkeye early warning aircraft roared to full power, its twin turboprops twin blurs. As it took off, the F-18s moved into position.

In primary flight control high in the carrier's island, anticollision teams worked diligently under pressure. Their job was to know and account for the position of every plane coming in, taking off, or parked, the handler closely watching his "Ouija" board, on which there were tiny models of the ship's planes. The deck was clear, the landing light red, the captain pushing the button for the harsh-sounding warning horn while a quarter mile out to sea the orange rescue Sea King chopper hovered.

Through the blur of rising steam, sea spray, and backwash of exhaust heat, the pilot of the first Hornet prepared to take off and watched the yellow-jacketed catapult officer, his hand up and open, signaling him to go to afterburner. The pilot saluted, then the catapult officer's left hand dropped behind him, his left leg fully extended at an acute angle to the deck, his right leg bent and his right hand thrust forward, wind speed and temperature and weight already in the belowdeck computer. The deck edge operator pressed the button, and a deck below, the catapult controller let her go, hurling the plane aloft in a cloud of steam—from zero to 150 miles an hour in less than three seconds.

As each of the Hornets climbed, one of the pilots saw a glint of reflected sunlight amid the carrier island's cluster of air, surface, and target acquisition radar masts. The pilot took it as a good omen, and the next second both Hornets, climbing, disappeared into the base of a huge cumulonimbus cloud, its ice-cream whiteness already bruising with rain.

CHAPTER FOURTEEN

THE VIETNAMESE DIVISIONS fought hard, but Wang and Wei's PLA infantry and artillery outnumbered the Vietnam regulars. As the pincer closed about Lang Son, the Vietnamese began a tactical retreat, the air full of the whirling and shuffling noise of artillery rounds overhead and the massed stuttering of heavy machine guns and T-56s, the Chinese version of the AK-47s, as the Chinese pressed their advantage.

In Washington the unexpectedly rapid Chinese breakthrough sent shock waves through the Pentagon. It wasn't supposed to happen this way, and it created a new sense of urgency in the White House. Bypassing the Security Council, stalemated as it was by a Chinese veto, the President, through his ambassador to the U.N., appealed to the General Assembly for assistance in forming a U.N. coalition. He made it clear, however, that if such assistance was not forthcoming, then the United States would act unilaterally and send in troops to assist the Vietnamese, in the interests of preventing a general war in Asia.

It was a sensation, more so because the American offer was carried by CNN to an audience of over 100 million, topping the 94 million who had watched the O. J. Simpson story and the Oklahoma bombing in the mid-nineties.

CHAPTER FIFTEEN

Whitehall, London

THE AMERICAN OFFER to send in troops came as no great surprise to the British Foreign Office. The Minister of Defense, Richard Tyler-Jones, had been told by the White House to expect some sort of declaration from the President pertaining to the Chinese-Vietnamese clash.

Tyler-Jones, looking out the window down Whitehall, spoke to his deputy minister, Ronald Nash, without looking at him. "What to do, Nash?"

"Well, I expect we should say something positive. Washington is clearly, however reluctantly, prepared to do battle with the Chinese because they realize that if the Chinese succeed, they'll not only occupy the border areas between the two countries, but they'll claim all the oil islands, the Paracels as well as the Spratlys."

"Not to mention what all the Chinese in Vietnam and Malaysia might do. We could have another Communist insurgency in Malaya, and who would stop it? Apart from that, it would turn the whole of the South China Sea into an Asian Yugoslavia."

"Ironic," Nash commented wryly. "The Americans are prepared to send in troops to help a Communist power."

"Not at all," Tyler-Jones said tartly. "They helped Stalin—worst Communist of all—a thoroughly nasty piece of work. We helped him too, remember? Besides, without *Uncle* Joe as well as Uncle Sam, we could have been in a rather sticky situation." He meant England would have lost the Second World War.

Tyler-Jones sat down and took up his letter opener, a cassowary bone dagger from an old patrol officer who had once journeyed up New Guinea's Fly River. The weapon made him think of another dagger, the famed curved Kukri knife of Britain's legendary Gurkha troops. They were fierce fighters, especially renowned for jungle warfare. Late in the 1980s, during a recruitment replenishment drive for just over sixty men, more than sixty thousand men applied. The Gurkhas took only the best of the very best.

"How about we offer them a Gurkha battalion and a squadron or two of SAS?" The Special Air Service commandos had carried out the lightning raid in London against the terrorists in the Iranian embassy in 1961 to rescue British hostages, and had performed sterling service behind the lines in Iraq.

Nash, though deputy minister of defense, couldn't recall how many men were in a squadron of SAS.

"Varies," Tyler-Jones told him. "Around seventy-two. I suggest we send two or three squadrons, and have a battalion of our Gurkhas in Brunei on standby—ready for deployment. Not many as far as numbers go, I agree, but top drawer all the same."

"And we should offer them without strings attached," Nash asked.

"Not visible ones anyhow," Tyler-Jones replied cagily. "I'm seeing the Prime Minister at Number Ten this evening. Don't do anything until I give the green light."

Nash looked surprised. "You don't think the P.M.'ll raise any objection, do you?"

"I shouldn't think so," Tyler-Jones answered. "You know, England and America—allies in two world wars, Korea, et cetera—Iraq. Our 'special relationship' and so forth."

"Some of the opposition don't think there's a special relationship anymore."

"They may be right to some extent, but there are the ties of blood Winston spoke about, despite the fact that we are separated by a common language."

Nash forced a smile. It was a very old chestnut but one that the minister still thought amusing. "Quite," he said. "I won't draw up the offer beyond a rough draft."

Tyler-Jones glanced at his watch. "Ten minutes? If so, I can take it around to the P.M. myself."

"It'll be ready, sir."

"Good . . . Tuesday, isn't it?"

"Ah, yes sir."

"Oh, God—the P.M. and his one-main-course dinner. An example to the nation in hard economic times. Tuesdays, Nash, arc corned beef, cabbage, and white onion sauce—none of which I can abide."

Nash's eyebrows rose. "Surely, Minister, the menu isn't as predictable as that?"

"Alas, it is. Our beloved leader, Nash, has not one of the more discerning palates in government. It's rumored—no, it has been *confirmed*—that he likes those awful American hot dogs."

"Perhaps there'll be a change in the menu—in your honor, Minister."

"Perhaps," Tyler-Jones replied, though his tone was not one of conviction.

"One could simply order the soup," Nash proffered with a smile.

"Yes," Tyler-Jones answered wryly. "And one could end up on the back benches. No, Nash, I shall do my duty, and you do yours."

"Yes, sir."

As Nash reached the door, Tyler-Jones, looking over his reading glasses at the deputy minister, said, "You see how much I trust you, Nash."

Nash glanced at the very rough draft of Great Britain's offer, one England could just afford, but one he was sure the Americans would like. However, if it were to get out before the P.M. had seen it . . .

Tyler-Jones, his hands forming a cathedral, was shaking his head. "No, no, not the offer of troops, old man. The bloody cabbage!"

"Oh—yes, Minister," Nash said, smiling.

"You mention a word of that and I'm for the high jump." He meant, for hanging.

"Don't worry, sir. Mum's the word."

The minister, his hands still in the prayer position beneath his closely shaved chin, merely nodded.

"Mr. Tyler-Jones, Prime Minister," announced the secretary at 10 Downing Street, and then, withdrawing in utter silence, deftly closed the door to the P.M.'s study.

"Richard," the P.M. said, smiling, taking off his reading glasses and extending his hand in greeting.

"Prime Minister," Tyler-Jones acknowledged.

"Sit down, Richard. I've been going over these budget

figures again. And your department is one that we'll have to trim."

"We've trimmed to the bone, Prime Minister. You may have noticed that we've reduced the number of our Gurkha battalions significantly. We've gone from eight thousand men to two and a half thousand."

"Yes," the Prime Minister interjected, "I realize that. It's not a criticism of you, Richard, but I've been wondering—do we really need them at all?"

Tyler-Jones was flabbergasted, and fought against his natural urge to respond sarcastically. "I think we do—need them, Prime Minister. Their fighting ability is legendary. Perhaps, sir, not being an avid student of the military, you might not realize the extent of their reputation."

"I realize full well, Richard. They are very very good soldiers. My father used to regale us as children with tales of their unquestioning loyalty and ferocity. That knife they carry, the—"

"Kukri."

"Yes." The P.M. smiled. "Sounds like something one would use in the kitchen, don't you think?"

"Perhaps, Prime Minister," Tyler-Jones said. "The Gurkhas use it to hack their way through jungle and to cut off their enemies' heads."

"Yes, Father did mention that, but can't they be replaced by British troops? I mean by that, of course, home-based troops?"

"Hardly economically viable, Prime Minister. All in all they're a bargain, and their morale—well, what can one say? In the Falklands War when the Argentinian units heard the Gurkhas were on their way, it caused mass panic—a 'withdrawal in force,' I think the Argentinians called it."

"Mass desertion?" the P.M. proffered.

"Just so," Tyler-Jones responded, adding, "Of course, during Mao's cultural revolution they also proved invaluable."

"Really? How?"

"Difficult to know where to begin. In any event, when the Red Guards let loose by Mao spilled over into Hong Kong and caused massive riots, we sent in the Gurkhas—had 'em draw their Kukris. Once they draw the big knife, you see, there's an imperative to use it before they can return it to the scabbard."

"Oh," the P.M. said. "That I didn't know."

Tyler-Jones saw his opportunity, and the moment the P.M. finished speaking, he added, "And I thought that if Beijing wants to foment more trouble on the Vietnamese-Chinese border, we might be able to assist our American cousins with Gurkhas."

"Very good, Richard," the P.M. responded, unwinding, both arms outstretched for isometric exercise, pushing hard against the edge of the desk. "Very good indeed. And of course the Gurkhas, black chaps and—"

"But Asian in appearance. They come from Nepal."

"Quite. That's what I meant. Asian-looking. And in Asia, Asian troops on our side would look much better than— Good." The P.M. was plainly pleased with himself, as if it had all been his idea from the first. "Excellent." A light on his console blinked silently. Not bothering to lift the scrambler phone, the P.M. spoke into the small intercom. "Very good. We'll be out in a moment." He turned to Tyler-Jones. "Dinner," he announced. "You'll stay to partake, Richard?"

"Thank you, sir." Any meal with the P.M. was a feather in one's cap, particularly when one had been instrumental in putting the P.M. in such a good mood.

"Corned beef, cabbage, and white onion sauce, Richard. How's that sound to you?"

"Delightful, Prime Minister."

CHAPTER SIXTEEN

THE DOT IN the distance looked like all the others, seabirds of one kind or other, some lazily gliding about a crinkle of white as turquoise swells broke upon a barely submerged reef like the one Mellin had drifted onto. Though his legs had been lacerated by the reef, he owed his life to the rocky outcrop. Mellin knew he could have lasted days without food, floating in his Mae West, but could not have survived without water, and in the higher depressions of the rocks, those not flooded by seawater at high tide, he found a few pools of rainwater from the downpour that had followed the attack on the drill ship. It wasn't much water, but it was enough to prevent what would have been a fatal dehydration. As for food, he'd forced himself to eat and swallow a slimy sea urchin from one of the tidal pools, and had almost thrown up.

Soon Mellin could discern another ship close to the dot, and then he saw that the two seemed to cohere and were now one. Several seconds later he could see it was a speedboat, most probably a patrol boat passing the almost completely submerged reef in the distance and coming toward him. Now, after the days and nights of hoping and waiting, he was suddenly afraid.

Would it be a rescue or a killing? He guessed the vessel, whoever's it was, would reach him in about twenty minutes. Then it occurred to him that maybe the boat wasn't Chinese or Vietnamese. Perhaps it was a speedboat coming westward from Brunei. It also occurred to him that although the reef wasn't large, only thirty to forty yards long and ten to twenty wide, he could, if he wanted to, hold on to the edge of it as one would grasp the edge of a swimming pool, all but his head submerged, to somehow hide and see them before they could see him.

Hanging behind a piece of coral that jutted out from the reef like a small peninsula, Mellin now realized how absurd it was to think that it mattered whether they saw him first or he saw them. The reality was that unless he wanted to die on the reef, he would have to go with them, whoever they were. He saw the flag of the Red Chinese—its five stars representing China proper, Manchuria, Mongolia, Sinkiang, and Tibet—fluttering from the stern of the ship, not a gunboat, but a frigate, its bow, a quarter mile from Mellin, slicing through the light swells with an effortless grace that belied her purpose.

On the frigate's bridge, an officer walked out to the port wing and, binoculars in his hands, began to peer more intently at the reef. Mellin knew they had to spot him. After thirty seconds or so it struck him that the ship might in fact be on a routine patrol of the Spratly Islands and reefs to check that no foreign structures or markers had been placed there, the Chinese and Vietnamese having had confrontations about such claims, and on several occasions firing upon one another. In one incident several years ago, in the early nineties, over fifty

Vietnamese had been killed by the Chinese. In a way, Mellin was relieved to see the Chinese flag, signifying that it was a PLA naval warship, rather than a fast patrol boat of the kind some pirates used in drug runs across the South China Sea to the countries that lay on its rim.

Now the ship leaned hard astarboard, turning away from the island. Suddenly Mellin was yelling out as loudly as he could, raising his voice above the slap and smash of the swells along the hundred feet of rock and coral.

The officer of the watch, however, had seen him, and the ship was merely coming about to better launch its rubber boat. It was with a mixture of gratitude and apprehension that Mellin saw this taking place. He could hear an outboard motor coughing, spluttering, and dying. Chinese maintenance, he thought, and grew more anxious now, not because of the temperamental outboard—he knew they would get him somehow—but because of what appeared to be spikes—rifles sticking up from two of the four men aboard. The outboard now sounded like an angry wasp as the Zodiac's bow rose, slapping the crest of a wave then disappearing for a second or two before reappearing again, the blue-and-white-striped shirts of the sailors standing out against the sea, now a gunmetal gray beneath a big cumulus that had obscured the sun.

The first thing that struck Mellin after they took him aboard was the stiff attitude of the four PLA navy types. Every face was solemn. The petty officer at the control console pointed to the middle of the boat and said in Chinese, "Sit there!" Mellin didn't know much Chinese, only what he'd learned as a POW in Vietnam, where he had been guarded by Vietnamese Chinese.

"Xie xie ni." Thank you.

No one answered him, two of the four using their rifle butts to push the rubber boat away from the reef, where it could easily capsize should a sudden swell rise high above the reef's edge then just as suddenly drop precipitously onto the coral below. Steadying himself in the middle of the Zodiac, he thanked them again. The unsmiling bosun, a rather sorry sailor, said something to him gruffly and pointed to the rest. The bosun waited till the water lifted the rubber boat high, then turning the wheel sharply to starboard, he gave full throttle and they were heading back at about eight knots toward the frigate.

The bosun pointed impassively toward the reef and again said something just as grumpily as before. Mellin couldn't understand the tone. As far as he knew, the Chinese and U.S. had cordial relations due to joint Chinese-U.S. ventures. It then occurred to him that even if they could have understood what he said, they might not know about the attack on *Chical*—or had they been part of it? There had been reports before, particularly in 1994, about pirates in PLA uniforms telling foreign vessels to stop, whereupon the pirates had proceeded to ransack the ship's cargo.

They were nearing the ship now, and Mellin made one more attempt at conversation. "Shipwrecked," he lied. Maybe it would be better for him to stick to a shipwreck story and say nothing about the *Chical*. None of them responded as they reached the netting ladder just forward of the bridge. "Well, you're uncommunicative bastards," Mellin said, smiling, "but thanks for picking me up anyway."

"Get up the ladder!" the bosun ordered in clipped but perfectly understandable English.

Mellin had a distinct sinking feeling.

CHAPTER SEVENTEEN

Fort Bragg

GENERAL DOUGLAS FREEMAN was in his tiny kitchen, emptying the last of his coffee around his aspidistra plant—an aspidistra was able to take anything and thrive—when the phone purred. It was the Pentagon telling him that the Emergency Response Force was to be activated for immediate deployment. Freeman knew it was for Vietnam, and a shiver of excitement rather than apprehension passed through him.

"Yes, sir," he answered crisply. The irony of Americans returning to the country where they had suffered their first and most humiliating defeat in the twentieth century was on his mind, and he knew it would be at large among the EMREF's troops; if not the British SAS contingent, then certainly among the rest of the force. But he welcomed the Pentagon's decision, for whatever the American troops' apprehension, Freeman saw it as an opportunity to exorcise once and for all the stigma that had been the legacy of America's Vietnam vets.

The Pentagon's view, however, was quite different. Its hope was that the very announcement of the American-led EMREF being activated, via Hawaii, would send a timely and clear message to Beijing—to stop the fighting and to withdraw its troops from Vietnam.

Within the closely guarded and vivid red-lacquered gates of Beijing's Zhongnanhai, the government's VIP compound, reaction was swift, with a message to Generals Wei and Wang to hold their positions at all costs, that "decisive" reinforcements were en route from Nanjing military district to the border. In fact, the Vietnamese supply line from Hanoi eighty miles to the south had been cut again, this time by PLA MiG-29 Fulcrums, so that Hanoi's ability to resupply its troops south of Lang Son and Dong Dang was even further impaired, inviting a fresh Chinese attack, with Generals Wei and Wang eager to seize the moment and press farther south.

CHAPTER EIGHTEEN

THE ADVANCE PARTY of the Emergency Response Force, a mixture of 2,150 Marines and three squadrons of 216 British Special Air Service and 200 Delta Commandoes, left Britain and the United States by air ahead of Second Army. Meanwhile, General "George Scott" Douglas Freeman was busy in the cavernous interior of the lead L-100-30 Super Hercules.

In addition to the 127 other combat troops in the first Hercules, another twenty of the aircraft would fly into Hanoi with the remainder of the advance party, which would chopper eighty-five miles north into the area around Lang Son. The advance units of Freeman's Second Army and all its material were already on their way from Japan aboard the fast 20-knot vessels of the Military Sealift Command, including amphibious assault ships, helo- and Harrier-carrying ships from the 40,500-ton Wasp class, a 39,300-ton Tarawa, and an 18,000-ton helo-carrying Iwo Jima class. They were escorted by 30-knot Burke-class and Spruance-class destroyers, two Ticonderoga-class Aegis cruisers, and two combination SSBN/SSN Sea Wolf submarines with cruise missiles and torpedoes.

Tokyo

At 9:55 Chong moved away from the temple of Asakusa Kannon to the phone booth nearby and dialed Tazuko Komura's contact number. When she answered, he knew she would be wearing white gloves. He asked for a Mrs. Yoshi. Tazuko Komura told him he must have the wrong number, there was no Yoshi living there. He rang off.

Before Chong had made his phone call, six JDF intelligence officers had been milling in the crowd around the Asakusa Kannon—the minimum needed to follow anyone. All of them had seen Jae go into the phone booth and dial. Immediately, two of the closest agents made their way to the phone booth, one of them rudely stepping in front of a woman waiting her turn to enter the booth.

"Excuse me," she said, "but I am going to use the phone." The agent said nothing. "I am going to use the phone," the woman repeated.

"No you're not, mother."

"I beg your pardon?"

"Be quiet," he said, "or I'll arrest you."

"Arrest me?" she said, surprised. "And who are you, please?"

The agent was losing it. Amid the murmur of the crowd around the shrine, their voices couldn't be heard, but if the old woman kept on nagging at him . . .

He *would* have to get the rare one, he thought, a woman who thought herself equal to men—the man they were watching, still in the booth, might hear them arguing as he came out.

"And who are you, please?" the woman repeated.

The agent had seen Jae dial four of the six numbers, but not the last two. It was something, but not enough. They'd have to feed it into the computer and have it print all the possible combinations of numbers.

"And who are you, please?" she said once again.

"Be quiet!" the agent hissed. He couldn't hear what Jae was saying.

The agent walked away as Jae hung up.

"I thought you were in such a big hurry," the woman called after him. "Did you hear him?" the elderly woman challenged the person lining up behind her. Jae came out of the booth. "And who is he? He's a lout, that's what he is. A shrimp brain!"

The person she was addressing, another woman, but much younger and prettier, smiled weakly but obviously didn't want to get into it.

"Moyashiko," bean sprout, the old woman said as she made her way into the phone booth.

The agent joined his companion, and both of them sought out the American agent, Henry Wray, who was waiting in one of the surveillance cabs. The Japanese agent lowered his eyes in a sort of obeisance. "I only got four of the numbers," he confessed.

"Did you?" Wray said, but the American's tone was more a hearty declaration than a question. "Well, we got the whole six!"

The agent's mouth was agape. "The truth?"

"The same," Wray said. "JDF boys had a bead on him the moment you saw him waiting. It's a number in the north of the city, in Kita-Ku."

"Do we pick him up?" the agent asked eagerly.

"No," Wray said. "He's just a messenger. We can get him anytime. What we want are the soldiers—who he calls—the action boys. Besides, we pick him up now, his friends soon know, the cell disbands, and then we're back to square one."

"But we still tail him."

"Your boss and I think that's the best way to proceed."

The agent nodded. Whether or not he agreed, it was impossible to tell. "Will we pick up the contact?"

"We'll do that," Wray replied, indicating the other four agents in the car.

Tazuko Komura, after walking away from the public phone, made her way back to her apartment block, and in her tiny, boxlike kitchen, which smelled of pickled cabbage and fish, she sat down and turned on the news. The yen had risen again, worrying Japanese business about the resultant high price of her exports relevant to other countries. Tazuko was struck by the irony that the Japanese yen—because it was one of the strongest currencies in the world—was now giving Tokyo a headache with millions at stake in exports.

She handled the TNT-based compound carefully but confidently, each malleable plastique piece of grayish-white C4 looking like a rectangular bar of putty except for its inverted-V-shaped bottom. Next Tazuko pushed in two aluminum blasting cap tubes, out of which came the detonating cord that would be started via a small, tubular, battery-operated electronic timer, its top resembling the rotary dial of a telephone except that instead of each hole moving ten spaces from operator to 1, the ten-holed rotary dial of the electronic timer was marked from one-quarter minute to forty-eight minutes. She would, of course, use the 48 setting, giving her ample time to walk away.

Now on the news, the CNN feed was showing the massive sea lift of the U.S. Second Army from Japan, each of the two corps making up the army of 108,000 men. But for every man at the front, several were needed in support functions, so the actual number in combat would be no more than 27,000.

Tazuko turned up the TV volume and heard that the American general in charge was someone called Freeman, but whether or not he was with the task force, they didn't say.

An hour after Jae had made his call, U.S. CIA agent Henry Wray and his Japanese colleagues arrived at the phone he'd rung. It was another public booth.

"Clever," Wray said. "I thought it'd be a residence. Should have known better."

"Yes," one of the Japanese agents said, but he quickly made it clear that this was not a slight against Wray, just an admission that they had all thought it would be residential.

Wray looked about him up at the forest of apartment blocks and exhaled heavily. "Where?" he asked of no one in particular. If they couldn't find the person who answered—and it didn't look as if they would—then they were, as Wray had said, back to square one.

The most senior of the Japanese agents spoke to the others, and just in case Wray's Japanese was a little rusty, he explained in English, "We'll dust the phone booth for prints. You never know."

Henry Wray nodded, his tone more one of resignation than expectation. "Might as well."

Next morning, Tazuko made herself a picnic lunch of sushi, and also packed a small bottle of mineral water. Normally she preferred to eat from one of the side-street stalls in Tokyo, but this day she didn't want to go into any shop, because afterward they would be looking for anyone who had been carrying a shoulder bag large enough to transport the explosive. It was highly unlikely they would find her, she thought, but it was best to avoid any contact with anyone. It was a bright, sunny day and Tazuko took this as a good omen. And from a purely practical point of view, it meant she could wear her sunglasses, which of course gave her more cover.

CHAPTER NINETEEN

"HERE!" THE PEOPLE'S Liberation Army bosun ordered, pointing brusquely to the portside entrance to the Jianghu frigate. On the bridge Mellin saw an officer immaculately dressed in white uniform and dark blue-banded white cap, a captain's gold insignia on his collar tabs and shoulder boards, the red star in the middle of his cap. He was a small man but carried a quiet authority about him.

"Why are you on this reef?" he asked Mellin.

Mellin was astounded by the question, his earlier moments of reverie when he knew he would be rescued now supplanted by a perplexed mood. Why are you on this reef? Surely a child could see he'd been cast upon the reef. What did the Chinese think—that he was just passing by on a ship and suddenly decided, Oh, I'll go and sit on a reef? Anyway, who in hell were they? Did they think they owned the damn reef?

As he was to find out, that's precisely what they did think— that they owned it and many more like it in the South China Sea among both the Spratly and Paracel islands, and it was not at all uncommon to have them station two PLA soldiers on a reef next to a lone four-to-six-foot-high marker claiming this or that particular reef was Chinese territory. If the published photographs of two hapless-looking PLA soldiers on duty atop a reef, unable to keep their feet dry, seemed humorous to others, they were deadly serious to the PLA. The two soldiers armed with AK-47s were ready to shoot anyone who tried to land.

"Where is the marker?" the officer asked.

Mellin looked from the officer to the bosun and back again. "What marker?"

"There was a marker on the island, proclaiming it to be the property of the People's Republic of China."

Mellin's throat was so dry he found his tongue sticking to his palate, and his first attempt to answer was garbled. The Chinese officer, still looking disapprovingly at the American, said something to the bosun, who disappeared and reappeared with a worn enamel mug of water. Mellin nodded, gulped it down, handed the mug back to the bosun with a nod of thanks and told the officer, "I don't know anything about a marker."

"There was a marker there," the officer said angrily.

"Look, I'm grateful for you picking me up, but I never saw any marker. Want to search me?"

"Do not silly man," snapped the officer, unaware of his grammatical mistake. Mellin, however, knew better than to show even the slightest amusement. This officer was not one for joking, the security of the marker amid competing claims for oil and minerals obviously his responsibility. Now Mellin understood what the Chinese who had taken him off the rock had so assiduously been looking for. Where had the marker gone?

"There is no sign of it," the officer said. "Did you use explosives?"

"Listen, Captain—"

"I am not the captain. I am second officer—Lieutenant Mung."

"All right, Lieutenant Mung. Look, I don't know anything about a marker. And if it's explosions you want to talk about, I have a few questions of my own. First of all—"

"You speak too much in haste."

Mellin slowed down. "I was on—" Mellin stopped. Whoever had attacked the *Chical* hadn't wanted to leave any witnesses alive. "I was on a fishing boat and it sank a few miles from your reef."

"This is Chinese territory," Mung interrupted. "All the Spratlys are Chinese."

"But it's hundreds of miles beyond your two-hundred-mile limit," Mellin said.

"Like your Hawaii," Mung said. The bosun thought that this was very smart, and a smug smile took him captive.

"Hawaii," Mellin began, "has been U.S. territory for more than—"

"So too with the Spratlys. Chinese were there long before anyone else."

"I don't believe that," Mellin said simply.

Lieutenant Mung spoke rapidly to the bosun, who then told Mellin, "Come with me."

A guard joined them as the bosun quickly led Mellin down below and forward to the paint locker and told him he would be given food shortly. Then the bosun slammed the door and left. Suddenly, Mellin was in utter darkness. He began to hyperventilate in sheer terror, his claustrophobia so intense that he thought he would go mad, his panic heightened by the overwhelming, cloying smell of paint, which caused his sinuses to all but close down, making it difficult for him to breathe. Within minutes he was drenched in perspiration, his clothes sticking to him like Saran Wrap, and all the while his anxiety heightened by the unknown. What were they going to do with him? The brusque way they had treated him, it was as if China and the U.S. were at war.

The fingerprints they got from the public phone in the Kita-Ku district were not helpful. The prints were smudged, and it was the forensic technician's guess that whoever had held the phone in response to the call from the Akasura Kannon Temple had probably worn gloves. Besides, it had taken them an hour to get to the booth—many people could have used it by then—and so forensics was at a loss as to why they had been asked to take prints at all.

The best they could do now, Wray thought, was to stake out the phone booth and run a security check on everyone who used it. In lieu of this long, tedious surveillance, Wray and his

Japanese colleagues were tempted to bring in Jae, but they held off for fear of making an arrest that would not stick. A crime had to happen before they could act on their suspicions that the Chongryun were up to no good. Meantime, there had been no letup in the coded radio messages from North Korea, and it was generally agreed among Western intelligence agencies that in Pyongyang the "great new leader," Kim Jong Il, like his father, the "great leader" Kim Il Sung, was about to turn up the heat.

They were wrong. Pyongyang had already sent its instructions for her mission to Tazuko Komura via Jae weeks before. The communication from Jae had been the final transmit.

CHAPTER TWENTY

FOR MOST OF the men with "George C. Scott," Douglas Freeman, the first sighting of Vietnam from the lead Hercules, a line of deep green broken here and there by palm-shaded beaches, was not particularly memorable. Only Freeman and a few others were old enough to really remember the Vietnam War, let alone to have fought in it. For most it was one of many wars America had fought, and America's defeat had not marked them as it had Freeman and others who could still recall Walter Cronkite entering their living rooms every evening to tell them the state of the war and, always, like a football score, the body count.

In any case, the predominant emotion in the plane was fear—fear of the enemy and fear of showing it. These were not conscripts, but well-trained professionals, some who had seen action in the Iraqi War and some in the invasion of Haiti, and so knowledge of both desert and jungle warfare traveled with them. But most of the 127 in the EMREF spearhead had never been in battle, and they feared that unknown. Already in the vast interior of the plane, the smell of perspiration was heavy in the air.

There was a flash!

"What the hell—" Freeman began, seeing it was one of the two reporters he'd allowed to accompany the EMREF spearhead into action. He'd chosen a CNN reporter because he knew that way he'd get a story out if he needed it for strategic reasons. The other was a photojournalist, a woman, Marte Price, from the little-known midwestern *Des Moines Register*. He disliked seeing all the big networks get all the scoops.

"I'm sorry," she began, blushing, "I didn't—"

But Freeman cut her short. "Ma'am, last thing we expect in an aircraft is a flash popping off—looks like a damn flash-bang grenade. Lucky someone didn't shoot you."

"I promise I won't do it again, General."

Freeman nodded and mumbled something about how there were going to be enough surprises to contend with once the EMREF had reached Hanoi then headed north to do business with the "red dragon," as he collectively called the Chinese.

"Huh," grunted Martinez, a Marine, formerly an auto mechanic, who hailed from Los Angeles. "That flash sure as hell frightened me. Damn near shit myself."

"You and fifty uvvers, mate," a Brit said, nodding, his cockney accent reminding Martinez of Mr. Doolittle, Eliza's father in *My Fair Lady*. The short, stocky Englishman's accent was a bit hard for Martinez to understand, but the man's eyes and gestures told most of the story. Martinez felt comforted by Doolittle's frank admission of fear, especially since the Britisher wore the simple but coveted beret of the Special Air Service, among the toughest of the tough. To be SAS was to be as handy with a parachute as with the Heckler & Koch 9mm submachine gun, to run miles with a heavy pack, to be able to live off the land from grass shoots to rats—raw, uncooked, for fear of the smell alerting the enemy—and then you had to pass the hostage exam.

The SAS were so tough that the U.S. Delta Force based their training on the English elite, who had worldwide and enduring fame not from the wars they'd stopped and Communist infiltrators they'd killed, from Aden to Malaysia, but because of the stunning raid they had mounted in full view of the TV cameras on the Iranian Embassy in London in 1961. They had all worn black, including balaclavas, to protect their identity. And then they'd melted back incognito, some of them to the regular units they were assigned to, their absence usually covered by compassionate leave or some other such conventional excuse. The Delta Force and the Green Berets didn't hop into a phone booth and do a "Clark Kent."

Both the U.S. and British phrase "Special Forces" covered all three—Delta Force, Green Berets, and SAS—in this operation, as Freeman thought equally highly of all of them. He'd fought with all of them before at different times and had admired all three, but as the Hercules crossed the coast heading for Hanoi, the ETA less than ten minutes, he had something else to tell them—not because of the common bond they shared with one another, but because they would soon be fighting against a common enemy, China's People's Liberation Army, an army which Freeman's and his men's forebears had fought back in the Korean and Vietnam wars.

"What I want you boys and ladies—" He smiled at Marte Price. "—to remember is that it isn't so strange to be asked to fight on the same side as the Vietnamese. A lot of your grandfathers fought with the South Vietnamese, and besides, two hundred years or so ago your ancestors and mine were fighting one another in the War of Independence, and we, the United States, lost more men in the fight between the Union and the Confederacy than we did in both world wars. So you see, as times change, old enemies become comrades in arms. It is the position of the United States of America and Great Britain that this Chinese attack on Vietnam threatens a hell of a lot more than Vietnam. It threatens, if it goes unchecked, the whole of Asia. And we've learned from history, if we've learned anything, that if you don't stand up to bullies in the first instances, you only encourage the sons of bitches to take more and more."

ETA Hanoi was another five minutes. Douglas Freeman saw Marte Price tucking strands of her short-cropped red hair into her helmet, but not even her camouflage fatigues could totally hide her figure. Freeman told her that once the plane landed in Hanoi the only pictures allowed would be "sans flash."

"I'm not that stupid, General," Marte said.

"Didn't say you were, ma'am. It's just that along with the truth, I don't want you to be our first casualty."

"In that case, thanks." She paused. "This is my big chance. To . . ."

She left the sentence hanging in the air. Freeman finished it for her. "To break free from the pack—be your own—" He paused. "—person."

"Yes."

"General, ETA seven minutes," Bob Cline told him.

"It was ETA five minutes—three minutes ago!"

"Yes, sir, but we've had to swing south before turning north. Captain's afraid the Hanoi triple A might let fly, mistaking us on radar for Chinese swinging west after hitting Haiphong harbor."

"Very well," Freeman said, then, turning to Marte, said, "Ms. Price?"

"Call me Marte, General."

"I prefer Price."

She looked surprised. He hadn't struck her as the formal type.

"Ms. Price," he began again, "don't take *any* photos till you establish where you are vis-à-vis headquarters."

"Where will that be?" she asked, nonplussed.

"Me," he said. "Stick with me, and whatever story you write, don't put anything about anybody saying 'over and out,' 'cause that's a contradiction in terms. Only those movie jokers in L.A. who rarely get out of bed write that guff."

"ETA four minutes," came the pilot's voice in the cavernous interior, the sound of the Hercules more thunderous than before, shaking more, but everything seemed to be going all right. As soon as they landed they would be met by the French chargé d'affaires, whose staff would direct them to camouflaged trucks already painted with the outline of a black triangle signifying a U.N. truck. Likewise, all the men's uniforms—both British and American—also sported the U.N. symbol on helmets and both shoulder patches.

"Man," Martinez's friend Johnny D'Lupo confided, "I hope those fuckers see it!"

"Balls," Martinez said. "You don't want 'em to see it. If they can see it they can shoot it."

"Bloody right," enjoined Doolittle, whom the others had dubbed "Doctor." "I hope they don't see me but I see them."

"Sir," Martinez called out to the general, his élan with a superior officer easy not only because he was American, but because he was one of the elite whose forebears' battle honors went back to the Halls of Montezuma. "Sir, how long you think we'll be goin' in the trucks?"

"Twenty-five miles from Hanoi to Thuong," Freeman said.

He meant Phu Lang Thuong. "Roads are pretty bad and we're coming in on the leading edge of the rainy season. I guess about forty-five minutes to an hour. No time to dip your—" He fell silent, and this was greeted with an assortment of catcalls, whistles, and cheers.

"What were you going to say, General?" Marte inquired.

"You'll have to excuse me," he said, mumbling something about conferring with the captain.

Marte asked Martinez what the general was about to say.

"It's kinda crude, miss."

"C'mon," she pressed, her notebook out, camera slung over her shoulder and her moving awkwardly in the seat belt H harness.

"No time to dip your wick," D'Lupo put in. "No leave."

"Oh," she said, and smiled. Farther down the row, D'Lupo turned to Dr. Doolittle, his voice hardly audible above the roar of the engines. "I'm in love with her, Doc!"

"You and everybody else, mate," Doolittle responded. "I've had a hard-on ever since we left the States."

"Yes," D'Lupo said.

"Well, don't worry, old son. Sooner we clean this lot up at Thuong, sooner we'll 'ave time to spend wiv young Marte."

They both knew it was bull, Martinez, like everybody else aboard except maybe Freeman, scared about going in. Only a few had seen sustained combat in Iraq—and hell, that was in the desert. In any kind of jungle, they knew, you couldn't see an arm's length in front of you.

"Well hell," D'Lupo said, "we won't be going in till the rest of the EMREF arrive."

Doolittle didn't know whether this was supposed to mean they'd have more time to ogle Marte Price or have more time to collectively steel their nerves. But then Doolittle and every other man aboard the Hercules was discovering once again that the company of your fellows could only go so far in comforting you—ultimately you were alone.

In the U.S. battle group, with the carrier USS *Enterprise* at center, steaming into the South China Sea, an echo was picked up by one of the Sea Kings' dipping sonar and relayed to the sub *Santa Fe* by advanced warning aircraft. The commander of the *Santa Fe* prepared to dive the boat.

"Officer of the deck—last man down—hatch secured," came the seaman's report.

The executive officer moved to his position as officer of the deck and in turn reported to the captain, "Last man down. Hatch secured, aye. Captain, the ship is rigged for dive, current depth one two fathoms. Checks with the chart. Request permission to submerge the ship."

"Very well, officer of the deck," the captain responded. "Submerge the ship."

"Submerge the ship, aye, sir. Dive—two blasts on the dive alarm. Dive, dive."

The alarm wheezed twice sufficiently loud that every crewman aboard could hear, but not so loud as to resonate through the hull. A seaman saw to the vents and reported, "All vents shut."

"Vents shut, aye."

For any visitor to a sub, the obsessive litany of the dive seemed to be unnecessarily repetitive—almost comical—but there would be nothing comical about it if a single order was botched and the ship were to dive too deep too fast. Within seconds it could be below its crush depth around three thousand feet, and the next minute would be hurtling down unable to reverse its course, the quickly mounting pressure of thousands of tons per square inch driving it in excess of a hundred miles per hour to hit the bottom like a bomb imploding, its giant frame no more than flat-pressed metal scrap.

A seaman was reading off the depth. "Sixty-two . . . sixty-four . . ." and a chief of the boat reported, "Officer of the deck, conditions normal on the dive."

"Very well, diving officer," acknowledged the OOD, who in turn reported, "Captain, at one forty feet trim satisfactory."

"Very well," the captain said. "Steer five hundred feet ahead standard."

The OOD instructed the helmsman. "Helm all ahead standard. Diving officer, make the depth for five hundred feet."

The captain glanced over at the ethereal blue of the sonar room and its half-dozen green video screens of yellow lines, each line in the "waterfall" a sound source from the ocean, a world not of silence but a cacophony of noise, from the frying sound of schools of shrimp to the steady deep beat of a submarine's cooling pump.

"Anything interesting, Sonar?"

"Negative."

"Maybe it's a diesel they heard. No pump."

"Could be, sir."

The captain knew he could go active, but then his own position would be betrayed. "We'll wait."

"Aye aye, sir."

The Chinese frigate was now in rough water, and Mellin, alone in the fume-laden darkness, was violently ill. He had experienced seasickness twice before—once in a friend's sailboat off the California coast near Big Sur, the other time during a ride up from the Mekong Delta aboard one of the U.S. riverine patrol boats. It was the most terrible sickness he could imagine, and he'd seen hardened combat troops humbled by the ordeal. And whereas normally the eyes became adjusted to darkness, the darkness of the paint locker was so absolute that he could not make out anything but the hard bulkhead as once more the ship's bow rose hard astarboard, shook as if it were coming apart, then fell through a gut-emptying space, colliding with the sea.

He heard a noise and prayed it was someone coming to let him out.

CHAPTER TWENTY-ONE

HIGH UP IN the Hong Kong tower that he owned by special agreement with the People's Administrative Committee of Hong Kong, Jonas Breem of Caloil surveyed Victoria harbor and the clustering of high-rise apartments and business offices, and imagined what it might be like ten years hence. Breem, gesturing with his large scotch and ice to his concubine, Mi Yin, said, "Beijing will make a mint."

"Maybe not," proffered Mi Yin, a diminutive five feet, the sheen of her black hair catching a reflection from Breem's opulent bar.

Breem didn't turn his head, but kept looking out the enor-

mous tintcd plate-glass window, swirling the ice in his drink.
"And what the shit would you know about it?" he said.
"You're paid to fuck, not forecast."

She shrugged, apparently not bothered by his vulgar outburst. "I was just thinking," she said matter-of-factly.

"Well don't," he cautioned. "Get your ass over here."

She got up from the couch, the midnight blue *qi pao* she
was wearing amply split at the thigh, revealing a brown slash
of flesh that Breem always found enticing. His drink in his
right hand, he steered her in front of him with his left,
unzipped the *qi pao* and slid his hand around, following the
line of her bra, cupping her breasts, squeezing them tightly.

"You like that?" he asked.

"Yes," she lied, and wondered how it was that such a man
had risen to the top of the heap in his cutthroat business yet
was so stupid about women as to think a woman liked having
her breasts squeezed tightly. Maybe he knew very well they
didn't like it, but he kept doing it anyhow, control of any situation being his nirvana.

Breem called her just one of his Hong Kong "fringe bene-
fits," though he knew she was highly intelligent as well as
beautiful, her sense of irony as subtle as her perfume, her timing deft as a lover of long experience. He was also sure Mi
Yin was an operative of the Gong An Bu, the Chinese secret
police—sent to keep tabs on him—her "accidental" meeting
with him no doubt carefully arranged by Beijing. Well, he'd
screw her on behalf of the people, he resolved, and she
wouldn't get any more out of him than he wanted to give. He
was convinced that after she'd taken off the sexy, thigh-split *qi
pao* and made love, and he lay back snoring, she'd be quickly
checking his briefcase for the seismic and drill reports he received daily by fax from the various drill sites scattered
throughout the countries of Southeast Asia. In one of those
quirky war situations not known to the general public, the Chinese had taken over all the drill sites, moving all the American
experts to a concentration camp, yet the daily drill reports from
the skeleton-staffed Chinese drill site crews were still faxed to
Breem in Hong Kong as the head of Chical Enterprises and
Caloil.

"Why, I wonder?" Mi Yin had asked. "I mean with America
and China fighting—"

"For Chrissake, you can't—" He began unclipping her bra

and peeling, sliding the *qi pao* down over her shoulders and buttocks. "—be that stupid."

"What d'you mean?" she asked like a petulant schoolgirl.

"China's one of the biggest goddamn investors on the Hong Kong exchange. That's one reason why they don't want this war to drag on. They're looking for a knockout punch early in the game to show the Vietnamese who owns what." He slid his hand down inside her magenta pink panties. "It's one reason they don't want to upset the agreement between Caloil and Beijing. C'mon, let's get into the sack."

"How about all the Americans from the drill ships?" she asked. "The ones taken prisoner."

"Hey, what the fuck is this—an interrogation? Since when do you give a shit who's taken prisoner? Anyway, the guys that came out to work the Caloil sites knew what the fuck they were doing. They got extra money."

"You don't care about them."

"Much as I care about you, sweetheart," which Mi Yin knew was not at all. "C'mon," he commanded. "Take off your drawers."

"Close the drapes," she said.

"Why? I want the whole of Hong Kong to see us fuck."

He was bluffing and she knew it. As chief executive officer of Caloil, he had to obey, at least publicly, the social mores of Hong Kong. He had to toe the line a bit more regarding sex. But even that didn't faze him because in the end, when the party's political purists, the cadres, had their say about good socialistic behavior, it would be the same old story—all a question of money, in this case Hong Kong dollars.

"C'mon," he said, "go down on me!" She sat on the huge water bed, its surface undulating like a small sea as she pulled her hair back and reached across his hairy body for a condom on the bedside table, her breasts brushing his face. He bit at her nipple.

"Ow—"

"C'mon, you beauty—you love it, right? Or would you like to be having it off with all these saps?"

She cocked her head prettily, like some rare and beautiful bird of paradise. "Saps? What does it mean?"

"You serious?"

"Yes," she said unapologetically. "I don't know what 'saps' means."

"Losers," he said. "All the losers the Chinese are putting in that camp."

"You really don't care about them," she said again, looking puzzled—or was she just putting on a Miss Goody Two-Shoes act? he wondered.

"No, I don't care," he answered. "Why should I? They're all over twenty-one, sugar. They don't know what makes the world go around by now, it's tough tit for them—right?"

She shrugged noncommittally.

"What do you think of that?" he asked, looking down at his erection. "That's what makes my world go round. That and money. Right? You don't do it for free, do you?"

Mi Yin didn't answer.

"You love me?" he asked. His laugh was hard and scornful. "You're a hooker, Mi Yin—an expensive one, but you're a hooker, right? But listen," he said, propping himself up on an elbow, grabbing her wrist, "just remember you're *my* hooker. Bought and paid for. Right?"

She nodded.

He fell back on the water bed, causing a wild wave in the water bed, which shivered before it started settling down. "But man, are you built." He grabbed her ponytail down over the front of her head and pulled her down on him. Her mouth was too dry. He reached out and poured from his drink.

"Now—" He laughed, struck by what he thought was a terrific pun. "—have a scotch on the cock!"

The things she did for Beijing—the safety of her parents in the balance.

So let her go through his briefcase, he thought, checking the seismic and drill reports he received daily by fax from the drill ships, making sure that he wasn't pulling a fast one—drilling, finding gas or oil, but giving Beijing a different seismic profile from somewhere else in the South China Sea, where there was little if any promise of gas or oil. The trick was to give them a seismic profile made in the same depth as where you'd found good promise of oil, and to return to the true position of the find later on, until ownership of all claims in the South China Sea islands had been settled either by the international court in The Hague or by what busy law professors were calling a "prevailing military presence"—which meant, CEO Breem had told his EOs, "which army in the area has the biggest fucking guns."

Those that might be involved besides the Vietnamese and

the People's Liberation Army were Taiwan, Indonesia, Malaysia, and the Philippines, all of whom claimed part of the islands and reefs scattered over the 35-million-square-kilometer South China Sea, nearly four times bigger than the United States, including Alaska. Breem dismissed Malaysia and the Philippines. The Malaysians didn't have the balls to start anything with Beijing, not with thirty-six percent of Malaysia's population being Chinese.

Then there were the Philippines, but Breem thought they had enough trouble at home trying to handle their terminally ill economy. Besides, they'd kicked out the Americans from the big base at Subic Bay and the American jets from Clark Field. "Stupid!" Breem had told his executives. No, the fight, if there was to be any, would be between the big military muscle in the region: China and such traditional rivals and enemies as the Vietnamese and the Taiwanese, with North Korea always a wild card.

Then again, it wasn't clear whether Taiwan and Beijing might not subsume enough of their differences to team up, making a joint claim for the islands, so rumor had it, along a proposed fifty-one, forty-nine percent China-Taiwan split.

And now the ex-Soviet republics were having a basement sale of everything from the upgraded MiG-29s to submarines, the PLA was modernizing, and part of the ex-Soviets' sales ploy was throwing in pilot training for the MiG-29s to sweeten the deal. "Smart move," Breem told his executives, noting that the Vietnamese navy was strictly brown water—coastal patrol—but since China had started purchasing more submarines from Russia to go blue water, so had Vietnam. With the forced withdrawal of U.S. naval forces from the Philippines, Breem said, "The whole region is a goddamn powder keg!" But he was sure he'd backed the right horse. China would win.

CHAPTER TWENTY-TWO

"STAND UP!"

It was said with the same bullying tone as the first time Mellin had heard it years ago in the Hanoi Hilton, the POW camp during the time some Chinese-speaking Vietnamese had helped staff the jail.

Mellin could hardly stand, his legs shaky from both dehydration and the continuing violence of the ship's peculiar corkscrew motion in the heavy seas. The Chinese sailor stepped back sharply, almost tripping over a hawser. The smell of the paint locker combined with that of old rope, sweat, and vomit hit him with the force of a physical blow. The sailor yelled something at Mellin, to which Mellin, whey-faced and unsteady, nevertheless answered, "Well, how the hell d'you think I like it, you bastard?"

The man struck him sideways with a closed fist, sending Mellin crashing through the doorway onto the deck, momentarily concussed, blood running from a scrape on his cheek. Suddenly, the foredeck and gun housing seemed to come alive with amplified sound as the officer on watch in the ship's bridge harshly reprimanded the crewman who had just hit Mellin, telling the crewman to help the American up. The man made a motion to help Mellin, but the American pushed the offered hand aside. "I can get up myself, you bastard!"

He saw the Chinese face flush with anger, and Mellin knew if it hadn't been for the intervention of whoever it was up on the bridge, he most probably would have been sprawled out again on the deck. The man grunted and, motioning roughly for Mellin to follow him, walked off, his legs perfectly balancing against the yaw and crashing of the ship, Mellin barely able to stand, his legs still feeling rubbery. The next minute he was left staggering like a drunk against the remainder of a huge wave that had hit the ship hard amidships, heavy and billowing spray draining off the superstructure and running down the scuppers like a flash flood. But unexpectedly, Mellin felt much better for the bracing, drenching water. The combination of cold water and fresh salty air partially revived him, and though he still felt woozy, he could feel his whole body benefiting. For the first time in hours, the sinus-stuffing stench of paint and associated odors left him.

Along with the rush of fresh air, he felt more confident, his determination returning, whereas in the stinking forward locker his seasickness had been so acute that all thoughts of the future, let alone hope for it, had vanished. He wasn't proud of the fact, but then he'd never felt that ill before either. And it was a matter of conditioning. When he'd been a young man in Vietnam as part of the U.S. Special Forces, member of an elite team whose élan was the best possible, he was in top physical condition, and as the rigorous training had toughened his body, it also toughened his confidence.

No matter how hard life had been in the oil business, from the deep freeze of an Oklahoma winter to the sweltering days high atop a deck in the South China Sea, life in the Special Forces had been tougher. And it was this that Mellin was harkening back to—imagining, if only momentarily, he was with his old team in the Delta and that they were watching him now.

Inside the ship he was taken to a small cabin aft of the mess. The cabin was crammed with supplies—cardboard boxes of cans—leaving room for only four men, one wooden stool, and two plastic chairs. The first thing Mellin noticed was how much better the ship was riding amidships than in the gut-wrenching paint locker forward. Though the chairs and the two men in them, both junior officers, threatened to tilt every time the ship rose to meet a new onslaught, the two officers remained all but motionless, letting their feet and legs adapt to the roll and pitch of the ship. The fourth man stood at the door, legs well apart, arms folded, his face larger than most, fat lips tight together, eyes staring. His whole demeanor was a threat, all but daring Mellin to make a try at getting out, though where he could go if he did break out Mellin didn't know.

"Why," began the older of the two junior officers, "were you on our reef?"

"*Your* reef?" Mellin countered.

"All reefs are ours," said the younger officer, a thin, short, intense man, probably in his mid-twenties.

"All the reefs in the world?" Mellin said.

"In the South China Sea," said the older, mid-fortyish, and stouter man, whose tone was not nearly as excited, but nevertheless more menacing in its carefully measured cadences, doing battle with the scream of the wind and crashing seas. "We have traditional rights to all the reefs. Chinese fishermen here long before anyone else."

"Is that right?"

"Yes."

"How do you know it's the truth? Could have been any of a dozen nationalities."

"Chinese were here first," the older man said.

"So you believe?"

"So we know."

"So you've been told."

The older man, without turning, said something in Chinese, but Mellin could tell it wasn't meant for him. He understood the word "now"—they were always telling you "now" in the POW camp. When the older man finished speaking, the heavier man guarding the doorway came quickly to attention and left the cabin. The stout man took a packet of cigarettes and offered one to Mellin.

"No thanks," Mellin said. The younger, thinner one eyed the pack of cigarettes—Camels—and when he saw his fellow officer take one then put the pack back in his jacket, he took out his own, a red packet of Fight for the People! cigarettes, and sullenly lit one.

"Who," the older man asked, "discovered America?"

"Christopher Columbus," Mellin said, nonplussed.

"Huh—" the older man said, blowing out the smoke at Mellin. "So you believe. It could have been any of a dozen nationalities."

Mellin said nothing.

"Yes, yes," the younger officer cut in, full of enthusiasm and victory. "Red Indians! Yes. Ah-ha! Yes, Red Indians!"

The door opened and the guard reappeared with a coil of rope and stood behind Mellin. The older officer took another long drag on his cigarette and asked, "What were you doing on the reef?"

"It looked a nice day for a swim. I was shipwrecked—as if you didn't know."

"What ship?"

They seemed so intent on knowing the details, Mellin intuitively felt that his refusal to give them answers might be his only chance of survival, remembering how easily the lives of those on the rig had been snuffed out. "Am I under some kind of arrest? If I am, you'd better—"

"*You,*" the old man said suddenly, "were aboard the drill ship *Chical.*"

"Was I?"

"Yes," the younger one chimed in. "On the drill ship *Chical.*"

Had there been no other survivors? Mellin wondered.

"The drill ship for *Chical,*" the older officer repeated. "You were working on her—yes?"

Mellin said nothing, and the older officer sighed, nodding at the guard standing behind the American, who now tied Mellin securely to the chair. The guard's right hand bunched into a fist, and he backhanded Mellin so hard the left-side legs of the chair came off the floor, the whack echoing in the small cabin.

"Were you on the *Chical?*" the older officer pressed, his creased forehead making it evident that his impatience was mounting. The guard struck again, the blow leaving Mellin with a ringing in his ears so loud that it smothered every other sound. In that moment the point of information as to whether or not Mellin had been on the *Chical* became academic, the quest for information now becoming a test of wills. The older officer looked tired, the guard watching him attentively, waiting for the order to hit the American again. But instead the older man rose, the younger one following suit, the guard bitterly disappointed.

"Take him back," the older man ordered, in a tone of finality.

With the younger officer in tow, he left the cabin. The guard untied Mellin as roughly as he could, but left the American's hands bound behind him and jabbed the prisoner up off the chair.

"Follow me," the guard ordered, and made his way forward out the door onto the well deck, his lean compensating for the sharp pitching of the ship, the fact that he allowed his prisoner to walk behind instead of in front emphasizing his contempt. The very thought of being taken back to the paint locker churned Mellin's stomach, his anticipation of the heavy fume-

laden locker enough to worsen the pounding of the headache
he had from the guard's blows to his head.

At the door of the paint locker Mellin stopped and turned,
waiting for the guard to untie him. The guard merely grinned
and shoved Mellin forward, the sill tripping him, causing him
to fall headlong into the semidarkness among half-used cans
of paint, dirty cleaning rags, and vomit, the nose-plugging
smell rising all about him, making it difficult for him to
breathe. The dampness above his right eye, blood from a cut,
now began to sting, and his body convulsed as he threw up
from the nausea brought on by the overwhelming stench of the
oil-based paint and urine. He was sure the guard was leaving
him tied up contrary to the older officer's intent but he could
do nothing about it, or at least everything that had happened to
him conspired to convince him nothing could be done.

He had never felt so low—not even in 'Nam. There, at least,
he could fight back. But here in the rolling, pitching darkness
of the tiny paint locker, he felt absolutely abandoned. Mellin
thought of his sister, Angela, who had been posted all these
years as MIA, wondering if her final moments had been like
this—utterly alone—or had she had it worse than he? Was she
perhaps still alive? A prisoner? Or was she dead? He clung to
the idea she was still alive, as if somehow he had unfinished
business, her unknown fate something to be settled, something
to concentrate upon in his own abandonment, something to
hold on to. Why? he asked himself as he lay sick on the cold,
metal floor. Why were the Chinese so bent on finding out
whether or not he'd been on the *Chical*? Had they been behind
the attack? What made the Chinese authorities so interested in
him?

The truth was, they weren't interested in Danny Mellin. The
ship's officers' Neanderthal interrogation of him was merely
the result of them carrying out Beijing's orders; orders which,
in the seething bureaucratic maze of the Chinese capital, had
now been forgotten in the sudden avalanche of paperwork oc-
casioned by the war.

The activation of China's twenty Main Force divisions—300,000 men, nine hundred planes, over a thousand
T-69 tanks, and fourteen hundred pieces of artillery, much of it
self-propelled—required a massive bureaucratic effort. An
army of clerks in the Great Hall of the People and beyond,
who, from the ministerial level of arranging finance through

Beijing's holdings on the Hong Kong stock exchange, to the more than twenty clerks required for each soldier at the front, complained that there were not enough computers to help reduce the task.

In fact, even Schwarzkopf's HQ with all its computerization still required no less than thirty million phone calls for the bombing offensive against Iraq alone, and still needed three *hundred* Americans behind the lines for every American soldier at the front.

CHAPTER TWENTY-THREE

THE MOMENT THE massive tires of the Hercules touched and screeched on the runway at the Gia Lam airfield southeast of Hanoi's center, the plane came under sniper fire, several rounds penetrating the fuselage, a ricochet striking and zinging off an EMREF trooper's helmet. "How rude!" Doolittle said.

"Jesus Christ," D'Lupo said, ducking. "Thought this friggin' place was supposed to be secure."

"Settle down," Freeman intoned coolly over the PA system, not showing his own surprise. "Bound to be a few Chinese insurgents—take a potshot in hopes of shaking us up, then trot off home to bed. Right?"

"Fucking shakes me up," D'Lupo told Martinez, the latter agreeing, gripping his rifle tightly. Doolittle meanwhile watched the photojournalist, Marte Price, quickly jotting down notes, stopping for a moment to push away a wisp of hair beneath her helmet.

"General," she asked Freeman, "how about a shot of the EMREF spearhead just before they deplane?"

Freeman nodded. "All right, boys, Ms. Price wants a photo of you heroes. Smile—and that's an order."

Marte Price was annoyed. What she didn't want was a

photograph of 126 troops grinning from ear to ear. The flash seemed to illuminate the whole plane. One soldier asleep—the tension having already drained him—suddenly sat up. "What the—"

It was good for a laugh, and Marte Price was satisfied. A startled soldier was a good pic for the next edition of the *Des Moines Register*. But already, even as the huge plane was coming to a standstill, she was feeling dishonest, somehow corrupted, knowing full well that the *Register*'s editor, unless told otherwise, would run the picture as one of a soldier in a moment of high combat stress. As such it would be taken off the wire by most major papers in America, particularly given the fact that apart from CNN, Freeman had excluded any major media network.

Two of the aircraft's crew stood by as the massive rear door/ramp was lowered and two Humvee "scouts," each armed with a TOW missile launcher and .50 caliber machine gun, rolled off onto the tarmac. They were followed by the two lines of troops, none of whom were below the level of E-7 Sergeant First Class when they volunteered for EMREF duty. The sniping had stopped.

"You figure this is worth fifty-five bucks a month?" D'Lupo said, referring to the Airborne's hazardous duty pay.

"No way," Martinez responded.

Freeman saw two Vietnamese, one a cadre—a political officer—coming toward him dressed in traditional black pajamas and lion-tamer hat, the other a senior military officer dressed in the camouflage green khaki of the new Vietnam uniform.

"General Freeman," the cadre said, smiling. "We welcome you and your troops to Vietnam."

"Cam on," Freeman said, extending his hand first, though he didn't like it, to the political officer and then to General Vinh.

"What'd he say?" D'Lupo whispered. " 'C'mon!'?"

"No, you fucking wop," Martinez said. "It's gook for 'thank you.' "

"You speak it too?" a surprised D'Lupo pressed.

"Yeah. Me and the general do our homework, see?"

"Oh yeah," D'Lupo challenged. "All right then, what's 'fuck off' in Vietnamese?"

"Easy," Martinez said. *"Chuc ngu ngon!"*

"All right, smartass, so you know gook."

In the penumbra of light about the ramp, D'Lupo saw a woman in Vietnamese uniform, then another carrying baskets toward the plane. D'Lupo couldn't take his eyes off the woman. It seemed as if her whole leg was showing. She was walking toward Freeman, who was politely but firmly telling his Vietnamese host, through an interpreter now, that he was given ample assurances by Hanoi via the Pentagon that the Hanoi airfields were secure and that if there were sniping around Gia Lam Field, why the hell didn't Hanoi tower divert the American Hercules thirteen miles north of the city proper to Noi Bai Airport?

Through his interpreter the cadre assured the general that the Gia Lam Airport was secure. There had been only one sniper, an ex-NVA regular who, the cadre explained, was mentally unstable, so that when he saw an American plane, and a huge one at that, as big as one of the B-52 bombers that had attacked Hanoi in the Vietnam War, he had had a false memory—the cadre meant "flashback"—and shot at the big plane.

"I believe," the cadre added, "that you have similar problems with veterans in the United States?"

"Yes," Freeman replied, tempted to say that as he understood it, Marxist-Leninism would make a balanced personality impossible, but realizing the cadre's explanation was an olive branch being extended. Freeman accepted it. "Yes, we shot up one another quite a bit, didn't we?" After the interpreter had finished, the cadre smiled, shaking Freeman's hand again.

By now almost every one of Freeman's 127-man spearhead had been given a lei of welcome by one of the female V.A. regulars, CNN already bouncing it off a satellite, beaming it back to the States, and Marte Price busily taking shots of the cadre and the two generals meeting, each handshake a polite but not overly warm gesture of willing cooperation. Once he realized the CNN camera was rolling, Freeman—the first note of anxiety present in his voice since he'd left Hawaii—called his aide over. "Bob, for God's sake make sure CNN gets a shot of the British SAS boys. Emphasize that this is a U.S.-led *U.N.*, I repeat *U.N.*, action, and that other countries will be making their contributions to the U.N. force within a matter of days. And make sure those—" He stopped, unable to think of the right word for a second.

"Gurkhas," Cline said.

"Exactly," Freeman said, slapping him on the shoulder.

"And mention the Aussies, New Zealanders, South Koreans . . ." He steered Cline away from the Vietnamese general and cadre and toward his heavily loaded troops, his voice subdued. "But Bob, for Chrissake don't say anything about the Japanese support—not even logistical support. These jokers in Hanoi, like much of Asia, hate the Japanese—figure the Japs still haven't made amends for atrocities."

"How about our My Lai?" Cline asked, reminding Freeman of the massacre of a whole Vietnamese village by U.S. troops.

"Bad as it was, Bob, it doesn't start to compare with the widespread rape and pillage perpetrated by the sons of Nippon—sons of bitches traumatized the whole of Southeast Asia. And Bob . . . ?"

"Sir?"

Freeman's voice was friendly enough as he smiled back at the Vietnamese general and cadre before saying quietly to his aide, "Bob, coming down the ramp I heard some joker use the word 'gook.' " Now Freeman was smiling broadly. "You tell 'em if I hear any disparaging remarks about our U.N. allies, I will personally cut the offender's prick off. You got that?"

"Yes, General."

General Vinh asked in heavily accented English how long Freeman wanted to rest his troops before moving up to the snake—the name given by the Vietnamese Army to the winding front line that snaked its way up, down, and at times around the base of the hills north of Hanoi.

"Rest?" Freeman responded. "General, we didn't come here to rest. Vietnamese people are being attacked by China, the U.N. sent us to help, and that means now. We can move out the moment my boys finish relieving themselves. Main body of Second Army in—" He almost said *Japan*. "—is already assembling for airlift. First planeload'll be here in a matter of days."

General Vinh understood most of it, except for the part about "relieving" themselves.

"Gia ve sinh," the interpreter explained.

"Yes," Freeman cut in. *"Gia ve sinh,"* adding, "Thunder box!"

When this was explained to General Vinh, he uttered an "Ah . . ." of recognition, smiling broadly. *"Toi*—Come," he said, motioning to a line of ten three-ton trucks—all American made—looking the worse for wear, their engines spitting and coughing in two lines beyond four portable toilets that had been rolled into the apron of light about the Hercules.

As the trucks, their "blackout" headlights mere slits of light in the enormous darkness, rolled north from the Gia Lam airfield, Freeman's spearhead troops, whose main function now was to carry out a recon in force for the benefit of Second Army, heard the sound of clapping in the darkness. Through their infrared goggles, against a soupy green background, they could see lines of Vietnamese civilians clapping here and there and waving tiny U.S. and U.N. flags.

"Ain't that somethin'?" D'Lupo said, taking his infrareds off, as he, like others, was prone to severe headache from the goggles if he left them on too long. "Gooks welcoming U.S. soldiers. I'm gonna tell my grandchildren 'bout this one."

"You'll tell nobody, D'Lupo," a Delta first lieutenant said, "if you keep callin' 'em gooks. Remember what the general said—he'll cut your prick off!"

"All right," D'Lupo riposted. "I'll call 'em 'Charlie.' "

"Shit," Martinez cut in. "You tryin' to sound like a vet?"

"Listen, dick brain, I figure in a coupla hours we'll start being vets."

"If you last that long," Martinez said.

"Thanks a lot, Marty," D'Lupo charged. "You're all laughs, you know that?"

Dave Rhin, a black man from Chicago, flicked up his IR goggles. "Man, there are thousands of 'em lined up. See 'em plain as day."

"Yeah," D'Lupo said in the rough camaraderie of soldiers. "Well, they're gonna find it hard to see you, Rhin."

"I told you," Martinez chimed in, "to use that fuckin' sunscreen, Rhin!"

"Hey, dick brain," Rhin retorted, "they gonna see you honkies all right. They don't need no IRs to see you, man."

"Oh," Doolittle said to his fellow SAS troopers in the truck, "isn't this nice? We're on our way to a punch-up wiv Charlie an' these blokes start a fuckin' race riot. Lovely, i'n'it?"

"Can't understand a fuckin' word you say, limey," Rhin said.

"No matter," Martinez joshed, flicking up his IRs. "Brits are full of shit anyway."

"You'll get yours, mite!"

"All right," the first lieutenant said on the cellular. "Pipe down. We'll be in enemy country before you know it. General wants you all quiet as of now."

The silence was deafening. Freeman had permitted them to let off steam on the way in from the Gia Lam Field. But now that they were past the Ho Tay—West Lake—approaching the Song Hong, or Red River, and Thang Long Bridge, a prime target for U.S. bombers during the Vietnam War, every one of the 127 men, including Freeman, was alone with his fear.

Marte Price had wanted to stay in Hanoi to cover the war, but the CNN crew of three had decided to go to the front, and being the only woman reporter, she felt she would lose face not only for herself but for all the women in the armed services if she didn't go with Freeman's spearhead recon group. Someone had joked she'd decided to go "all the way," but there were no laughs.

Sitting in the second armed Humvee behind the vehicle carrying Freeman, Cline, and the two Vietnamese, Marte Price was sick with fear. She found, to her astonishment, that one's teeth really do chatter in the face of a danger so overwhelming that she felt a shortness of breath—a rapidly rising surge of panic that momentarily convinced her she was having a heart attack.

Southwest of Hanoi, in the Vietnamese People's Army indoctrination center at Xuan Mai, Vietnamese militia and reservists were being told once again that it was not the American people in the sixties and early seventies who had declared war on the freedom-loving peoples of Vietnam but the "imperialist criminals" Kennedy, Johnson, and McNamara. The fact that the U.S. had never actually declared war, attested to by the Pentagon's insistence on still writing about the war with a lowercase w, was not mentioned.

The American people, continued the cadre, had had their own civil war and a war of independence against the British imperialists. Very few of those listening were paying much attention to the cadre's harangue. All they cared about was that in Vietnam's never-ending struggle—the first Indochina War, the second Indochina War, and the wars against the Chinese—war had been the way of life. Peace was the abnormal condition.

This time it was again China, which had had its eyes on the lush Red River Delta since two hundred years before Christ. The Vietnamese soldiers didn't need a cadre to tell them the obvious: their country was again under attack by the Chinese. No one bothered raising the theoretical contradiction of one Communist state waging war on another Communist state, for everyone understood that this was a war not of ideology but for territory, the rich deposits of oil beneath the hundreds of offshore islands from the Gulf of Tonkin to Borneo. In any case, the Americans had helped the Vietnamese once before, giving them arms and money to fight the Japanese in Vietnam. War was the way of life.

The militia and reservists were told that should it become necessary, they might have to fight side by side with the Americans to plug any gaps the Chinese attack might open. Most of the subdued talk among the young militia and reservists, many of them women, was of how anxious they were to fight with the Americans. Most of them were too young to have fought in America's undeclared war against North Vietnam, and the same would be true for many, though not all, of the Americans. Besides, it was a well-known fact that Americans had everything, and there was a collective craving among the Vietnamese militia and reservists for American cigarettes. Not only were they the best cigarettes in the world, but in many transactions throughout Southeast Asia they had become the currency of exchange, a prime cargo for the South China Sea pirates.

The indoctrination session ended with several militiamen dozing off, the general belief being that there would be no further Chinese breakthrough, that their Vietnamese regular army would soon counterattack and with the help of American bombers force the Chinese back from the Lang Son line across the border.

The arrival of the EMREF recon spearhead was known to Beijing within half an hour of the Hercules landing, CNN having beaten the transmissions of Chinese Vietnamese agents who radioed the news to the Chinese capital. But CNN, as part of its "deal" with Freeman, hadn't disclosed it was only one Hercules, and had it not been for the agents' transmissions, Beijing would have been under the impression that the total EMREF force of several thousand had already arrived in Hanoi.

In any event, the news jolted Beijing, and within minutes the HQs of the Chengdu and Guangzhou military regions had been notified that the gains made so far by Generals Wei and

Wang must be consolidated as soon as possible on both flanks of the Lang Son front—*before* the American genius for logistical buildup could be exercised.

"It is like," General Wei's cadres explained to his troops, "attacking a loaded bullock cart—kill the bullock driver first before he can unload his weapons and ammunition." In this instance, Wei explained to his HQ personnel, the carts—the U.S. air supply line—might not be stopped by the Chinese air force, but the lead driver, Freeman, was already here and could be killed.

The Chinese general announced that any PLA unit wiping out Freeman's advance spearhead would receive a "thousand commendations from the people." This phrase was officialese for the fact that any unit that wiped out Freeman's spearhead force would receive a monetary reward—one thousand dollars U.S. It was a small fortune, and on the black market it would buy many American cigarettes. Some senior cadres objected that this was unworthy of the people's army ideology and was a "capitalist corruption" of the troops, to which Generals Wei and Wang responded that they were responsible for the military tactics and that the cadres, with all due respect, should keep out of it—it was a military not a political matter. A senior cadre continued to object, and Wei told him in very unpolitical terms to perform a sexual act on himself with a pointed stick.

CHAPTER TWENTY-FOUR

A THOUSAND FEET below the surface of the South China Sea aboard *Santa Fe*, a sonar analysis confirmed the earlier Sea King's contact as a "Sierra Four," or probable enemy surface vessel.

"Possible hostile by nature of sound, bearing one four six! Range eighteen miles!"

"Very well," the captain said calmly, already at the control room's attack island. "Man battle stations."

"Man battle stations, aye, sir," a seaman of the watch repeated, pushing the "yellow" button that sent a pulsing F sharp slurring to G throughout the ship.

The captain turned to the D.O. "Diving officer, periscope depth."

"Periscope depth, aye, sir."

The captain quickly, quietly, took the PA mike from its cradle. "This is the captain. I have the con. Commander Rogers retains the deck. Up search scope."

"Ahead two-thirds."

"Scope's breaking," reported one of the watchmen. "Scope's clear."

The captain and the search scope's column became one, moving about, looking for a dot on the flat metallic-colored sea.

Now the sub's sonar had picked up the cavitation, or sound of water bubbles caused by the turning propeller of the unknown ship. At first it was suspected that it might be one of the destroyers of the carrier battle group, but within seconds the noise, having passed through the acoustic spectrum analyzer, suggested the craft was either a fast 32-knot Luda-class destroyer or a Jianghu-class frigate. In any case, her speed was now 23 knots, the details on the computer screen quickly giving the two classes' dimensions and armament, both equipped with antisubmarine depth charges, surface-to-surface HY2 missiles and mines. The ship was now on a heading not for the *Santa Fe*, whose presence she had probably not detected, but in the direction of the *Enterprise* carrier battle group, an enemy mission that clearly fell under the *Santa Fe* rules of engagement and within the parameters of the sub's mission orders to protect the CVBG.

"Make the tube ready in all respects," the captain ordered.

"Make the tube ready in all respects, aye, sir."

The Luda class had now increased her speed to 25 knots.

The sub's captain stopped moving the scope. "Bearing. Mark!"

"Range. Mark! Down scope!" He heard the soft whine of the retracting M-18 search scope equipped with infrared. "I hold one visual contact. Range?"

"Seventeen point two miles." On the green "waterfall" of the display screen the target's sound was represented by a vertical white line. Forward in the torpedo room, 650 pounds of explosive in the nose of a Mark 48 advanced-capability torpedo, equipped with twenty miles of control wire—capable of 67 knots and a range of twenty-five-plus miles, and known by *Santa Fe*'s crew as "heavy freight"—was loaded and ready in number 7 tube on the port side.

"Range?" asked the captain.

"Seventeen miles—decreasing." Every man on the boat went about his business with a deft, quiet approach to everything, including the placing of the compacted garbage container into a freezer. Any ejection of it could immediately have signaled the sub's position to the enemy, and the captain did not know if the Chinese ship was alone. There could be another one lying silent, its cavitation not yet picked up by *Santa Fe*'s passive sonar.

"Torpedo in port tube one, sir."

"Very well. Angle on the bow," the captain said. "Port, three point five."

"Check," came the confirmation.

"Range?" the captain asked.

"Sixteen point seven miles."

"Sixteen point seven miles," the captain repeated. "Firing point procedures. Master four five. Tube one."

"Firing point procedures, aye, sir. Master four five. Tube one, aye ... solution ready ... weapon ready ... ship ready ..."

"Match bearings and shoot."

The Mark 48's ram jet shot the torpedo into the sea. At 65 knots, given the varying salinity of the water and the relative speed of the two ships, it would take the torpedo plus or minus fifteen minutes to reach the target.

Now, in the predawn darkness, the Vietnamese welcome seemed as if it had never happened. Gone were the lines of villagers, whether sent out by the Hanoi government or not, and in their stead there were only the flitting images of the night, a constant stream of misbegotten shapes that, with a little fear and imagination, could be anything and everything, from a Chinese T-59 tank to a squad of PLA moving up ready to fire. But except for the noises of the aging trucks, it was a quiet ride for the EMREF spearhead for whom the only indication of battle was the occasional thump of distant artillery from the direction of Lang Son.

"This is far enough," Vinh's interpreter told Freeman, who quickly alighted from his Humvee, the first two vehicles in the following ten-truck convoy also slowing to a stop. Tail boards were lowered rather than dropped, as quietly as possible, and now what was called the "great humping" began, as each soldier prepared to "saddle up" for the reconnaissance patrol to probe the Lang Son line.

General Vinh's intelligence reports, as good as they might be, hadn't provided Freeman with enough information for any confident and immediate deployment of Second Army once it arrived. And as Freeman told Robert Cline, he couldn't afford a mistake because of something lost in what the interpreter might or might not say. He had to find out for himself, and so eighteen miles northeast of Hanoi, just before the town of Ba Ninh, the 127-member spearhead of the EMREF task force company split into four platoons of thirty men each. Freeman's intention was to proceed toward the Lang Son front in cloverleaf pattern, seven-man patrols from each company constantly moving out on the flanks, circling to prevent ambush as the whole company of four platoons, one behind the other, moved forward. A five-man radio and rifle squad remained with the trucks already helping the Vietnamese drivers and guards to camouflage the vehicles, mainly against the possibility of Chinese recon planes from the border area seventy-eight miles away, beyond Lang Son.

Vinh introduced Freeman to a group of five Vietnamese guides before he shook hands with Freeman and stepped into a Long March staff car to take him back to Hanoi, from whence he'd rejoin the battle on the western front.

In one of the strangest verbal exchanges in his career, General Freeman was engaged in a whispered "shouting" match with Marte Price of the *Des Moines Register*. "General, give me one good reason for me not going—a reason you can give that CNN cameraman and that CNN reporter."

"Ms. Price, I don't have to give reasons to the press. You stay with the trucks. You should have gone back with Vinh, goddamn it! I'll have you disbarred from the press pool."

"There is no pool, General."

"Goddamn it, you could get shot!"

"I know the risks."

"You certainly do not."

"General, when you said, 'Stay by the headquarters group,' I assumed that was all the way up to the front."

"Well, you assumed wrong, goddamn it."

"Give me one *good* reason, General, and I'll stay behind."

"You're a woman, goddamn it!"

"You've used women chopper pilots before, and I wish you wouldn't keep saying that."

"Well, you *are* a woman—aren't you?"

"I mean saying 'damn it' all the time."

"All right," Freeman said. Major Robert Cline thought the general was about to give in, but Freeman took a breath and said, "You smell!"

"I *what*?"

"The Vietnamese guides," he said, nodding in their direction, "have complained that you're a hazard to the operation, and I agree. They told me they could smell your perfume before the first truck rounded that curve a hundred yards back. Chinese regulars'd sniff us coming from a hundred yards away."

For a moment Marte Price was lost for words, but then suddenly she knew she had a counterattack. "General, I can smell cigarette smoke, and none of your troops are smoking now. Ever walk into a motel room where there's been a smoker? You can smell it right away."

"I'm not in the habit of going to motels," he replied grumpily. But she had him and he knew it. Despite all their instructions in training Special Forces like the Delta Force and SAS about not using deodorant and so on, a smoker carried the stale smell of cigarette or cigar smoke wherever he went.

"All right," Freeman said, more fiercely than before, and in an uncharacteristic non sequitur that would become part of Second Army lore, he added, "Don't blame me if you get killed! Goddamn it!"

"I won't," she said quietly, smiling, her features more distinct now as the predawn light stole upon the clearing in the black jungle by the road.

"I'll rub mud in my armpits," she said.

As Freeman turned to walk over to the Vietnamese guides, he confided to Major Cline, "By God, I hope the Chinese aren't as tough as her. We'll get our clock stopped."

"PLA use women in combat, General."

"We're not the PLA. We're Americans."

"With some Brits and Aussies to come, plus the British Gurkhas—"

"Yes, yes, I know—we're a United Nations force."

According to lore, it was similar to what George Patton had said, Cline thought, when he complained about Eisenhower being an *ally* and not an *American*. The general liked everything his own way, and after Freeman's spirited exchange with Marte Price, Cline had a sneaking suspicion that his intent to carry out a recon in force and return within four days was being done not just to better deploy Second Army, now arriving in Hanoi, but for some other reason, which no one, including the Pentagon, knew about. "Letting her come along with us, General, will win you a lot of kudos back home—and 'round the world via CNN."

"I'm not interested in kudos from the femisphere, Major. Far as I'm concerned, those rampant feminists—"

"I meant from the Pentagon, General. There's been a big push for equal rights."

"Damn it, Bob, the army's not a democracy. Even the Chinese know that. After years of that comrade crap, they've now reinstituted rank—'different pay scales.' "

"Maybe so, General, but my guess is having a woman reporter at the front'll do you more good than harm back home."

Freeman turned to Cline. "You make it sound like I'm running for office."

"General Eisenhower did."

"I'm not a political animal."

"Maybe not, General, but I still say your decision to have Marte Price will raise your profile—promotionwise."

"I didn't decide. She did."

"Even if she did, I don't think you'll regret it. It's politically correct."

"I don't give a dog's turd about political correctness and you know it."

Cline knew it, but the general had an ego as big as an M-1 tank, and it enjoyed being refueled every now and then with a headline or a TV sound bite that would keep the legend alive.

The general pulled down his IR goggles to take another look at the topographic map between Bac Ninh and Lang Son near the Vietnamese-Chinese border, about thirty miles of it across part of the lush Red River delta and then into the hilly jungle country of the border range. First he'd send out one patrol along the sides of the road for five miles. There was no point "hoofing" it, as he put it, if he could use the trucks for another few miles or so. He was confirmed in this tactical decision after one of the Vietnamese guides got off the radio with Hanoi to say it had been reported that Chinese units were pulling back from the delta ten miles or so up the road toward Kep, only nine miles from Lang Son.

Freeman's smile was a wry one, the kind he used when a colleague played chess with him and thought he'd baited a trap. Besides, part of the Freeman legend was "speed."

"Well, I'll tell you one thing, Bob. We're going *slowly* up that road in cloverleaf. If the Chinese have pulled back that quickly, then it's for one of two reasons. It's because their attack into Vietnam has been so successful that they've outrun their supply line, or it's a trap."

"Think we should stay put awhile, General?"

"No, you don't win wars by sitting on your butt. Either way, we'll have to find out what's going on. The thing is to be ready for whatever happens. But before we do send out a patrol, I want our flyboys in that *Enterprise* battle group to be ready for some TACAIR if we need it. We're not going to get arty," he meant artillery, "for a few days, until the self-propelled guns can get up here from Hanoi."

"General!" Cline said in amazement.

"What? What's wrong?"

"Nothing. That Marte Price woman undid her blouse and stuck some dirt under her arm."

"For Chrissake," Freeman said.

CHAPTER TWENTY-FIVE

ABOARD THE CHINESE frigate there was a rising sense of panic. The lookout had seen the wake of the American torpedo through his binoculars and given the captain a three-minute warning. With the torpedo coming midships, the frigate quickly began a standard "shake off" procedure, turning hard astarboard to run parallel with the torpedo's wake and then, as the latter changed direction, hard astarboard again. Next the captain ordered a fan pattern of depth charges off the stern's starboard side.

The turbulence of the resulting semicircle of explosions bothered the torpedo's advanced seeker head's computer, but only for a second or two. And then, like a hound suddenly recovering the scent, the Mark 48 locked onto its prey. As the frigate made its last attempt to run parallel, its helicopter lifted off from the stern pad only seconds before the *Santa Fe*'s torpedo exploded starboard midships, lifting the bow high and dumping it, the ship's back broken, fire already raging about the stern, orange-black flames leaping wildly, the sea about the stricken ship literally boiling white from the intense heat of the explosions and fires.

"Abandon ship!" the Chinese captain called, and within seconds a good quarter of the 195-man crew were jumping overboard, some of them accompanied by the white plastic drums of the Beaufort self-inflating rafts.

As the paint locker's door opened, two crew were almost stuck in the opening, such was their rush to reach the life jackets stowed in the locker. Neither one, nor the crew members who followed, snatching life vests and running out again, gave a thought to Danny Mellin. Stunned by the concussion of the explosion, he wandered around, bumping into and pushed aside by the panicky sailors.

Eventually, blinded by the daylight, Mellin felt his way to the forward starboard railing by letting his hands follow the line of the bulkhead. His vision cleared enough for him to see the sea afire off the starboard side. He turned, made his way over to the port side, and jumped, hearing the screams of several men who either in their haste or panic had dived into the boiling caldron. The portside water was hot, but as Mellin used his hands to paddle himself away from the sinking ship, the water cooled rapidly. He kept pushing himself to get farther away from the frigate so as not to be dragged under when she plunged. All around he could hear men shouting frantically as an oil fire, having spilled through the gaping hole that had been the midships, began to spread.

The moment he'd taken off from its stern, the frigate's helicopter pilot knew his landing pad on the Jianghu was gone. He now had one of two choices. He had fuel enough to go east and make the PLA navy's base at Yulin on the southern coast of the big island of Hainan, or he could head south, following what was now a pale but nevertheless quite clear wake left by the super-fast American torpedo. He turned south along the wake, only meters above the sea with two of the latest homing Yenchow ASW depth charges. Their shadows skimmed over the water like two dragonflies, the torpedo's wake broken here and there by different salinity patches racing up at the pilot in an endless blur on the wider blur of the cobalt-colored sea.

Now four hundred feet below the surface, the watch crew of the *Santa Fe* could hear the Chinese ship going down, her bulkheads popping as she sank farther and farther down to her sunless grave. There had been a second or two of celebration—the *Santa Fe* having done her job. But now all was silent in the control room save the sounds of the dying ship crackling and moaning over the sub's PA. The captain turned it off. He could only imagine what was happening to the Chinese crew. He had taken his boat down fast after the explosion fifteen miles away, because some of the Chinese ships, like all surface navies, sometimes carried a Recon/ASW helo. Depth alone wouldn't help him, but speed might, and now *Santa Fe*, without any discernible noise or tremor, had gone from 15 to 30 knots in an evasive zigzag and S-shaped pattern.

When the helo neared the end of the wake, or where the wake had been dissipated by the motion of the sea, the pilot didn't drop magnetic homing mines, for he was aware that the Hunter/Killer sub would now be well away from its firing position. Normally following such a wake was risky business, for it was believed that the American and British SSN sensors now had the capability to pick up chopper noises if they were near the surface, where sound would travel up to five times faster in water than air, and that in this case the enemy could launch a surface-to-air missile either by torpedo tube or vertical launch tubes forward of the sail. But the pilot dismissed this from his thoughts, for he knew that the sub's sensors, no matter how sensitive, would be overwhelmed and smothered by the sounds of the frigate breaking up.

The chopper pilot was now radioing his position to Zhanjiang, the headquarters of China's Southern Fleet, and at the same time, while hovering a hundred feet above the sea's surface, feeding out his dual magnetometer to sense any magnetic anomaly such as that caused by a ship's metal and/or microphones. All he got on the dipping mike was the hissing of the sunken frigate's oil fire still raging amid a slurry of flotsam and debris. The magnetometer showed a fairly consistent reading of seabed magnetics for the area. He reeled in the dual magnetometer/mike unit, which looked like a three-foot piece of pipe suspended from the end of the cable.

As the helo darted forward to continue its dipping, it looked for all the world like a dragonfly hovering one minute then skimming, hovering over another spot, the pilot receiving radio confirmation that two PLA air force Ilyushin-H5 light ASW torpedo bombers with an intensive torpedo/bomb load of 2,205 pounds were approaching the area, escorted by two Shenyang J8s, versions of the Mach 2, MiG-21 upgraded by the purchase of U.S. avionics. The Shenyangs were armed with three NR 30 30mm cannon and air-to-air missiles on wing hard points. They would not save the helo, as for every new dip the helo pilot made trying to locate the Hunter/Killer, the lower he was getting on fuel.

The best he might hope for would be to ditch after giving his last position and maybe get picked up by a PLA navy patrol ship. But unlike the extraordinary lengths that the Americans and British would go to to save a downed pilot, the PLA—navy, air force, or army—would do so only if it constituted no more than a minor alteration in course.

The *Enterprise*'s forward air combat patrol was notified by the *Enterprise* group E-2 Hawkeye advanced warning aircraft of all radio traffic between China's Southern Fleet HQ at Zhanjiang and of the dot on the AWAC's radar screen, which could only be a helo. Computer translation took fifteen seconds longer than usual, but it was quite clear that the Chinese ASW bombers were coming out from Yulin to search for the *Santa Fe*, and the *Enterprise*'s team of two F-18s were now put on an intercept vector to first meet the two Shenyang fighters.

The sharks of the South China Sea were no different from any other of their breed—they would not attack unless they were hungry. But blood in the water was an attraction they could not ignore, and Mellin, exhausted from hauling himself onto one of the rubber rafts, saw that the predators were now among the survivors of the Chinese frigate, ripping and gulping, turning the roiling waters crimson.

Mellin and the two oilers in the raft with him lay exhausted. One of the men's breathing was so strained from his lungs being covered in oil, Mellin could hear the rasping sound he made above the cries of terror as crewman after crewman thrashed in sheer panic, in frantic efforts to reach a raft, anything that would hold them. Mellin could see dozens of dorsal fins cruising about amid the material and human flotsam. Now and then a dorsal fin would suddenly move much faster as another shark in the school made its sudden attack. Not far from the raft he was on, Mellin could see one of the Chinese crewmen in a Mae West, his right arm unable to move because of burns, trying to make for the raft. Mellin reached out to him, but the current and turbulence of the water kept widening the distance between them.

"Oars!" Mellin yelled to the two others in the raft. "Where are the damn oars?" The two Chinese looked at him in bewilderment. There were no paddles. "C'mon," Mellin yelled, using his right hand to paddle, his head indicating the man in the water. "Paddle! Paddle with your hands! C'mon!"

One of the Chinese unenthusiastically joined Mellin. The other, covered with oil and still wheezing, did nothing. The man in the water—the sailor who had beaten Mellin aboard the ship—kept drifting away toward the frenzied, scream-filled cauldron that was the shark attack. Mellin took off his life jacket and slipped over the oil-greased side of the raft, striking out in a breaststroke toward the badly burned crewman. He grabbed the collar of the man's Mae West and, turning about, struck out for the raft. When he reached the raft he told the two crewmen aboard it to help him. They didn't understand English but they knew what he wanted. The one covered in oil did nothing. The other man started to panic, yelling and shaking his head. It was clear that he thought if Mellin tried to drag the burned crewman aboard, the raft would capsize.

"Grab his arms!" Mellin yelled, near exhaustion himself. "Now!"

The man aboard the raft was terrified, shaking his head. "No, no!"

In utter exasperation, Mellin heaved the burned man up against the raft's gunwale, the man's weight already tipping the raft as he slid back into the water. Out of the corner of his eye Mellin could see several fins coming his way. With a last Herculean effort he pushed the burned crewman up against the raft. The able-bodied crewman in the raft, out of sheer fright that if he didn't help, the raft would capsize, hauled the burned crewman as Mellin, still in the water, pushed. Next Mellin tried to haul himself aboard. But he was out of breath, his strength momentarily drained until he felt something pass him and touch a leg. The next thing he knew he was aboard the raft, water pouring off him, the rescued man flat on the bottom of the small craft, his reluctant co-rescuer screaming hysterically at Mellin at the near capsize. Mellin couldn't have cared less. All he cared about was the next breath.

When he recovered a few moments later, he looked at the guard who was stretched out beside him and moaning in pain. "Should've let you sink, you bastard!" The man covered in oil was dead, the remaining Chinese talking excitedly, pointing skyward where he could see two H-5 Ilyushin bombers, and high above them, the glint of two fighters, the jabbering crewman in a reverie of anticipation for now they were sure to be rescued. Several men in other rafts, floating among the limbless dead, were also cheering.

The frigate's helo had skimmed a few miles west and dipped the magnetometer/sonar, registering a magnetic anomaly. It could be unusually strong metallic deposits on the seabed, or it could be a submarine. The pilot dropped two depth charges, went higher, waited for the sea to erupt into two mushroomed columns of greenish-brown water, didn't see any signs of a hit and so dropped two floating orange marker flares for the Ilyushin bombers to see. He then headed off toward Yulin, the PLA's naval base in southern Hainan, dropping a purple parachute flare over the thirty or so crewmen from the sunken ship, some of them waving to him as he glanced anxiously at his fuel gauge.

Sitting up now in the raft, Mellin could see the thin spirals of orange smoke marking the spot where the helo pilot had dropped the depth charges, and he said a prayer for the sub that the Chinese were now searching for. Despite the sub nearly having killed him, it had told Mellin that there was war with China, and now at least he knew where he stood.

The dogfight between the two Shenyangs and the two F-18s of *Enterprise*'s air combat patrol was short and stunningly unequal.

"Tally Two! Tally Two! Afterburners!" came the first American pilot's voice, indicating he could see both Shenyang fighters. "Five miles. Select Fox Two. Four miles . . . three miles . . . lock 'im up . . . lock him . . . shoot Fox Two Fox Two."

The Sidewinder missile took off from the American plane, streaking out toward one of the enemy, the other American plane also firing a Sidewinder. Within seconds of one another each missile found its target. There were two orange flashes, one many times the size of the other, as the second Shenyang's fuel tanks went up.

"Splash one!" came the excited voice of the first American pilot, "Splash two!" following only seconds later.

Aboard the carrier's combat information center there were shouts of jubilation. "Good kill! Good kill!" the air boss said, echoing one of the pilots' exultations. "Outstanding!" The pilot of the lead F-18 acknowledged the congratulations from the carrier. The other pilot said nothing, part of him exhilarated by the kill, the other half feeling sorry for the downed Chinese pilots, only one having a chance to eject. In a way, attacking the two Shenyangs, whose maximum speed was 957 mph, with two F-18s at 1,190 mph, was a little like Mario Andretti's Formula One chasing a pickup. Unless the Chinese fighters happened upon F-18s with complete surprise—highly unlikely, given the F-18s' multimode air-to-air and air-to-surface tracking radar—the Shenyangs didn't stand a chance, despite their having jettisoned "hot spots"—magnesium flares—to decoy the U.S. missiles.

But if the two American pilots from the *Enterprise* had good reason to be supremely confident of their aircraft's ability, they gave the Chinese pilots top marks for courage. Neither Shenyang pilot had run from the fight, but had kept coming head-to-head to do battle. Both American pilots and those back in the *Enterprise*'s CIC knew how different the outcome might have been had the Chinese sent out their MiG-29s—the Fulcrums—now being purchased at bargain basement prices by China from Russia and other republics within the CIS.

The Fulcrum, with a maximum speed of 1,518 mph, was faster than the F-18s by 328 miles per hour and was considered by many, particularly by the modern German Luftwaffe pilots, as the world's preeminent fighter. Without the Shenyangs as cover, the two H-5 bombers were embarrassingly easy for the two F-18s to shoot down, one exploding in air, the other afire and in an uncontrollable spin, one crewman ejecting, his white chute blossoming against the blue expanse of sea and sky. For some reason the spiraling H-5's two 23mm nose cannons kept firing, their aimless bullets striking the sea like errant pebbles scattered over the water.

"All right!" Danny Mellin said as the H-5 smashed into sunglinting pieces as it struck the sea in excess of 500 miles per hour. The Chinese crewman who had refused to help Mellin rescue the guard, who was only now coming around, looked at Mellin with an expression of sheer hatred for the American. He said something to Mellin, but despite Mellin's basic knowledge of Chinese from his POW days in 'Nam, he couldn't understand, though he guessed it was some kind of insult. The Chinese crewman repeated himself, this time jabbing his finger at Mellin. Danny, his eyes squinting in the harsh glare of the sun on water, nodded as if he understood. "Yeah, well fuck you too, Sheng."

"Sheng," the first thing that came into Mellin's head, means one liter, and the Chinese crewman was utterly perplexed.

"Sheng?"

"Oh Sheng fuck!" Mellin said, not feeling as cavalier as his tone suggested. He knew for sure that once he fell asleep, the crewman would push him off the raft. He had to stay awake, and so a deadly waiting game began. The guard, alternately coughing and moaning, still lay in the fetal position on the undulating floor of the raft.

"Sheng?" the crewman said.

"That's right," Mellin replied, both men watching each other as intently as two cats with territory in dispute. The raft should have had several liters of water as part of its supplies, but the only thing attached to the gunwales was an ancient packet of hard crackers and salt tablets. Mellin looked about for other rafts to hail, but the half dozen or so he could see were too dispersed, several bodies—or rather, what was left of them—floating up and over the swells, which were growing in intensity and height.

A Chinese container ship, the *Wang Chow* from Shanghai, en route to San Francisco via Honolulu when hostilities broke out, had been turned back by a U.S. Navy destroyer northeast of Maui. The destroyer escorted the *Wang Chow* back to Honolulu, where its cargo, mainly cheaply made cotton clothing destined for the American market, was impounded and its crew of thirty-two interned.

That evening produced one of the Hawaiian Islands' legendary sunsets, an incandescent orange turning to a crimson, the streaked high cirrus clouds giving the promise of another splendid day in paradise as the USS *Madison*, a combination Hunter/Killer/Ballistic submarine of the Sea Wolf III series, egressed out of Pearl Harbor past degaussing ships—the magnetic signature of the ship "wiped," lest an enemy pick up the signature and file it in its threat library.

Had the *Madison* been in any foreign port, no matter how urgently she was wanted elsewhere, her departure would have been delayed until four divers—it used to be three—had "swept" her acoustic-tiled hull and declared her "clean." But given it was in COMSUBPAC's home port, and the urgency of the situation in the South China Sea, the USS *Madison* set off promptly.

Once having cleared the safety nets in Pearl, she headed up the channel, her sleek shape, more like a cigar than a teardrop, slicing through the water as easily as any behemoth of the deep. The explosion took place at 1109 hours as she was preparing to dive, shattering the hull underneath and forward of the fairweather or sail, ripping out the torpedo room, water tank, forward trim tank, and Tomahawk vertical launch system. It also ruptured two of the three forward starboard-side ballast tanks, whose implosion doused some of the forward sub's fires, but not all of them.

Within a minute firefighting teams had donned their white asbestos-hooded Nomex fire suits, some strapping on the emergency air breathing apparatus hose, others the more portable OBX, oxygen breathing apparatus. Temperatures were already 52 degrees Celsius and climbing, fire control crewmen trying desperately to make their way through choking, dense smoke with their infrared thermal imagers. Had it not been for the quick action of a Charles F. Adam–class destroyer nearby, with her fire hoses and her bravery in coming alongside despite the acute danger of the torpedoes in the *Madison* blowing, the whole sub and its crew might have been lost instead of the sub being badly damaged with thirty-three of her 132 crewmen reported killed.

It had been a torpedo attack right off the mouth of Pearl Harbor, or more precisely, it had been a mine, a U.S. acoustic Mark 60 Captor mine—in effect a long, tubular sheath housing a Mark 46 torpedo, its computer control programmed to lie in wait for certain classes of sub with their telltale cavitation. Upon sensing this, the torpedo would be let loose from its housing.

From now on, as directed by the CNO, all U.S. submarines, including all deep-diving submergence rescue vehicles, had to be swept, along with egress lanes, whether in a home or foreign port.

The extent of *Madison*'s damage would keep the boat in dry dock for at least three months, as well as necessitating an undersea and an evaluation center test. The Chinese ship *Wang Chow* was soon swarmed by SEALs and other underwater demolition teams, and they'd found brackets for a half-dozen Mark 60 Captor mines underneath, set into her hull.

"Thank God they didn't sink it altogether," a petty officer said. He meant the *Madison*.

"Might as well have," an ensign said. "It's going to slow down one hell of a lot egressing out of Pearl—sub or surface vessel. Damn Chinese might just as well have sunk her." Two of his best buddies had died during the mines' attack. COMSUBPAC's naval intelligence confirmed from serial numbers on remaining U.S.-made Mark 60 Captor mines that they had been among those purchased and then resold in East Asia prior to hostilities by a South Asia Industries owned and operated by a Mr. Jonas E. Breem.

CHAPTER TWENTY-SIX

WHILE TAZUKO KOMURA was packing some food and juice in her kitchen, she thought about a man in the phone booth she'd seen the night before below for what seemed an unusually long time. Through the small telescope in her tiny, three-room apartment she'd been able to see that the man wasn't using the phone, but was dusting it with a small brush. It both frightened and reassured her—frightened her, because it meant police or JDF agents were closing in, altogether too close, but reassured her because they were dusting for prints. Obviously they didn't know who had used the public phone. And what would they have heard when they tapped it? A man's voice asking for a Mrs. Yoshio, and a woman's voice, hers, answering that there was no Yoshio "living here." And anyway, the police who were following up the call couldn't possibly know it was the signal for her to act, to do what her cell of three had spent months planning.

Even so, Tazuko knew she would be in grave danger the moment she stepped out on the street. If anyone searched her shopping bag, they might find the explosive. Or would the way she had camouflaged it fool them? As she finished her coffee she noticed her right hand was trembling, half from fear, half in excitement. She knew she must control it, and in order to do that she first had to lose control. She was wound up tighter than a spring.

Tazuko lay down on the carpeted floor, placed a pillow beneath her head with her left hand and slid her right hand under her skirt and taut, white nylon panties. Very soon she was moaning softly, moving ever so slowly at first but then increasing the pressure until she was rolling back and forth in her mounting ecstasy. Suddenly her back arched, and it was as if she was suspended in time, her free hand clutching the air.

When she woke fifteen minutes later, she felt drained of all tension, her nerves calmed for the task ahead.

In the South China Sea, approximately halfway between the Spratly and Paracel island groups, the helo from the now sunken Chinese frigate ran out of gas and dropped like a stone into the sea.

Naked in his recliner, belching after draining another scotch on the rocks, Breem farted, told Mi Yin to "get the fuck outta the way" of the TV, and switched from the local Hong Kong station to CNN, where they were showing more shots of the PLA herding prisoners they'd taken from various "liberated" oil and gas rigs into a makeshift POW camp "somewhere" in China.

"More fucking losers," Breem proclaimed, taking a handful of beer nuts, trying to pop them in his mouth one at a time and missing now and then, some of them rolling down into his crotch. "Fetch them, baby. Go on, fetch!" This was followed by laughter that rippled through his belly. "Hey hey hey!" he said, abruptly sitting up. An ABC "scoop" window was superimposed on the lower right corner of CNN pictures of the Chinese destroyer picking up "victims" of a "warmongering attack" in the South China Sea by what was believed to be an American submarine. Breem zoomed in on the superimposed

ABC window, the New York anchor reporting that a "Sea Wolf" SSN/SBN had been sunk off the Hawaiian island of Oahu by what naval sources were "unofficially" describing as an American-made Captor 60 mine or mines. It was suspected that the mine or mines that had gutted the U.S. sub had apparently been laid by a Chinese merchantman, the *Wang Chow*, en route to the U.S. West Coast when hostilities broke out between China and the United States. Now ABC's "Nightline" was reporting over forty crew aboard the 132-man submarine had been killed, due largely to a subsequent fire-created explosion in the forward torpedo room.

"More fucking losers!" Breem proclaimed, his mouth half full of beer nuts. "Oh well, more yuan for B.I." He was talking about Breem Industrials, listed on the Hong Kong exchange as one of the South Asia Industries group.

"How come?" Mi Yin asked.

"Come any way you like." Breem thought this bon mot hilarious and laughed so hard, scotch and beer nuts sprayed the carpet. He tossed Mi Yin the empty glass. "Ice, my little juicy fruit. More yuan for me, my lovely, because who is the biggest seller of marine munitions—among other things—in the Near East?"

"You are," Mi Yin said, handing him a glass of crushed ice turned golden with Johnnie Walker.

" 'Course," he added, "manufacturers of Captors, et cetera, don't know I've cornered the market. They only sell through 'legitimate' firms. Saps!" Breem knew he was drunk and that he was talking too much. "But hey, Juicy Fruit. What fuckin' good is success if you can't share it, right?" He meant "flaunt" it.

"Yes."

"Right!" he bellowed.

"Right."

CHAPTER TWENTY-SEVEN

DANNY MELLIN COULDN'T walk properly. Conditions on the PLA navy destroyer that had picked him, Sheng, and the guard from the raft along with other survivors of the torpedo attack against the Jianghu frigate had been so crowded that his right leg had gone to sleep. As he walked, or rather limped, down the gangplank toward the waiting POW trucks, he had little sensation in his right leg. He didn't know where he was except that it was a Chinese naval port, given the number of destroyer frigates and fast-attack patrol boats moored there. As they parted company, Sheng said something to him, laughing at him, dismissing him with the contempt of a man who had been down a little while before but who was now clearly on the winning side.

"You prick!" Mellin said. "Should've let the sharks—" The next instant he was down on the dockside, his head numbed by the blow, blood oozing from the left side of his face. A PLA soldier clubbed him again with the AK-47's stock, this time in the stomach.

Somebody, an Australian by his accent, helped Danny up. "Easy does it, mate. These jokers 'ave no bloody sense of humor at all." The same guard pushed the Australian in the small of the back. Both Danny and the Australian kept quiet, half climbing, half pushed up the tailgate of one of the three-ton trucks loaded with an assortment of captured rig workers. Two PLA navy guards, including the one who'd just struck him, rode at the end of the two benches of about ten POWs each, the AK-47s unslung, ready to fire. As the truck took off with a jerk that jarred everybody aboard, the Australian held up his hand. "Hey, Thumper," he called out to the guard who'd just clubbed Mellin. "You got any water? Me mate here," he indicated Mellin, "looks pretty badly dehydrated."

"Up shut!" yelled the other guard. "You up shut!"

"All right," the Aussie said. "Piss on you too."

Mellin could see the guard starting to move toward the Australian, but the ride was so rough the guard stayed where he was, glaring at them, holding on to one of the truck's two high roll bars. The Australian waited till the truck was climbing a hill, its engine in a high scream, the guards glancing at some peasant women walking along the roadside.

"Name's Mike Murphy. What's yours?"

"Mellin, Danny."

"You a rigger?" Murphy asked.

"Yeah. You?"

"I tease Chinese."

"Yeah, well, be careful."

"Not to worry."

"You been—" Mellin's mouth was so dry he could barely talk. "—interrogated yet?"

"No," Murphy said, and for the first time a shadow of alarm crossed the Aussie's face.

CHAPTER TWENTY-EIGHT

Tokyo

CIA LANGLEY'S FAX to its Tokyo field agent, Henry Wray, was to the point: EXPEDITE SONGBIRD IMMEDIATE STOP MESSAGE ENDS.

Wray asked his JDF colleagues to bring in the Korean prisoner, Jae Chong, "and put him in the paper box." It was three feet square, two feet high, and made of slotted cardboard that could be dismantled and reassembled in seconds. The suspect or prisoner had to squat in the middle of the square, and God help him if he moved.

"We may have to wait a long time till he talks," one of the JDF agents said.

"We can't wait too long," Wray countered. He thought of the danger that one person, one mishap, could have on the complicated and vital logistics tail of Second Army that would stretch from Japan to Hanoi. "Give him an hour on his haunches," Wray suggested. "If he hasn't talked by then, beat the shit out of him. No bruises."

"Hai," agreed the youngest of the two JDF agents. He didn't like *gaijin*—foreigners—including Americans, but he especially disliked Koreans, particularly those from the north.

That afternoon at a quarter to three they picked up Chong from his job as a janitor for an apartment complex not far from the Ginza strip. The timing was important for Chong, who knew that sooner or later they would get him. But had they arrested him an hour earlier, he probably would not have withstood the beating until the 2:38 departure of the Joetsu Shinkansen, bullet train, from Tokyo's Ueno Station to Niigata on Honshu's west coast, over two hundred miles away. As it was, by the time the beating started, the 2:38 to Niigata was well on its way across the Kanto Plain north of Tokyo, speeding toward the fourteen-mile Daishimizu tunnel, which would take Tazuko Komura from Japan's "front" or the *omote Nihon*, to *ura Nihon*, the "inner Japan" beyond the alps.

Before she had moved to the frenetic glitter of Japan's east coast, the west coast around Niigata had been Tazuko's home. In its own way, Niigata was as flashy and as fast as Tokyo, but not far from Niigata you were in the small villages of Japan, hundreds of years old. It was a Japan in which having a life of *yutakasa*—of great value—was not measured in yen or worldly possessions, but in the spirit of harmony one experienced with the rhythm of the seasons and the wisdom of traditions passed down from one craftsman to another.

For Tazuko, it had still been a land in which she was one of the *gaijin*, but its affinity for things rural and old captivated her. Her nostalgia, however, was a fantasy, at odds with the often harsh reality of modern industrial Japan, with the kind of industrial wealth Pyongyang wanted to emulate. But Tazuko felt no such contradiction, and knew if she was to give her life to help thrust North Korea onto the stage of major world powers, then she would give that life. And should anyone doubt her courage, then they would soon doubt no longer.

At first she hadn't planned anything even remotely heroic,

but heroism, if it meant self-sacrifice, had more or less been forced upon her by the stringent security carried out by the automatic rail "scout" machines that constantly monitored the tracks of the bullet trains. Had anyone wanted to put the sausage-shaped explosive on the rail tracks or supporting structures, they would have had to do it in darkness, for the moment they used a light, their position would have been immediately identified by the infrared track cameras. Besides, the way to inflict the most damage on the Japanese psyche was not to blow up part of the track, but to stop the train itself, to puncture their much vaunted and worldwide reputation for speed, safety, and quality. Also, if they expected an attack, it would be on the southward Tokyo-Hakata line, where U.S. and JDF troops would most likely travel as part of the buildup of force in Vietnam.

"Tell him," Wray said, lighting another cigarette, "that if he doesn't tell us the name and whereabouts of his contact, he's going to have an accident—a fatal one."

"I've already told him," the JDF agent replied.

"Maybe he thinks we're bluffing."

"No," the JDF agent assured Wray. "He knows." The other JDF agent indicated to the American that they should go outside.

In the hallway they talked about how far they really wanted to go. Wray said he didn't want to kill the son of a bitch, but with the segmented air/sea Second Army supply line stretching from Japan to Hanoi over 2,200 miles away, any sabotage would be disastrous for what the U.N. hoped would be Freeman's counterattack against the Chinese. The JDF agent said he didn't mind beating the crap out of the North Korean—it would be a message to the Gong An Bu, Chinese Intelligence, that if they insisted on using *gaijin* to do their dirty work in Japan, this is what would happen to their agents.

Wray, now that his bluff was being called, wasn't so tough. He said the trouble with killing the little bastard was all the fucking paperwork involved, but what he really meant was "killing the little bastard" was a contradiction of what they were supposedly fighting for—inconvenient stuff like habeas corpus. Without wanting to sound weak, Wray wanted to convey this to the JDF agent. "Chinese'd just take him out and shoot him in the neck if he was one of ours."

"We don't have to shoot him," the JDF agent said. "There wouldn't even be a bruise."

"Yeah, yeah," Wray said. "But like I said—too much friggin' paperwork."

"It's up to you," his Japanese colleague said amicably.

"Well, stick a barrel against his head and tell him to tell you who he contacted and why—I mean their specific target."

The JDF man made a face. It was a question. What happens if he still doesn't answer? You've lost all credibility. Right?

"Try it," Wray said. "I've got a hunch the little bastard'll sing like a bird."

"Do you want to try it?" the JDF agent asked. What he meant was, *You* lose face if you want to, Wray-san, but not me.

"All right," Wray said. "I'll do it. Give him another fifteen minutes to think about it, then call me."

CHAPTER TWENTY-NINE

ON THE POINT of Freeman's recon patrol, D'Lupo's squad of seven men from the first platoon had moved out to the flanks and back again in cloverleaf pattern, a rifle platoon between them and the HQ section behind them, the warm jungle dampness causing their shirts to cling to them like Saran Wrap under the Kevlar bulletproof vest, each man wearing a patrol harness, pistol belt, two ammo pouches, one smoke and two fragmentation grenades, and a K-bar knife, in addition to bandoleers of machine-gun bullets, a poncho, C-rations for the ninety-six-hour probe of Chinese positions, a claymore mine, and a collapsible shovel. But all this mountain of gear, except for his M-16, was ready for instant jettisoning if necessary by a quick ruck release strap, leaving the grunt as free as possible to fight.

Behind the HQ squad of General Freeman, Major Robert

Cline, Marte Price, the radio operator PFC Rhin, and the two CNN crew, was a weapons platoon led by Martinez, made up of SAS and Delta veterans. They were a rear guard, but moving as cautiously as the men on the point, lest they get caught in an ambush, should the enemy try to sucker them in by allowing the point, the HQ and rifle platoon, to pass before springing a trap.

The haunting night sounds—thousands of birds and some of the millions of bats from caves like those around Lang Son—filled the darkness with such a flood of noise that was both unnerving and reassuring, since neither side would hear the other in the middle of such a racket, unless the Chinese tried to move tanks or self-propelled heavy artillery units down the road.

The noise of the bats and the general confusion they'd caused in the undergrowth amid a variety of animals, from wild pig to small deer, serow goats, and flying squirrels, seemed to cease almost as quickly as it had started. Then it began to rain, a deluge dumped on the jungle, immediately washing off much of the insect repellent on exposed flesh. In ten minutes the downpour too had ceased, and now masses of insects, mainly mosquitoes, buzzed, and rain could be heard plopping from the trees into pools and onto the canopies of broad-leafed plants as the soldiers unavoidably brushed against them.

There was a dull thump, followed by another, then another.

"Mor—" But the mortar rounds had already landed, splitting the air, their explosions throwing up earth in huge, dark convulsions of undergrowth and fire—men screaming all around, the frenetic chattering of machine guns opening up—another scream and the purplish veined explosions of grenades, the crash of more grenades, mortars—the air hot, coming in bursts whose concussion stunned and whose shrapnel lacerated the thick vegetation like hail.

Though the farthest ahead, D'Lupo's squad was only now coming under attack, the trap being sprung, men yelling on the perimeter, "Two o'clock—five five!" and another explosion, the air acrid with the stink of cordite and muddy earth. Hunkered down, Freeman was calling back to the trucks for a relay message to Hanoi for TACAIR from wherever he could get it.

It came, but not quickly enough. By the time four Tomcats roared in from *Enterprise* as dawn broke, their ordnance bristling on hard points, their vapor trails sculpted golden by the carly sun, the fighting was over, the enemy had withdrawn, and Freeman's recon force was left with nine dead and about an equal number wounded. Medevac choppers now appeared like black bugs descending. As Freeman stomped about, Marte Price, badly shaken by the attack, moved behind him from corpse to corpse. She could see his eyes moisten, but whether it was from suppressed rage, compassion, or both, she couldn't tell.

"Goddamn it," he said to no one in particular. "For Second Army to get mauled like that first time out in 'Nam—"

"Excuse me, General," Robert Cline interjected. "It's hardly Second Army. I mean this recon force is only—"

"Numbers aren't the point, Bob, goddamn it! I was led to understand that our approach to the snake—as our Vietnamese colleagues call the front line—would be—"

He heard a soldier moan but couldn't see him. One of the Delta contingent had given the soldier, or what was left of him, a shot of morphine, but it couldn't hold the pain. He was lying in the cool morning shade of a hardwood tree, his head hidden in a triangle of leaves. When Freeman neared the man and saw what was left of his face, he clamped his jaw muscles so tightly Marte Price could see them bulge. Freeman took another couple of paces toward the man and knelt beside him, gently pulling away one of the broad leaves that had acted as a curtain. The man's face was gone, from the bright bloody pulp that had been his nose to the deep purplish red of where his eyes had been. The miracle to Freeman was that the body was still alive, its lips, lacerated, moving like some obscene puppetry. Freeman put his right ear near the man's mouth, and he could smell the rusty metallic odor of blood and a vile stench of excrement. He nodded, looking to Marte like a priest listening to the confession of a bedridden believer. Freeman took the man's limp right hand in his and squeezed it slightly, nodding his head. "Yes," he said to the soldier, and with that unclipped his side holster and pulled out his .45.

"Medevacs," Marte said. "In a few hours the wounded'll be—"

"I know," Freeman said without looking up. "Would you go away now—please," and he let the .45 slide back into his holster. "Go away," he told her, still watching the mash of bone and raw flesh. "Now!" He heard a click—a camera—and Bob Cline took her by the arm.

"My God," she told Cline, reluctantly following him away

from the tree. "For a moment there I thought the general was going to shoot him."

"He was," Cline said matter-of-factly, "but it would've panicked everyone and given our position away to any—"

They heard a scuffle behind them. "Don't look," the major said, but she already had and clicked her camera again. "Oh my God—"

Freeman had cut the grunt's throat, the blood bubbling out, the man's legs kicking about with such force they were splashing the mud up and about what was now the corpse. It wasn't that uncommon in combat, and seasoned correspondents had seen more than one mercy killing, but it was something Marte Price hadn't seen before, and it was always terrible to see.

Grim-faced, Freeman walked over to her. "You use that and you'll end my career."

Now reports were coming in from D'Lupo's men on the front of what had been the cloverleaf formation, and from the second and third platoons, of the number of enemy killed—fourteen, and five wounded prisoners.

The terrible shock of that morning, however, didn't fully occur until one of the four medics in the EMREF, having done all he could for his wounded buddies, moved on to help the enemy prisoners. The first was bleeding badly from shrapnel-caused lacerations to the arms and chest. The medic bandaged the wounds and gave the soldier a shot of morphine. It was only when he saw the second prisoner, the man's upper right leg hit by an M-16 round, that the medic realized he wasn't treating Chinese. Freeman was called, and arrived just as Cline was having a look at the wounded man.

"What's up?" Freeman asked curtly, his face still creased by the strain of having put one of his own men out of his misery.

"General," Cline replied, looking up from the wounded prisoner, "you're not going to like this."

"Like what, damn it?"

Marte Price's camera clicked and whirred as it advanced the film. Freeman turned on her. "Goddamn it, lady, can't you use a quieter gadget than that? You can hear it whirring from thirty feet away." Marte Price said nothing—she was watching Cline exchanging a worried glance with the medic. Cline straightened up. "Sir, I think we ought to get one of our Vietnamese guides over here."

Freeman looked down at the corpse, grimly adding, "So he doesn't look Chinese. Probably from one of the hill tribes near the border. Chinese have Vietnamese sympathizers from the border regions. I—" He stopped, as if he'd just run out of breath. "A lot of PLA sympathizers were probably wearing those goddamned pajamas. Peasant garb. Could even be from the Laos-Vietnam border."

The HQ phone crackled and a hushed voice from the third platoon told Freeman and his force that there was movement in the heavy underbrush at eleven o'clock, four hundred yards off on the left flank behind them and coming from the direction of the Hanoi–Lang Son road, a creaking, metallic noise.

"Tanks?" Cline asked.

"Freeman! General Free-man!" It was a high-pitched woman's voice piercing the heavy jungle growth, but there was no reply, the EMREF's reconnaissance force having gone to ground the instant they'd known of an approaching force. It was an old Vietnamese ruse—to learn someone's name on the opposing force, particularly that of the commanding officer, and to call out the name, giving the impression they knew a lot about you. Even among battle-hardened veterans it was a nerve-racking experience, for no matter how many times you might be reassured by your own commander, the fact was that somehow they had discovered your name—somehow they were getting inside information and had found out exactly where you were.

"General Freeman!" The voice was coming from about a hundred yards back. "General Vinh is here."

"Yeah, right!" D'Lupo whispered. "And I'm fucking queen of the May."

"General Freeman. Do you hear me?"

In the HQ platoon Freeman, via radio, ordered his first platoon to swing around hard left in a cloverleaf patrol, while the remaining three of the four platoons settled in defensive posture. "Okay," said first platoon's sergeant quietly, turning to D'Lupo, "you take the point, queenie," and the patrol moved out.

"General Freeman!" The woman's voice on the left flank of the HQ platoon seemed closer now, and seven and a half tense minutes later the HQ radio crackled to life, a report coming not from the left flank but from D'Lupo's platoon up ahead. "Alpha One to Mother Hen. We've got a white flag fifty feet in front of us."

"Alpha One," Freeman ordered, "do the same. Fly a white flag."

D'Lupo was watching the woman. She looked Chinese. At first sight she appeared to be alone, but now that his eyes had been fixed on her for several minutes, D'Lupo and others in the squad left and right of him also saw the two men materializing on either side of her, one of the AK-47s looking for all the world like a stubby branch of a tree.

Slowly D'Lupo, wondering why Freeman had been so ready to answer a white flag with a white flag, reached up to the elastic khaki band about his helmet and felt for the field dressing package, the only ready white material in his kit. "Cover me," he whispered, hoping that the two of his men nearest him on the flanks about thirty feet away from each other and either side of him had heard him. They didn't, but they saw D'Lupo rise slowly, the white bandage wrapped loosely around the end of his M-16.

The woman, her hands held high in surrender, advanced slowly toward D'Lupo, and now the two Vietnamese guides moved forward, stopping by the four dead Vietnamese men in the black pajamas. There was a short, rapid exchange between the guides, its tone more revealing than any translation, telling Freeman that his worst fear—any commanding officer's worst fear—had been realized. It had been a "blue on blue," the innocuous-sounding phrase the Army used whenever there had been a clash between "friendlies" or "allies."

The wounded men in the black pajamas were now talking rapidly at the guides, confirming that they were part of Vinh's men, not part of the Chinese army. The Americans had fired upon their allies—or had it been the other way around? Whatever, the failure of one side or both to properly identify the other had led to the disaster of twenty-nine Americans and Vietnamese killed and fourteen wounded. To make matters even worse, Vinh's force on the Americans' left flank, which the Americans had thought was the creaking noise of PLA tanks, was in fact a Vietnamese relief column moving along the Hanoi–Lang Son road, riding their bicycles—some with tires punctured, riding on the rim.

"Malaya," Freeman said, his tone terse.

"Malaya?" Cline asked, nonplussed.

"After the Japs hit Pearl Harbor," Freeman answered, "they drove south on the jungle roads through Malaya. Get a flat tire—they'd just keep going on the rims. Sounded like armor on the move to the Aussies and the Brits. Scared the hell out of 'em." It was a throwaway comment, but it reminded Captain Boyd, Freeman's press officer, just how encompassing and particular Freeman's knowledge of military history was.

Marte Price was having a war of conscience about whether or not to file her fax report on Freeman's mercy killing and his use of "Japs" instead of "Japanese," when she saw the two Vietnamese guides talking fast and gesticulating wildly, looking down at and up from the dead men in the black-pajamas-cum-uniforms. She knew, then, she had a really big story: two legendary old foes—the United States and Vietnam—represented by Freeman and Vinh, both commanding "specialist forces," had screwed up.

Marte Price's story about "friendly fire" would be avidly picked off the wire service by hundreds of newspapers in the U.S. But it was CNN, with its four phone and "umbrella" antenna, that almost instantly sped the pictures of the American dead to its billions of viewers all over the world via satellite.

Both Freeman and Vinh refused to be photographed for what they both—Freeman vociferously, Vinh less so but just as firmly—referred to as propaganda for Beijing. And they were right. The blue on blue or "friendly fire" episode that had killed the four Vietnamese gave way to charges by GIs that yet another Army situation was definitely FUBAR—fucked up beyond all recognition.

Other mild pejoratives, courtesy of CNN, rained down from U.S. soldiers and Chinese alike, and for the first time since the terrible tank battles at Skovorodino in another U.N.-sanctioned intervention, General Douglas Freeman, though still not knowing who had fired the first shot, took full front-on responsibility for the debacle. In private he was fuming, knowing that his overall command of the U.S. forces in Vietnam was in jeopardy.

The only good news he received that day was the ringing endorsements of his corps commanders of Second Army, now en route to Vietnam from Japan. Many of them had been with him at Skovorodino in Siberia, where his armor was lured into a trap by "false" tanks that U.S. aerial reconnaissance had spotted, and those in Second Army who remembered the humiliation also remembered Freeman's audacious comeback in some of the largest tank battles since Kursk.

In Washington there were congressional calls for his, Freeman's, removal as C in C of the U.N. force, but the President and Joint Chiefs held firm. All of them knew the pitfalls of command—particularly the huge psychological bridge that had to be crossed by old foes, such as Vinh and Freeman suddenly having to form a coalition.

Vinh was hardly criticized at all by the American left, the latter's venom directed almost solely on Freeman, whom the left saw as a warmonger who "must surely harbor old antagonistic feelings toward the Vietnamese people." General Vinh immediately came to Freeman's defense, saying that mistakes had no doubt been made "by both sides," adding that the fault lay with the "aggressive imperialist" policies of Beijing, whose determination to "steal" Vietnamese territory in the Spratly and Paracel islands and whose claim of ownership of the whole of the South China Sea started the conflict in the first place.

And in one of the strange paradoxes of modern politics, General Vinh—who had fought so hard as a young man against the Americans, in particular the American Division in the Vietnamese War—was now welcomed aboard by Rush Limbaugh and others on the political right of the media, and within days Vinh's defense of Freeman was used to batter the democratic left into virtual silence. But Greenpeace complained that the U.S. transport ships carrying Second Army toward Vietnam were flushing out their bilges at sea and thereby endangering the delicate sea life ecosystem in the waters off the China coast.

Freeman, who was clearly meant to be cowed by this second public salvo against him, responded via Marte Price, that Greenpeace's complaint sounded like a lot of "bilge" to him and that Greenpeace might better occupy itself with concerns about the "delicate ecosystem of human beings in and around Lang Son" who lay dead and dying as a direct result of the worst pollution of all—invasion by what was now over ten divisions—over 130,000 Chinese shock troops.

"How do we know they were shock troops, General?" press officer Boyd asked afterward.

"Because," Freeman replied, "they gave us a hell of a shock, that's why."

"Yes, sir," said Boyd.

"Another thing, Captain Boyd."

"Sir?"

"I want you to find a few good stories about the flagrant Chinese violation of the environment laws—in particular the violation of the law prohibiting the killing and or transport of wild animals. You know the sort of thing I mean. Believe eating crushed-up tiger's balls'll give 'em a dick big as a tiger's."

Boyd blinked. "Ah ... I mean, sir—you sure about that?"

" 'Course I'm sure. Anyway, you can flesh out the details. Make sure it gets on CNN. Get the bastards working for me for a change—instead of all those damn fairies and Commie fellow travelers in State."

"Ah, General, the Vietnamese are Commie—"

Freeman waved the objection aside. "Not like the Chinese they aren't. You get that story out, hear me? I want those animal rights people raising shit, with Greenpeace moaning about the damn fish our supply line ships are supposedly traumatizing. Take the heat off us." He winked at Boyd. "Can you handle them?"

"I think so, sir."

The general smiled. "Do so, Captain—or I'll fire you. And Boyd?"

"Sir?"

"I want that report in an hour."

"Yes, sir."

CHAPTER THIRTY

Tokyo

HENRY WRAY WOULDN'T have beaten the North Korean prisoner—at least not as badly—but the man had said *"Migook!"*—American—and spat at him. With his overtime robbing him of sleep, and contrary to all the rules and practices for self-control he'd learned at Langley, Wray snapped and punched the Korean off his haunches, the man falling over, crashing into the two-foot-high wall of cardboard that had formed the "disciplinary square" about him. At this, the Japanese interrogater went wild, kicking the man in the head twice before Wray, his hands trembling with the strain of the war between the anger and common sense raging inside of him, yelled, "That's enough!" at his JDF colleague. But the North Korean spat again and Wray lost it. Besides, what was it that detective used to say on "NYPD Blue"? he thought afterward. At some point in the interrogation room you take off your belt and leave the Constitution outside.

Wray and the JDF agent had gotten each other going, and once or twice their blows coincided, they were so frantic to give it to him. Little bastard was probably holding the key to an attack on the Second Army convoy, which was now out over the Macclesfield Bank, 350 miles east-southeast of the PLA's Yulin naval base on Hainan Island.

"Who did you contact?" Wray yelled. "Who did you call?"

The North Korean either couldn't or wouldn't talk.

That night, Wray signed out and faxed Langley that he was ill and would have to be relieved from—in effect taken off—Songbird.

He went home and opened a bottle of Johnnie Walker Black Label, an expensive escape in Japan, and drank long into the night, occasionally flipping channels but mostly watching CNN for up-to-date news of the war. He saw a raging argument going on among demonstrators of various political stripes in the front of the White House, then a zoom shot showing the state of play between a Greenpeacer and an animal rights advocate. The animal rights lady, who looked remarkably like a cat—where did CNN get this stuff, he wondered, from some casting agent?—was complaining loudly about the barbaric practices of the Chinese, their crimes against animals, and the Greenpeacer was arguing just as loudly about how Greenpeace was for animal rights too, but that the animal rights issue was a red herring put out by the fascist administration in Washington to divert all attention away from the real war—against the environment.

"If this was a fascist administration—" said the woman.

"It is," the Greenpeacer charged.

"If it *was*," the woman replied, "the police would be dragging you away right now."

"They'll be here. You wait."

Another demonstrator, an unkempt redhead, shoving her way into the fray proclaimed, "It's not the Chinese who started this—it's the Vietnamese. They're the real aggressors."

"Bullshit!" someone called out.

"Yeah—piss off, lady!"

Wray didn't know which lady was being referred to—the animal rights one or the redhead. Now there was a special news bulletin reporting that there had apparently been some "naval activity" in the South China Sea. Wray grunted in drunken disgust. It was about as helpful as saying there was a weather disturbance somewhere in Texas. The nonspecific nature of this newscast upset Wray much more than it normally would have. He was a perfectionist, and vagueness about anything irritated and at times disturbed him, especially when he'd been drinking heavily. On top of this, there had been the day's dismal failure of not getting anything out of the Korean, and on top of that, of losing his cool and the unspoken, maniacal encouragement he'd given the JDF man. Which made him, Henry Wray of the CIA, no better than the North Koreans, he told himself. Worse.

He finished his scotch and walked over to a map of southern Japan, surprised there had not yet been any kind of attack on U.S. and Japanese shipping by North Korea. Maybe the Korean had made contact about something else? But not knowing what it was, even what it might be, filled Wray with a despair, despite all his years with the firm, made infinitely worse by the booze—a plunging feeling deep in his gut, his conscience telling him that he had stood far too long at the edge of the abyss, and now it was staring back at him—that he was out of control. He reached inside his jacket, took out the 9mm Beretta automatic, and fingered it like a blind man for a few minutes, as if it was something he'd lost touch with, as if he was reacquainting himself with an old friend. Then he put it atop the TV.

CHAPTER THIRTY-ONE

Dalat, Central Highlands

IT WAS NEAR dusk when a policeman pulled up to the American visitor by an alley off Duy Tan Street and asked for identification and the special permit to be in Lam Dong province. Though the American lifting of an embargo against trading with Vietnam had meant better relations for several years, old habits died hard among some of the highlanders who, as young men, had fought the Americans in the Vietnam War. The American, Captain Raymond Baker from the U.S. legation in Ho Chi Minh City, was dressed in civilian clothes. He presented his passport with three ten-thousand-dong notes—about three U.S. dollars—sandwiched in the middle. The policeman moved back a few paces into the alley, said nothing, took the money, handed back the passport and began walking eastward down Duy Tan Street. Baker slipped the passport into the waistband money belt he wore and called out to the policeman, "Which way to Lang Bian Mountain? They tell me the views are—"

"Bac," the policeman answered. North. His thumb jerked back over his shoulder. "Twelve kilometers. You must hire a guide."

Baker didn't know whether this was official policy or simply well-meant advice. In any event he decided he would hire a guide. The policeman had already seen that he was a cultural attaché at the U.S. legation and might therefore already suspect him of spying around Dalat, though now with the U.S. and Vietnamese allies against the Chinese, it was difficult for Baker to imagine what military mission the Vietnamese policeman might think he was on. Unless the policeman had guessed that he was up here possibly searching for MIAs. The discovery of an MIA would be highly embarrassing at the moment, not only for the Vietnamese, but for their American allies as well. A hitherto MIA suddenly turning up would prove extraordinarily damaging to the U.S. public's support for U.S. assistance against the Chinese invasion, rekindling memories of the interrogation and treatment of U.S. POWs during the Vietnam War.

It was too dark now to start out on the twelve-kilometer journey to the five volcanic peaks of Lang Bian Mountain that rose to over six thousand feet above lush countryside, and Baker went instead to the nearest mid-range hotel, booked a room for the night, and asked if he could hire a guide from there to go to his ultimate destination of Lat village near Lang Bian.

"*Co, phai*—yes," the desk clerk replied, "but first you must buy permit."

"Who from?"

"Dalat police."

Baker wondered why the policeman who had stopped him hadn't told him about the permit. "How much?" he asked.

"One hundred thousand dong. Ten dollars U.S."

Baker nodded and started up to his room when the clerk called after him, telling him that he had to leave his passport at the desk for security. Baker brought out an expired but unpunched passport that he kept specifically for such purposes. It wasn't his first time looking for an MIA. He knew they wouldn't bother looking at the date, so long as it had a lot of the right-looking stamps.

Tiredly—it was unusually warm for the central highlands— Baker made his way up to the second floor of the People's Palace and spread out a local tourist map of Dalat on the mattress atop the old, creaky French-colonial style, wrought-iron bedstead. The map was poor in quality and seemed to have no scale, but he did discover that Lat village was in fact not a single entity, but consisted of a half dozen or so hamlets. Which hamlet had the old man on the sampan meant? Perhaps Lat village had been the only description the old man had been given. Most of the villages were inhabited by the Laks, the others by Kohos, Mas, and Chills, and so now he saw more sense in the hotel clerk's advice about a guide. And given what were bound to be the different dialects of the villagers, he might need more than one guide.

Already his mission to ask about any possible MIAs in the village was becoming complex, and there was no early bus from Dalat to Lat, so he would be obliged to hire a car. He suddenly wished he'd stayed in Ho Chi Minh City. His colleagues at the legation there were probably right—the MIA tip was probably a waste of time and Baker knew he wouldn't get any encouragement from Washington now that the Americans and Vietnamese were allies against China. A live MIA still being kept as a POW would be embarrassing all around. On the other hand, Washington had enough on its mind with the war that MIA search policy had more or less been forgotten about.

Baker estimated he'd need at least a week to visit the hamlets alone, for though he spoke Vietnamese, he wasn't familiar with the dialects of the central highlands. He reflected momentarily on the only hard evidence he'd ever unearthed about an MIA—two sets of dog tags and a pile of bones which the U.S. Army forensic lab had determined were human. But he still remembered the phone calls, then the letters, of the two GIs' parents.

And while more and more the question of MIAs—2,392 of them—from the old Vietnam War was receding and being shunted aside, Baker knew that if a young soldier of about twenty had been taken and was still being held, he would now be in his late forties or early fifties, and that the pain of his loved ones, like that of the parents of any missing child, would still be there.

He unpacked his suitcase, took out a glass jar of boric acid, and like someone marking a tennis court, tapped out a line of the white powder until the rectangle he made about the bed was complete.

Around midnight he thought he heard someone outside his door—or was it someone in one of the next rooms? He sat up and listened. The noise ceased and all he could hear in the background was the faint tinkle of a radio—probably from one of the rice stalls in the street below.

CHAPTER THIRTY-TWO

SUSAN D. BASEHART was an American who had tired of having most of her money invested in small-yield blue chip stocks. Diagnosed as having inoperable cancer of the bowels, her life expectancy at most a year, she had decided—along with other American and Asian investors—to gamble most of her money on a new stock in ASAM Industries, a firm sold on the promising research carried out on the feasibility of high-speed maglev: magnetically levitated train travel on commuter routes. With tests of banked speeds up to 250 mph and 1,000 mph on straightways, the commuter run from Penn Station in New York to Union Station in Washington, D.C., averaging 300 mph, would take less time than it took to take a limo from Manhattan to La Guardia. And you could move hundreds of passengers at a time, no matter what the weather. ASAM shares jumped from ten dollars to $86.50 within a month of being issued. At a hundred dollars, fourteen percent of the shareholders sold, but Susan Basehart held on, sure it would very soon climb to over a hundred dollars.

As the Tokyo-Niigata express raced through the countryside at over a hundred miles per hour, Tazuko Komura took care not to look in the foreground that was receding in a dizzying green blur of fields and supporting trestles of the fast-line track. Instead she looked beyond at the steadier scene of long, variegated rectangular sheets of newly dyed kimono linen stretched out on the green fields to dry. They looked like strips of exotic flags. The train was now on the flats going in excess of 100 mph. She pressed the button.

The flash of the explosion could be seen for miles, the sound of it now rolling thunderously across the countryside, like thunder, the forward section of the train split in half as if

143

struck by some enormous cleaver, bodies incinerated, the rear sections of the bullet train telescoping into one another in excess of 100 mph, then shooting off the elevated rail ten meters above a field into mangled tubular heaps of smoking metal and upholstery that were giving off columns of toxic smoke. There were no survivors, body parts strewn across the field and among the trees of a small wood outside Sanjo.

NHK, Japan's national network, got to the story first, then CNN. Within forty-five minutes of the crash Susan Basehart's stock in ASAM industries tumbled. She lost over $350,000 and was effectively wiped out.

Subsequent media investigations pointed out that sabotage had almost certainly been the cause of the catastrophe in which all 372 passengers and crew were killed, and that bullet-train railway technology was markedly different from that used in maglev vehicles. But these reports had little or no effect on the stock markets of the world—confidence in supertrains had crashed with the Tokyo-Niigata express. As Susan Basehart's health grew worse, exacerbated by the shock of her near financial ruin, she was told that due to medical bills, only some of which were covered by her health plan, she would spend her last days in a public ward at Bellevue.

The effect of the bullet train disaster in Japan was to produce a chilling recognition among the Japanese public, and in particular in the Japanese Defense Force, of just how vulnerable rapid transit movement of supplies and people was to terrorism. In the interrogation room of Tokyo's JDF offices, the North Korean agent Jae Chong was shown a video of the train wreck and given a single sheet of paper by one of the JDF agents, who told him that if he didn't start writing down contact names and numbers, he would be beaten again.

"It's no good protecting the bastard that blew it up," the JDF agent told Jae Chong, acting on a hunch that because of stringent security on the bullet trains, and with no package being allowed to stand unattended, it had probably been a suicide bomber.

Jae Chong sat there immobile, only the muscles in his face and the blinking of his eyes giving any indication of his nervousness. He slowly took up the ballpoint pen and then just as slowly put it down.

"Bastard!" the JDF agent yelled, and punched him in the

temple, knocking him off the stool. A call came through for the JDF agent from CIA agent Henry Wray.

"What's the story?" Wray asked. He sounded drunk.

"Nothing yet."

"I just saw the Shinkansen wreck on the TV."

The JDF agent waited—was he supposed to say something?

"Well," Wray said, "has our songbird started to sing?"

"No."

"I'll come down."

"I will send a car for you," the JDF man said.

"No—I'll be all right. Grab the *chikatetsu*." The JDF man thought quickly—that's all he needed, the American half pissed on the subway, turning up downtown. Reporters had already staked out Tokyo police HQ, pressing for news about the Shinkansen wreck. "Please let me send a car, Wray-san."

"All right," Wray said. "You're paying for it."

Wray took the Beretta off the top of the TV. Now that so many people had been killed on the bullet train, he felt justified in having told the JDF to smack the North Korean around. "Hell!" he said, talking to himself in the tiny hallway's mirror and grabbing his hat from the rack on the second tray. "Should've beaten the prick earlier—fuck the cardboard box!" It only gave a suspect more time to think—to weasel their way out of it. Well, Henry Wray was going to put the 9mm's barrel right against the son of a bitch's head, and he'd better start talking.

"Over three hundred people," Wray said, hands in his pockets. "Almost four hundred—men, women, and kids—were killed on that Shinkansen, you little prick—so you'd better start writing, Chong. Understand?"

The JDF agent could see that Wray had the Beretta in his shoulder holster so that Chong would get the message.

"Understand?" Wray repeated.

"Hai," Chong answered, nodding.

"Good."

Chong bent over the small table in front of the stool. His shoulders slumped, then with a sigh of defeat he began writing down a phone number. "I don't know the name," he said. "I just call the number—somebody answers and I leave a message."

"If you don't have a name," Wray said, "what happens if

you misdial—get a wrong number?" The JDF agent was impressed. For someone half hungover, the CIA man was on the ball.

"Whoever answers," Chong said, using his sleeve to wipe off a trickle of blood running down his chin, "says the number. Then I leave my message."

"Huh!" Wray grunted, leaning forward to pick up the paper. Chong's left hand hit him in the face, Chong's right hand pulling out the Beretta. He fired once before it cleared the holster, the shot hitting Wray's heart at point-blank range, the second shot lodging in the JDF agent's stomach—again at point-blank range—throwing the agent back against the wall, streaking it with blood. The Japanese's legs buckling, he slid down to the floor, blood spurting out from the gut wound. The interrogation door swung open and Chong fired again, dropping another JDF agent, others scattering in all directions.

Chong ran out firing two shots at random, clerks and other agents diving for cover behind desks as Chong reached the elevator. It wasn't open. Immediately he ran for the stairwell, where, taking a terrorized woman hostage, pressing the gun's barrel against her neck, he made his way out into the street. It was now dark and raining, the Ginza strip's neons coming to life as he walked down the street. Suddenly releasing her, he made a dash down an alley and disappeared into the nighttime crowds of shoppers, the wail of police and ambulance klaxons filling the air.

Chong's escape and the three men he left dead in the JDF building provided a field day for the press and a nightmare scenario for those officials responsible for the Japanese end of the logistical supply trains that were to provide the American Second Army in Vietnam with vitally needed supplies. The JDF now knew that as a hunted man, Jae Chong had nothing to lose. There was no doubt that he would be recaptured, but the question was where he and/or other North Korean agents would strike next.

CHAPTER THIRTY-THREE

NORTH OF HANOI along the road to Lang Son, General "George C. Scott" Freeman, to his acute embarrassment, found it necessary to halt his advance recon cloverleaf patrol because of lack of information about where General Vinh's forces were.

To make matters worse, the Chinese Fourth Division had penetrated the Vietnamese Army positions along the fifteen-mile Lang Son–Loc Binh front, pushing Vinh's regulars back along the Lang Son–Ban Re railway, creating the possibility of widespread confusion between the EMREF's advancing reconnaissance patrol and the retreating Vietnamese.

For now, Freeman and Vinh decided to have the EMREF recon force withdraw sixty miles south to Phu Lang Thuong along the hundred mile Lang Son–Hanoi road so as to avoid any further blue on blue incidents. One of the deciding factors in the U.S./U.N. Vietnamese decision to have the American and U.N.-led force pull back was the lack of good radio communication between dispersed Vietnamese positions, creating the ever-present danger of a unit of withdrawing Vietnamese running into allied or their own units in the thick jungle.

Freeman could have easily rationalized his forces' pullback, as press officer Boyd advised, by pointing out the inferior Vietnamese communications ability, which posed the greatest danger of a blue on blue. Instead, Freeman, in a CNN interview that night, explained the pullback as a *joint* tactical decision made by him and General Vinh. It was a face-saving gesture for the Vietnamese which General Vinh would not forget. Freeman's pullback of his EMREF spearhead, however, received less than fair treatment in most of the world press. It became an opportunity for all those who either disliked and/or were jealous of Freeman's reputation as one of the most, if not *the* most, aggressive U.S. field commanders since George Patton.

"Will you be withdrawing any farther south, General?" a British news pool reporter asked. With Vinh looking on, Freeman hedged his bets. "We may find it necessary to regroup to Bac Ninh, ten miles farther south, but—" He turned to General Vinh. "—I don't expect anything more than that."

General Vinh nodded his agreement immediately, which told Freeman the Vietnamese general knew more English than his interpreters had led the U.S.-U.N. team to believe. Freeman held up his right hand to signal that the press conference was over. *"Cam on rat nhieu."*

Press officer Boyd, surprised, looked at Major Cline. "I didn't know the old man could speak Vietnamese."

Cline smiled. "There's a lot you don't know about the old man. He does his homework."

"Well, do you know what he said?"

"Some form of thank-you, I think. But he sure didn't like that limey's question about maybe pulling back farther. Apart from Skovorodino, it's the only time I've seen him pull back. It's against his religion."

"Which is?"

"His creed is Frederick the Great's. *'L'audace, l'audace—toujours l'audace!'* Audacity, audacity, always audacity!"

"Maybe," Boyd said, "but he didn't get off to much of a start."

"Stick around," Cline advised. "He'll surprise you."

"For instance?" Boyd challenged.

Robert Cline thought for a moment. "Freeman was in a winter battle once, leading U.S.-U.N. forces. One of the many wars that've erupted since the Berlin Wall came down and we got the 'new world order.' Anyway, Freeman gave the order to withdraw his armored corps of M-1 tanks—retreating from Russian-made T-72s. Everybody thought he was nuts—cracking up." Major Cline paused to light a cigarette.

"And?" Boyd pressed.

"And," Cline continued, "as the temperature kept dropping—minus fifty degrees, minus sixty—Freeman kept pulling the M-1s back. Until it got minus seventy with windchill factor—then he suddenly orders all the M-1s to stop and attack the T-72s." Cline took a deep drag on the cigarette. He liked this part, wanted to tease it out a little, show how the Freeman legend had grown, that it wasn't all bullshit like some of the Johnny-come-latelies thought it was.

"So?" Boyd said, anxiously awaiting the outcome. "What happened?"

"M-1s slaughtered the T-72s. Knocked out over ninety percent of them."

"I don't understand," Boyd said.

By now Marte Price had come in on the fringe of the conversation. "I remember," she said. "The oil in the Russian tanks froze at minus sixty-nine degrees, right? And the waxes separated out in the hydraulic oil lines—clogged the lines like lumps of fat in an artery. Russian tanks couldn't move. Seized up, and Freeman's tanks knocked them out."

Major Cline blew out a long stream of smoke. "Thanks for ruining my story, Ms. Price."

"Call me Marte."

"All right. Thanks for ruining my story, Marte."

"You're welcome, Major," she answered impishly. "You're not the only one who knows Freeman's a stickler for detail."

CHAPTER THIRTY-FOUR

THE TRUCK CARRYING Danny Mellin, the Australian Murphy, and a dozen or so other POWs, including several Vietnamese and Caucasian women, abruptly stopped, the prisoners told to get out by the two AK-47-toting guards.

Once down on the crushed coral road, the prisoners, despite some of them limping and showing other signs of wear and tear, were ordered to start marching down the whitish road toward a clump of trees from which the noise of construction issued forth, along with Chinese shouts. The stubby trees were more like tall brush, and soon through gaps in the trees the prisoners, most of them Vietnamese with two Australians and three Americans, could see a long line of men in black pajamas, about fifty or so, passing what looked like variegated stones on a fire-dousing line.

As Mellin and Murphy got closer to the gaps in the scrub, they could see that cement powder was being passed as well, and was being used to build hut walls about ten feet high.

Up to this point Mellin, like most of the other POWs, thought he was somewhere on the southern coast of China. But then, rounding a bend in the road, Mellin, Murphy, and the others were astonished to see an endless expanse of ocean.

"Jesus," Murphy said. "We're on a friggin' island."

"Up shut!" shouted one of the PLA guards, jabbing the Australian in the ribs with the Kalashnikov.

"Okay, mate," the Australian said with a conciliatory smile. "Don't get your balls in an uproar."

The guard smashed him in the back with the rifle butt, sprawling the Australian on the crushed coral road, his arms lacerated and bleeding. Mellin bent down and, despite the fierce headache he was suffering from his earlier altercation with the same guard, helped the Australian back to his feet. "Be quiet," he whispered to Murphy. "They'll kill you."

The next second there was what sounded like an enormous underground explosion, the crushed coral road beneath them trembling momentarily, and now the sound of the detonation hit them in a series of gut-punching waves. The guard who had hit them, and who would soon be known to the POWs as "Upshut," was laughing, calling out to the other guard at the head of the line and pointing to the stunned disarray of the prisoners.

Mellin and Murphy, like the rest of the POWs who had been landed by the destroyer, would find out the next day, after spending a very uncomfortable night in the open, that the explosions, which were underwater and offshore, were part of the PLA's plan to use the blown-up coral to add height to what was essentially a reef island, one of the many in the Nansha or Spratly Islands, which at high tide was covered with several inches of water, large parts of it becoming visible only at ebb tide.

But building up the island reef and maintaining it with a company of over a hundred PLA marines was only part of the PLA's plan to occupy all islands in the Spratly and Paracel islands. A more pressing purpose was at hand, but it was one neither Danny Mellin nor Mike Murphy would discover until the sun rose on another perfect tropical day. It would be a day that would turn into a nightmare for all those taken prisoner by the PLA's invasion and occupation of rigs and islands scattered throughout the two strategic groups of South China Sea islands, cays, and atolls.

For Mellin it was like being back in 'Nam, and as he lay there beneath a bloodred moon, caused by the pollution of rig fires, he became disgusted with himself, for his hands were trembling and he feared that the guard's brutality had not yet reached its peak. It was the only thing he was sure of; everything else—why they were here, for instance—was an open question and laden with anxiety. He'd given up smoking years ago, but right now he craved a cigarette, the stronger the better, to calm his nerves. Incredibly, next to him Mike Murphy was fast asleep and snoring, "to beat the band," as the Aussie would have said, but then the Australian hadn't been in a war before, and as yet hadn't suffered the soul-breaking loneliness of the POW in solitary. Perhaps the PLA wouldn't separate them—and perhaps when you'd finished doing whatever they wanted you to do, they'd shoot you in the neck. He heard a prisoner urinating and the never-ending crashing of the sea on the reef.

After Jae Chong's escape—during which he had killed two JDF agents and Wray of the CIA—the ambulances raced through the city to help those injured by flying glass during the melee. In the JDF's HQ there was special consternation among the staff. How was it that the American, Wray, was permitted into the room while he was still armed, a direct contravention of internal JDF regulations? Someone was going to get it in the neck for that violation, and never mind about the possibility of the families of the deceased suing, even though the JDF officially had no office of Intelligence.

In all the confusion of how to word the official report of the shootings that would have to go to the minister, it was a junior clerk who found what looked like a phone number written on a piece of paper that had been lying, blood-soaked, in the interrogation room. He gave it to his section chief, who immediately punched out the number on his computer, waiting for the number/address correlation listings. It came up on the screen as a local number for Kentucky Fried Chicken.

"Very amusing," the section chief said, decidedly unamused. The headquarters staff got the distinct impression that the chief was more interested in recapturing Chong for ridiculing him than for killing the two agents and the American. To be on the safe side, the chief ordered a stakeout of the Kentucky Fried Chicken outlet. It wasn't beyond the range of possibility, he told his staff, that the *gaijin* Chong had written down an actual contact number—that some other *gaijin* working for the KFC outlet was in fact a spy.

For a few days, however, the chief's loss of face could be measured in the number of chicken and cock-a-doodle-doo jokes doing the rounds of the Japanese Defense Forces HQ. That is, until the funeral of the two agents and the return of Wray's body to the United States, reminding everyone that Jae Chong, the uncooperative comedian, was also a killer, and a killer who now had nothing to lose as one of the biggest manhunts in Japanese history got under way.

CHAPTER THIRTY-FIVE

Taipei

"YOU TURD!"

"You've been looking in your mirror, you asshole!"

This edifying exchange was not unusual. It merely signified that yet another day of "debate" had begun in the democratic life of the Li-fa Yuan, Taiwan's legislature, between the Nationalist and Democratic Progressive parties. The subject of discussion was whether or not Taipei would contribute any of its well-equipped and superbly trained armed services to the U.N. force under the command of General Douglas Freeman. Taiwan, as the congressman, Shen, from Kaohsiung in the south put it, was caught between a "rock and a hard place" about what to do in the conflict between the U.N.—in effect, the United States—and China. If Taiwan did not contribute to the joint U.N. force, Congressman Shen pointed out, then Washington would be angry, but if Taiwan did furnish troops and matériel to the U.N. force, then Beijing would be furious. Indeed, Beijing had already cautioned Taiwan about getting involved on the American side. "Remember," the Communist Chinese had warned them, "after the war you'll still be there and we'll still be here—only a hundred and sixty kilometers away. We can wait. *Fen-shen-suei-ku*—we will break your bones."

A member of the Nationalist opposition party rose and suggested that if the government was too "gutless" to throw Taiwan's hand in with the Americans, who, during the hard times of the fifties, had contributed enormous amounts of aid as well as putting the U.S. Seventh Fleet between Taiwan and mainland China to thwart a Communist invasion, then the very least Taiwan could do was contribute money to the U.N. cause.

"Like Japan!" a Nationalist party member charged, springing to his feet. "As gutless as Japan in the Iraqi War. War by checkbook!"

"*You* talk of war by checkbook! *You*, the ardent followers of Chiang Kai-shek!"

The joke was a pun on the English phrase "Cash My Check," the name Harry Truman had given to Chiang Kai-shek. That such an aside could be made in the Li-fa Yuan, no matter that several legislators wanted to punch Mr. Shen in the nose for making it, was a measure of just how far—or, for the Nationalists, just how low—Taiwan had come in its surge to a multiparty democratic system.

"We'll break *your* bones!" shouted another legislator in warning that there was a dire risk of war with the mainland should Taiwan assist the U.S. or the U.N. In *any* case, another warned, the Americans wouldn't want a war on two fronts— Vietnam and Taiwan.

"On *three* fronts," another legislator said. "Don't forget the Spratlys—Beijing certainly hasn't."

In addition to risking war with the mainland, Taipei had another serious matter on its mind, namely the fact that because Taipei had prohibited direct offshore investment in the mainland economy, which would constitute a de facto recognition of Beijing, the only way in which Taipei businessmen could do business with the burgeoning entrepreneurs of the mainland was to either become petty smugglers or, if they were big investors, to funnel their money through middlemen in Hong Kong, such as Jonas Breem, within his South Asia Industries Group.

* * *

When the Taiwanese noninterventionist decision reached the White House, there was disappointment on the part of the President, but not surprise. Americans had not had to live under the guns of the PLA for almost half a century. However, among the Joint Chiefs of Staff there was resentment in view of the fact that U.S. forces and billions in foreign aid had helped Taiwan develop into one of the powerhouses of Asia with one of the highest levels, if not *the* highest level, of personal income per year. CIA chief David Noyer helped put the situation in perspective when he advised those present at the morning intelligence briefing that despite Taiwan's official refusal to become involved in the U.N. stand against the People's Republic of China, the Republic of China could still be helpful in maintaining and, where possible, activating its covert network on the mainland and in the South China Sea.

"Submarines?" the President inquired. "They only have four, and none of them are nuclear."

The Chief of Naval Operations, Admiral Reese, was impressed by the President's recall of Taiwan's status in the military balance of power.

"No, not subs," Noyer said, "though I've no doubt they could prove useful in helping us with guarding our Japan-Vietnam convoys, and Beijing'd have no physical proof of their intervention. But what I mean, Mr. President, is their clandestine operations on the mainland—saboteurs. If they could help sabotage the Ningming–Lang Son railway in the south, we could sever the head of their logistics line."

"For how long?" Ellman asked.

"Depends on what kind of job the Taiwanese agents can do. However long it is, it'll help Freeman's force."

"Fine," the President said. "But what if the Taiwanese are captured and talk?"

Noyer shrugged. "Beijing's hardly going to go to war with Taiwan over that. Besides which, Taiwan's agents on the mainland are mostly mainland Chinese. For most of them it's not a matter of ideology—it's just another way of making money."

"Like the smuggling," the President said, "that goes on between Fujian province on the mainland and Taiwan."

Ellman suppressed a grin. The President was showing off. Fair enough—it wasn't a bad idea now and then to let the Joint Chiefs and Noyer know that he knew more than he told them in his briefing papers. "And besides," the President continued, "there's already a tremendous amount of jealousy in China between the north and the more prosperous south. The northerners are seen as snobs in power, while the south is prone to much more capitalistic-type economic drives. And there's one hell of a lot of resentment by the minority groups and the non-Mandarin-speaking groups against the north."

All right, Ellman thought, that's enough—we read the State Department memos too.

Even so, Noyer appreciated the President making the point. It was surprising how few congressmen fully appreciated the fact that there were serious divisions within China, which, if handled adroitly by agencies such as the CIA, could help the fight against the PLA.

The President turned to Noyer. "Have we enough operatives of our own in China?"

"No, sir. That's why it would be good to have some liaison with Taipei on this."

"We already have liaison with them," CNO Reese cut in. "Unofficially, of course."

"Yes, Admiral," Noyer replied. "But I mean at the highest levels."

"Such as?" the President inquired.

Noyer decided to press a little. In the firm it was called covering your ass. "I mean, sir, that if we had the chief executive's authorization to negotiate a deal with Taipei."

The President was doodling on his desk's leather-bordered blotter. "All right," he replied. "You have the chief executive's go-ahead, Dave, but I caution you that if it's screwed up in any way, no one in this room'll remember anything about authorization." He looked at Ellman and the Joint Chiefs. "Is that understood?" They nodded their assent.

"We'll be discreet," Noyer put in. "I have just the person in—"

"No!" the President cut in. "I don't want to know whether it's animal, vegetable, or mineral. Nothing! Nada!"

They all smiled in agreement. They were the President's men.

"Of course," the President added, his tone much lighter now that the serious decision had been made to help foment trouble in South China—or anywhere else along General Wei's and General Wang's supply line—"knowing you, Dave, you'll probably have one of their goddamn pirates representing us."

There was hearty laughter except, Ellman noticed, from

David Noyer, who merely smiled politely. "The main thing," the President said, grasping Noyer affectionately on the shoulder, "is that we help Freeman. Until he gets up to proper strength over there with men and matériel, he'll need all the assistance we can give him."

It was the understatement of the year.

CHAPTER THIRTY-SIX

THE CHINESE WERE pushing south all along the fifteen-mile Dong Dang–Lang Son front, with follow-up divisions from the Chengdu military region's Fourteenth Group Army pouring through the hole punched out by artillery at Lang Son. Troops spilled down into the patchwork quilt fertile valley southwest of Loc Binh, eleven miles southeast of Lang Son.

Here they were joined by forward elements of several divisions, 34,000 men, from Guangzhou's Fifteenth Group Army of 56,000 men. The remaining 22,000 troops were split between an infantry division of 13,000 and an airborne division of 9,099 officers and enlisted men and kept in reserve in and around Lang Son to help repulse any breakthroughs in what the PLA commanders knew would be the inevitable American-led U.N. and Vietnamese counterattack.

The two commissars—the political officers—of General Wei's and General Wang's armies had joined forces and convinced Wei of their argument to keep pushing south to Hanoi. Wang, however, was arguing that both group armies, while still north of Hanoi, should pivot eastward near Phu Lang Thuong, and instead of worrying about Hanoi, should head for the vital port of Haiphong, thirty-five miles to the east.

One of the political officers interjected, "Comrade, your plan to turn east toward Haiphong is most commendable militarily—"

"Commendable?" Wang cut in. "It is in my view essential." His fingers jabbed at the map of northern Vietnam. "Haiphong is the tail of the American supply line. If we capture Haiphong, we can prevent supplies from Japan from ever reaching Freeman's troops."

"I have already said, comrade, that militarily this is sound—as far as it goes. But Hanoi is the *capital* and is only twenty-five miles from Phu Lang Thuong. The capture of the Vietnamese capital would be of major psychological significance. Once the capital falls, morale collapses."

"*That,*" Wang replied, "is a hypothesis, comrade. Haiphong is a fact."

"Only another twenty-five miles south, comrade."

Wang pointed to the map. "Twenty-five miles, comrade, can be a life's journey. Yes, we have done well so far—because we have had the element of surprise—but now that is gone, and the Americans will soon launch an attack."

"If we keep striking south, General, we will overrun Hanoi, and then the Americans will withdraw as they did once before, when Saigon fell. They will flee like rabbits, and Vinh's Vietnamese will withdraw ever southward."

"Will they?" Wang asked, his skeptical tone indicating quite clearly what he thought of the political officer's conclusion.

"Yes," the political officer answered, his confidence as evident as Wang's skepticism. "The Americans, comrade, have no more stomach for another long war in Vietnam."

Wang shook his head. "The Americans have no stomach for another *defeat* in Vietnam—or anywhere else, comrade. Iraq revived their confidence. And Haiti."

"Haiti," the other political officer responded, "was nothing. Our young Communist pioneers could have taken Haiti."

"I disagree, comrade."

"I am not interested in Haiti," the political officer said.

"But I'm interested, comrade," Wang replied, "about your—" Wang thought carefully. "—your preoccupation with Hanoi. Is this truly your view or is this Beijing speaking?"

"I am with the party on this," the political officer said.

There was a long, tense silence. No one wanted to lose face. Wang lit a cigarette, offering the packet around, the other three accepting graciously.

"I will go this far," Wang proposed. "I will keep attacking south with General Wei's army group on my right flank. If we meet strong resistance at Phu Lang Thuong, I will turn east

toward Haiphong, calling on our reserves of the Fifteenth
Group Army to reinforce my spearhead. I will use armor to
race for the port and destroy the Americans before they can organize a full-scale counterattack. We will move at night and
rest during the day, as General Giap did, and the North Koreans in their civil war—to avoid American air attacks."

The political officers conferred. A compromise was reached:
the generals would have ten days to take Hanoi. If they did not
succeed, they would accede to General Wang's strategy, and
support him in a drive east to Haiphong. Wang was not satisfied, but it was two against one, with General Wei ready to follow whatever would be best for his career prospects.

"All right," agreed Wang, "but I wish to draw your attention
to the Americans' industrial capability. I was a very young
man when my grandfather told me stories about the American
devils in Korea. They were all but driven into the sea, and for
their Marines trapped at Chosin reservoir, it was the longest retreat in their history. But they counterattacked, comrades, and
drove *us back* across the Yalu. Their industrial capacity is—"
He thought for a moment. "—something which has to be seen
to be believed."

"They had this capacity in the Vietnam War, General, and
they were driven out."

"The American public was not with them then."

It was the political officer's turn to be skeptical. "You think
it is with them in this war, General?"

"The U.N. lackeys are with them," Wang replied.

"Perhaps," the political officer said, "but that can evaporate
overnight. Is the American public with them?"

General Wang conceded the possibility that the American
people's support might be only transitory at best, that it might
vanish overnight if he could inflict unacceptable casualties on
the Americans—kill as many of them as possible in the short-
est time. That was an aim both political officers and both generals could agree on. Wang was heartened by this thought—the
fact that while the PLA had sustained 26,000 casualties in the
three weeks of the 1979 war with Vietnam, the American public would simply not tolerate such losses. Finally, in the matter
of numbers, China would always win. Every day in China another sixty thousand babies are born.

CHAPTER THIRTY-SEVEN

PULLING BACK FROM where the blue on blue had occurred, D'Lupo's seven-man point squad, the first rifle platoon HQ, and three other platoons behind them—including Martinez's Special Forces group and the retreating troops of General Vinh—ran into some isolated sniping but managed to establish a half-moon-shaped defense perimeter. It was about three hundred yards in diameter, its edge just beyond a V-shaped gully formed by a creek bed which the PLA would have to cross before climbing fifteen feet at a forty-five-degree incline if they were to attack the allied force. Behind the half-moon-shaped perimeter there were the burial mounds of a deserted village. The villagers, terrified of the PLA, had left, heading south for Phu Lang Thuong well before the retreating advance patrol of the EMREF and Vinh's troops had arrived.

On the lip of the gully, EMREF's Special Forces had planted antipersonnel, puck-sized disk mines. Using K-bar knives, they'd gently lifted patches of grass, not cutting out the patches but lifting them up carefully from one side, as one would gently prise up a scab, then scratching out a two-inch hole beneath the grassy trapdoor, placing the disk mines, and covering them with the patch. Farther back from the gully's lip, members of the two rifle platoons placed claymores, just as cautiously laying the trip wire. Johnny D'Lupo ordered some claymores on the flanks and in the rear.

"You think they're gonna get behind us?" Dave Rhin asked.

"What d'you think, man?" Martinez, from the Special Forces platoon, replied. Rhin was on the field phone to HQ platoon, reporting that everything was set up and confirming that, in their capacity as the advance patrol for the EMREF, they were now in contact with Vinh's forces, who had joined

the defensive line above the southern side of the gully. After
further consultation with Vinh's English-speaking operator, the
HQ squad ordered the flank mines to be dug up lest either of
Vinh's flanks gave way under a PLA attack and were forced
into the American perimeter. Instead, the mines were to be
placed on the Vietnamese flanks, several hundred yards away
from both EMREF flanks.

"Shit!" one of D'Lupo's seven-man squad complained.
"Nothing I like better, man, than to dig up mines we just laid."

"Right," D'Lupo agreed. "Some fucker oughta thought of
this 'fore we started laying the fucking things!"

"Stop your whinin', man," Rhin advised. "Go take the
fuckers to the Vietnamese flanks. They'll love yer for—"

There was a high, whistling sound followed by the crash of
an explosion, then another and another, men screaming, scram-
bling for cover as more explosions of red earth and undergrowth vomited skyward. The soil fell like rain for several
seconds after the first mortar salvo, the smell of cordite and
freshly uprooted vegetation pungent in the hostile air.

Some of the EMREFs who had been digging slit trenches
lay unmoving, dead now, one beheaded, another sitting quite
still, the victim of the tremendous force of the concussion and
perhaps shrapnel as well. D'Lupo dived behind one of the
loamy burial mounds, an 82mm Chinese mortar round landing
close to the lip of the gully, sending shrubs and sticks into the
air. Immediately, he moved to a mound in front of him that had
been hit dead center, D'Lupo noting that there was an advancing pattern of small, mortar-made craters in front of him. He
now dived into a burial mound, the peak of its cone blown off,
the incoming round he'd just fled landing ten yards behind
him. To his amazement, as he came up for air, he noticed his
arm covered in blood.

He had no recollection of being hit. Despite the explosions
of incoming and the steady *Bomp! Bomp! Bomp!* of outgoing
81mm rounds from the Special Forces platoon, D'Lupo pulled
his bleeding arm quickly from the protective burial mound. He
was staring at a completely emaciated skull, a sandy-white
loam spilling over it like sand in an hourglass, the skull's teeth
red where D'Lupo's arm had scraped them as he'd dived for
cover.

As suddenly as it started, the heavy mortar barrage ceased,
only to be replaced by the tearing tarpaper sound of light and
medium machine guns using not only the heavier 7.62mm am-

munition of the old Type 68 assault weapon but also that of the newer 5.6mm CQ automatic rifle.

Following the blare of a Chinese bugle, someone on the west U.S.–Vietnamese side of the gully shouted, "They're coming!" Rhin cussed like the trooper he was, disgustedly releasing his radio pack, which was now so much junk, the only thing intact being the handpiece, which he now tossed away. Through the undergrowth, they could see Chinese regulars, whose "piss-pot" helmets were covered in camouflage netting, branches of leaves draped from them, and whose black-green-brown combat uniforms were so difficult to see against the background of the gully's bush-lipped opposite bank.

Even knowing that his platoon was cut off from HQ—they'd have to use runners, if necessary—Rhin was impressed by the Chinese assault. No sooner had half of them, fifty or so, been chopped down by the American and Vietnamese fire than the remaining fifty, having rushed across the shallow streambed, were out of sight, now at the base of the forty-five-degree-angle dirt cliff. The ocher-colored dirt cascaded down like a waterfall as the Chinese, without stopping, immediately began scaling the steep incline of loose soil by running up as far as they could go with supporting machine-gun fire from the bank behind them, from which they'd descended.

At the apogee of their climb, unable to make it alone up an almost vertical dirt face of ten to twelve feet, they took hold of long, arm-thick pieces of bamboo stilts shoved up to them as an assist from the men below.

Up and down the creek a hundred yards in either direction, more and more Chinese began scaling the cliff. Those first up to the edge were machine-gunned immediately and fell down amid their comrades at the base of the cliff. But without a pause, others took their place on the cliff and held ground, helped by a rain of stick grenades being flung up and over the cliff's edge, lobbed amid the forward American and Vietnamese U.N. troops.

The explosions and concussions of earlier mortars had set off many of the antipersonnel mines. One Chinese at the middle of a ten-man-line charge tripped a claymore, and all ten were killed either outright or fatally felled by the ball bearings that had exploded toward them in a steel curtain at supersonic speed. But the Chinese kept coming and dying. D'Lupo and Martinez's Special Forces knew that unless the Chinese resupply of troops could be cut, numbers alone would soon overwhelm them. Some of the USVUN machine guns were so hot, rounds were cooking off.

D'Lupo and Special Forces platoon were firing flares down into the gully, knowing that some of the units behind them must have gotten through to U.S.-Vietnam-U.N. troops headquarters at Kep or Phu Lang Thuong, and they hoped that despite the poor visibility in the low ceiling of stratus, TACAIR would be on the way. D'Lupo, by prior agreement with TACAIR's forward air controller, had an understanding that should radio contact be lost, the enemy position would be indicated by a white/red/white flare combination.

Early in the Vietnam War, such arrangements were often made on the spot via radio contact between pilots and the men in trouble on the ground. But "Charlie," as the enemy was then known, had often listened in on the U.S. radio messages with English-speaking radio interpreters, and would quickly fire the flare sequence onto American and ARVN positions, creating a blue on blue.

Now D'Lupo's forward squad fired a white/red/white sequence into the gully's eastern sector to the right of them. TACAIR, if it was on its way, should make visible contact in plus or minus two minutes, coming in beneath the blankets of the gray stratus.

Down in the gully, the Chinese immediately began a barrage of small-arms fire, shredding the flares' chutes so they fell faster, giving the Chinese more time to pick up the unburned section of the smoke flares and, having cut their chute straps, lob them into the brush beyond the western side of the gully. Nothing like this had happened in Iraq, where, not surprisingly, there was no bush.

Some of the Chinese, already ensconced in dugouts along the lip, kept up a sustained fire into the American positions, making it impossible for the Americans to rush forward and secure the flares, now burning furiously, supposedly marking the enemy position to be bombed. As a result, two Intruders sent in from the *Enterprise* dropped their ordnance, including two free-fall pods of napalm-jellied gasoline, within forty-three seconds killing sixteen Americans in the EMREF's advance recon force. Nine of them were burned to death, running torches of fire in the brush, setting it afire before they collapsed, or throwing themselves onto the earth in futile attempts to smother the fire with soil. Friends used their cupped hands, digging with spades, whatever, to save two men who were so horribly burned they now wished they were dead.

At least three of the stricken men had made a rush toward the gully to try to extinguish themselves in the water holes of the gully bed. They were cut to pieces by Chinese small-arms fire before they got beyond the lip, falling, rolling down the steep red dirt slope, Chinese troops immediately stripping them of what weapons they could, some of the Americans' flesh sticking to their M-16s like melted cheese.

The remainder of the USVUN were also hit by napalm, and seconds after the terrible beauty of an enormous orange flame rolling through a backdrop of green fields and brush, five Vietnamese had been burned black with five U.N. soldiers, including two from the British SAS contingent. Only their badges, "Who Dares Wins," were recognizable after their own ammunition packs exploded.

By now the forward air controller had seen the Chinese rush the gully, realized about the flare balls-up, and redirected the Intruders. This cleared the gully nicely, an even more devastating attack than upon the USVUN line, since the sharp-angled sides of the gully made it a natural conduit for the flame that raced like a flood of molten hot steel from a furnace down the gully floor. Over two hundred Chinese assault infantry were incinerated, and the presence of the American planes ready to bomb again had dissuaded the PLA from any further rushes, the air filled with a stench of burned chicken.

To further dissuade the PLA, the planes on another run dropped napalm pods a hundred yards in from the gully on the PLA side. The screams of those caught in the swath of burning gasoline attested to the pilots' having guessed right that the next wave of PLA assault troops had been assembling not far from the gully's edge. The hesitation this caused the Chinese, along with the fact that much of the underbrush had been set aflame, thus denying troops cover close to the gully, saved the USVUN force, which had pulled back after several units found themselves badly mauled and their positions untenable, though in numbers lost the Chinese had suffered considerably more than the USVUN.

For Douglas Freeman, the retreat was a decision he abhorred. His intuitive reaction was to hold ground and take the gully while TACAIR kept the Chinese pinned down with napalm and rocket fire. But he was too good a soldier to pretend he could hold the gully against the PLA if he had no backup and/or no support from the flanks. He'd trusted the Vietnamese to fight if they were ordered by General Vinh to hold. But it was systematically built into the Communist cadre, as it had been in the PLA by Mao Zedong in his Little Red Book, to attack only when one had overwhelming strength, to withdraw when the odds of winning dropped. You struck where you thought the enemy was weakest, but withdrew once the maximum amount of damage had been achieved and *before* the enemy could rally in force against you. Though he knew this tactic well enough, Freeman hoped that Vinh's troops would stay and assist his own men in securing and holding the gully while more USVUN troops could be brought up on the Lang Ro–Lang Son road.

Vinh disagreed. "No," he explained through the interpreter, "the Chinese main force would come south down the Lang Son–Lang Ro road, so it would be unwise to withdraw USVUN troops from there to come here. It is vital," he continued, "for the Chinese to take the road if they wish to move supplies quickly to feed the head of their snake."

Major Cline asked whether he might not have a word with General Freeman.

"What is it, Major?"

"Sir, with all due respect, we'll get nowhere if you argue with Vinh, particularly in front of his political commissars. He'll lose face and then he won't agree to anything."

"Of course," Freeman said, nodding, beaming at Vinh and his advisers. "I have full confidence in the fighting ability of the Republic of Vietnam's armies—" He deliberately left out the *Socialist* before *Republic*. "—they've proved themselves in battle against us many times." He paused, then smiled politely. "All I want to be sure of is that if we commit ourselves to an overall strategy, we stick with it till we have a touchdown."

Vinh and the others were unsure about this term, and the translator had to spend some time imitating the huddle, et cetera. "Ah!" Vinh finally said, nodding and smiling. "Football."

"Right," Freeman said. "No good agreeing in the huddle, then having some joker suddenly decide it's not for him—ruin the whole goddamn play. Right?"

There was a huddle of Vietnamese advisers while Freeman explained softly to Cline, "Point is, we've got to have the will to stand ground and use it as a launch pad from which to direct our heavy stuff—arty and TACAIR. For that I need those around me to hold the goddamn perimeter and not suddenly decide to retreat 'cause we're taking heavy fire. I meant what I said, Major. These Vietnamese troops are first-rate, but this constant hit-and-run business could suddenly leave me with a flank in name only."

"We agree," General Vinh said in heavily accented English, "but . . ."

Here the interpreter took over. "The general," he told Freeman, "agrees but wishes to point out that what the Americans might think is a good strategic move, the Vietnamese might see as a simple tactical move in a local battle and therefore wish to break off if casualties are too high."

Freeman could have spit wood chips. "Please tell the general that he and I must first agree on the overall strategic plan. My strategy is simply this—to pulverize the border area around Lang Son and Dong Dang by bombing, and then to roll forward along the road with arty until we clear the area once and for all and reestablish the correct political line between the two countries.

"Christ," Freeman said in an aside to Cline, "I'm sounding like one of their damn commissars!"

The interpreter begged the general's pardon, but what was the meaning of this word "arty"?

"Artillery!" Freeman replied. "Pound the area flat— reestablish a cordon sanitaire—hopefully secure a DMZ."

Vinh nodded agreement but asked whether the other USVUN forces would agree to it or not, given what, in time, would have to be their countries' postwar relationships with China.

Freeman was getting annoyed with what he perceived to be the Vietnamese preoccupation with minor players, and he told the translator straight, "You tell General Vinh that there are really only three players on this field: his forces, mine, and the PLA."

"You have no respect for your allies?" Vinh asked.

"I have respect," Freeman replied honestly, "but I won't always have time to consult with my South Korean allies or the Japanese, for example. I know what I can expect from the British and Australian troops. Besides, their numbers aren't high and they're integrated with my command."

Vinh understood Freeman's underlying concern and brought the conversation to an end by saying, "I am not against nonconsensual decisions or massed fixed battles *if* they strategically make sense."

Freeman smiled. "You mean the battle for Khe Sanh?" The Americans had dug in, in and around the airstrip, ringed as it was by Vietnamese artillery, and aided and abetted by U.S. airpower, had won by breaking the siege.

"No," Vinh said without a smile. "I meant Dien Bien Phu."

Vinh extended his hand, and Freeman, a sardonic look on his face, as if to say, You old fox, took it in the spirit it was offered.

Vinh bowed and said, "We will try to agree in the 'huddle.' A consensus. Yes?"

"Right," Freeman said, thinking that Vinh would make a hell of an adversary.

Press aide Boyd looked, puzzled, at Major Cline. Boyd had noticed that this general agreement to work together on one plan rather than two had somehow been sealed by the mention of this Dien Bien Phu.

"Who's this Phu anyway?" Boyd asked Cline.

"You dork," Cline said good-naturedly. "Don't you know any history? It's a *place*—a valley 'bout 230 miles west of us—near the border of Laos. During the French-Indochina War in 'fifty-four, French were always bitching about the Viet Minh's hit-and-run tactics, never being able to fight a one-place pitched battle with them. Well, the Viet Minh decided on just such a battle, and General Giap ringed twelve French battalions with more than thirty of his own. Viet Minh had brought in artillery—and I'm talking 105mm and triple A—a lot of it piece by piece on their backs through the jungle. French commander called for reinforcements, and six battalions of paratroops were flown in. The French were dug in, and the Viet Minh dug miles of tunnels around the French firebase. Often they came right up to the wire, fired a burst, then disappeared before the French could get a bead on them. French were finally overrun. Over twelve thousand Frenchmen were killed or taken POW. Absolute disaster. Put an end to all the crap about the Vietnamese not being able to win a set-piece battle."

"What'd it cost the Vietnamese?" Boyd asked.

"Well over twenty thousand. Some on both sides were never found—blown to bits by the artillery." Cline paused, glanced at Vinh and Freeman and explained to Boyd, "That's why old Vinh mentioned Dien Bien Phu. He was telling Freeman that he can play it either way—hit-and-run or dig in. He's flexible."

"Well," Boyd said, adopting an air of authority beyond his

years, "they'd better agree on something pretty soon. All we've been doing so far is falling back."

CHAPTER THIRTY-EIGHT

IT WAS DIFFICULT for reporter Marte Price to know who was more surprised by the Chinese breakthrough south of Lang Son: General Vinh or Freeman. Both commanders were well-practiced in their ability to keep their innermost thoughts to themselves, and while Freeman was less inhibited about acknowledging defeat to a press conference than was the Vietnamese general, he, like Vinh, was not about to cause a plummeting morale in the U.S.-led U.N. forces.

Vinh, a veteran of the Chinese-Vietnam border clash in February of 1979, during which the PLA suffered more than 25,000 casualties in just three weeks of fighting, did say, however, that the PLA advance was "somewhat unexpected" by Hanoi, given what he described as the "corruption." Beyond that he had nothing to say to either Marte Price, the CNN reporter, or to any of the other news correspondents who, under pressure from the U.N. to allow a larger press pool, were now flocking into Hanoi. Given General Vinh's reluctance to elaborate any further, several reporters turned to Freeman to explain the Vietnamese general's terse charge of "corruption."

"Several years ago, in 1979 to be exact," Freeman answered, "the Republic of Vietnam defeated the PLA in a border war. The Chinese premier, and thus the commander in chief of the PLA—which includes, by the way, the Chinese navy and air force—told the PLA that it had better get leaner and meaner. He reduced the force size by almost a million— that still left him with plenty—and he told the PLA chiefs of staff that if they wanted to upgrade their capability, they'd have to find the extra money themselves."

"You mean," an obviously surprised British reporter asked, "that the Chinese generals were told to go into business?"

"That's exactly what I mean," Freeman answered. "It's long been practice for many of the PLA armies to grow most of their food, but now they were being told to get busy making whatever would bring in hard cash." Freeman paused. "And it wasn't only growing and selling excess vegetables on the open market that they got involved in."

Freeman had anticipated a knowing chuckle or at least a nod from some of the more senior correspondents, but none came, and he realized, from the frantic scribbling in his audience, that for many in the press pool this background information he was giving was something new. For a fleeting second or two Freeman had an uncharacteristic moment of anxiety as he wondered whether he was revealing information he'd gotten from classified intelligence sources. It was a professional hazard. Then, just as quickly, he realized that the information he was giving out was the result of his own "homework," and that he wasn't revealing anything the Pentagon had on its secret list.

"Problem was," he continued, "that many of the PLA armies, particularly those who, with the government's blessing, got involved with the making and selling of arms to make money, also got involved with a lot of kickbacks and the like. From privates who were making ten times as much money as an ordinary private's pay to officers who were getting brown envelopes under the table from middlemen in the arms sale business, there was one hell of a lot of corruption."

The CNN reporter had his hand up. "General, you mean that because of this so-called corruption, you underestimated the PLA's ability in this war. Thought they'd gone soft?"

"Soft?" Freeman's tone could barely conceal his anger. This son of a bitch was trying to ambush him. If he said no, he hadn't thought the PLA had gone soft, his spiel about corruption wouldn't be believed, but if he said yes, the PLA had gone soft, then the next question from the monkey gallery would be, Well, if the PLA has lost its combat readiness, General, what are your troops doing retreating south from Lang Son?

"I never said the PLA was soft—nor did General Vinh. Why, the PLA's one of the toughest outfits in the world. Their training is hard, their morale is high, and they keep coming at you—ask anybody who fought in Korea. No, they're sure as hell not soft! What I think my distinguished colleague had in mind in referring to corruption was that the PLA soldier has been corrupted politically by a lot of propaganda about his neighbors to the south—that their political leadership is 'corrupt.' "

Freeman pulled out his retractable pen-sized pointer and moved it in a huge semicircle, starting from the Spratly Islands in the South China Sea, going west, north up to Russia and then east to the Siberian republic. "In the Spratlys, Vietnam, Burma, India, Tibet, Russia, all the way to—" He almost said, "Black Dragon River," the northern border between Siberia and China, but Black Dragon was the Chinese name, and instead he used the Siberian name. "—all the way to the Amur River and to Vladivostok, the Chinese have been fighting neighbors for years. Now we've had enough, and we won't put up with it anymore."

"Who's *we*, General?" the CNN reporter asked in his follow-up question.

"*We* are the United Nations." Cunning bastard, Freeman thought, but at least he'd got them off their damn fixation with Vinh's remark about corruption.

Press officer Boyd and Major Cline were likewise impressed, and after the press conference congratulated the general on his adroit handling of what could have been a loss of face for Vinh.

"General, sir," Boyd inquired, "why did the Chinese manage to push us back down the Lang Son road?"

Freeman telescoped the long pointer back into its pen's sheath, simultaneously looking about him to make sure no reporters were within hearing range. "Because, Captain," he answered, "we got the shit kicked out of us. Because General Vinh's boys, tough as they are, like our boys, haven't been in a major battle for years. For them it's been since 1979—not counting the naval battle they had over one of the Spratlys in 'eighty-eight and again in 'ninety-two. Meanwhile, the Chinese have been keeping in practice in Tibet and all their other border disputes. But don't worry. Second Army'll be up to combat strength very soon, and then my boys'll kick those Chinese asses back across the border beyond Dong Dang where they belong."

One of the reporters, a Frenchman, Pierre LaSalle, now well back in the room, couldn't suppress a smile. For a few American dollars in Manila on a stopover en route to Hanoi, he'd bought a pickup mike, one of those that advertisers boast can capture a whisper from thirty feet away, and he had Freeman's answer to Boyd on tape.

The Frenchman, who had always resented American presence in Indochina after the French had lost it all at Dien Bien Phu in '54, didn't want a French paper to have the tape. They could easily trace it back to him. No, he thought, the North American market would be best. The only problem for LaSalle was how long he should wait. It would be nice to get ahold of that photo the American woman, Price, was said to have taken of Freeman. No one could tell him exactly what the photo was, but it was rumored to be pretty embarrassing for the American general.

The next explosion that Mellin, Murphy, and the other prisoners heard on the island was followed at dawn by the agonized howl of a mobile claw crane, its tracks in several inches of water, its long neck stretched out beyond the edge of the partially submerged reef. Its claw brought up huge lumps of coral that had been blasted out by underwater dynamite charges, then swung inland and deposited the coral and sea bottom mud on a pile on part of the reef that was now submerged beneath a few inches of water in the high tide.

Dozens of variegated fish—grouper and red snapper among them—some stunned, some dead, a few sharks and hawksbill turtles as well, lay floating on the sea's surface. Several PLA soldiers who, apart from thongs on their feet, were stripped naked—despite the presence of three women among the thirty POWs—were wading out to gather up the fish, one soldier carrying an AK-47 over his head to make sure of the sharks. Quietly, Mellin, his temples still pounding from the headache he'd suffered as a result of a PLA guard hitting him with the rifle butt the day before, nudged the Australian. "See all the heaps of coral they've dredged up?"

Murphy was looking to the west. "No," Mellin told him. "Other way—east of us." When Murphy saw them, he could also see a line of what he thought might be prisoners, all clad in peasant-style black pajamas, passing baskets of coral from one of the heaps along the line, several of the black pajamas emptying the broken coral on a part of the reef covered in a few inches of water. The mud, or rather sea bottom ooze, was being carted away by another line of black pajamas to one main heap a few hundred yards inland, amid the scrubby and stunted bushes.

"How big d'you reckon?" Mellin asked. "The island?"

Mike Murphy shrugged and a guard saw it. " 'Bout half a mile long, maybe less, five hundred yards wide."

"Up shut!" shouted the soldier.

Murphy saluted the guard. "Sorry, shithead."

"Jesus," Mellin murmured, looking away from the guards. "For Chrissake, shut up, Mike." But Upshut seemed impressed by Murphy's elaborate show of obedience and the snappy salute.

Now Mellin could see several pairs of the black pajama figures leaning, straining forward like beasts of burden, pulling cement rollers behind them over the coral that had been spread out over the tidal pools.

Upshut and his cohort were looking away from Mellin, Murphy, and the dozen or so other prisoners in their charge when Mellin heard a soft and distinctly British woman's voice—one of the other rig prisoners—whispering to them to be careful, that Upshut understood more English than the American or Australian realized.

Mellin checked out the guards. They were talking to one another at about a hundred decibels, pointing at the fish dinner provided by the latest explosion. It was the Englishwoman doing the translating.

"You know a lot of Chinese?" Mellin asked the woman.

"I speak Mandarin, a little Cantonese," she said. "I was radio operator on *Chical 3*."

Mellin nodded. As far as he could remember, *Chical 3* was a rig—or at least what had been a rig—off Livock Reef about a hundred miles northeast of the island they were now on, one of the more than 220 island reefs, cays, and shoals that made up the Spratly, or, as the Chinese called them, the Nanshan, island group.

"What's your name?" Murphy asked in a low tone, looking not at her but rather at the two guards she'd warned them about.

"Fortescue," she answered. "Shirley Fortescue."

"Well, Shirl," Murphy responded. "Thanks for the tip."

Danny Mellin could see the woman, in her mid-thirties, didn't like the Australian's easy familiarity with her name. "Shirley," she corrected Murphy.

"Righto, luv," Murphy said, smiling. "No problem."

Mellin watched the Australian eyeing her more closely now, taking note of an hourglass figure which even the drab black

POW pajamas couldn't hide. "Things could be worse," he told Danny with a wink. There was a growling sound nearby—one of the other prisoners' stomachs complaining of hunger.

"Hey, Shirl," Murphy whispered. "How 'bout using a bit of the old Mandarin and asking Upshut when we get a feed? We're all bloody starving."

"No," Danny said quickly. "Don't let them know we've got someone who can understand their lingo. We might find out what—"

Upshut swung about. "Who talks?" he shouted. No one said anything, and for a moment there was silence between the sounds of the dredge claw bringing up more dislodged coral, water, and kelp streaming from it, and dumping it. One of the prisoners, a Vietnamese, got up and, holding his hand up like a child in class, asked, in what Shirley Fortescue could tell was a border dialect of Cantonese—the Chinese spoken in the south—when they would be getting some food and drink.

Upshut's cohort gave a long, loud answer, after which the Vietnamese who had asked the question sat down desultorily, shrugging his shoulders.

"What'd he say?" Murphy asked.

"I think," Shirley Fortescue said softly, "that the guard said we'll get some water but no food until we finish our work."

"Work?" Murphy said. "What fucking work? Ah, sorry, Shirl, but I'm not working for these assholes."

Upshut was coming straight at him, clicking the fold-out butt of the Kalashnikov to use the AK-47 as a club.

"Sorry!" Murphy said, quickly raising his hands. "Sorry."

The Australian's raised arms stopped Upshut, who made a show of folding the butt, shortening the weapon, and grunting, pleased by the Australian's surrender, nodding his head as if to say, That's better, now you know who's boss.

CHAPTER THIRTY-NINE

GENERALS WEI AND Wang were pleased by their armies' southward offensive but were by no means complacent. The Vietnamese Army had given them a bloody nose in '79, no matter what Beijing told the Chinese people. And neither general wanted a repeat of that performance—when the supply line had simply not been able to keep up with their own advance units, so entire battalions went without water for several days and were as much in danger from dehydration as from the Vietnamese.

Another factor that the PLA generals had to take into consideration was that what had begun with a four-mile-wide front spearheaded by the Fourth Division of the Nanning army had now spread out to a ten-mile front. The two PLA generals were concerned that if Vinh's Vietnamese divisions managed to launch a concerted counterattack, they would be able to punch a gap in the PLA line and do a "breaststroke." That is, the Vietnamese spearhead would first punch a hole in the PLA front, then divide into two arms, both swinging back southward like the arms of a swimmer doing the breaststroke, first cutting off elements of the PLA's Fourth Division, then encircling segments of the advance Chinese troops in a "scissors handle" maneuver. They would isolate the PLA troops for piecemeal destruction and rush more Vietnamese north from the Hanoi military region.

Despite this risk, elements of Wei's army heading south on the eastern flank of the ten-mile front knew they must push forward down the valley beyond Lang Ro to capture and/or render the airstrip at Kep inoperable, then swing eastward to Haiphong, the port for Hanoi in the Red River delta. But here lay another possible bone of contention between the PLA's military commander and their political officers. Generals Wei and Wang had their political officers, equal in rank to the generals, and both political and military officers had to come to an agreement about strategy—right down to the tactical level—before the troops could be given specific orders. The Vietnamese Army under Vinh, as Freeman had discovered, was run in much the same way.

At first sight Westerners were unimpressed by the system, so cumbersome, so different from their own. Or was it? Freeman asked his staff as they prepared the plans for the deployment of Second Army, whose supplies were now being unloaded at Haiphong.

Freeman, to the consternation of his aide, Major Cline, answered his own question about the similarity of the PLA command structure and that of the West. Typically, he overstated the position by pointing out how General, later President, Eisenhower had ordered General George Patton to halt what Freeman called Patton's "magnificent end run" into Eastern Europe in 1944, and how Ike had not wanted the Americans, British, and Canadians to beat the Russians to Berlin, so that "the goddamned Russians' noses wouldn't be out of joint."

"That, gentlemen," Freeman said, "was nothing less than a political decision by Ike. Another thing—it was Harry Truman who tied Doug MacArthur's hands behind his back when the general wanted to cross the Yalu in Korea and hit the red bases inside China—another political decision. Don't look so stunned, gentlemen. I just want you to know that we have our own commissars in the West. We just put 'em in the State Department and call 'em experts!"

Cline and Boyd had been equally startled by the general's analogy.

"Jesus!" Cline told Boyd. "If a reporter ever heard him say that, the shit'd really hit the fan."

It hit the fan anyway, but for a different reason. Someone, somehow, had gotten hold of what the general had said to Cline and Boyd immediately *after* the press conference. A highly profitable and thoroughly disreputable tabloid in the United States used its morning edition to scream via a four-inch block headline, in capital letters:

USVUN FORCE IN DISARRAY
'WE GOT THE S--T KICKED OUT OF US!' —GEN. FREEMAN

Soon the general's remark had been carried via cable network news to every country in the world. Anti-American sentiment was buoyed by the U.S. embarrassment, which caused red faces from the Pentagon to the White House, whose "spokespersons" were pressed by a media frenzy to explain why the advance elements of the over two and a half thousand U.S.-led U.N. emergency response team had bungled their first engagement in Vietnam. Were they exhibiting the same deficiencies that had afflicted an earlier generation of Americans in Vietnam?

It was like a spark to a powder keg of emotion as American Veterans of Vietnam and others, from as far away as the Korean and Australian contingents that had fought alongside the Americans in Vietnam, rallied to the defense of their younger compatriots, most of whom, outside Freeman's emergency response team, had just arrived in Vietnam and had not yet engaged the "Great Wall of Iron," alias the PLA.

Freeman was furious with both Boyd and Cline, reminding them that they were the only ones to whom he had made the remark that was now drawing fire from "every son of a bitch liberal in the country!" Both men assured the general they'd had nothing to do with it—hadn't said a word. Cline was brave enough to draw the general's attention to the unpalatable fact that the cries back home for firing the general were not confined to "every son of a bitch liberal," but in many instances were coming from the right wing because of his admission that the U.S.-led force had met with failure the first time at bat *and* that he had already, *before* this remark, personally taken responsibility for the action in which Americans were killed by "so-called friendly fire." Also, several large evangelical groups loudly objected to the general's use of "scatological references" in his speeches.

Within twenty minutes of the political storm breaking about him on CNN and the U.S. networks and their affiliates around the world, a phone call came into the U.N.-EMREF HQ now at Phu Lang Thuong, twenty-eight miles north of Hanoi on the Hanoi–Lang Son road. Captain Boyd's face looked pale as he said, "Yes sir, yes sir, Mr. President," and handed the receiver to Freeman.

"General."

"Mr. President."

"You know why I'm calling. I can't have my military commander making public comments of this kind. Now, I don't want to tell you how to do your job in the field, but I must remind you that I can't very well support you being C in C of the USVUN forces when you go around—albeit unintentionally—undermining the American public's confidence in the American army."

Nothing had hurt Freeman in years as much as the President's last comment.

"Mr. President, I apologize. I'd never willingly bad-mouth my men. That's not what I meant sir. I was merely giving an off-the-cuff assessment, a military man's assessment, of the Chinese breakthrough at Lang Son. S'matter of fact I was referring to General Vinh's forces more than I was ours. Why, our men haven't really closed with the enemy to any—" Freeman stopped. What was it the French said? *"Lui qui s'excuse, s'accuse."* He that excuses himself accuses himself! "I'm sorry, Mr. President."

"Well, I'm going to accept that, General, but I have to tell you that I'm under one hell of a lot of pressure here to fire you." There was silence. "I wouldn't want to do that, General, but I might have to. You must understand my position."

"I do, sir."

The President tried to end it on a note of levity. "Trouble is, General, you're one heck of a good field commander, but I have people here from Defense as well as State telling me you're another Georgie Patton—just great when it comes to getting the job done in the field, but you're a bit, ah, bullish in a china shop when it comes to political nuances. Am I being fair?"

"I'm bullish on America, Mr. President." It wasn't meant to be a joke, but the President liked it anyway.

The next morning, under increasing political pressure, the President fired Freeman from his position as C in C Vietnam USVUN forces, relegating him to command U.S. Second Army on the ground but putting the U.N. task force under the command of U.S. General Dean Jorgensen, en route from Washington to Hanoi.

"By God," Freeman said in conference with General Vinh when he received the news. "They're sending me a commissar."

General Vinh, with barely any emotion, said, "Welcome to the club."

Major Robert Cline knew if he didn't say what was on his

mind to Douglas Freeman right now, he'd never have the guts to say it again. The major begged General Vinh's pardon and asked Freeman if he could speak to him privately for a moment. Freeman, frowning—which almost destroyed Cline's resolution—excused himself from Vinh and his party. "Yes, what is it, Bob?"

"Sir, can I be utterly frank with you?"

"Yes."

Cline inhaled deeply and said, "General, you've got to be more—I don't know—politically sensitive."

"Politically correct you mean!" Freeman responded, glowering at the major, the general telling Cline that, "goddamn it," he had been the first U.S. general in history to use women as chopper pilots.

"No, sir! I don't mean 'politically correct,' I mean politically sensitive. General, that crack you just made about Washington sending you a commissar, and yesterday your remarks to the staff about there being commissars in the State Department—and we don't know how that remark you made to Boyd about the Chinese kicking the shit out of us first time to bat got out—but if your comments about 'commissars in the State Department' leaked to the press—" Cline paused for breath, his shoulders tight with tension. "—you'd be ruined, sir. They'd fire you as field commander as well."

Freeman was still glowering, his cheek muscles bunched up, his jaw set in a look of ferocious determination. "Are you finished, Major?"

"Yes, sir."

For what seemed like an eternity to Cline the general stood there in the tent. Freeman's head was nodding, the rest of him immobile. "All right, Bob, you've made your point. Oh, hell—I agree I'm not politically—*sensitive*—that the word you used?"

"Yes, sir."

"Well, you're right, damn it! I'll try to be more—" He exhaled heavily. "—'sensitive.'"

Cline smiled with relief. Boyd entered the HQ clutching a sheaf of faxes. Freeman turned to him. "What've you got there, Captain? More bad news?"

"And some good news," Boyd replied.

"Give me the bad first."

"Beijing radio is using your, ah, demot—ah—"

"Demotion."

"Yes, sir. They're using it as a sign that Americans will fail against the PLA the same as we did in Vietnam earlier—in the Vietnam War. . . ." Boyd hesitated.

"Go on!" Freeman ordered.

"Sir, they said we'll be crushed like beetles."

"Did they?" Freeman said, raising an eyebrow.

"Yes, sir."

"Well," Freeman said, turning to Cline, "they're being very insensitive about beetles, Major. You think we should make a protest on behalf of the beetles of the world?"

Cline shrugged and smiled. "They've probably got a beetle lobby on Capitol Hill, General."

"By God!" Freeman riposted. "You're probably right." He turned to Boyd. "So what else are they going to do to us American beetles?"

"I don't know, General."

Freeman pointed at the pile of faxes Boyd was holding. "Well, what else do you have for me, son?"

"Messages, sir, from various veterans' associations all around the country. Basically they're all saying—" He looked down at one. "—It says, 'Tell it like it is, General. Give 'em hell!' "

"Huh!" Freeman laughed. "Who? The PLA or Wash—" The word died on his lips, his right hand giving the stop signal. He smiled at Cline, then turned to Boyd. "Thank them on my behalf, Captain. Much appreciated."

"Yes, sir."

Freeman glanced over at Cline. "Is this century crazy or what? I've just been demoted for being politically insensitive—for telling the truth—and now Vietnam vets from our most unpopular war in history are telling me to hang tough and help the Vietnamese."

"It's the new world order, General."

"Huh—in some ways I prefer the old. Least you knew what was what." Freeman made his way back to the operations table, where Vinh's staff were obviously impressed with the 3-D computer graphics of the terrain up north from the Red River valley and the high country about Lang Son, showing the last known disposition of Vinh's army. But Freeman observed the graphics with a jaded edge. He knew how pretty it all looked, but he also knew that the computers were only as good as the information going into them, and right now the information had to be highly suspect, as Vinh's forces and the advance elements of the U.S.-led U.N. force were fighting desperately to form a defensive line to somehow stop, or at the very least slow down, the PLA's advance. And tactical air support from the carrier group was not yet possible because of heavy overcast curdling in from the Tonkin Gulf.

Even if the weather changed immediately, TAC support would have to be guided in to bomb pinpoint positions at night via infrared sighting, and at the moment all Vinh and Freeman knew was that their respective forces were in retreat. Until the situation stabilized, his airborne infantry and artillery now being deployed from Haiphong to Hanoi couldn't be used effectively.

Most of Freeman's staff, including Major Cline and Captain Boyd, were amazed by the general's stoicism in view of what they, like many others, saw as a humiliating demotion, overall command being given to Jorgensen. But if Freeman appeared sanguine about his fate, it was in large part because he believed in destiny and knew that now he would be freer to do what he knew he was best at—fighting—directing and leading his men at the front. For Douglas Freeman, his demotion was to be seized upon as opportunity, and he thanked God for it.

CHAPTER FORTY

" 'ELLO." IT WAS said with a distinct French accent followed by an offer of French champagne and two tulip-shaped glasses.

Marte Price had just finished using a gravity shower that a helpful Marine had erected outside her tent, and she was now drying off as the French reporter LaSalle poked his head farther into her tent. "Anyone 'ome?"

Startled, not yet having dried herself, Marte stood draped in Army khaki towels. "What do you want?"

"Some company—yes?"

"No. Get out!"

LaSalle gave a shrug worthy of Maurice Chevalier. "But I cannot. The champagne, she is opened—how do you say? Ah yes, opened for business."

"Well, I'm not," Marte retorted. The Frenchman was handsome, no question about that, the archetype of the kind that women fell for—tall, lean, very physical in his movements, but with eyes sensitive to the slightest nuance. And he could see that she had seen the outline of his erection as he gazed at her sleek, long thighs before they got lost in towels.

"Very well," he said accommodatingly. "I will leave the champagne for you and no offense. Okay?"

He reminded her of Hawkeye in the "M*A*S*H" TV show. "Look," she said, "I'm sorry. I didn't mean to be rude. Maybe another time?"

It struck her that LaSalle could give her some general background for her stories—after all, it had been French Indochina till 1954.

LaSalle shrugged, smiling. " 'Ow about in ten minutes? The champagne will 'ave lost some of its bubbles perhaps, but—"

"All right," she said, "but let's keep it strictly business."

LaSalle spread his hands as if asking what other possible motive he could be thinking of. "*Certainement.* Business, sure. But—" He wagged a finger at her. "No monkey business—I promise. *Oui?*"

"*Oui,*" she responded, adopting his friendly tone. As he left, she was still thinking about what she'd thought was his erection, or was it simply the way the crotch of his pants had bunched up? It was something that even as a young girl used to fascinate her—to think that women had the power to make it stand up like that. She toweled herself vigorously, throwing her hair back in abandon and feeling herself getting moist.

When Pierre LaSalle returned, she was much more hospitable, and her khaki uniform, meant to hide any feminine aspects, had failed miserably by making the size of her bust a tantalizing guessing game.

The champagne was poured, the stream of tiny bubbles ascending like chains of golden pearls winking at the brim.

"Cheers," she said, raising the glass.

"To peace," he responded, neither of them meaning it and each knowing the other had said it merely as a social nicety. They liked war—not being in it, but watching it, being close to it, being in less danger than the front-line fighter but close enough to smell it; to be scared and exhilarated by the rumble of the heavy guns, by the threat of it, the way it had of putting everything else into perspective, of showing just how thin the thread of life could be, of how you might as well enjoy yourself wherever and whenever you could.

"That was a good piece you did," LaSalle said, complimenting her.

"Which piece was that?" Had he read any or was this just bullshit too?

"The one about the difficulties of commanding a U.N. force. It's hard to do, I know. No pretty pictures, and the editor always want to show the viewers, eh? Not tell them. Explanation is much 'arder."

"Isn't that the truth?" Marte said appreciatively. She was weighing it up, considering the possibilities. No way was she going to let him in her, even with a condom. He'd have one, of course. With his looks, he probably ordered them by the gross. But even a rubber, which most men hated anyway, wasn't any guarantee against catching something like AIDS, hepatitis B, syphilis, gonorrhea, or any of a legion of subtropical and tropical sexually transmitted diseases.

"What do you think of Freeman's demotion?" LaSalle asked.

Marte took another sip. "I think it was a blessing in disguise—for the U.N."

"Oh? You think this Jorgensen will be much better, then?"

Marte shrugged. She wasn't going to let the Frenchman slobber all over her either. You could catch stuff that way too. "I think," she said, "it doesn't matter a shit whether Jorgensen is here or not. He'll be Washington's man, a figurehead—press conferences. Freeman'll do the actual work, only now he'll be able to do it without Washington and Hanoi breathing down his neck." Now Freeman, she thought, was a man you could get laid with and not worry. She didn't know why, but she intuitively felt he'd be safe. With young Pierre here, however—what was the expression the EMREF boys on the plane had used? "Dipping your wick." Well, young, or maybe not so young, he had probably dipped his at every stopover between here and Paree.

He was filling up her glass again and saying something now about some sensational photograph he'd heard she'd taken.

"Of what?" she wanted to know, figuring that as she'd been drinking her champagne, he'd been only sipping his. She could read him like a book—didn't want to get too pissed, then the old wiener would just lie there.

"Some picture of Freeman I heard about—somewhere near the Lang Son road during the—" The Frenchman sneered. "—the so-called 'friendly fire' incident."

"Huh," she said, affecting puzzlement. "I took some shots of him giving orders—that kind of stuff."

He lifted the bottle again.

"Uh-uh," she said, shaking her head. "You'll get me drunk."

"Not at all," he said, pouring more champagne anyway. "So," he went on, as if that piece of business was over. "You do all your own developing?"

"No," she answered just as easily. "I send all my film to Hanoi Kodak. That way anyone who wants to see what I've taken can have a peek. You know, sort of supermarket—take what you like."

Pierre LaSalle laughed. Was it a response to a joke or the truth?

"You want to embarrass Freeman—that it?"

"Oh," he said with a Gallic shrug. "Don't be silly. It's nothing personal. You're a good journalist. You know 'ow it is. We get what we can."

This time she put her hand over the tulip glass.

"Ah," he said. "You think I'm up to no good. Yes?"

"Yes."

Suddenly his whole tone, comportment, changed. "I want you, Marte. That is what I want."

"So why didn't you say so?"

He moved closer to her. "We French are more subtle than that."

"So I noticed," she said, "when you first came in the tent. Looked like you had a bazooka in your pants."

"Marte!" He sat up, genuinely shocked.

"Well, didn't you? Or did you just want to dance?"

"No—I mean yes, I was aroused."

There was a pause as she let her hand trail along his thigh. "So was I," she said.

"Oh, Marte!" He had his hand under her shirt, exploring, gently squeezing her breasts. "Oh, Marte!"

"You can't go in me," she said.

"I have a con—"

"Doesn't matter. I'll let you lie on me if you like, but no—"

"All right, all right," he murmured, almost incoherently, unzipping her slacks, pulling them down.

"Mon Dieu!" She was wearing skintight scarlet lace panties. *"Mon Dieu!"* Still gazing at the panties, he took off her bra.

As they began to move together, his weight between her legs, his elbows propped to keep his weight moving on her there and nowhere else, she could feel him sliding against her with more and more ease. She joined him in the rhythm of it. There was an idiotic smile on LaSalle's face, as if he was genuinely surprised, enjoying it more than he thought possible.

Soon her hair began to whip from side to side as the excitement in her mounted and he could feel her growing abandonment beneath him. His fingers started to pull down her panties. "No!" she gasped. "No," pushing his hand away.

"All right, all right," he said quickly, sensing that if he tried the same move again, she'd stop. "All right," he said. "Oh, Marte—"

He heard her whimper, felt himself going and, her back arching suddenly, they climaxed together, now as one, now as two separate beings, each enjoying the fishtail arching of their bodies, each in its own orgasm.

"My God," he gasped. "That was wonderful. I never believed—" His mouth was too dry to speak. He watched her, eyes closed, her body still moving against him until finally she gasped, utterly exhausted, utterly spent, her eyes closed in a sleep of reverie.

CHAPTER FORTY-ONE

IN DALAT, RAY Baker had been awakened by yet another noise, again outside his door. He quietly got out of bed to check, his feet crunching the dead cockroaches that had fallen victim to the protective line of boric acid he'd put around the bed, and opened his door. A small fleeting shadow was going down the exit stairwell at the far end of the hall—a huge, gray rat, one of the hundreds that staked out the moderate- to low-income hotels.

It wasn't till Baker stepped back into the room that he saw the piece of paper, some kind of note written on the back of a can label. Even those who could afford it couldn't easily get their hands on writing paper, one of the casualties of the Vietnam War and Agent Orange having created enormous deforestation of parts of the country. The note said, "MIA—come market."

It told Baker that the ever-vigilant Dalat police force must still be at work regarding MIAs, that someone dare contact him only in this way, that despite all the officialese about more mutual understanding and more economic aid since the U.S. had lifted the postwar blockade, there was still reluctance among the lower regions of the Communist bureaucracy to aid Americans, or at least a reluctance to be seen aiding Americans seeking MIAs and those who some Americans thought might still be POWs hidden in the jungles of 'Nam.

No one who wanted to help, it seemed—for a price, of course—would be seen lingering around hotels to make contact. It had probably been considered a great risk by the note writer just to try to get the message to Baker's room. Baker slapped himself on the forehead. "Stupid!" He wasn't properly awake. It wouldn't have been the man who made contact who left the note, but a runner—a kid—one of those thousands left homeless by the war with those who had been their enemies and were now their allies.

Baker collected his expired passport from the front desk and went out in search of a good coffee and pastry, one of the better legacies of the French colonial era. He found what he wanted at a sidewalk café. He sat first enjoying his *trai quit* juice. He had no intention of squandering the U.S. taxpayers' money, but damned if he was going to hurry. He'd been chasing shadows for years and hadn't found one of the more than two thousand MIAs or POWs.

At the same time, because of his lack of success, his search to find at least one MIA or, less likely, a POW to justify all his efforts had now become an obsession. He ate the pastry, which was filled with fruit, and lingered over the remains of his coffee, watching the new Vietnam roll by.

At a glance nothing much had changed—the ever-present fish sauce smell, more scooters, more noise, only now the sound, instead of coming from jukeboxes, came from a jungle of video games emitting horrible screams of victory or defeat. So absorbed was he by the hustle and bustle of Dalat that it took Baker a couple of minutes to realize he was being watched intently by a boy of about twelve, in dirty T-shirt and ragged blue shorts, who even at this age appeared to be addicted to betelnut, now and then spitting out arcs of bloodred saliva on the sidewalk.

Whether it was the good weather, the pastry, or the rich, dark coffee he had lingered over, Baker was in no mood for a complicated day. He made a writing gesture to the waiter and at the same time with a dollar note he signaled the boy to come over to his table.

"You speak English?" he asked the boy.

"Sure."

"Who are you watching me for?"

The boy either didn't understand or didn't want to answer. Instead he looked covertly at the dollar bill Baker was holding like a lure. "Who sent you?"

"A man."

"Really," Baker said. "Listen, boyo, tell me or no money."

"Two dollars, okay?" the boy interjected.

Baker nodded.

"A man in the—" The boy couldn't think of the word in English. *"Cho."*

"Market?" Baker said. "There are a thousand people in the market. I want you to point him out to me."

"Okay," the boy said, holding out his hand.

"Khong," Baker replied. No. "Not until you show me who."

"One dollar now," the boy said, spitting out another jet of saliva and betel juice, his smile a brownish gash, his teeth already stained by his addiction.

"Okay," Baker said, and gave him a dollar. For any Vietnamese, it was good money—for a boy, a small fortune. As they walked past the Red Tulip restaurant toward the Mai Building, Baker wondered if they were being followed by either the police and/or the person who had hired the boy, who perhaps wanted to make sure that he, Baker, wasn't being followed by someone else. As Baker followed the betel-spitting boy toward the market, he had no chance to double back or stop to see whether or not someone was following him. Just before they reached the market the boy glanced back at Baker, made eye contact, spat, and walked toward one of the stalls selling every kind of fruit from green dragon fruit, lychee, jujubes, and Chinese dates, to water apple. The boy leaned across the counter and said something to the woman serving the customer, her hands full of cherries she was dumping on the scales. She said something quickly to the boy, and he made his way back to Baker.

"You go now," the boy said. "Ask her for *chanh*—lemon, you understand. She will tell you she has none but to come back tomorrow. She will have some. Other dollar."

"What? Oh yeah. Here." He gave the boy the dollar. "Am I to come see her tomorrow?" Baker asked.

The boy shrugged with an insolence that had broken out once he'd secured the second dollar, his shrug saying, How the hell do I know? "You go see her," he said, spat once more— perilously close to Baker's shoe—and melted into the crowd.

Baker asked the old woman for a lemon.

She promptly gave him one and held out her hand for payment. It had happened so fast, so unexpectedly, that he barely had time to think, but he immediately looked about for the boy. The woman repeated the price impatiently. The boy was gone.

"Damn!" Baker said, counting out the money and giving it to the woman. "Damn, I've been had."

"Eh?"

"What?" He turned on the old woman, realized he was childishly taking it out on her. *"Cam on"*—Thanking you—he said, and walked back to his hotel, every youth he saw raising his ire. *"Chia khoa phong!"* he all but shouted at the desk clerk, who, despite the American's bad temper, took his time getting the room key and sliding it across to Baker.

The room was a shambles, every drawer of the small chest pulled out, what few clothes he had strewn about the room, white streaks of boric acid all over the floor, the mattress upended and slashed open, its stuffing oozing out. Also strewn about the floor was the distinctively sweet smell, not at all stale, of an American cigarette, in itself signifying that whoever had hired the kid must not have been long gone. Had he or they left satisfied? Did they suspect him of having information on POWs or MIAs, or whatever it was that they could sell for a high price to more parents of an MIA, or were they looking for something else, or was all this mayhem among the dead roaches and boric acid simply for effect, a warning to quit his trip to the hamlets of Lat village below Lang Bian Mountain? As he looked out the window that framed the warm gold of morning light, Baker felt clammy and cold.

LaSalle, none the worse from the champagne he'd consumed, wanted to make love again. Marte Price didn't. Once a night, she figured, was quite sufficient for any nice girl. Besides, no matter what all the sex manuals said, the second time more often than not proved to be a huffing, puffing affair— more a measure of fitness than passion—and plain wore you out, but not in that wonderful, satisfying, spent way. Besides, she was still languorous, in a warm, safe cave mood, and wanted it to last, and she told Pierre to leave her alone, she wanted to sleep. The Frenchman was happy to oblige, and rolling away from her, surveyed the tent with a more discerning eye, namely to see where she might hide her most prized photos.

Almost asleep himself, LaSalle had to concentrate hard to stay awake, his eyes searching the small tent, looking for something that would withstand the rigors of war. His gaze settled on a gray metal box about a foot square and a foot high. He'd seen that kind of box before. Usually they were asbestos-lined and waterproof. Problem was, there was no key in the lock. The more he thought about it, the more certain he became that the photos he wanted to see were in the gray box. Or did she play the fox and keep the photos in some very ordinary place—her Army-issue passport side pouch that he could see hanging from a suction hook on the tent's center pole? Easing himself off the bed, looking back to make sure she was still asleep, he took down the pouch and quietly unzipped the rear passport section. Apart from the passport, Army press pass, and a sheaf of two thousand dollars' worth of American Express traveler's checks in hundreds and fifties, there was nothing.

The second, smaller section of the pouch contained Chap Stick, lipstick, a two-pack container of tampons, a card of Midol capsules, Band-Aids, and assorted hairpins. The front section, which LaSalle left till last, it being no larger than a change purse, contained a hodgepodge of American quarters and tight bundles of red ten-thousand-dong bills, each bearing a flattering portrait of Ho Chi Minh, the man, LaSalle was reminded by the picture, who had started life as a waiter in Paris and ended up as the president of the republic. Then LaSalle saw a small safety-deposit-type key taped to the inside of the change pouch. In his eagerness to undo the tape, several quarters dropped out, clanging against the tent pole.

"Merde!" he hissed as he heard her moan and roll over toward him. He replaced the pouch.

"Pierre?" she called.

He was pulling on his pants. *"Oui?"*

Her eyes looked over at him dreamily. "I—" She yawned and stretched. "I thought you'd gone."

"No, *chérie*. I fell asleep."

"Hmm," she murmured, happy that it had been good for both of them. "What time is it?" She yawned again.

"Eight o'clock, or twenty hundred hours if you're military."

"Christ!" she said, flinging the sheet off.

"What in—" LaSalle began.

"Freeman's giving a press conference in half an hour."

"I know—so?"

"So, *mon cher,* it takes us gals a little longer to get ready, especially after being violated."

"Violated?"

"Just a joke, honey. I have to be ready for hookup in fifteen minutes. I'm doing a spot for CNN."

"What's wrong with their reporter?"

"Down with the runs. Too much tit."

"What?"

She was dashing into the shower stall. "I wish you'd stop saying 'What?' every time I say something. Too much tit."

He still didn't get it, or at least if he did, he wasn't saying anything.

"Banh bao," she called out. "Pastry stuffed with veggies and meat. Looks like a boob—nipple and all. You must have had it."

"Yes . . ." There was a pause as if he was thinking about it. "Probably."

He was trying the key in the gray box. *Bien!* It fit, and he dropped it in his pocket.

"Probably what?" she called out above the noise of the gravity rinse that came in a torrent over her body.

"Probably I have eaten it, yes."

She was out of the shower, and her nakedness aroused him again.

"Oh no, you don't!" she said, throwing his shirt at him.

His Gallic shrug told her there would be another time. "Probably." She shrugged playfully in return. "Maybe." He forced a smile.

CHAPTER FORTY-TWO

NUOC—WATER—WAS the first word some of the more than a hundred Caucasian POWs learned. The water was tepid and tasted metallic, but at least it was liquid, and the POWs, on what they were by now grimly calling "Upshut's Island," drank it gratefully yet resentfully, realizing as they did so that their dependence on him meant that Upshut's power over them had been tightened another notch. Even Murphy, the outspoken and garrulous Australian, was wary of the PLA guards' displeasure, though they were now a good fifty yards away, and was wondering how he and his fellow prisoners could survive on the meager rations being handed out. Despite the ample supply of fish that was the result of the explosions in the coral reef, the Chinese were giving the prisoners only enough to sustain them, and not bothering to cook the fish, which they simply tossed among the POWs as if amid a pack of dogs.

"Bastards," Murphy said, but quietly enough that the guards couldn't hear him. "Hope none of these are bloody stonefish." He waited for a response but none of the other nineteen prisoners in his group said anything, some frantically trying to figure out how best to deal with raw fish with your bare hands. "Stonefish'll kill you in less than five minutes." Only Shirley Fortescue balked at what lay in front of her. "Don't worry," Murphy said. "None of these are stonefish."

"Why bring it up, then?" she said tersely. "You enjoy frightening people?"

"Don't get your knickers in a knot, Shirl. Just somethin' to say, y'know."

"And I've told you before my name's Shirley, *not* Shirl."

"Piss on you, lady."

"Hey, Mike," Danny Mellin interjected. "Ease up."

"No problem, Dan, just trying to pass the time."

"Well, don't," Shirley said. "It's going to be tough enough as it is. We don't need your warped sense of humor on top of it."

"Listen up, you two," Danny cut in. "We've got trouble enough without *you* two starting another war." Mike Murphy was using a sharp-edged shell to scale the rockfish.

"War's already started," Murphy answered petulantly.

"Yeah," Danny said, "but we're in the middle of no-where—"

"We're in the Paracels," Shirley cut in. "Far as I can tell, somewhere near Pottle or Woody islands."

"Whoopee," Murphy said.

"Mike," Danny said, "put a lid on it. What I was saying was that we have to start figuring a few things out because when they're done building this airstrip, what are they going to do with us?"

"What makes you so sure it's an airstrip?" Murphy asked, tearing hungrily at a piece of fish.

"Well," Danny said, "it's the wrong shape for a baseball di-amond."

Shirley Fortescue laughed.

"Yeah, well," Murphy said, feeling foolish in light of Mellin's repartee. "Why in hell would the Chinese be blowing up a reef and rolling it flat when there's already an airstrip on Woody Island?"

"Because," Shirley answered in as civil a tone as she could manage with the Australian, "Woody Island's airstrip was wrecked by the Vietnamese in the first few days of the war. It was blown up and the island occupied by Vinh's marines within a few hours of *Chical 3* getting hit."

"The rig you were on?" Danny said.

"Yes. We got the news on the distress channel from a few foreign rigs drilling offshore."

"So now Upshut Island is to replace Woody Island," Danny said.

"Right."

"Ah, rats!" Murphy said, his tone trying for a jauntiness that he knew the others were either too thirsty or too hungry to share. "Your lot," he told Danny. "Seventh Fleet won't let 'em build an airstrip here—middle of bloody nowhere or Paracels—whatever. Yanks'll bomb the crap out of it."

Neither Shirley Fortescue nor Danny Mellin said anything for a few moments. The Australian was indisputably brave, as his helping Danny earlier in their capture had demonstrated, and he was clearly intelligent enough to have been working on one of the South China Sea rigs before the war had started, yet he was surprisingly naive politically, as evident from his remarks about the Seventh Fleet bombing Upshut Island.

"Haven't you noticed, Mr. Murphy," Shirley began, "how many Americans, British, and Australians have been brought to this island?"

"Yeah, Miss Fortescue, I have. So?"

"You don't see any reason for that—the fact that there must be over a hundred of us here?"

"All right, so they're using us as bloody coolies," Murphy retorted. "Wouldn't be the first time, would it?"

"Mike," Danny said calmly, "they're using us as bloody hostages." He paused. "As well as coolies. The President isn't going to order the Seventh Fleet or any other fleet to bomb the 'crap' out of this speck in the ocean. Not with so many American and British and—" Murphy looked thunderstruck, so Danny tried to lighten it up. "They won't even bomb Aussies!"

Murphy was still silent.

"Lookit," Danny continued, "even when we bombed the crap out of Hanoi, our guys never went near the Hanoi Hilton." Shirley Fortescue looked nonplussed. "Hanoi Hilton," Danny explained to her, "was the POW jail in Hanoi. During 'Nam."

"Oh . . ."

"Bloody hell!" Murphy pronounced. "Then how the dick are we gonna get off this bloody island? I mean, I thought we'd at least be traded or something."

"What do you suggest meanwhile?" Shirley asked. "We swim for it?"

"Very bloody funny."

"Actually," she riposted, "it isn't bloody funny *at all*."

"*Hoy! Hoy!*" It was one of Upshut's guards jabbing his Kalashnikov at the prisoners, indicating that they should get up and back to work hauling great loads of coral, then straining on the ropes of the cement rollers to flatten it.

CHAPTER FORTY-THREE

Tokyo

IF IT HAD been handheld computer games that had taken Southeast Asia by storm, then in Japan it was the craze for karaoke, patrons of bars singing to recorded music. And this night Jae Chong was foot stomping and humming along to a raucous rendition of country music, including a tub-thumping version of "Ghost Riders in the Sky." Jae ordered another drink, and though several other people had their hands up ahead of him, he was the one the waiter decided to serve first. The waiter, Jae thought, probably despised him for being Korean, but he was a Korean with money, and that made all the difference. For more yen, the waiter would treat him like royalty, and Jae was spending big. Why not? He was convinced that by now every police station in Japan had his photograph or artist's likeness and yellow sheet.

The only thing keeping him off Japanese TV's "Most Wanted" program was, ironically, the very press that had been so vocal in calling for the capture of all terrorists responsible for the bullet train wreck. For while it was widely known that there were Korean terrorists in the country, it was not known that the Japanese Defense Force had a CIA-type agency, and to keep the press off the scent, the JDF had to arrange a cover story for the killing of the three policemen, including the American agent Wray. There were Japanese constitutional restraints forbidding an intelligence agency from having links or even liaison with the U.S. CIA.

But Jae Chong was under no illusion. Once the JDF had its story watertight, then his photo would be flashed across every TV screen in the country as *the* Korean terrorist responsible for the murder of two Tokyo policemen and a visiting American specialist, ostensibly in Japan to "collect information on American gangs," a growing problem in North America.

And Jae Chong knew that once his face went public, he'd be lucky to last a week. In any event, his cover was now completely blown. Whatever Pyongyang's assurances to its agents in South Korea, he knew Pyongyang would make no effort to recover him, because, unlike Moscow's rules in the old cold war, Chong and other "abroad agents" were considered expendable. There were only two Pyongyang rules, the first being that if you were caught, no recovery effort would be mounted. Second, if you talked, your next of kin would be shot. Not surprisingly, it encouraged North Korean agents to commit suicide when blown.

Jae faced the inevitable in a drunken stupor and a cloud of Lucky Strike, without rancor, without remorse. He hated the Japanese deeply for what they had done to his grandparents during the Second World War, and besides, to tell the truth, he'd enjoyed the relatively rich consumer life in Japan as compared to the hardships of home, where all the money possible had been drained off and funneled into North Korea's nuclear program. Trust the U.S. President to have believed that a final "understanding," in short, a financial buyoff in terms of U.S. aid, had caused North Korea to "deconstruct" its nuclear weapons program. True, the factories in question had now been effectively gutted of any nuclear potential, but with Pyongyang's old ties to the Soviet Union still largely intact with Russia, the men who ran Pyongyang now had Russian and North Korean scientists going back and forth on mutually beneficial cultural exchange programs. Only one thing was needed—a conventional Soviet submarine with its nuclear missiles intact.

The problem now, with the old Soviet Union in disarray, wasn't the price. There were a half-dozen admirals one could do business with. No, the problem for Pyongyang was simply one of procurement, and enough terrorism in capitalist countries like Japan to play havoc with transport systems, such as the bullet trains, that kept supplying the USVUN convoys that sailed from Japan to be used against Beijing's soldiers. Whatever North Korea's agents could do to impede the convoys would be gratefully, if not publicly, acknowledged by Beijing by according Pyongyang increased access to its nuclear secrets.

As Jae Chong contemplated his end, he included in his calculations the chance of pulling off one more coup—something maybe not as spectacular as the bullet train. To go out into the field with this in mind was foolish, of course. Transport police, especially, would be on the lookout for him. No, he decided he would do something less risky but equally devastating. He ordered more scotch and another packet of Lucky Strikes. Even the old tightwads who ran the Japan circuit in Pyongyang wouldn't begrudge him having a bit of a party, in exchange for what he was going to do for good relations between Pyongyang and Beijing. Jae lit up another cigarette before one of the prowling bar girls giggled and pointed out that he already had one going. He lifted his glass to her and laughed. No, no, he didn't want any company just now. He was so pissed, he said, he probably couldn't get it up, but maybe she should come to see him in the morning.

"The morning?" She looked surprised. "That's a bit odd, lover."

Yes, he agreed, it was—about as odd as a Japanese twerp singing "Ghost Riders in the Sky," and now the silly bastard was going to punish everyone with an encore, "The Streets of Laredo."

CHAPTER FORTY-FOUR

"NO," THE LETHARGIC hotel clerk told Baker, he hadn't seen anyone hanging around the hotel. And no betel-chewing youth either. Baker pulled out two dollars to help his memory. It didn't, and the clerk didn't seem as upset over a burglarized room as perhaps he should have been, but then maybe the new Republic of Vietnam, like everywhere else, was experiencing more crime than usual.

"You'd better call the police," Baker said.

At this suggestion the clerk seemed to suddenly come to life, his alarm evident. The police would not be good for business. Besides, was Bac Baker sure he wanted to get involved with the police who, as Bac Baker must know, were often—he paused and looked about—"very difficult to deal with if you are a foreigner—and especially if you are American"?

"My understanding," Baker said, "is that Hanoi has issued directives to this specific problem—that foreigners—potential investors, customers, especially Americans—who are here helping them fight the Chinese aggression are to be accorded all respect. Is this not so?"

The clerk spread his hands in the universal plea for understanding. "Yes, yes, of course," he answered. Everyone knew about the official directives, but the police were sticky beaks, shoving their noses into all kinds of things that didn't concern them.

"I don't care if you call them or not," Baker said. "Nothing of mine is missing, as far as I can tell." The clerk seemed relieved. "How long," Baker asked, "would it take me to get to Lang Bian and the nine hamlets that make up Lat village?"

"Ah!" The clerk was smiling, showing a row of dark brown stained teeth. "I can be of assistance. You cannot walk—is too far. You must take bus. Round-trip, you understand?"

"Never mind the bus. I'll get a taxi."

The clerk was shaking his head, eyes half closed. Baker sighed wearily. Couldn't anything in this country be done simply, without either a bureaucratic hassle and/or money under the table?

"How much?"

"You will need a permit. This is fifteen dollars."

Baker said nothing, waiting.

"Ah, yes. Twenty-five dollars for rental car. Bus take too long."

"Who do I rent the car from?"

"Government office," the clerk said, smiling. "Or you can ride bicycle."

"Yeah, right," Baker said. "Where do I get the permit?"

"Ah, Bac Baker. Here I can be of assistance."

"I'll bet."

"No, no, no betting allowed. Strictly forbidden in—"

"How much?" Baker cut in.

"Forty dollars," the clerk said, now the epitome of helpfulness, hastily adding, "Lat village very beautiful."

"Where can I get the permit?"

"At police station. But you no worry. I can fix."

Baker shook his head resignedly and paid half the total of forty dollars.

"You wait here, Bac Baker. I will arrange for car to come here."

"The permit?"

"Permit also."

"All right. But hurry it up." The clerk was already on the phone. "Can I stay overnight in Lat?" Baker called out.

The clerk made a face. "Difficult, I think."

"How much?"

"Twenty dollar. Maybe no stay is possible."

"Then how come you know it's twenty dollars?"

"Ha ha."

"Ha ha," Baker imitated. "You wouldn't have a connection with a hotel in Lat, would you?"

"Ha ha."

"Look," Baker demanded, "stop screwing me around. Fix the police permit, fix the goddamn rental, and fix me up overnight."

"Yes, yes, of course, but why overnight?"

"Well, you tell me. Lat village"—he pronounced it correctly now as "Lak," as a way of showing "Ha Ha" that he was more familiar with Vietnamese practices than Ha Ha had given him credit for—"is very beautiful, you told me. Maybe I want to take the walk up K'Lang in the moonlight." K'Lang was the eastern peak of Lang Bian Mountain's five peaks.

"Yes, yes," Ha Ha agreed readily. "Beautiful in the moonshine."

"Right. Now I want all this fixed up—" He glanced at his watch. "—by eleven this morning or I'm out of here. Understand? I'd just as rather be back in Saigon." Baker still refused to call it Ho Chi Minh City—a little private rebellion.

"Okay—you pay ten dollar more. Overnight stay."

"No I don't. I don't pay squat till I see a vehicle, a permit, and anything else I need. Understand?"

" 'Squat'?"

Baker didn't elaborate. After a few seconds Ha Ha had figured it out.

"I will fix," he said, and went out.

"Good," Baker said, but there was no enthusiasm in his voice. By now his obsession with trying to find just one MIA or POW from 'Nam was waning, at least for this morning. It was unusually hot for Dalat, normally an ideal climate year-round, and the haggling one had to go through to get the simplest government approval seemed twice as oppressive in the heat. Officially, Hanoi had issued more of what amounted to "help American" directives, and while this was being practiced in the north with regard to the USVUN alliance, to the south there were still many old former North Vietnamese Army regulars and cadres who were either too corrupt or too resentful of their old enemies to be of much help. Right there and then Ray Baker vowed that if nothing turned up in Lat village or Lang Bian Mountain, he'd head back to Saigon and turn his attention to some other problem that was more satisfying, maybe helping with the American Vietnamese adoption agency.

When the clerk arrived, he came in beaming. He had everything Bac Baker needed, and was especially proud of the rental. It was a jeep, either U.S. Army surplus, or as the Vietnamese had done with all the helos the U.S. had left behind, it was made up by cannibalizing the wrecks of several jeeps. The fact that he was now hiring a U.S.-made jeep to look for U.S. MIAs and POWs captured by the Vietnamese who were now allies with Americans struck Baker as an irony that only Vietnam vets would fully appreciate.

"Four-wheel drive!" the clerk announced proudly.

Baker nodded. "So I hear."

"Good luck."

Baker thanked him, then immediately wondered what the clerk had meant. Good luck for what? Did Ha Ha know more about his reason for going to Lak village, or had he, Baker, let it slip somehow? Then again, there wasn't anything particularly secretive about an American official investigating a report about U.S. MIAs and POWs. In fact, maybe Ha Ha could help him. "You know anything about American MIAs and POWs?"

"No, no, nothing," Ha Ha said.

"I'd pay good money." Baker held up a twenty, and could have sworn he saw the clerk salivating at the prospect of more American dollars, but the Vietnamese's answer was still no.

It was odd, Baker thought, because the clerk could have made up any old story and taken the twenty.

CHAPTER FORTY-FIVE

"IT'S ABOUT TIME we got a break," Freeman told his HQ staff. He was referring to an intelligence report from one of General Vinh's reconnaissance patrols that had revealed the reason so many Chinese had so suddenly appeared at the beginning of the war around Dong Dang and Lang Son. Vinh's patrols, most of which were badly mauled, returning with only half their strength, were reporting that the exits of an elaborate tunnel complex had been found just south of Dong Dang and that Chinese regulars apparently moving at night through the tunnels had holed up in the caves around Lang Son, ready for the massive attack on the Vietnamese Army. And the same had apparently happened eastward near Loc Binh.

" 'Course, it shouldn't come as a surprise to Vinh's boys," Freeman pointed out. "They're probably the best damn tunnelers in the world." He reminded his staff of the vast tunnel complexes, not only the maze of over a hundred miles at Chu Chi in old Saigon, but those that the NVA had dug in the north, tunnels that not even the bombs of the B-52s could penetrate or uproot, and the tunnels that honeycombed the earth beneath Beijing since the time when China had feared nuclear attack from the Soviet Union.

"We've been hit," Freeman told Vinh, "with the old 'one slow, four quick' strategy."

Vinh agreed, leaving it to the interpreter to explain the technique to Freeman's HQ staff. "The method is simple, very slow at first and extremely effective. One slow means take time to plan logistical needs to the smallest detail, the amount of rice for each soldier, the number of rounds, amount of bandages, morphine, dried fish—everything needed for an offensive from battalion to divisional level. And practice, practice, practice for the attack—all the tunnels ending up in areas directly beneath the target. Once all is set, then the Chinese carry out the four quicks: mobility, attack, tactics, and withdrawal. It is a massive hit and run."

"Only this time," Freeman interjected, "there was no 'run.' They caught the Viet—" He stopped. "They caught the Vietnamese and U.S. with our pants down while we were trying to defend the Lang Son road. Coming up all around us. For all we know, gentlemen, our blue on blue with General Vinh's force might have begun with legitimate fire from PLA gophers. They pop up here and there in the jungle long enough to draw our fire, confuse us with the possibility of an ambush, then disappear down their warrens while we're still firing at anything that moves."

Freeman stepped back to the Play-Doh mock-up of the area between Dong Dang and Loc Binh in the north down to the airfield at Kep. "One thing's for certain, gentlemen. We're going to have to retake what we've lost, but first we have to stop the advance, and then we're going to have to engage the sons of bitches in the tunnels as we—" He almost said, "As we did in 'Nam," but with Vinh present, he thought it was more diplomatic not to say it. Major Cline couldn't help a wry smile. Perhaps they'd make a diplomat of Freeman after all.

General Vinh said something, but the interpreter balked. Vinh, a chain-smoker, gestured to the interpreter to tell Freeman exactly what he'd said. The interpreter faced Freeman. "General Vinh said you are correct—that sooner or later you will have to rid the tunnels of the PLA, the same as you tried to do with the Viet Cong sons of bitches."

Freeman looked at Vinh, the latter's face in a cloud of smoke, nodded and, smiling broadly, extended his hand to Vinh. As they shook hands in the camaraderie of soldiers, both men's HQ staffs clapped appreciatively. It was a rare moment in which old animosities were forgotten and only the task at hand mattered: to defeat the enemy.

Freeman circled the low country east of Ban Re and southwest of Loc Binh. "I propose sending in elements of First Division Air Cavalry along these ridges above the valley—a battalion westward to sever the Ban Re–Lang Son railroad and get enough artillery in there—" He bracketed the valley area between Loc Binh and Ban Re. "—to pour down fire into the valley. Give Wang and Wei something to think about in the north besides their main force advance. Meanwhile, General, your divisions can go in with my Second Division east of Kep. That way we'll hit 'em back and front."

Vinh looked unconvinced and ventured a few words in English on the subject. "You like high ground, Americans?"

"We do," Freeman responded.

"I remember."

"So do I, General."

Vinh now told Freeman through his interpreter that he thought the plan was sound and simple and he endorsed it, but he wondered if his battalions might be landed along with the Americans to deal with the tunnels. Otherwise what the Americans would win by day would be lost by night, the PLA using the tried-and-true method of Mao—of not attacking until one had overwhelming strength and retreating if one didn't, a tactic that might tie down the Americans for weeks, particularly if the PLA, as the general was sure they would, retreated en masse to the labyrinth of tunnels. Why not leave the artillery and the lower, wetter regions of the valleys to the Americans and leave the infantry fighting at night to the Vietnamese?

Freeman was mulling it over. Vinh said something else to the interpreter, the latter telling Freeman with a tone of apology, "General Vinh intends no insult to the American forces who have so generously come to help stop the Chinese aggression, but in the unfortunate war between the Republic of Vietnam and the United States, many of the Viet Cong spent their lives in the tunnels, where there were first aid stations, ammunition dumps, kitchens, dormitories, wells—that these men lived in and operated from the tunnels."

"Cu Chi," said Freeman, and Vinh and his staff immediately showed pleasure in the recognition of Freeman's knowledge of the Vietnam War, Major Cline explaining to the much younger Captain Boyd that the huge American base at Cu Chi had unknowingly been built on an extensive Viet Cong tunnel complex from which VC would emerge at night, kill, steal, and generally create chaos, then disappear back down the tunnels, leaving the Americans demoralized and their commanders puzzled as to how in hell the VC were getting through the base's extensive razor wire and machine-gun-defended perimeter.

"Of course," Freeman said, "don't forget that our boys went down after—them." He had almost said "after you."

Vinh acknowledged the bravery of the U.S. "tunnel rats" but pointed out that the unfortunate war was now long ago, and he wondered whether the skill of tunnel clearance was still with the Americans. The Vietnamese, on the other hand, had been using the tunnel complexes almost continuously since that war against China's aggressive forays into the Republic of Vietnam. Again Vinh explained that General Freeman must not take this as an insult, for the American tunnel rats had shown great bravery and were fearless despite the booby traps.

Freeman thanked the general for his suggestions, saying that he, Freeman, would welcome all the help he could get from Vinh's tunnel clearers but that he thought it important that wherever possible, Americans and Vietnamese should work together with a view to better future relations between the two countries.

This met with general approval by the Vietnamese staff, who were eager to get their hands on some American equipment. It was especially welcomed by Vinh's political officer, who was keen to keep improving Vietnam-American relations. After the details of the forthcoming operation, code-named "Tiger," had been discussed from divisional, brigade, regimental, battalion, and company level, and things were wrapping up for the day, Major Cline complimented Freeman on his diplomacy.

"Diplomacy, hell!" Freeman said as he, Cline, and Boyd walked out toward the press pool tent. "I want Americans with them so I damn well know what's going on. Their radio communications compared to ours are primitive, and I don't want our boys in our arty batteries on those ridges left on their lonesome because Vinh's boys are fighting a hit-and-run Maoist war."

Captain Boyd looked worried about the upcoming press conference. Since Freeman's demotion to field responsibility, General Jorgensen, recently arrived, was opening the press pool to as many as the tent would comfortably hold. And he was letting reporters fan out to battle zones for live reports. Hadn't Jorgensen learned anything from Schwarzkopf's tight field control of the press in the Iraqi War? Boyd complained to Cline that the press shouldn't have been allowed as far north as Phu Lang Thuong. "Should have kept them in Hanoi," he opined.

"Well, they're here, Captain," Freeman interjected, "and you and I are going to have to deal with 'em."

Boyd now looked twice as worried. "Sir, what if I'm asked about the tunnel rat business?"

"What about it?"

"Well, sir, I haven't had much background in that area."

"None of us did, son. All you had was a knife, handgun, and a flashlight. And down you went."

Boyd nodded but seemed unconvinced. "Were they fearless?" he asked. "As General Vinh said?"

"Some. But very few. At first a lot of men ordered down refused to go. Those who did, often came up and told the squad leader there was nothing down there. So we had to create 'tunnel rat' units. Guys who volunteered."

"You ever go down, General?" Boyd asked.

"Yes, I did. Not in 'Nam but in another op."

"Scary, sir?"

"Son," Freeman said as he approached what he called the "bullshit" tent, "never been so friggin' scared in all my life. Damn near shit myself, but I got the bastard—right in the belly!"

"What kind of booby traps were there?" Cline gave Boyd a back-off look, but the young press aide was too interested in hearing Freeman's answer.

"Captain, do you want to have nightmares?"

"No, sir."

"Then don't ask me about booby traps and don't go asking any of the troops. Most of them haven't ever seen a tunnel, and I don't want to spook their morale unnecessarily."

In the press conference, the first such joint conference ever shared by a Vietnamese and U.S. general before so many reporters, Marte Price's was the first question taken by Freeman. "General, there've been rumors going around about tunnel complexes occupied by the PLA in the border areas. Will our men be involved in fighting them?"

"We—"

"USVUN," Boyd whispered.

"Ah, I don't know where you could've gotten those reports from, Ms. Price, but it will be the task of the USVUN forces to engage the enemy until he withdraws his forces beyond the Vietnam-Chinese border. That's all we're here for."

ABC had his hand up. "General Freeman, how do you feel being relegated to field command from overall command of USVUN forces?"

"Suits me fine. General Jorgensen is a fine soldier. This is like a football game. Coach can change anyone to any position he likes."

Cline winced inwardly but outwardly looked unperturbed.

The general, he knew, would be quoted by someone somewhere as comparing the war to a game.

A CBS reporter was identified. "General Vinh, this is a follow-up from a question asked earlier. Will U.S. forces be fighting in the tunnel complexes?" There was an audible murmur of surprise among the assembled press corps, the question being all but a direct accusation that Freeman was holding back. General Vinh's interpreter took the question, waited for his boss's brief reply, and announced, "We know nothing of a tunnel complex."

"But what if there were tunnels?" Marte Price interjected.

"Then we'd fill them in," Freeman said, smiling.

This got a laugh until Marte said, "You mean you'd just suffocate men without giving them a chance?"

"No," Freeman said good-naturedly. "We wouldn't do that." He turned from the podium as another question about tunnels was addressed to Vinh. Still smiling, Freeman told Boyd quietly, "I want to see her in private, off-the-record." His troops called it the George C. Scott look. Cold fury under a camouflage net.

Vinh spoke to the interpreter again, and the interpreter told Pierre LaSalle of French television that he knew nothing about tunnels.

Freeman announced the news conference was over. There was an uproar from the press.

Freeman was in a rage. "Boyd, you get Ms. Price here right now! This instant! You hear me?"

"Yes, sir!"

When Marte Price entered the general's tent, he knew Boyd must have told her he was furious, and he made no attempt to hide it. "Against my better judgment," he stormed, "I gave you clearance to accompany the EMREF, and the first thing you do is try to undermine my credibility—and General Vinh's—let alone that of the entire USVUN force!"

"Off-the-record, General," Boyd warned, in the bravest advice he had yet given the general.

"What—yes, off-the-record, Ms. Price. Can I tell you—can I *trust* you—with something off-the-record?"

"Yes, Gen—" She couldn't finish, her throat and tongue dry as parchment.

"All right," he thundered. "I know what you and those other—*reporters*—are after. You want to do to me what you did to our field commanders in 'Nam. You want grisly descriptions of tunnel warfare so you can get on prime time and worry the hell out of every parent and family of our men over here. You want to serve up blood and guts for dinner and upset our boys' folks so bad that they'll be demanding we be sent home."

Marte Price tried to speak, but he rolled over her like a monsoon.

"What you don't realize, young lady, is that these boys are here because the most populous country in the world, and the only other world power militarily, is eating away at its neighbors like a goddamned jackal, and if they're not stopped, they'll be encouraged to war war instead of jaw jaw over every goddamn territorial claim they make. Hell, don't you realize the Chinese have had wars with everybody anywhere near their fence—India, Pakistan, the Russians, Siberia, Laos, Vietnam. Now they're laying claim to every goddamn island and reef— over *five hundred* of them—in the South China Sea. And what do you want to do? You want to do a goddamn liberal dance about our boys going down some goddamn tunnel because it makes good copy for your rag. Now piss off!"

An hour later General Freeman called on Marte Price. He couldn't tell whether she'd been crying or whether she was being deliberately cold.

"I apologize for losing my temper. I apologize for telling you to—to 'piss off.' That was ungentlemanly of me and I regret it."

"And the rest, General?"

"I don't withdraw a word of it. It's true. I wouldn't trust you people as far as I could kick you."

The road to Lat village, or rather the nine hamlets that constituted the population of just over seven thousand, was in bad repair following heavy rains, and Raymond Baker was glad that Ha Ha had got him the jeep for the seven-and-a-half-mile journey. He was stopped twice by police who demanded to see the required permits and who, in the second instance, argued that the date stamp on the Dalat permit was for tomorrow and that therefore he should not be on the road and should be fined one million dong, about ninety dollars U.S.

Exasperation barely under control, Baker told them about the clerk at the hotel and that perhaps what he should do is have the U.S. legation in Saigon ring the officials of General

Vinh in Hanoi. That did it. Albeit grudgingly, he was allowed to proceed, and once in the first hamlet, in the early afternoon, he let it be known that he was looking for information about U.S. MIAs and POWs from 'Nam, appealing to their patriotism, telling the village headman that "our soldiers and your soldiers are fighting side by side to repel the imperialistic ambitions of the Chinese," and that therefore the Vietnamese people and all those who had been exploited by the Chinese no-gooders had a patriotic duty to help him find any missing MIAs or POWs from 'Nam. Then they could rejoin their comrades in the fight against the Chinese invaders. Baker had particularly balked when it came to using terms such as "imperialist," "no-gooders," and "patriotic duty," but then again, why not use anything he could? He added that there would also be a substantial reward for helpful information leading to any POW or MIA.

A lot of villagers on their way back from market stared at him as they had stared for thousands of years at barbarians who smelled like dog and often, to the Asians' disgust, grew facial hair. But beyond that, no one took much notice, other than a crowd of boys who, despite the village's relative prosperity, soon clung about him, their hands out for money or whatever he might have had to give. The only thing he wanted to give was hope to at least some of those parents back in the States who simply did not know for sure whether their kin were alive or dead. If they were dead, then at least they would know for certain, and the grieving could begin. Police, he noticed, were everywhere in Dalat, and suddenly in the beautifully rich, clean air that had followed the downpour he realized how futile it all was.

Who would dare approach a stranger with such information with policemen sniffing everywhere? Perhaps he could do better by forwarding a request to USVUN HQ in Hanoi, or was it now in Phu Lang Thuong? Baker wished he could give MIAs' next of kin some idea of how frustrating it was trying to follow a single lead through the tangled web of bureaucracy. It always ended like this, despite the most optimistic beginnings. And who could blame the Vietnamese? What would he do in their position, with officialdom ever ready to swoop for some reason that might rest on nothing more than a petty whim or vindictiveness?

Baker decided he would return to Dalat in the morning if he failed to get anything that would substantiate the old Chinese's claim, made on his sampan, that there was an MIA in one of the Lat villages. There was no hotel in Lat, but for the twenty dollars he'd given Ha Ha, it had been arranged that he would stay overnight in one of the village thatched-roof houses built high on stilts. Without knowing it, at least at that moment, the American was among people who, if they knew anything, would most likely tell him, for the Lat villagers were made up of old men who, along with other minorities, had helped the Americans in the early seventies.

The evening meal was rice and some kind of meat that they told him was pig—which he doubted—and black beans. They told Baker through a local translator that "you see the hill people, the Montagnards, were correct. They always said the Americans, the green faces"—they meant Green Beret commandos' face paint—"would not desert them, that they would come back."

"It's been a long time," Baker said by way of apology.

"What is time to us?" the family elder said, smoking his pipe at full blast. "The important thing is they came back."

One of the younger men shook his head from side to side. "The important thing is, will they stay?"

"No," another man said matter-of-factly as he held the rice bowl close to his mouth, shoveling with his chopsticks. "The question is, what will Salt and Pepper do?"

"Who cares what they will do?" the old man said angrily. "There is always one rotten banana in the bunch."

"One!" the younger man said. "In this case there are two."

"Who are they?" asked Baker. "Montagnards?"

"No, no," the old man said, waving aside the mention of Montagnards. "They are rebels."

"From what tribe, then?" Baker inquired.

No one spoke, busily eating and drinking tea, the silence growing heavier by the second. Baker felt his gut tighten as if he'd swallowed a slime ball along with his rice. Slowly he put down his bowl. "Are they Americans?" he asked quietly.

"Yes," the young man said.

"Do you know where they are?"

The old man's chopsticks waved in a wide gesture toward the peaks of Lang Bian Mountain. "Up there."

"Why do you call them Salt and Pepper?"

The young man shrugged nonchalantly. "One is white, one is black."

"You're sure they're Americans?"

"Yes," the old man said, offering more tea.

Baker was simply lost for words. He'd come looking for MIAs and possibly POWs, not renegades. He blew on the hot tea. "Could you contact them?"

The old man shrugged. "I don't know. Who wants to talk to such vermin?"

Baker conceded the old man's point. Who *would* want to find two turncoats? He'd sure as hell get no thanks from Washington. The Chinese would of course relish the propaganda value, despite the fact that whoever this Salt and Pepper were, they must now be near middle age.

"What do they do?" Baker asked. "I mean, so they turned and ran for the other side—the Communists—but they can't still be running against our men—I mean the U.S. has been long gone."

"The U.S. has come back," the younger man said. "The renegades will run with whoever runs against the U.S.—the Chinese or the Khmer Rouge. Sometimes they transport heroin from Laos into Vietnam."

Baker felt himself sweating despite the cool air of the Lat village. The very mention of the Khmer Rouge from Cambodia—the Khmer Rouge being one of China's allies in the south—filled him with the kind of fear and loathing some of his Jewish friends experienced upon hearing the names Auschwitz and Buchenwald—run by power-crazed madmen bent on genocide. China would welcome a Khmer Rouge attack against the Vietnamese anywhere on Vietnam's western border.

"Have you heard any rumors of a Khmer Rouge invasion?" he asked.

"Yes," the old man said. "Porters are being recruited to move ammunition and supplies along the Cambodian-Vietnamese border and the Laotian-Vietnamese border using some of the old Ho Chi Minh trails."

No one spoke for several minutes, the only sounds those of the fruit birds from the hill country and the sipping of tea. Finally Baker, still trying to absorb the shock of the information and the implications of it for the war should the USVUN forces be hit on another front, determined that the USVUN field commander, General Freeman, should be advised of the impending likelihood of an attack on his left flank. But Baker's thoughts immediately returned to the subject of the two American renegades.

"Do you know what rank they hold?" Baker asked. "These two?"

"No."

"Have you seen them yourselves?"

"I did," the young man said. "Once. It was a drug line moving toward Saigon."

"Ho Chi Minh City," the father corrected.

"Saigon," the young man repeated, and Baker knew he had an ally. "I saw them for only a moment. They were in NVA uniforms with the big metal rings on their backpacks. Remember? The rings were for attaching camouflage—leaves and such—so that, unlike an American, an NVA soldier could move his head around without any camouflage moving. They had gone past so fast you could not see them clearly. But the white one was much smaller than the black one."

"Would you recognize them again?"

"No, though I have heard they never separate and the white one is bigger than most Vietnamese. Sometimes they move from place to place by air, but it is said they only transport drugs on foot."

Baker sat still, both hands cradling the cup, accepting the offer of more tea. Then he sipped the tea, and a crisis had passed because he had resolved what to do. The moment he got back to Dalat—hopefully tomorrow evening—he would send a message to USVUN's HQ. He'd get shit for not having notified State first or the Pentagon, and not going through normal channels, but he took comfort from the words of Field Marshal Von Runstedt, who once declared that "normal channels are a trap for officers who lack initiative."

He thanked his hosts for the meal and went outside to bring in his sleeping bag from the jeep. Despite the fading light, he saw that all the tires on his jeep had been slashed.

"Vandals!" the old man pronounced. "Hooligans—from Dalat, no doubt."

No matter who it was, Baker told them, it meant he would have to go back to Dalat by bus in the morning. "What time does it leave?"

"Seven."

From habit, Baker unzipped his sleeping bag to make sure that no bugs or snakes had set up shop, then laid it down on the palm-matted floor, sat down and, by candlelight, wrote down a summary of all he'd heard that night. He folded it when he was finished, took his boots off, and stuffed it down his right sock until he could feel the square of paper under the arch of his foot. Then he quietly begged pardon and asked the young man who had said "Saigon" instead of "Ho Chi Minh City" whether it was possible for him to get a weapon—a pistol, anything.

The young man said this was possible; caches of arms had been buried by many villagers during 'Nam, but Bac Baker must understand that this would cost money, not for himself, but for those who sold such things illegally. Two hundred American dollars.

"Traveler's checks?"

"Sure, American Express or Visa, okay, fine."

The young man soon returned and handed Baker a .45 service revolver and two full clips. Sure, Baker admitted to himself, he was feeling a little paranoid about it all, but it was just in case the tire slashers weren't simply vandals after all.

There was a scream—the old lady who had come to clean up the kitchen. Someone had placed the chopsticks Baker had used upright in his rice bowl—since time immemorial a Buddhist sign of the dead.

Moving quickly, Baker removed his raincoat, flashlight, and what few other belongings he had in the jeep, and bunched them in his sleeping bag to resemble a body. He turned out his lamp, then sat in a corner of the room where he had a clear view of the open doorway, his ears straining for the least sound, the gun in his right hand resting on the left for instant use. All he had to do was stay awake till morning.

He tried to remember what they had told him on the firing range back in Washington, but all that seemed, and was, a world away. He thought about the chopstick sign. The message didn't worry him so much as who'd done it. He'd heard nothing. Could someone have come up to the high house without making a sound? If not, it must have been someone in the family. Was the young man's use of "Saigon" instead of "Ho Chi Minh" merely a ploy to build confidence in him? Was the young man an agent provocateur?

In any case, Baker hoped he wouldn't have to use the gun— merely having it in Vietnam was highly illegal—and hoped the tire slashing and the sign of the dead were merely two unrelated incidents. Perhaps the chopsticks being put in the bowl like that—sticking up like incense tapers—was a nasty bit of teasing by someone else in the village. All right, Baker told himself, so it was a cruel prank by some spiteful neighbor and had nothing to do with him. The problem was still the stealth it took for someone to come up to the house, creep up the ladder steps, do it, and leave without being noticed by either him or his hosts. Which brought him back to the family again.

He heard a soft thud, like a rubber ball thrown in through the doorway. A grenade? He switched on his flashlight, ready to kick it out the door, and instead saw nothing but a slash of brilliant green slithering toward him. He fired with one hand holding the flashlight, the other pulling the trigger, until he'd emptied the .45, his hands shaking uncontrollably from his phobia of snakes, the snake having disappeared under the mattress. By now of course it was as if the house had been bombed, everyone running and talking excitedly, lanterns coming on and swinging through the hamlet.

Baker tried to talk but couldn't. Instead he pointed the handgun at the mattress. Finally he could manage a few words. "*Con tran!*" he said. "*Con tran!*" It meant python, but he couldn't remember the word for "snake." "*Con tran*—green. You understand *con tran*?"

Sure, everybody understood. Who didn't understand? Pythons, said one of the contemptuous teenagers, are known for their great flying ability! "Must have been a bat!" another said.

The young man, his host's oldest son, who called Ho Chi Minh Saigon, carefully lifted up the riddled sleeping bag and straw mattress with a stick in one hand and a long knife in the other. There was no snake there, only a wild pattern of holes that the bullets had made after passing through the sleeping bag, mattress, and thatched floor.

Soon the rest of the villagers went home. They needed sleep for their work in the fields more than they needed stories of flying pythons from a mentally ill American. And in his city-bred panic, the American had totally lost face.

Yet the next morning, when a policeman arrived wanting to know who had been firing a gun last night, none of the villagers could answer him. They were all asleep, they told him. No one wanted trouble for the hamlet. Oh yes, they said, they'd heard shots coming from the direction of Lang Bian's peaks, but Vietnamese had lived with the sound of firing for a thousand years. A poacher, perhaps. Everyone knew that since the Vietnam War deer, wild pig, and even tigers had begun to repopulate the area. "Saigon," as Baker had begun calling his host's oldest son, was apparently the only one who believed

Baker that a snake, despite the height of the house's stilts, had been in his room.

"What color was it?" he asked Baker.

"Green."

"Then it wasn't a python."

"No—No, but I couldn't think of your name for snake."

Saigon asked, "What kind of green?"

"Very bright."

"A bamboo viper," Saigon said.

Baker didn't want to ask the next question, but his need to recover face at least for himself after his outburst of panic forced him to. He asked Saigon if a bamboo viper was your ordinary elephant grass, nonpoisonous creepy crawly or what?

"Had it bitten you, you would have been dead within the hour. You had better keep the gun."

In one sense, it was the last thing Baker wanted to hear, yet it reassured him to know that someone at least believed his version of what had happened. "Someone is after you," Saigon said. "You've come too close, I think, to Salt and Pepper. I don't think they are directly involved—otherwise you'd be dead. They are probably off west somewhere in Cambodia or Laos, but I think the slashed tires, the rice bowl and the chopsticks, this is all—how do you Americans say it?—'low-tech.' The word has been put out, but now with the Americans helping us in the north, no one wants to do it overtly—" He paused. "—to kill you in the open. They wish it to seem like an accident."

"Slashed tires are hardly *covert*," Baker said.

"True. But that might have nothing to do with it. Teenage bad types."

And why, wondered Baker, are you telling me all this? Is it you? Are you after me? Are you just telling me all this so as not to make me suspicious?

It was as if Saigon could divine what Baker was thinking. "I'm helping you," Saigon said, "because you are here helping us. I wasn't born until after the war. For me it is history. I do not dislike Americans."

"Thanks," Baker said. "I feel awkward with the gun. What if the Dalat police stop me? They'll stop you because you're breathing."

It was the first time since last night's meal that Saigon had laughed. "It is true. They would stop their grandmothers. Give it to me. You will be safe on the bus going back to Dalat. I'll send someone to your hotel with it. I think you should have it."

"You think I should pursue this matter of Salt and Pepper?"

Saigon shrugged. "This is up to you, but till you're back safely in Saigon, I think you should keep the gun. I will keep the sleeping bag. If the police saw that, they would be suspicious."

"Yes." Baker walked a few paces, then stopped. It was six-fifty, and the first bus out would be in ten minutes. He took out a note he'd written about the existence of Salt and Pepper and of the possibility of a Khmer Rouge flank attack against Vietnam. He gave the note to Saigon, telling him that if anything should happen to him, Saigon should give the note to a senior cadre in Dalat to be passed on to USVUN HQ.

As the crowded bus began its bumpy journey back to Dalat, Baker felt the loneliest he had in years. In going *to* Dalat, he was running *away* from Lang Bian Mountain.

CHAPTER FORTY-SIX

IT WAS AN awesome sight even for seasoned chopper patrols: over two hundred helos carrying two thousand of Second Army's Assault Helicopter Battalion and Airborne into battle, fifty miles north of Phu Lang Thuong to the edges of the valley southwest of Loc Binh. From a distance to the fighters and bombers already plastering the scrubby ridges around Loc Binh with H.E. and napalm, the choppers made it look as if the sky was full of gnats.

Marte Price had wrangled a ride on one of the helos. General Jorgensen, she discovered, was a much easier obstacle to work around than Freeman. Jorgensen, at pains to be politically correct, had also allowed several other reporters, including LaSalle, to be in the first wave. Marte Price now wished

Jorgensen had refused permission. The noise of over two hundred helicopter engines and rotors chopping the thick, humid air, and the distant thunder of heavy ordnance being dropped to clear the ridges of the PLA, combined to fill her with a fear she had never felt so intensely.

The members of the nine-man squad she was with were mostly silent, all but two sitting on their bulletproof Kevlar vests instead of wearing them, fearing shots from below that could easily penetrate the skin of the chopper and hit their genitals. The minutes before deplaning were filled with apprehension, each man knowing that the PLA might well be ready to spring a trap around the landing zones, holding their fire till the helo's soldiers were spilling out on the flats between the ridges and then opening up in a murderous ambush.

As the First Battalion of Airborne went in led by Colonel Smythe, Freeman was in the control chopper high above the swarm of helos below, with F-14 Tomcats from the *Enterprise* riding shotgun, making sure that the helos were properly dispersed to ensure the perimeter about a half mile across.

Normally a colonel or a one-star brigadier general would have been directing the local deployment, but this had been Freeman's plan, and if he was going to take responsibility for it, he wanted to personally direct it. Besides, like Patton, he was known as a front-line general, no matter whose plan it was. Furthermore, Second Army was his until told otherwise by Washington.

Then it happened. Bravo Company of the First Battalion were deplaning close to a dike running along the edge of a rice paddy when the field seemed to erupt in fire, the fusillade of bullets coming from a scrubby and partially treed ridge that sloped down to the valley floor of green fields. Even as a star, or six-point 105mm howitzer, gun position was being set on the ridges south of the landing zone, with 105mms slung under the bellies of an equal number of heavy-load Chinook choppers, the PLA infantry were laying down a murderous fire on the Americans.

How did the PLA know there would be a major force attempt to secure the valley as a hub from which to "spoke out" attacks against the PLA's supply line between Lang Son and Loc Binh and the road between Loc Binh and Lang Duong? In fact they didn't know. The PLA had guessed that Freeman, a general known for his "keep-moving" tactics, wouldn't be satisfied waiting for a set-piece battle about Phu Lang Thuong.

He wouldn't wait for his enemy to come to him, but would probably try to leapfrog, overflying the PLA's spearhead on the Lang Son–Phu Lang Thuong road, to hit Wang's and Wei's forces deep in their own territory. That would stop the Chinese supply line, splitting their forces and allowing two divisions from Second Army's I Corps to close in from Phu Lang Thuong.

Wang and Wei, while having made spectacularly impressive gains so far, had not managed to take Hanoi. The U.S. artillery was too formidable. The Chinese generals now had to decide whether to recall those PLA elements to the south now wheeling before Phu Lang Thuong for the attack on Haiphong on the USVUN eastern flank. If these PLA regiments were able to reach the allied port of Haiphong, then the winding, seventy-mile-long Haiphong-Hanoi road, the allies' vital supply artery, would be cut, and with that would come a bonanza of allied supplies for the PLA. And whatever the PLA couldn't find dockside at Haiphong could be supplied along the southeast coast from the Chinese city of Mong Cai.

On the other hand, if the PLA regiments did not pivot before Phu Lang Thuong toward the Red River delta, but stood their ground to prevent the other units of Second Army's I Corps from pressing north toward Ban Re and Lang Son, the oncoming Americans would soon meet up with Freeman's Airborne, allowing the Americans in the north, now reinforced, to split into two spearheads, one swinging west to take Lang Son, the other right to Loc Binh.

The two Chinese generals knew they had the numbers, but also knew that if their supply line could be cut this far north, then Freeman's Second Army I Corps would not only advance but would be constantly reinforced by Haiphong. Wei was still ready to go along with the two political officers and make an all-out assault on Hanoi.

"Imagine," Wei said, "if Washington fell—the terrible effect on American morale."

Wang arrogantly waved his comrade's comment aside. "Washington did fall, comrade. The British burned it to the ground, and look at it today. If anything, its fall hardened American resolve to counterattack."

"This is another time," Wei responded.

"Exactly!" Wang retorted. "In any case, it was our agreement that if we did not take Hanoi by the tenth day, we would turn to Haiphong."

"Yes, Comrade General, but we have been held up on the highway to Hanoi by American and Vietnamese saboteurs. We've not really begun our attack on Hanoi."

"Enough of this wrangling," Wang said. "I demand a vote." It was two for going on to attack Hanoi, two for Haiphong.

"Very well," Wang said. "Beijing must decide."

"What do we do meantime?" one of the political commissars asked.

Wang's knuckles rapped the map, his regiments red-flagged, the enemy's blue. "I suggest we crush Freeman's helicopter assault at Loc Binh."

One of the political commissars had the temerity to point out that it would not be correct to report that the Americans were attacking with helicopters. This would give Beijing the impression that the assault was a gunship attack by American Comanche and Apache helicopters when in fact it was an infantry attack, albeit airborne.

Wang said nothing that would injure his career, but merely smiled at the commissar. The other three took this to be a sign of acquiescence. In fact it was a well-camouflaged expression of contempt for the tendentiousness of the political officers. But clearly, neither commissar detected his true feelings about them. He was glad they were deceived and was hopeful that Freeman's forces were about to be equally deceived by his camouflage at Loc Binh.

Apache gunships came to the fore as those who had deplaned their troops flew westward of what were now being called the Loc Binh fields, the Apaches spraying machine-gun fire into the scrub and bamboo that came down to the edges of the fields. In a confusion of communications, some choppers got the order to withdraw with their full complement of troops so TACAIR could be brought to bear, while others still a few feet above the field, their blade wash flattening the elephant grass along the edge of the field/ridge interface, deplaned their troops into a maelstrom of small-arms fire directed at the troops just landing, their most vulnerable moment, the helos also drawing heavy fire.

Up on a ridge held by the Chinese, a battery of 12.7mm machine-gun-cum AA fired had already downed three choppers: one after its troops had alighted, the other two while fully loaded, approaching hovering position. Two Tomcats came in low, dropped napalm on the batteries, and rose quickly as an enormous, roiling orange-black ball of flame engulfed what just seconds before had been enemy positions.

But meanwhile the PLA were "walking" 82mm heavy mortar rounds across the fields, telling Freeman that the PLA crews must have had time to angle—prepare their trap. Then the walking would stop, the rounds hitting the Americans with "unison" rounds in which up to ten mortar rounds landed together, shrapnel whizzing through air, immediately followed by the screams of men being hit.

Freeman, seeing he was between a rock and a hard place, had to decide to cut and run or drop more men into the maelstrom of fire. There seemed to him a better than fifty-fifty chance that he could hold position with a stream of troop-carrying helos keeping up the supply of men and matériel into the LZ while its perimeter was being established. "We keep going," he ordered. "Hold the perimeter." Already more helos were taking off from Phu Lang Thuong.

Meanwhile Wang was on the phone with his Loc Binh field commanders, ordering them to commit several reserve battalions from the Chengdu military region—over four hundred men—down the ridge and *into* the fields, by which his commanders understood that he meant them to penetrate the perimeter. Wang put the phone down and yelled, "Weather report?"

"Clouding over, sir, but clear for helos below two thousand feet."

"Then," said Wang grimly, "he will keep pouring troops into the area until he pushes the perimeter uphill. It must have been a terrible shock for him to find us waiting, to have forecasted this probable landing site, but now that shock is over—" Wang was pacing anxiously. "—I think he will stay, at least so long as the cloud ceiling makes it possible to call in air support." Wang ordered another battalion, another eight hundred, down the ridge into the fields to where PLA mortars had cratered an area of about fifty yards across, through which platoon-sized elements of Wang's Chengdu army were penetrating.

By now several hastily emplaced U.S. 105mm batteries were opening fire, and Freeman's men saw several volcanolike explosions of scrub bush and red earth. Still, the PLA's mortars were proving the more deadly fire, screams of "incoming" causing the Americans to scramble to what cover they could find in the detritus of war, from empty ammo boxes to the dead.

Now it was hand-to-hand where the mortars had broken the Americans' defensive ring, and D'Lupo, Rhin, and Martinez found themselves in a firefight through clouds of smoke grenades they'd tossed into the breach. It wasn't much, but it was enough to slow down the PLA regulars rushing through the clouds of dense white smoke, their shadowy figures cut down by the U.S. infantrymen's best friend, the "pig," the M-60 machine gun.

"Two o'clock! Two o'clock!" Martinez yelled. D'Lupo's M-16 fired and the figure fell. In a rush of three PLA soldiers through the smoke, one was unlucky enough to run across the field of fire of Private First Class Walter B. Sloane. Sloane had a twelve-gauge pump action shotgun and fired twice, the Chinese soldier's head gone, his blood-splattered torso still running around. "Sit down, ya silly prick!" some GI yelled out, and that was it—Martinez, D'Lupo, and even a harried radio operator Rhin couldn't contain their fear-bred laughter, Martinez laughing so hard he could hardly change magazines. Rhin could barely be understood by one of the following air cavalry companies coming in with priority landing status.

"What the hell's the matter with you, soldier?" a major bellowed.

"We jus'—man, Sloane just blew his head off—"

"Now you listen to me, goddamn it. Get a grip on yourself, fella!"

Rhin told Martinez they were to get a grip on themselves, and Martinez, having just fired off a three-round burst, said, "What parta me would he like me to grip? Shit, man, I can't—"

Rhin only got under control when a mortar shell landed yards away. Miraculously, he wasn't hit by any shrapnel, but the concussion knocked him to the ground, a large, ocher-colored sod of earth from the dike along the edge of the field hitting him in the stomach, completely winding him. He was gasping for air, unable to speak, so Martinez had to take the field phone.

"Identify your Lima," a voice yelled. "Identify your Lima. Over."

"Far as I can tell," Martinez answered, "we're at the northern edge of these fields. Lot of white smoke. Over."

"There's white smoke everywhere. Mark the LZ with purple smoke. Can you do that? Over."

"Roger. Can do. Over."

"Out."

It was a terrible mistake for Martinez not to know that day's prearranged signal for an LZ. As the Americans had the enemy wavelength and were using Vietnamese/Chinese interpreters, so too did the Chinese have the American wavelength and Vietnamese/Chinese/English interpreters. Within seconds of the transmission between the air cavalry major and Martinez, the helo pilot saw a purple column of smoke curling up from the swirling hell of shrapnel-infested white smoke and ground fire. He started to descend and saw purple smoke rising, this time in the northern sector somewhere farther east.

"Jesus Christ," the air cav major said, "which fucker is ours?"

"I say we go in on the first one, Major," the pilot said. "If it's a PLA dupe, we gotta assume our boys were the first to lay purple."

"Guess you're right, Lieutenant. Take us in."

"Yessir."

The blades of dozens of choppers above them, the never-ending cracks of small-arms fire and roaring machine guns around them, D'Lupo's platoon was in a cacophony of sound and confusion. Farther east, unseen by their fellow soldiers on the ground, the helo with the cavalry major descended into purple, the purple smoke now buffeted away by the downwash, the helo no more than ten feet from the ground.

"Jesus!" the pilot yelled, recognizing two or three PLA regulars below him, rifles raised. It was too late. An 85mm Soviet-made RPG7 round exploded into the guts of the chopper. Aflame, it fell like a brick, its blades broken and spinning like a scythe through the field, the explosion of its gas tanks an enormous saffron cloud, the bodies of its crew and squad of air cavalry curling grotesquely into wizened black fetal positions. The small-arms ammo inside the fiercely burning shell of the helo was popping off, the smell of cooked flesh, oil, and burning gasoline wafting across the battlefield.

From this point on, no LZ identification procedures were to be given in plain language over the field phones, only prearranged phrases or strips of cloth that would confuse the enemy.

The men pouring out of following choppers were now doing so in the center of the field and running out to relieve and/or reinforce the troops on the perimeter. Freeman kept pouring men in. "Don't let 'em bear-hug you!" he ordered his commanders as he landed in some tall elephant grass growing along part of the dike.

"What'd he mean?" Marte Price asked a private who was busy seeing whether it was possible for a human being to melt into elephant grass by will alone.

"What's he mean, bear-hug?" she repeated, only now noticing that the recorder in her hand was shaking uncontrollably. She dared not ask Freeman, his aide Cline, or even his somewhat—ironically—timid press officer Boyd.

"Bear-huggin', ma'am," someone with a southern accent explained, "is when tha enemy gets in so close to ya ya can't use arty—that's artillery, ma'am—as covering fire for your men, 'cause if you do, you'll kill as many of your own guys as the enemy—maybe more."

Marte Price spun around and crashed into a soldier's M-16 rifle, a hole and a large splotch of blood on her left breast.

"Medic!" a soldier near her shouted. "Medic! Reporter's been hit!"

Freeman moved her as gently as speed would allow, the pain of it making her gasp, a medic barely out of a chopper by her side. He slit open her blouse, cut her bra off, and gave her a shot of morphine, then taped her with a thick wad of field dressing. Then, with Freeman's help, the medic carried her to one of the relay choppers about to take off back to Phu Lang Thuong.

"I'm sorry," she told Freeman, who merely patted her on the other shoulder, shouting, "You'll be all right—a million-dollar wound!" She had heard him clearly despite the terrible confusion of the battle, and she vowed then that her wound would not be a ticket out of the war. She would get well and she would cover this war as she had first intended—at the front.

At the northern edge of the perimeter the fighting was hand-to-hand with rifle, knife, and bayonet, and the American artillery couldn't help. But the perimeter was bulging here and there, no longer the circle of Freeman's plan but larger in area, if only the bulges could hold and not be squeezed by the PLA. Here the American ability to reinforce and resupply with a speed unmatched by any other army proved the decisive factor, along with the fact that Freeman's troops knew he was there. They also knew Marte Price was there, a woman whose very presence not only commanded their protection, but also meant that their performance would be reported that day.

But if, as well as the bravery and training of the Airborne

troops, there was one weapon that turned the tide at approximately 1500 hours, it was the U.S. flamethrower, which not only arced toward the PLA it could see, but set a deep "pie slice" of underbrush afire, and soon the high canopy of forest on the hill and its ridges were ablaze, forcing the PLA infantry back, where they simultaneously became visible to Freeman's Forward Air Controller, who, in his Cessna Bird Dog spotter plane, was now directing the heavy ordnance from three F-14 Tomcats from *Enterprise* right on top of the retreating PLA. On the next bomb run, however, the Tomcats couldn't see any more targets for the fire's smoke, and neither could the FAC. Freeman ordered the First Battalion into the burned-out pie slice that had now become a charred three-acre patch on the southern side of the ridge that slanted up from the wet, muddy fields, over which thick, white smoke was now pooling, having been blown away from the PLA positions. But neither the advancing U.S. infantry battalion nor the FAC or Tomcat pilots could see any Chinese on the far side of the ridge.

Freeman grasped the field phone and coughed roughly to rid his throat of "smoke scrape."

"Now listen, Colonel, I want your boys to do two things simultaneously. First I want Alpha Company to get up to the ridgeline facing Loc Binh—watch for booby traps and dig in. Then I want rats from Bravo Company to go down after the PLA, and Charlie Company to stay in reserve so when those tunnel maggots come up for air after we smoke 'em out, we'll have reception for them. You got that? Over."

"Roger. Alpha top of the ridge, Bravo farther down, and Charlie covers the rear. Over."

"How many tunnelers you got there, Colonel? Over."

"Half a dozen trained, General. Over."

"Not enough. You grab anyone—Vietnamese or U.S.—under five-four and weighing under 145 and send 'em down. Over."

"I'll do my best, General. Over."

"No you won't. You'll flush those chinks outta there for us to shoot or I'll have your ass. Out!"

LaSalle had made a special note of Freeman's use of the word "chinks." *Mon dieu!* If he could get that pic he'd heard about of Freeman finishing off one of his own wounded, along with this "chink" gaffe, he'd probably get the lead story for *Paris Match.* Then it suddenly hit him. What in Hades was he doing up here at the front while Marte Price was back at the first available field hospital, a first-rate opportunity for him to really search her tent?

He waited till he heard the next Medevac chopper come in, its prop wash dispersing the smoke as several medics loaded two badly wounded men on its side litters. The sergeant told the Frenchman he couldn't ride this one out. They had several walking wounded with serious enough "bleeds" that he'd have to wait.

"No sweat," he answered loudly as Alpha Company's mortars pounded the top of the Loc Binh ridge. LaSalle waited. He didn't care if they thought him a coward, bolting from the battle. Not if he could get time to really do a cinema verité, as it were, of the great American general, Freeman. LaSalle didn't like Americans, never had. If the French were too proud, the Yankees were much too cocky. He planned to take them down a peg or two. He could see his prizewinning article now: "Pierre LaSalle at the Front! Exclusive!" LaSalle had never forgotten Freeman's comments about the French unwillingness to let the USAF overfly French airspace during the bombing attack on Khadafy in Libya. "The frogs only care about the frogs. Their idea of collective security is to have a multinational force protect France, and to hell with quid pro quo!" The only American LaSalle liked was Jerry Lewis.

Battalion leader Colonel Melbaine had Alpha Company atop the ridge, as Freeman had ordered, and Charlie Company was spread west to east at the base of the slope, forming a backup line about three hundred yards long.

Several of the tunnel rats from Bravo Company, stripped to the waist, were preparing themselves with field-phone transmitting throat mikes and transmitter packs that nowadays obviated the need of spool wire trailing behind. In addition to the mike and 7-shaped flashlight, each rat went down with a .45, spare clips in side pockets.

Colonel Melbaine said he had only five qualified rats ready to go. He needed more to go down, but guys he'd thought were around five feet four and around 145 pounds had suddenly grown fatter—said they'd "love" to go down but, fuck it, they were too wide.

General Freeman turned to Major Cline. "Bob, get me a kit. I'm going down."

"General, Jesus, sir—pardon me—but you'll get stuck down there."

"Don't be so goddamn rude. I'm in top physical shape."

"But sir—"

"C'mon, Bob, don't give me dance. Get me a flashlight, a .45, and a mike/transmitter unit."

With the five other rats ready, he signaled the six of them to go down. A second later each man was down a hole in the fire-ravaged earth.

In the darkness, Freeman found the arched tunnel, dug by the PLA for the PLA, as much a squeeze as Bob Cline had predicted, his heart thumping so hard that he felt sure the whole of Bravo Company must now be privy to his fear. He felt carefully in front of him, using his knuckles to rap the damp, cool earth, the PLA known to set punji sticks, razor-sharp angled bamboo that would go right through a man's boot, the earthen top of such traps often built to support the lighter PLA troops but not the generally heavier-built Americans.

His flashlight fell on a Z-shaped corner, constructed to prevent grenade shrapnel or concussion from wiping out a whole length of tunnel rather than just a portion of it. "Twenty feet in," came Freeman's subdued voice, "passed a Z, going toward a U bend." Like a bomb squad member or test pilot, he was recording everything for them. Should he get killed, the next rat down would know how far to go before he could expect anything new. He heard a crack like a stick breaking. One of his tunnel rats had made a contact, the shot echoing through the tunnel complex, but whether left or right of him, he couldn't say. He was halfway around the U bend when he came across something he had never seen or heard about in the tunnels before—a saloonlike bamboo door.

Breathing hard, sweat breaking out on his neck, he took a moment to compose himself. Then he noticed another tunnel veering off to the right, so that he had a choice, either straight ahead into the tunnel or to veer off to the right. He heard a noise, the scurrying of some animal, and felt the wet rush of a huge gray rat along his side that caused his whole body to shiver. "Am at a bamboo door," he reported to those topside. "Have probably gone in eighty feet. Another section of tunnel goes off to the right."

Which way to go? Bamboo door looked fishy, as if it was inviting him to come in. Perhaps it was a PLA sign that beyond lay a dead-end storage area. Was that where the rat or whatever had scurried past him had come from? He turned the flashlight on and off just long enough for him to see that below the door there was some spilled rice. "Huh," Freeman said gruffly, desperately fighting a growing sense of claustrophobia and the stench of rotten air. "Door definitely looks wrong. Ten to one you touch it and you trip a grenade."

His throat was bone dry, despite the cool dampness of the fetid tunnel. "Will use white smoke to make vertical shafts visible if I find any. Am resting awhile before I move. Out." It also gave Freeman time to listen for a few minutes to hear, despite the steady thunder and staccato of battle overhead, if there was any movement coming his way.

The door drew him toward it, but he resisted the temptation—it was a sucker's trap if ever there was one. He took the right tunnel instead.

CHAPTER FORTY-SEVEN

THE MOVE OF prisoners from Upshut Island to the mainland was as abrupt as it was unexpected. The South Chinese Intelligence Bureau had suddenly been apprised of the disposition of American naval forces in the South China Sea. It was impressive, with at least six Hunter/Killer Los Angeles subs within range of the island, which was merely another way of saying that if any PLA aircraft took off from the island against the U.S. Seventh Fleet, they would immediately be brought down by the Seventh Fleet's surface-to-air missiles.

And so, in one report by the Chengdu Intelligence Bureau, the reason for keeping U.N. POWs on the island as hostages against the U.S. air attack no longer made any sense. What was the use of having allied hostages on Upshut Island to protect the runway from U.S. bombs if the PLA planes on the airstrip were rendered unusable because of the Seventh Fleet's missiles? Much better, it was decided by Beijing, to move the

POW hostages to a location where they could be of more use as hostages and/or coolies.

And so, in a stench of sweat and kerosene fumes, and as quickly as they'd been brought to Upshut Island, the American, Australian, Vietnamese, and other U.N. POWs were placed aboard PLA transports clearly marked with a red cross, blindfolded and handcuffed to the inside lugs on the plane's fuselage, and flown north from the Paracel Islands, then east into Chengdu province. They were then taken to yet another airfield in the making, one not invulnerable to missiles such as the Tomahawk, but a field in China proper, not in the disputed islands of the South China Sea.

It was thought that though the Americans might drop bombs on their own if strategic considerations deemed it imperative to do so, the U.S. would not sacrifice the other POWs—the Australians, Vietnamese, and British. It would create an uproar within the United Nations coalition. In any event, the Americans would think twice for another reason. To bomb an internationally recognized "dispute island" was one thing, but to attack an airstrip in China proper would be an enormous leap into the political unknown. It would create the kind of political maelstrom in the offing when MacArthur wanted to cross the Yalu into China during the Korean War. The mere suggestion that, because of strategic and tactical considerations he was thinking about it, was enough to bring U.N. criticism, and led to Truman firing him. To be part, albeit the major part, of a USVUN force was one thing, but to allow U.S. airpower to cross the Vietnamese-Chinese border to hit inside China proper went way beyond the mandate Jorgensen and Freeman had.

Two F-14 Tomcats on combat patrol two hundred miles from the USS *Enterprise* were told by the carrier AWACS about the Red Cross plane, and the F-14s swooped down to have a look-see. "The Chinese have painted red crosses all over," the patrol leader reported.

"Do not engage," *Enterprise* advised. "I say again, do not engage." That'd be all the USVUN would need—the downing of a Chinese Red Cross plane—though the *Enterprise*'s skipper was willing to bet a month's pay the bastards were using it to ferry PLA troops back and forth from all the islands claimed by the PLA for the People's Republic of China.

For those in the Chinese transport plane, a PLA C-46 made to carry forty fully armed troops but now jam-packed with ninety prisoners, the sleep-inducing drone competed with the anxiety of not knowing where they were going.

"Where the fuck are we?" Mike Murphy demanded above the steady roar of the engines, and trying to use his facial muscles to work down the blindfold.

"Well, we're not in Hawaii," Shirley Fortescue whispered.

"Well," Danny Mellin said, "my money'd be on China. Somewhere on the southeast coast."

There was a thud, followed by an agonized expulsion of air.

"Up shut!" commanded Upshut, and now from a slit of light Mike Murphy could see Lieutenant Mung, the interrogator aboard the destroyer. It looked as if they were moving from Upshut Island lock, stock, and barrel. Through his tiny window on the world, Murphy could get only a tantalizing glimpse—a trace of silver—that would be somewhere in the northern sector of the Gulf of Tonkin, if Mellin was correct.

Soon they began their descent. Ears began to pop, and some experienced needle-sharp pains in their sinuses, their faces contorted as they leaned forward in a vain attempt to get away from the rapid change in pressure, hands straining against roped wrists.

There was a banshee howl as the undercarriage came down and engaged, then a sharp bump, and a second or two when everything felt out of control.

A political officer was already aboard before the props stopped turning. "Welcome to Ningming. You will work hard and prosper!" the cadre announced, smiling.

Mike Murphy stood up. Lieutenant Mung wanted to knock the Australian down, but stopped when the commissar held up his hand. "Whaddya mean by prosper, mate? You mean you'll let us go free?"

The cadre's smile showed yellow-stained teeth. "Yes. When you work hard, you help fight American imperialists. This will help win war. Then you go home. Everybody happy!"

"Yeah, well, what if we don't want to work—for you or any other bloody cadre?"

The eagerly nodding cadre was still smiling, his features thrown into gross relief by the flashlight he was holding. "You not work, you will be shot."

"Yeah," Murphy said sullenly. "Well, how we gonna work with our bloody hands tied up? Christ, you lot are straight from the bloody goon show—ya know that?"

"We do not understand this," the cadre said.

"Back off, Mike," Mellin warned.

"Well, shit, we aren't prisoners of war, for Chrissake. We're just a poor bunch of bastards picked up off the rigs."

"You will have your hands unroped," the cadre said. "In the morning you work—two hundred of you. You will help make Ningming large airport."

"From which to bomb the USVUN forces," Murphy charged.

"This," the cadre conceded, "is correct, but first you will build your accommodations." He said something sharp to Upshut, who unclipped the stock of the AK-47, walked over, and clubbed Murphy to the ground. With the Australian in a protective fetal position, Upshut kicked at his groin and missed, his boot crunching the Australian's cupped hands. Next, Upshut walked about Murphy and started in on his kidneys, ending with a final vicious kick at Murphy's face, catching the Australian on the right cheek, now bleeding profusely. Upshut handed his rifle to a soldier, still looking down at Murphy.

"Always big mouth. Never up shut! Always for girl, yes? For girl." He pointed at Shirley Fortescue. "For her—yes? Yes?" he bellowed, and took his foot back for another kick.

"Yes," Murphy said.

"Yes," Upshut said. "For girl."

He knelt down next to the bleeding prisoner. "You lose face, Australian. Next time you die. You understand?"

"Yes."

"Tell me you full of shit."

Murphy wet his lips, but before he could speak, Upshut stopped him, telling him that he wanted everyone to hear. Mung nodded, and Upshut kicked him in the base of the spine. Murphy groaned with pain. "Tell them!"

"I'm—"

"Louder!" Mung ordered, holding his hand out for the AK-47.

"I'm full of shit." All the prisoners averted their eyes to lessen his humiliation, but in doing so they too lost face.

Ningming, a railhead with one airstrip, was thirteen miles from the Vietnamese/Chinese border, twenty-six miles from Dong Dang and Lang Son in Vietnam, and twenty-five miles from Loc Binh, where Freeman's Second Army was waging war on the ridges south of Loc Binh.

CHAPTER FORTY-EIGHT

IN TEXAS, MRS. Mellin received yet another letter from the head office of the Veterans Administration in Washington, D.C.

Dear Mrs. Mellin:

Thank you for your letter of March 6 inquiring about the possible whereabouts of your husband, Daniel E. Mellin, who has been missing since the fire at an offshore drilling rig in the South China Sea. I fully empathize with your frustration at not receiving any solid information regarding your husband's whereabouts beyond the information given us earlier by the Royal Bruneian Government that the fire at the scene was so intense that many bodies were burned beyond recognition. We are of course continuing to investigate the matter, but given the present hostilities between China and the USVUN forces, our inquiries to date have been met with silence.

On another front—that of the MIA status of Mr. Mellin's sister Angela—there is the possibility, albeit a faint one, that increased contacts between the Republic of Vietnam and the United States necessitated by the USVUN coalition, will yield long-awaited information on some of the more than two thousand MIAs and suspected POWs still held in Vietnam.

The director has asked me to assure all those family and friends of MIAs and POWs that the department is doing its utmost in this matter. He has also suggested that public appeals through the media, phone-in shows, and privately written letters to the government in Hanoi tend to inhibit our inquiries rather than help. Rest assured, however, that we

will not cease in our efforts to ascertain the whereabouts of
Mr. Daniel Mellin and Ms. Angela Mellin.

CHAPTER FORTY-NINE

NOT HAVING HEARD anything for several minutes in the
tunnel, Freeman, still on hands and knees, edged his way from
the bamboo swing door into the first curve of what turned out
to be an S and not a U bend. Somewhere above him he heard
the faint stutter of what he guessed was an M-60, probably
chopping down a PLA soldier who'd felt trapped on hearing
tunnel rats coming for him from two directions at once. At the
end of the S turn, Freeman came adjacent to an alcove about
four feet deep, four feet high, and six feet long, containing two
bunk beds of bamboo, and, set into a small recess, an oil wick
candle. Beneath the bottom bunk were several dozen plastic
hoops, known to the Americans as "Beijing hoops." When
twigs and leaves were attached to the plastic rings, a soldier
wearing them could turn his head 180 degrees without the
camouflage moving.

At the end of the bottom bunk was a small first aid kit.
Freeman knew that whether your enemy had morphine was
one way to tell how well-equipped he was. But to find out that
bit of intelligence would have meant opening the box, which
he didn't do. Seeing a deep shadow off to his left about three
feet away, he determined it was another alcove and made his
way toward it. Its three walls contained rolls of curtainlike
muslin that could be unrolled to form cloth walls insects
couldn't penetrate.

In the middle of the alcove, taking up about half its length,
was a bamboo operating table with various instruments laid
out, including forceps, suturing needles, scalpels, and clamps.
There was a large light overhead, its socket set into the earthen

ceiling. The wire leading from it went across the roof of the tunnel to a smaller alcove, no more than two feet deep, five feet long, and five high, where Freeman found an old Flying Pigeon bicycle on rollers. When pedaled, the turning wheels would produce electricity to light the small operating theater.

Seeing a cone of light ahead of him at right angles, the beam moving farther to his left, Freeman released the safety on his .45, lay flat, and held the revolver in two hands. The beam went out, its images still dancing on Freeman's right retina, the general, from experience, having kept one eye closed. He opened it now, shutting the right eye. "Delta two!" he called.

"Lima!" came the correct response from one allied tunneler to another.

Freeman could hear his own sigh of relief. "Nothing is better than hearing a friendly voice down one of those godforsaken gopher holes," he'd once told Bob Cline. He switched his flashlight on then off. The other tunnel rat did the same. Freeman could see he was approaching a T section, with the other soldier about to cross it. Though becoming more claustrophobic by the minute, he whispered, "I'll take it, son. You head back. Make sure you let our boys know it's you coming out."

"Don't worry," the soldier whispered. "I will."

Freeman patted the youngster, then crawled cautiously across the junction to cross the T and follow the tunnel to its end, and in so doing added to his legend, to the mystique of those commanders before and since Caesar whose men knew they would never be asked to do something by their commander that he would not be prepared to do himself.

When Freeman crossed the T and was alone again in the enemy's subterranean world, an involuntary shiver passed through his body. He felt the claustrophobia worsening, the ever-present danger of suffocation so heavy upon him that he had to fight not to throw up. Combined with his own body stench, he smelled the damp mold of the tunnels themselves, and felt an overwhelming urge to go as fast as hell and get out. But speed, he knew, was as sure a killer as a hidden grenade or trip wire. "Carefully does it," he told himself, and when he moved forward, felt the rush of gut acid up his esophagus and cursed himself for not bringing antacid pills—next to his .45 and knife, a tunneler's best friend.

He felt ahead with the base of the flashlight in his right hand, careful of any traps. The ground was holding. Now he gave it the full weight of his right hand as he moved forward with his left. Suddenly the ground went from under his left hand, his body driving it down hard on the punji sticks. It was the first time anyone had ever said they'd heard Freeman scream. Two punji sticks, each tipped with excrement, had penetrated his left hand. Simultaneously he saw a shadow flitting ahead left to right. He challenged, got no answer, and fired two rounds that echoed eerily in the subterranean world. Freeman slumped for a moment, then regained his composure enough to back up out of the tunnel, his hand bleeding profusely.

CHAPTER FIFTY

IT SEEMED AS if the bus back to Dalat had no springs. It was certainly overloaded, and despite a sign—albeit a small one—warning of fines for expectorating on the people's buses, Ray Baker could hear the loud guttural rumbles of spitters about to take aim through the open-air windows.

Some of the children in the back of the bus were yelling with glee as the vehicle bumped and rattled on its way to Dalat. It made Ray Baker nervous. All the noise and the disease of Saigon had spread to the north—ghetto blasters blasting everything within earshot, the sound amplified by the interior of the ramshackle bus. He suddenly had a case of déjà vu—a bright morning like this, bodies pressing up hard against one another, the smell of people jammed together, engine fumes and dust, kids squalling then screaming, an American collapsing in the aisle, eyes bulging, falling flat on his face, adults screaming, reaching for their children to get them away from him, the American facedown, a knife protruding from his back, no one helping him. Baker had been unable to reach him because of the stream of hysterical passengers pouring from the bus as it skidded to a stop, several passengers climbing out the open side windows. A stampede, no one but him wanting to help the American, no one wanting to get involved.

Suddenly, the flashback over, he turned around. A baby saw his face from less than a foot away and began screaming. There were only other children and harried parents trying to maintain some sense of order while balancing the various fruits, vegetables, and village wares they were taking to Dalat. It was then that he saw the boy from yesterday running by the bus, sending out a long crimson stream of betel juice and waving happily to him.

"Oh yes," Baker said, smiling maliciously at him. "I want to see you too, you little bastard!" It was the boy who must have fingered him, or at least suckered him away to the market while they did over his room, whoever *they* were.

When Baker got out of the bus, the boy was nowhere to be seen. Then, on his way back to the hotel, he saw the boy nonchalantly coming toward him, not even pausing as he spat the next stream of betelnut juice onto the dusty street. Baker wanted to ask the youth a pile of questions, but all that came out was "Hi!" in response to the boy's greeting. Only then did Baker ask, "Who are you?"

"Friend, Bac Baker. Friend of Americans. Okay?"

True, the kid had indirectly got him the info about a couple of MIAs, but how about the woman and the lemon? Baker confronted the boy: Wasn't that just a dead end to allow whoever was paying him time to ransack his hotel room?

The boy didn't understand "ransack," but thought he understood after Baker had given him another dollar.

"I don't know who did this," he said.

To believe him or not? Baker wondered. He asked the boy who had hired him this morning, or did he just happen to turn up at the bus stop at that particular time? The boy was astounded by the question. Whether something had been lost in the translation or not, Baker didn't understand. But in any event the boy said, "Same man yesterday, today. Same man, Bac Baker."

"Yeah, all right, but *who*?"

The boy shook his head. "I tell you that, no more money. Bad for me. Okay? You understand, Bac Baker?"

"Yeah, yeah. So are you going to tell me why you're here at the market right now?"

The boy spat a long, crimson stream at a bug crawling on

the sidewalk, missed, and told Baker, "He say to tell you Salt and Pepper be back."

Baker felt a surge of exhilaration with an overlay of panic. "Salt and Pepper will be back?"

"No, be back."

"You mean they are back."

"Yeah, sure, that's what I tell you. Okay?"

"Okay," Baker said. He suspected the warning as well as the initial contact made with the note came from the villager's son, "Saigon."

"Tell whoever hired you, thanks."

"Sure, okay." Baker gave him another ten thousand dong. The boy snapped the bill and smiled, showing his brown-stained teeth.

As Baker walked across the pedestrian overpass from the Mai Building on a deliberate roundabout route to his hotel, he told himself to calm right down, as his mom used to tell him. "Just calm right down—don't get so excited, all worked up." Yes, it looked like the first solid info on MIAs he'd had in years, but it might be bullshit too. People everywhere wanted to make a buck and would tell you anything, right? But then how about the hotel room all messed up, and the damn snake in the village? All right, buddy boy, calm down. Call Saigon—not the guy, Ho Chi Minh City—tell them what you have, the people you've seen and so on.

He dialed 01-8, then moved his body so that Ha Ha, the good friend of the police permit department, on shift again behind the counter, couldn't tell the number he was dialing in old Saigon.

"United States Legation. How may I help you?"

"Jean, it's Ray Baker here. Got some info on MIAs."

"Shoot!"

"I hope not," he joked, aware of the .45 in his coat pocket.

"What?" Jean asked.

"Nothing. Listen, I might be a bit soft-spoken and oblique here, but try to follow me. All right?"

"Roger."

"Two MIAs. No evidence, only verbal, but a bit of monkey business with yours truly."

"A lot of business, Ray?"

"Not so far, but definitely business."

"You want us to extend your personal liability coverage?"

"Let me see. Hmm ... could you do that by tonight?"

"Might be difficult, Ray. We're sort of busy up north."

"Yeah, of course. Ah, don't worry about it. I've got enough coverage for tonight."

"You sure? I could always try our Hanoi rep."

"Nah, I'll be fine. I might even grab a flight down tonight."

"I can tell you now they're full—a lot of civil officials transferring south."

"Okay. I'll book tomorrow. I'll be fine. Friends coming around anyway."

"You sure?"

"Positive. One more thing, Jean. There's been a complaint. Same two MIAs ran with the opposition. Now info is they're guides for that movie *The Killing Fields*. They're apparently doing a remake."

"In their own studio?" Jean asked, right on the ball.

"Nah," Baker replied. "Apparently they want to use the opposition's."

"Oh. So is that all?"

"No. They're known as Salt and Pepper."

"Oh?"

"One black, one white. That's all for now. See you tomorrow night."

"You sure about the extra liability coverage?"

"Yeah. 'Bye."

Yeah, sure he was sure about extra liability coverage. Like hell he was, but what did it sound like to Jean—scaredy-cat! Look, the .45 was in his pocket. What the hell anyway? There'd be enough damn beetles on the floor, you'd hear anyone tiptoeing in. Besides, he'd crush up newspapers and throw them about—they'd make a hell of a rustle if someone tried to sneak in. And he'd use the dead bolt, sit with the .45 in his lap—on the toilet too. No way he'd take a shower or bath.

After he walked up and put the key in the door, he took a couple of steps to the side so he was braced against the wall and pushed the door open with his toe. A few dead roaches, a couple of them live but stumbling. Everything looked normal. He did a check on the chest of drawers, having put a hair where the second drawer closed on the first before he'd gone to the village. The hair was still there.

He went into the bathroom and washed his face, surprised by how dark the bags under his eyes were. He put a finger under each eye and pulled out to the sides. It took at least ten years off him. Was he vain enough to get a face-lift? He had always wondered why people bothered, but now, in his early fifties, he had a different perspective on it. He was starting to go bald—not a lot, but he could tell the difference. Jean was going bald too, and right now she was his best chance for a relationship.

After a shave, a meal of *cha ca*—charcoal-broiled fish fillets with roasted nuts—salad, noodles, and fish sauce washed down by a bottle of Tsing Tao beer—the Chinese were being a real pain in the ass, but they sure as hell could make beer—he felt a lot better. The dangers he'd imagined during the day now seemed grossly overblown, and he contemplated the difference a good meal could make to one's disposition.

He ordered coffee and started worrying about how much he'd already gotten through to Jean in his semiplain language code. He decided to book out on the earliest flight available—the next day at noon.

In his room, coat off, in his undershirt and trousers, Baker sat up on the bed as if on a desert island, ready to indulge one of his sins, and lit up a Camel no-filter, sucking the smoke in so he could feel it deep in his chest and see it flowing lethargically out in curlicue patterns, then watching it slowly dissipate above the land of the roaches. And if any creeps came through the door or from the side veranda, he would pump the bastards "so full of lead" that, in the words of James Cagney, when they fell they'd write!

Later, the night clerk said that the beer had probably made him sleepy. Whatever it was that put him temporarily off guard, by the time Ray Baker got off one shot, his throat was cut, blood bubbling from the carotid artery, his attacker having slid up from behind, coming out from under the bed. He was dead inside a minute.

CHAPTER FIFTY-ONE

THE MASH UNIT had to be especially cautious when attending to Freeman's wounds, not because he was a general, but because his Medic Alert disk showed he was allergic to certain antibiotics. When they got his wound cleansed and his hand bandaged up, they put his arm in a sling, which he immediately dispensed with. He walked back to the armored personnel carrier he was using as a mobile HQ, which, along with an armored cavalry unit, had made its way north along the Phu Lang Thuong road, then been airlifted into the west-east valley between Ban Re and Loc Binh.

Freeman was worried about the fading light. Soon it would be dark, and the Chinese still in the tunnels would be able to exit *within* the USVUN area and create havoc. Freeman and Vinh knew that if this occurred, there were bound to be many more blue on blue incidents. But to withdraw from the hillside would simply mean giving up the territory, the high ground, that the USVUN had fought so hard for all afternoon, and going back to the fields from which they'd started.

Freeman, like Patton, said he never liked "paying for the same real estate twice," and elected to hold the high ground. Vinh, however, cautioned that it was possible the Chinese might simply elect to retreat through the tunnel system on this side of the southern slope of the ridge to the ridge's northern side. Freeman readily acknowledged the possibility. At least if the Chinese did slip out of the battle, he wouldn't have to worry so much about blue on blue, but he would be faced with the prospect of more than five thousand PLA troops slipping north across the border, troops which—like those who slipped across the Yalu River in Korea—could not be pursued by his Airborne cav units because of the political decision in

Washington and Hanoi that USVUN forces could not cross the Vietnamese-Chinese border, which was only a mile and a half north of the ridge.

Vinh suggested through the interpreter that perhaps there might be a way of the USVUN "having cakes and consuming them." He meant "having your cake and eating it." Vinh said that if TACAIR attacks from the carrier USS *Enterprise* could keep up a steady bombing of the northern side of the ridge, bottling Chinese up in the vast underground tunnel system that traversed the ridge, then at least they couldn't exit.

"So they can't crawl out and head north?" Freeman asked.

"Yes," Vinh said. "Then tomorrow we smoke out the tunnels through the camouflaged entrances and exits we found on the southern side today."

Now Freeman saw the extent of the Vietnamese general's strategy: bottle their northern escape route overnight by ceaselessly bombing the northern side of the ridge, and in daylight man all entrances and exits you could find and smoke them out—with "white phosphorus" if necessary.

Freeman ruled out white phosphorus, but not purely on humanitarian grounds. After all, the USVUN forces and the Chinese were already using white phosphorus grenades. But a regular grenade was one thing, a phosphorus grenade was something else. You couldn't pump white phosphorus down into a tunnel system when you weren't sure where the hell it was going to come up. If it got on your own men's skin, you might kill more USVUN troops than those of the enemy.

"Very well," Vinh concluded, "we will use purple smoke. Blow that down, and wherever it comes up we'll seal unless they agree to surrender."

"What if they decide to backtrack?" Freeman asked. "I mean what if Wang decides to come back through the tunnels to the fields behind us?"

"Why go back to old ground you have lost?"

"To try and escape south," Freeman answered. "We don't know how far south the tunnels go, do we? Besides, they have two battalions at least from their Fourteenth Chengdu Army down there in Disney World. Around a thousand men— infantry and some engineers."

"Why engineers?" Cline put in.

"Because the bastards know how to dig, damn it! General Vinh here'll tell you. Hell, his boys had over two hundred miles of tunnels in the Chu Chi system down south during 'Nam. And despite all our technology, we couldn't rout them."

"What makes you think we can do it here, General?"

"Because—" Freeman hesitated. He was proud of his Second Army and he was loath to take anything away from them. "Because, Major, the Vietnamese have been at it a hell of a lot longer than we have, and in the tunnels, they're better than we are." He held up his bandaged hand. *"Capiche?"*

Cline nodded. "All right, but meanwhile where's General Wei?"

Vinh pointed at the map. "Last intelligence reports say he is still proceeding down the Lang Son–Lang Ro road three miles to the west of us. But our—I mean, the USVUN heavy artillery is lined up along Lang Son–Ban Re railroad and are pounding shits out of them."

Freeman roared with laughter at the interpreter's phrasing, adding, "By God, General, I hope you're right. We don't want our left flank penetrated."

"No."

That night the ridge became known as Disney Hill, not only to the men of Freeman's Second Army and the USVUN forces, but by the pilots of the fighters and bombers preparing to take off from the *Enterprise*, even now before the sun went down. The great carrier was at the center of the battle group, along with other ships—submarines and combat air patrols included—pledged to the protection of the carrier as she turned slowly into the wind of the Gulf of Tonkin, her catapults already bleeding steam. She was ready to thrust her warplanes aloft, the aircraft a careful mix of A-6E Intruders, F-14 Tomcats, and F-18 Hornet fighter-bombers, loaded with everything from two-thousand-pound bombs and Sparrow air-to-air missiles to fuel air explosive bombs.

There were no laser-guided bombs on this mission, for while the north side, and not the south side, of Disney Hill was to be hit, it would not be pinpoint bombing that was required to either kill or trap the Chinese in the southside tunnels, it would be power bombing—brute poundage. This was to be excavation by high explosive.

Already in Primary Flight Control, the "handler," PRI-FLY's second in command, whose job was so complicated and many-faceted that it often could not be computerized, watched his models of the aircraft on his grid-crossed table. Nowhere is war as complicated as on the flight deck of a carrier when men and machines move in a rough ballet of hand signals amid a forest of constantly moving, different-colored jerseys.

Two of these, gunner's mates, Albright Stevens and Elizabeth Franks, a "grape" who in her purple jacket was helping to fuel one of the F-18 Hornets with JP-5 gasoline, had been lovers ever since he'd taken her to the movie at the beginning of the voyage. Both of them had since found time together in some of the hundreds of nooks and crannies aboard the huge ship, which, as well as launching planes in any weather, had to feed and minister to over five thousand crew members.

"Lucky we ain't on a sub," Albright had told her.

"You'd find a way," she'd said.

"Believe I would."

But that was then, and now they were in the Gulf of Tonkin, not a happy place in the annals of American history, and around them they knew the PLA navy was determined to somehow penetrate the carrier's protective shield.

CHAPTER FIFTY-TWO

HOPES BY GENERAL Jorgensen's Hanoi HQ that relief might come to Freeman's USVUN troops through sabotage by proxy—by having Taiwan-run saboteurs hit China's southern supply route on the Ningming–Dong Dang railway—began to fade as night fell upon the battle zone.

The vote in Taiwan's Li-fa Yuan was close, with several nonpartisan or independent members swinging the slim majority to the side of the Democratic Progressive party against the "old ones," the second-generation right-wing remnants of the old Kuomintang party of Chiang Kai-shek.

In one of the strangest ironies of politics, the Kuomintang on the far right agreed with the Communist party on the far left that Taiwan was still a province of China. But here the

agreement between left and right ended, for while the Kuomintang supported the USVUN presence against the Beijing
regime, the Communist party was vehemently opposed. The
majority of votes swung to the left, crucial independents afraid
that any Taiwanese support for the USVUN would not only in-
furiate Beijing but be the end of the "understanding" between
Beijing and Taipei. The understanding was a promise from
Beijing that in return for Taipei's support for China's South
China Sea claims, Beijing would split certain oil concessions
in the northern part of the South China Sea, with fifty-one percent de facto control for Beijing, forty-nine percent for Taiwan.

"We can't wait," Douglas Freeman said, "for the Taiwanese
Chinese to make up their minds." His HQ staff were looking
at the red pins that stood for PLA positions on and around
Disney Hill.

"But our State Department boys might be able to swing a
few of the independents over to our side," Cline remarked.
"Then maybe the Taiwanese'll authorize some of their agents
in China to blow the Ningming–Dong Dang rail line."

"Huh!" Freeman grunted dismissively, his right fist punch-
ing the map of the southern China–Vietnamese border area.
"Too many maybes, mights, and what-ifs for my liking. By
the time those fairies in State get off their butts, Chinese
reinforcements'll be trundling down from the Ningming railhead—in their goddamn thousands."

"Sir," his nervous press aide interjected, "it's not, ah, politically correct to refer to people as fairies. And if you mean
gays, I'd advise you to modify—"

"*Modify!* To hell with political correctness. Wasn't talking
about gays anyway—long as they keep off one another and
keep shooting at the enemy, they're as good as any other soldier. The fairies in State I'm talking about are those dithering
old farts who can't make a decision. One desk jockey talks to
another, and that's all they do—*talk*—until it's too late to do
anything!" He slammed his fist against the map again, the
Ningming–Dong Dang road shuddering violently.

Freeman paused, but only to get air. "All right, look, here's
what we do. We send in a Special Forces squad to blow the
shit out of the Ningming–Dong Dang line, and I don't mean
just in one place, I mean at least three breaks west of
Ningming proper. Then again at Xiash and Pingxiang. They'll
have to mend the line in so many friggin' places it'll give 'em

a nervous breakdown!" Freeman turned to Vinh. "You concur, General?"

Vinh nodded and said something to his interpreter. "The general says this is a good idea but that Chinese nerves are very good. In 1979 they lost more than twenty-five thousand in just three weeks, and still reinforcements came through this area."

"Well, maybe so," Freeman answered. "I don't underestimate them for a second, but chopping up their rail line'll slow them down—give us a chance to secure the border here."

"Why," General Vinh asked, "cannot the American carrier planes bombard the rail yards at Ningming?"

"Politics, General," Freeman answered. "The White House categorically forbids any bombardment in China proper. They don't want to risk the war spreading any further than it has already."

"Is that the U.S. decision or the U.N. mandate?" inquired Vinh's political officer.

"Does it matter?" Freeman asked them. "Whoever's mandate it is, I'd get fired if I authorized beyond the border bombing. Only thing we're allowed to do is send out patrols when our positions on this side of the border line are threatened."

The political officer looked nonplussed. "But the planes from your carrier, they are allowed to bomb the northern side of the hill. It is very close to the border."

"Yes," Freeman said. "But our flyboys'll be able to drop their ordnance just where we want it."

"And what if some bombs land beyond the border?"

Cline held up his hands. "One or two won't start an international crisis."

"Exactly," Freeman concurred.

Vinh had such a determination about him that Freeman in private was starting to refer to him as the "bulldog."

"What will happen if your Special Forces are discovered sabotaging the Ningming–Dong Dang line? That would be considered by your White House and the U.N. as 'in China' surely?"

"Our Special Forces won't be caught," Freeman reassured him. "USVUN teams I'll send in will be made up of crack American and British commandos. Special Air Service from Britain, Delta Force from us. They'll go in NOE—choppers, nap of the earth flying. It'll be drop in, set charges, and get out. Low and fast, General."

Vinh nodded. "And what about this—" He momentarily forgot the English phrase he wanted. The interpreter listened to Vinh intently, conferred with their political officer, and when there was agreement, told Freeman, "—these condiments—salt and pepper number two."

Freeman looked blankly at Cline, who looked just as blankly at Boyd, the press officer.

"Condiments?" Freeman repeated.

"Salt and Pepper," Boyd interjected suddenly. "Condiments—they mean Salt and Pepper, the two MIAs—that report that came to us from our legation in Saigon—I mean in Ho Chi Minh City—about the two American deserters, one white, one black."

"Yes, yes," the interpreter said. "But this name, Salt and Pepper, is taken from long ago when there were two other Americans who came over to our side. This is why we call these ones Salt and Pepper number two."

"Call them bastards," Freeman said, infuriated by the possibility, no, the certainty, of Americans who had crossed over. "They must be damn near old men by now—I mean if they went over during 'Nam."

General Vinh began to talk, but his voice was drowned out by the sonic booms of the planes from the northern side of Disney Hill. Vinh raised his voice. "What will you do about them if this report is correct about them leading the Khmer Rouge up from Cambodia to attack us on our western flank?" Before Freeman could reply, Vinh went on, "The Chinese would be very happy about this. Two Americans fighting against the USVUN."

The political officer was nodding vigorously. This topic was obviously of far more importance to him than the immediately pressing military situation on Disney. He spoke rapidly and passionately to the interpreter, who explained the political officer's position to Freeman and his staff. "Hanoi is very concerned about the Khmer Rouge infiltration across the Cambodian-Vietnamese border while we are fighting here in the far north of our country."

Freeman was also concerned about a war on two fronts, but he'd also seen photos of the Khmer Rouge's tortured victims piled high at Tuol Sleng extermination center. He had once told the reporter Marte Price that if anything like the mass murder at Tuol Sleng had happened to a white population, there would have been U.N. action almost immediately. "The

Khmer Rouge are the scum of the earth," Freeman had told her bitterly, "and if I'd had my way, I would have turned Khmer Rouge staging areas into a parking lot, but of course, politics. You see, that would have offended their great ally—China."

"General Freeman," Vinh said, his expression of bland noncommitment now replaced with the look of an old warrior who, as hard as he'd fought against the Americans in 'Nam, had never hated a foe as much as he did the Khmer Rouge. Yet as he talked to Freeman—at times using the interpreter—he was putting this hatred aside. It was not hatred that led him to uncharacteristically plead with his American counterpart, but military prudence. "If the Khmer Rouge are not stopped crossing over into Vietnam, all kinds of insurgents from Cambodia and Laos will be encouraged to start yet *another* war against the new Vietnam, which will quickly demand more USVUN intervention."

Freeman knew Vinh was right. It was like one of the old oil change ads for your automobile—a case of "pay me now or pay me later," the inference being that later would be one heck of a lot more expensive in lives and matériel. Either Freeman stopped them now, or at least made a determined thrust into the Laotian staging areas as an unmistakable sign of the USVUN's commitment to stopping the insurgency, or he would pay heavily later.

"You—" Major Cline began, then changed it to, "*We* can't make that decision, General." Cline had said "General" in such a way that it was impossible for either Vinh or Freeman to know whom he was addressing. In fact he was talking to both, but was being careful, trying not to offend either one. "General Jorgensen," Cline continued, "is the only one who can authorize such a move out of our immediate sector." Cline paused and looked at Vinh's political officer. "In fact, as far as I recall, Jorgensen would have to confer with the Joint Chiefs and the White House for permission to—"

"Find two of our MIAs?" Freeman interjected, another idea already forming on how to bypass the Joint Chiefs. "American people won't stand for any delay on that score, Major. Over two thousand POWs and MIAs still missing. You think the American people are going to stand still for one minute if we know where our boys are and we say, 'Oh wait until we're finished with the Chinese'? Hell, they won't put up with that for a second."

"General, we're talking about two guys who went over."

"For what reason?" Freeman snapped. "Those Khmer bastards could be holding dozens of our boys." Before Cline could answer, Freeman's voice had taken on a terrible urgency. "By God, Major, these two you're talking about may have been forced to run with those bastards, for all we know. An old story, right? 'You don't help us, we'll kill your buddies!' "

"But," Cline stammered, "you don't *know* that, sir—with all due respect."

"With all due respect, Major, *you* don't know the truth of it either." Freeman looked at Vinh. "Matter of fact, quite a few volunteers in *your* army were more or less there because of families or friends held hostage."

The political officer quickly responded. "This was a political necessity—at the time."

"Oh," Freeman said, "I see. So that's what it was."

Cline obviously didn't like the turn the conversation was taking. "Perhaps you're both right," he put in. "I mean, I see why it's militarily important to send a strong message to the Khmer Rouge, some of our MIAs involved or not. All I'm saying, gentlemen, is that we're going to have to go through Jorgensen and the President."

"Jesus Christ, Major," Freeman said. "Haven't you been listening to what I've been saying? If those fairies in State and the Pentagon get hold of this, they'll take forever. Meanwhile we could be taking body blows from the Rouge."

"Then what do you suggest, General?"

There was a pause as Freeman looked at Vinh and then Cline. "Leave it to me. Meanwhile I want you to make sure our boys stay on the southern side of Disney. Don't want them getting pulverized by our own TACAIR."

"Yes, sir."

"And remember, no one moves forward till 0600. Everybody stays down till dawn. Then we'll smoke out those who haven't been blown out."

"Yes, sir."

Freeman turned to his press officer. "Boyd, sink that coffee you've got and come with me."

Outside, the darkness seemed to be vibrating as F-14 Tomcats and F-18s flew in low, dropping their loads amid curtains of red and white tracer crisscrossing the sky. The AA tracer was coming from those Chinese who had made it through the tunnel system from the southern side of the hill to the northern slope of Disney Hill, only to find their exits blocked by the bombing. Even so, several of them managed to hastily man what triple A they had managed to hide in the northern complex.

Meanwhile those Vietnamese regulars and the American forces nearest the hill's summit began "walking" their mortars across the PLA's triple A positions at a nice, easy, murderous fire of ten to fifteen twelve-pound 82mm shells a minute. To an outsider, the fact that the Americans were using 82mm rounds instead of their standard 81mm rounds might have seemed inconsequential, but Freeman's decision, indeed his insistence, that all U.S. front-line units from Second Army in the USVUN line trade their standard-issue 81mm mortars for North Vietnamese Army 82mm mortars proved to be a brilliant tactical move.

Freeman had always been a keen student of past battles and Benjamin Franklin, how for the want of a nail the horse wasn't shod and for the want of a horse the battle was lost. He had also remembered the lessons of Korea and of 'Nam when, with American GIs running out of their heavy 81mm mortar rounds, they overran enemy positions to discover piles of unused mortar shells, but shells that were useless to them because that extra 1mm diameter of Russian, Vietnamese, and Chinese 82mm rounds would not fit into the U.S. 81mm barrel.

Now the mortar positions the USVUN forces had managed to capture or overrun on their way up from the rice paddies to the southern slope of Disney Hill provided the Americans with lots of extra "help-yourself" mortar rounds, courtesy of General Wang's retreating units.

As Douglas Freeman set out back down the hill with Boyd, giving him a running commentary on what they must tell the media pack, which had now exploded in size due to Jorgensen's "come one and all—nothing to hide" policy, the press officer suddenly fell in the darkness. Freeman, crossing over so he could use his right arm rather than his bandaged left to help, heard Boyd moaning and cussing—unusual for the press officer. As Freeman reached down to help him up, he felt a sodden, metallic-smelling warmth, with the consistency of a firm sponge—the brain's pulse, like a thing breathing, not yet ended. Freeman kept moving, hearing bullets cracking past him as he crouched low, wondering why in hell the USVUN's bandages were all white instead of khaki.

Boyd's death told him something else, something he didn't

like at all, that some PLA sons of bitches were still in the tunnels on this the southern USVUN side of the hill. Not only were they there, but they had the balls not to sit quiet but pop up, God knows where, and were conducting sniper attacks using the momentary but brilliant light of white phosphorus and fuel air explosive against which to silhouette their USVUN targets.

When he reached the rear MUST area—Medical Unit Self-Contained and Transportable—where several reporters were stationed, most wanting to go up forward, Freeman immediately reported that Boyd had been killed.

"I'm sorry," said Marte Price, who was in the MUST, her flesh wound well on the mend.

Freeman said nothing, sitting down on a box near the MUST's long, snaking hoses that led from the refrigerator-sized gas turbine unit, unraveling his bandaged hand, now soaked in blood, the wound having opened up as he'd run down the hill, his adrenaline pumping. "Look," he told Marte as a medical corpsman came toward him. "You've been in the thick of it on the road up to Lang Son. You deserve a break." The corpsman took a pair of L scissors and cut the dressing from Freeman's wrist to his fingertips.

"You've got this dirty again, General, sir. I'll have to—"

"All right," Freeman said. "Do what you have to, but if you repeat what you're going to hear now, I'll have your hide. Got it?"

"Yes, sir."

"Right." The general waited for ten seconds or so to catch his breath, then told Marte Price that it had been reported there were American MIAs who'd been sighted in the south. She said nothing. She knew that there were still over two thousand MIAs unaccounted for. She took her notepad out.

"Rumor is," Freeman told her, "that they're yeller-bellies, crossed over, betrayed their country for preferential treatment." Marte Price remembered reading about Korea, where dozens had gone over to the Chinese, so many that the government ordered an official inquiry. "How many?" she asked him.

"I don't know. Two kingpins we know about and we want to get, but we've got a problem. Jorgensen."

"Why's he a problem?"

"You obviously don't know Dangerous Dean Jorgensen. He's a nice guy, but not too much in his top story. Career man. A yes-man. Pentagon sent him to Hanoi GHQ because he'll do whatever Washington tells him, no matter how stupid it may be in the field. He won't rock the boat." Freeman paused for a moment. "I should tell him we have to go get these jokers, make an example of them. They're supposedly helping the Khmer Rouge, trail finders on the Cambodian border, which means they were probably Special Forces, if they know the area's trails that well. Might have been with the Montagnards—hill people—before they crossed over. I don't know, but if we let 'em lead those murdering Khmer bastards to hit our left flank, out of Laos, well, neither Vinh nor I want a two-front war. But if we stop them now before— Christ!"

The corpsman was dousing the punji stick wounds with iodine.

"Go on," Freeman told him, then turned back to Marte Price. He could tell in the spill of light from the MUST hospital that she was excited by the story, her bosom rising and falling fast in the sweat-drenched khaki. He felt himself getting aroused.

"How many do you think there are, General—I mean MIAs?"

He grimaced as the iodine seeped deeper into the wounds. "I honestly don't know. Two, two hundred, who knows for sure? But we have a definite sighting. A guy—liaison officer from Ho Chi Minh City—apparently picked up their trail in a place called Dalat—hill country a ways south of here."

"General," Marte said, "I appreciate the scoop—it'd get me on CNN—but I'm not some hick in from the sticks. You're using me to bypass Jorgensen—and Washington."

"Am I?" The corpsman was putting a new bandage on.

"You bet your sweet ass you are."

"That's no way to talk."

"It's what you understand."

Freeman exhaled heavily. "All right, but it's no game, Marte." It was the first time he'd called her by her first name, and she didn't need to make a note of it. "If we can get the green light," he said, "to send a recon party to, say, the Laotian-Vietnamese border, we could kill two birds with one stone."

Marte saw where he was going, a chance to actually find two MIAs while serving notice to the Khmer Rouge to stay in their own backyard. She also saw herself in her mind's eye on the "Larry King Show" via special hookup with Hanoi. Just one MIA found would be one hell of a story amid the present inconclusive seesaw battle between the PLA and USVUN.

"All right," she said. "I'll run it if the networks okay it."

"*If?* Pull the other one, Marte. MIAs found would be the biggest story since the Oklahoma bombing."

"Think so?"

"I know so. And if you get the public demanding immediate action, our reconnaissance down there'll send a strong message to Beijing, and the Khmer will hopefully stop a second front or at least prevent a fifth column from attacking us on our left flank."

"One thing I don't get, General. What's in it for the Khmer Rouge?"

"What's always in it for those psychos? More killing? Power? Those guys are on another planet."

"Thanks," she said quietly. "How's the hand?"

"It'll be fine. If I were you, I'd bounce your story from an unnamed source off the satellite right now." She started walking away, and he caught a glimpse of her derriere in a residual stutter of flare light. He felt as hard as a rock.

She stopped, walked back to him, and spoke softly. "Is a dawn attack still on?"

He was hugely disappointed, for as she'd turned to come back, he would have sworn it was going to be to utter some term of endearment. "Yes," he answered, "it's on."

"You think you'll be able to push them back—all the way down the north slope?"

"Piece of cake," he said, and gave her a smile she couldn't see in the dark.

As she left, he berated himself for such an adolescent moment. But damn it, he hadn't had a woman for—he couldn't remember. And probably neither had young Boyd. It was ever a mystery why some men got hit and others didn't. Freeman had never believed it had anything to do with God. It was a matter of pure luck and something he called survival know-how, which had to do with knowing what to do in the absence of luck.

CHAPTER FIFTY-THREE

AS JAE CHONG staggered out of the karaoke club into Tokyo's Ginza district, the forest of neons became a blur of light, the cold night air that made his nose run doing nothing to sober him up as he made his way, smiling, through the crowds, which dutifully ignored him.

Ironically, it was the fact that he *was* drunk that allowed him to go unnoticed, as Japanese in general, while disapproving, were used to the outflow of drunks in the all-but-mandatory swill that up-and-coming young male executives took part in with their bosses after the working day. Chong, though he knew perfectly well he was drunk and had difficulty even reaching in his pocket for tissues, felt invulnerable. If any Japanese dare fix him with a disapproving stare, he was ready to stare back and stare them down. To hell with the lot of them. They had never conceded that the Second World War was *their* doing in the Pacific, all their revisionist historians busy writing tracts about how Japan was a victim. What they did in Korea was unspeakable. They deserved the atom bomb, and now the Americans were their friends. Well, sort of. Damn them all, the Japanese and the Americans and—

A policeman approached him, but Chong's air of confidence stayed with him, there being no discernible difference in his pace or manner. The policeman pointed at the pavement behind Chong. "You dropped your keys."

"What?" Chong said. Usually when they saw Koreans, they wanted to see ID. "Oh," Chong said. "Thank you," and he bowed before he bent down to retrieve the keys and two or three tissues that he'd dropped, wondering as he did so how it was that facial tissues always ended up in tight little balls in your pocket, and knowing instinctively that the cop was going to recognize him before they got much farther apart.

The air of confidence he'd had evaporated suddenly, and he turned right, into the first alley he saw, and ran down the dimly lit canyon. He turned right once more, stopping, slamming himself back hard against a cold brick wall, panting, fighting hard to slow down his heart, which was banging inside his chest so loudly he was afraid someone would hear it.

It was only a second later that Chong heard the whistle and the cop running. But would the cop turn into his ill-lit alley, or into the one on the left? He could hear the policeman stopping momentarily, could hear him breathing—or was it his own breath? Then the cop started running again. Chong saw the policeman's shadow the moment he turned right. He leapt forward then, and stuck the knife in the cop's heart. He wrenched it out, the policeman sliding down, his eyes bulging, his left hand clawing in the dim-lit air, his right trying futilely to grab the brick wall. Chong stabbed him again, leaving the knife embedded deeply in his chest.

Chong was half running, half walking, attempting to slow down his excitement. Plunging the blade into one of his persecutors had been one of the most satisfying things he'd done in a long time. But with it came fear too, gobbling up his earlier confidence, and he was afraid that when he hit the stream of pedestrians and late-night shoppers, he would have that hunted look that hunters so easily spot.

Relax, he told himself. Breathe the air deep into your stomach. That's it. No, don't force a smile or even a grin. Try to adopt that slouched, anonymous, expressionless look—meld into the crowd. Now he had two phone calls to make to confirm a rumor he had heard from the third agent in his political cell, the second agent having been Tazuko Komura, who had been killed along with all her other victims on the bullet train. The rumor he'd heard concerned the loading of supplies aboard the U.S. hospital ship, the SS *Tampa*—specifically, blood supply.

It was a common enough guide to impending war for a country's intelligence community, especially NATO and the Warsaw Pact, to keep tabs on such things as the movements of VIPs in departments of defense and associated industries and on the present state of blood supplies, any sudden increase of plasma and blood supplies a sign that hostilities were about to take place. In the case of the SS *Tampa*, it was only natural that blood supplies would have been maximized before she had set sail for the South China Sea to serve as USVUN's hospital, but Chong had wanted more telling information. Though he'd intended to make the two calls in the morning, after he had sobered up, the fright of his knowing that the death of the policeman, in addition to the JDF agents and the American he had killed, would be sparking the biggest manhunt in Tokyo's history quickly persuaded him to risk using a public phone booth to make the confirmation calls under the guise of being a furnace salesman.

The first number rang until the message machine came on. Chong hung up, watching the reflections in the Perspex bubble of the phone booth. When he dialed the second number, one of the man's children answered. No, her father wasn't at home. Could she take a message?

"No, thank you," Chong replied and hung up, conscious of two things simultaneously: that he was starting to get a pounding headache and that someone was standing behind him. He whirled about, only to frighten a teenage schoolgirl who stepped back a few paces and stared at him. He mumbled an apology and walked off, joining the crowd, where he became aware of people now looking at him, glancing down at his trousers. Holding his aching head, his gaze followed theirs and he saw a long streak of blood from his crotch to the knee of his right trouser leg. "Shit!" he groaned, and kept his eyes open for a drugstore. There, he took a plastic shopping bag to try to hide the blood, bought a package of acetaminophen gel capsules, and went over to the store's fridge for a guava juice. The druggist had a good look at him, and when Chong left the store, rang the police.

The censors in General Jorgensen's HQ in Hanoi knew they couldn't stop the story of the MIAs getting out, but they tried, under Jorgensen's instructions, in "the interests of security," by which Jorgensen meant in the interests of the Pentagon MIA and POW office, to limit the damage. Jorgensen insisted that from CNN Center in Atlanta the satellite feed, sped all over the world to millions of viewers, would consist of a two-part story: first, that turncoat American MIAs from the Vietnam War had "reportedly" been sighted in Vietnam's central highlands; second, that a column of fifty to one hundred Khmer Rouge had "reportedly" crossed the Vietnamese-Laotian border. In this way, Jorgensen hoped that in the viewer's mind the renegade MIA story would be connected with the Khmer Rouge, so that any public demand to have the MIAs found would not automatically become a call to commit U.S. forces to fighting the Khmer Rouge—with whom the Pentagon had no intention of closing.

But Jorgensen had been too clever by half, as American viewers coast to coast were jamming Washington's and CNN's fax lines, clamoring for the return of the MIAs immediately, because if they had been turncoats in 'Nam, weren't they now "allies" with the U.S. against China? The spirit of forgiveness was across the land and the call was, "Bring 'em home."

It didn't occur to anyone except Freeman, Marte Price, and a few others on the spot that "Salt and Pepper Two" might not want to go home. But Freeman didn't care. In a roundabout and unpredictable way, Marte Price's report had done what Freeman had hoped for. It galvanized U.S. public opinion to send in U.S. troops if necessary to bring out those two MIAs and the others the Vietnamese would now be hopefully willing to release—if they wanted to count on continued USVUN assistance in repelling the Chinese invasion.

Freeman immediately requested and received, albeit reluctantly, permission from Jorgensen to send in an "MIA reconnaissance force," but Jorgensen insisted that Freeman change the name from "Operation Eagle" to "Operation Homecoming."

"I don't give a damn what it's called," Freeman said on receiving Jorgensen's instruction. "It'll be carried out by a Special Forces task force of about a hundred men, assorted USVUN commandos chosen mainly from the U.S. Delta, British SAS, and the British Gurkha regiment."

"I thought you'd only need ten men," Jorgensen countered on the secure phone, the explosions of U.S. TACAIR from the carrier and Chinese triple A in the background making it difficult for Freeman to hear the commander. Jorgensen waited for a lull in the bombing. There was none and so he shouted again, asking why Freeman was sending in so many men.

"We might accidentally bump into the Khmer Rouge," Freeman answered.

"Now, Douglas, you listen to me. This is purely a recon patrol to find out about those two MIAs."

"Exactly!" Freeman yelled, not bothering to duck as enemy mortar rounds exploded in the trees around the MUST tent. "It's a reconnaissance in force!" Before Jorgensen could object, Freeman added, "I'm sure you'll agree, General, we owe it to the folks back home to give it our best shot, to rescue any MIAs. Be a feather in your cap, General."

"I don't care about feathers in my cap, Douglas."

" 'Course not, sir—" Suddenly the line was frying with static, and it was several seconds before contact was reestablished and Jorgensen made it clear that under no circumstances was his Special Forces group to engage the Khmer Rouge.

"That's a political decision," Jorgensen said, adding, "That's Washington's call."

"Of course," Freeman said, and they signed off amicably enough.

"What's up?" Cline inquired.

"I'm sending a force west. We're gonna kick ass, Major."

"You heard what General Jorgensen said, sir?"

"It was a bad line," Freeman replied.

"Witnesses," Cline said.

"Our boys'd have no option if they were attacked."

Cline paused and from habit looked about for the press aide. "If young Boyd was here, General, I think he'd point out—"

"Young Boyd was a good officer, Major. So are you, but you've got to remember you're in the field. Here we've got a chance to teach those Khmer Rouge bastards a lesson. Leave it up to the politicos, and they'd wine and dine the sons of bitches."

"It's possible we could rescue some MIAs."

Freeman looked exasperated, like George C. Scott with a cigar between his teeth. "What the hell's the matter with you, Major? *Some MIAs*—you know as well as I do that by now most of those MIAs are long dead and buried or went nuts, paddled off upriver, and shot 'emselves. 'Sides, the only damn MIAs I'm interested in right now are those two shitbags running with the Khmer Rouge. By God, I'd like to meet those two—gentlemen."

"We couldn't allow them," Cline began, "I mean, our reconnaissance force—to cross over the Vietnamese border—into Laos."

"Who said anything about crossing over into Laos?" With a cigar in his mouth, Freeman gave Cline the impression that he was grinning.

CHAPTER FIFTY-FOUR

MARTE PRICE HAD not yet returned from Hanoi to Second Army's rear HQ in Phu Lang Thuong. Even so, Pierre LaSalle knew he had to hurry if he was to find the photo of Freeman shooting one of his wounded men. There was no doubt in LaSalle's mind that such a photograph existed. There were simply too many rumors for it to be untrue, and LaSalle didn't know a photographer in the world who wouldn't keep such a shot. He'd had a duplicate key made from the one he "borrowed" from her purse in the aftermath of their lovemaking, and now he had it in the lock of the gray metal asbestos-lined box. In another second he had the lid open and was rifling through its contents: several nine-by-twelve brown envelopes filled with blowups and negatives, each print marked and numbered according to what roll of film it belonged to.

Even so, LaSalle could tell at once that there were considerably fewer photos printed than there were negatives. *"Merde!"* It would take him hours to examine every negative. There were hundreds of them. Like most professionals, she'd taken dozens of shots in an effort to capture a story she wanted to file. He was avidly searching through the box for some kind of master index but could find none, only a Sharp electronic organizer notebook. Excitedly he pressed the On button, but couldn't access it, as it was asking for a password. *"Merde!"* The Frenchman heard a noise outside, a Hummer coming to a stop, then voices, hers among them, thanking someone for the ride.

"Anytime, ma'am, *anytime!"*

Quickly, LaSalle's hands shoveled the contents of the gray box back in, closed the lid, took out the key and sat on her bed, grabbing a magazine from a small pile she had by the bed.

"What the—Pierre!"

"At last!" he said, rising from the bed, taking her hand and gallantly kissing it. "I thought you'd never come. So—how was Hanoi?"

"What are you doing here?" she asked, still in a mild state of shock.

He straightened up and looked at her with a surprised, quizzical gaze. "Waiting for you, of course. I hope you don't mind. It was raining earlier on, so I let myself in." He was still holding her hand. "You look—positively ravishing."

She took off the Vietnamese-style cap and shook her hair loose. "Raining?"

"Oh," he said, "just a little, but I have an aversion to rain." He paused, took a step back and gazed at her with mock concern. "Oh dear, you are angry with me for letting myself in."

"What? Oh, no, not really," she said. "Just surprised, I guess."

"Pleasantly, I hope?" he said, a grin passing into a wide smile.

She visibly relaxed and threw her cap over onto the bed. "I didn't know you're a fan of *Cosmo*."

"What? Oh, the magazine." He winked at her. "I only look at the pictures."

"Hmmm," she said, smiling. "I suppose you're too sophisticated to read the love advice?"

He glanced down at the pouting beauty dressed in a tight gold lamé dress and read aloud, " 'How to keep your man— once you've landed him.' " LaSalle shrugged. "I don't need advice."

"Oh," she answered playfully. "Really?"

"Really. But that's easy to say. Perhaps we had better put me to the test—yes?"

"Hmmm, maybe," she responded. "I don't mean to be unkind, but maybe you should give me time to shower. I'm perspiring like a—" She hesitated.

"Go on," he said. "Like a what?"

She sat down on the bed, shucked off her Army-issue walking shoes, and began massaging her foot. "Let's just say I'm sweating, okay?"

"Okay. I love it."

"What—perspiration?"

"In a woman, yes. How do you say it? It turns me on."

"You're sick."

"For love—yes."

"Be a sweetie and come back later. I really am dog tired."

"Dog tired?" He approved of the phrase but wasn't quite sure why it involved a dog.

"Oh, gimme a break," she said. "Let me shower and rest for a while. I'll see you tomorrow."

"Tonight?"

"Tomorrow."

"I am—" He thought hard for a moment. "—devastated!"

"You'll live," she said, and changed the subject. "How are things on Disney?"

LaSalle gave a Gallic shrug, his bottom lip saying it all. "Who knows? They are bombing the turd out of—"

"The shit," she corrected him playfully.

"The what?"

"They're bombing the shit out of the Chinese."

"No, out of the northern side of the hill to keep the Chinese in their tunnels till morning. Jorgensen is sure the Chinese will have had enough by dawn, that they will surrender in droves. Freeman—" He shrugged again. "—he's not so sure. The ones not damaged by the bombing might come out fighting."

Marte yawned. "So, can you give me a lift up there tomorrow?"

"Of course—but we won't be allowed close to Disney."

She winked at him. "I have ways."

"I know," LaSalle replied.

"Ah," she said in mock disgust. "Don't you guys think of anything but sex?"

"*La guerre* and sex!" he proclaimed, spreading his hands in the air. "What else is there, *chérie?*"

When he left, Marte began to undress, sniffing at her underwear to see if it would last another day unwashed and looking down at her khaki pants. She'd been walking through fairly tall elephant grass, yet there were no water stains on the pants. It must have been a short shower of rain Pierre had sought refuge from, or maybe he thought that being there, ready for her, she'd fall into his arms. He *was* a little conceited in that way. Weren't most Frenchmen, thinking they were the best lovers? Of course, she admitted to herself, Pierre was no slouch. Hell, neither was she. And that bit about him saying he liked women perspiring was disgusting and deliciously naughty.

CHAPTER FIFTY-FIVE

JAE CHONG SOUGHT refuge in a four-movie-theater complex off the Ginza strip, and in the flickering darkness he had time to think. The difficulty would now be how to get out and make his way home, let alone make the two calls about the blood supply shipment. He tried to remember whether there was a phone in the lobby, but he couldn't recall. He'd been moving too fast for the clerk in the box office to look down and see the bloodstains on his pants.

Inside the theater the smell of the fake leather seats triggered a smell memory in him, and momentarily he was back during his first meet with the other two agents in his cell, eleven years before. Tazuko Komura was just fifteen then, and Chong recalled that the last time he'd seen her, only a few days before she blew up the Tokyo-Niigata express, her eyes were those of an old woman, weary and frightened that the next knock on the door or the person behind you was from Japan's counterespionage service.

Chong had thought then that she wouldn't risk leaving her bag—any piece of unaccompanied luggage would immediately raise suspicion, inviting the conductors to inspect it. No, he'd known then that she'd stay with the bomb till the end. And that's what he'd do too. Only a crazy would think he had a chance, now that every cop in the Tokyo prefecture would be looking for him.

Maybe there was a phone in the rest room. The movie, which he hadn't been following, now moved from a vast field of corn and blue sky into a dark passage. He eased out of his seat then and made his way out toward the men's room, passing several teenagers and an elderly couple sitting down in the lobby waiting for the next show in the adjoining theater to start. None of them took any notice of him.

There was no phone. Another man entered, in his late sixties or early seventies, suit and tie, and stood at the urinal two down from him, trying to hit the piece of camphor ice with his stream. He'd do nicely, Chong thought, noting that the man was alone and about his size. The man had a paunch, but better too large than too small. Chong waited until the man was behind him, then struck out with his elbow, slamming him against one of the cubicle doors. Chong's right foot followed, smashing the man on the right side of his face, the force of the kick driving him straight into the cubicle. Chong went right in after him, stamping on the flush ball set into the floor, causing the toilet to roar as the old man began to push himself back from the cistern. Chong hit him with a left. The man fell again, knocking himself out on the edge of the toilet. Chong heard the washroom door open. He stepped out of the cubicle, kicked the kid he saw in the groin and smashed his right fist against the boy's temple, knocking him unconscious. Then Chong returned to the cubicle, pulled off the old man's jacket and pants, put them in his plastic drugstore bag, and walked out. A teenager, a boy, was approaching the washroom.

"I wouldn't go in there," Chong said. "Drunk's been sick all over."

The kid, frowning in consternation, nodded and backed off, not quite sure what to do. Chong disappeared back into the theater. The damn cornfields were back again, but he didn't mind; the light helped him find a seat in an empty back row, where he slipped off his trousers, put on the old man's trousers and jacket, and walked out. It was only now that he felt the bump in the jacket's left inside pocket. He took it out and saw it was thick with hundred-yen notes, a small fortune to a worker like Chong. The irony was that there were no coins for a phone. He'd have to break one of the yen notes.

Colonel Melbaine still had Alpha Company on the top half of Disney Hill's ridgeline waiting for the TACAIR bombardment to stop before they could sweep forward and force the remaining dug-in Chinese to come out or die in the tunnels.

"I ain't in no hurry," D'Lupo told Martinez.

"Neither am I," Doolittle added. "We've got a ringside seat, mate. Besides, far as I'm concerned, they can bomb till hell freezes over." Just then they heard sporadic firing behind and below them.

"That's a friggin' AK down there," D'Lupo opined, turning his head to look a hundred yards or so down the slope. Now, added to the explosions of the TACAIR bombs, they could hear the distinctive popping of USVUN M-16s, followed by the *boomp boomp boomp* of mortar rounds taking off, then the sound of a bugle.

"Fucking hell!" Martinez said, swinging his rifle from the top of the ridge, pointing it downhill instead.

"What the fuck's that, man?" a greenhorn called from the next group of foxholes on their left flank.

"It's a fucking Chinese bugle, man," D'Lupo informed him. "That way they don't have to use no radio."

"They ain't got no fucking radio," Martinez said.

"What the fuck's going on?" came another voice.

Then, whether or not it was a wild guess or whether he'd seen the outline of a PLA soldier illuminated by the burst of his Kalashnikov, Doolittle yelled, "Chinese!"

"Where the hell they come from, man?" a black soldier asked.

"From the fucking tunnels, you dork."

"Must've crept down past us, man."

D'Lupo had already switched off his safety. "Past us, crap, man. They're coming out of the tunnels at the base of the hill, so's they come right up in the middle of the fucking battalion, man, and behind us." A figure came running at them from the direction of the bottom of the hill. D'Lupo fired and brought him down with the first shot.

"No—no—no!" came a frantic, screaming voice. "Americans! Amer—"

"Flares!" a platoon lieutenant from Bravo yelled, coming up on D'Lupo's right. He didn't want to illuminate his own troops, but with one blue on blue already, he had to chance it, yelling out "Flare!" again so that all those in Alpha, Bravo, and Charlie companies at the hill's base could get their heads down and/or freeze to deny the Chinese any sign of movement. D'Lupo saw at least four or five PLA within a hundred feet of his nine-man section. Added to the noise of the air bombs there was now a cacophony of machine-gun bursts, purple and white flashes of exploding grenades, the firing of rifles, and amid them the crash of 82mm mortars, falling trees, and bushes blown sky-high, the fresh-smelling dirt from their roots coming down with other debris of stone and shattered wood on the helmets of the USVUN troops, most of whom were the Americans from Melbaine's battalion.

In the dying and flickering gray of flare light, Martinez cut down two PLA rushing his foxhole from the cover of low shrub while the American that D'Lupo had shot was being dragged by his buddy toward the foxholes of D'Lupo's Alpha Company squad.

"What the fuck you doing, man?" the buddy yelled at D'Lupo. "Oh, man!" The soldier was crying with rage. "You dumb bastards! You killed my buddy! You—"

"Shut up, man!" the black soldier said, reaching out toward the downed man's body. The soldier released his buddy and let fly with a left that missed the black soldier, causing the puncher to overbalance and fall. The black soldier grabbed the man's collar. "Listen to me, man. Your buddy ain't dead. Still a pulse, man! Get a grip on yourself. Now git down and shut the fuck up! Medic!" he yelled. "Man down—"

Abruptly, he stopped shouting. One of the shots crackling overhead had hit the wounded man's head, exploding his brain over other members of the squad. By the time the medic made it through the whistling shrapnel of a mortar round, the crying soldier's buddy was dead, Martinez dragging the two bodies in front of him for extra cover. Martinez saw a Chinese fifteen feet away coming at him with a Kalashnikov look-alike, a T-56, on full automatic, its bayonet catching flare light. Martinez and Doolittle opened up, an M-60 tearing the air to the right of them, and they saw the Chinese soldier's body stop, torso and legs lurching, an arm separating, the T-56 crashing to earth. Martinez, exhilarated by the kill, heart thumping in fear, cast a sideways glance at D'Lupo. "You all right, Lupe?"

D'Lupo was throwing up. Martinez put his hand on his buddy's shoulder. "Fucking accident, man. We all thought it was Charlie."

"Yeah," Doolittle chimed in. "What're we s'posed to do when the fuckers are amongst us? Ask for fucking ID? Son of a bitch shoulda yelled at us 'fore he started running."

"That's right," Martinez said. "Gotta put it behind ya, Lupe." But Martinez knew that D'Lupo would never be able to put it behind him.

"Wish to Christ it was me," D'Lupo said, his voice taut with anxiety.

"Aw, rats," Martinez said. "Listen, I'll tell the captain."

Doolittle saw a shadow in flare light. Was it a tree or a well-camouflaged gook or one of his own? He fidgeted with his rifle, holding his fire. "We don't have to tell anyone, Marty."

"Yeah, we do," Martinez said.

"Yeah," D'Lupo said, his voice barely audible in the bedlam erupting all around them. "Yeah—we do."

D'Lupo was right, not just about having to report his blue on blue, but in having quickly assessed what had gone terribly wrong amid the USVUN units on the long southern slope of Disney Hill. The Chinese, instead of fleeing north of the ridge atop the hill or lying low until the TACAIR bombardment ceased, had come back, streaming through the tunnels like so many ants erupting out of exit-cum-entrances at the base of the southern slope and in the middle of the Americans. There were more U.S. infantry killed by friendly fire in the predawn darkness than all those accidentally shot in the Vietnam War.

The Chinese showed no fear and no mercy, taking full advantage of the fact that, having burst forth from the tunnels—sometimes only yards from an American position—they were immune from the American artillery some miles south of the hill because of the well-known American and USVUN refusal to shell their own troops.

With dawn approaching and the end of the *Enterprise*'s bombing runs just north of Disney Hill, Freeman's forces were in sudden danger of catastrophe if the Chinese came out of their tunnels on the northern side and counterattacked. The Americans and other USVUN troops would then be caught in a "crush" movement between the Chinese who'd poured out of the southern sections of the tunnels and those who might still be alive under the bombed northern section.

Major Cline opined that he didn't see how anything could have survived the bombing on the north side. Freeman, who had been in an optimistic mood after having seen off the Special Forces, which were heading west on the mission to the Laotian-Vietnamese border, was now a man who knew Second Army and his career were a step this side of a military disaster if the Chinese counterattacked from the northern side. It was already a highly dangerous situation, with God only knew how many PLA already among his troops.

He had to do something—quickly.

CHAPTER FIFTY-SIX

FROM WHAT HE liked to call his eagle's nest, Jonas Breem, in his wine-red velour robe, gazed down on the blue early-morning reaches of Victoria harbor, pouring coffee from the sterling silver pot and pontificating on the stupidity of the Russian inventor, Kalashnikov, who had designed the most popular assault rifle in history, with millions now sold around the world, without Kalashnikov receiving a single royalty.

"Now, if the doddering old fool had done business with me," he told Mi Yin, who was just waking up, "he would have been one of Moscow's millionaires. But no, with the mind of a peasant and true revolutionary, he gave the patent to the party, and some other old fool laughed his way to the bank."

Kalashnikovs were on Breem's mind this morning because he had just brokered yet another delivery of five thousand K-74s between Moscow and Beijing for the PLA, and was reveling in his latest profit in excess of a hundred thousand dollars.

Ironically, not all of the shipment had come from corrupted Russian factory managers, but from U.S. sellers who had seen the end of the U.S. market for the assault weapon following a congressional ban on the Kalashnikovs and others of their ilk. Breem was highly amused by the certainty that many of the rifles sold to him at bargain basement prices in the U.S. were now killing Americans, or "army suckers," as he referred to them.

"You want to be a loser, Mi Yin? Join the army. All the fucking same, babe. Nowheresville. Know what I mean?"

Mi Yin murmured something, but Breem, turning from the enormous grand-view window of his skyscraper, could tell she hadn't heard, and when Jonas Breem spoke, everyone was supposed to sit up and listen. He picked up a tulip glass, still half full of champagne, and taking a step toward the huge, king-size bed, threw the silk sheets aside and emptied the contents on her crotch. "Hey, that woke you, eh?"

Her mouth open in shock, Mi Yin shot up in the bed, quickly clasping a pillow protectively against her.

"Oh, spare me the modest virgin bit," Breem said, walking back to the table. "You've been gone through more times than—hey, what are you doing?"

"Going to the bathroom," she said petulantly. "Do you mind?"

"Yeah," Breem said. "Come here." Tossing her hair back, the pillow still in front of her, she looked to see if he was serious. He was—he nearly always was.

"C'mon. Come here."

She walked toward him, around the bed, trying to affect a nonchalant air of self-assurance, but she was still clutching the pillow.

"Put that fucking thing down."

"I—I have to have a shower."

"You have it with a pillow? For Chrissake—" He snatched it away from her and tossed it on the bed. "You stink like a wino. You know that?"

"If you say so."

"I say so." Holding a cup of coffee with one hand, he gestured toward the bed with the other. "Go on, spread out. I feel like a dawn breaker."

"Can't I shower first?"

"You don't get it, do you?" He smiled maliciously.

She understood him all right. She was supposed to lie flat on her back and let him lick her.

He undid the robe and flung it away from him, pressed a remote on the bed stand and the drapes opened wider. He liked to imagine everyone was looking up at him performing cunnilingus, "pissing themselves with envy," as he put it.

"Know what I'm gonna do to you?" He waited. "You know, babe?"

"No," she had to answer, even though she knew very well what they were going to do. They'd done it enough.

"I'm gonna lick your cunt till it's dry."

"No," she said.

He knelt over her. Suddenly his hand flashed out, slapped

her hard on the cheek. Her face flushed with the pain and humiliation. "What?" he said indignantly. "What'd you say?"

"No," she repeated.

"You little bitch!" He hit her again, so hard she began to cry.

"Hey, hey!" He suddenly became solicitous of her well-being, kissing her. "You're all right, babe—it's all right." The next instant, he slid back down her breasts, her body, and buried his head between her legs, his tongue darting hungrily like a lizard's inside her, his hands bunching the sheets up beneath her to get her higher. Now he began licking her, his slurping noises like a cow with a salt lick. He stopped his breathing short, excited. "You like that, babe?"

She knew yes was the answer he wanted, but he liked her to pause a moment as if teasing him.

"Yes," she said. "It's beautiful. Don't stop."

"Love—you, babe—I—" He couldn't say all the words, he was so aroused. Panting, he raised himself onto his elbows, his head sinking beneath her shoulders like a wildebeest at water. "Know what—I'm gonna do now?"

"Yes," she said. Oh God, she'd made a mistake, but before she could recant, he was raging at her. "You stupid bitch! What do I pay you for, eh? What—"

"No," she said quickly. "No, I don't know."

"You don't know what I pay you for?"

"No, no," she said frantically. "I mean I don't know what you're going to do to me."

"Ah . . ." He was on his feet, his tumescence already subsiding. She'd fucked up the script. It had to be perfect—goddamn it.

"You stupid bitch—go on, get! Into the fucking shower, you—incompetent whore!"

Mi Yin let the shower cascade over her, cleansing her, out of his grip for a few precious moments. The things she did for Beijing. She'd had enough. If she didn't find out whether he was faking the well surveys, she'd tell Beijing he was anyway. The risk was they might want to see an original forged chart from which he'd made copies and on which potentially rich oil finds were hidden. It was a risk either way, but better be in the bad books with the party than stay any longer with this pig.

She could see him naked through the curved, bubbled, and transparent glass wall of the shower. She saw his hand on the handle, and so she quickly turned off the shower. "Turn it back on!" he commanded her. With the water falling on both of them, he pushed her against the glass-bubbled wall, and she stiffened as she felt him rubbing the bar of soap between her buttocks. He was hard again, pushing into her rectum.

"You like this, babe?"

"Yes."

"You want it deep?"

She hesitated.

"You want it deep?"

"To split me," she said.

"Atta girl."

CHAPTER FIFTY-SEVEN

CHONG RODE THE subway for the next two hours. Perhaps he could send the message to Pyongyang immediately on his own recognizance, assuming the rumor to be true. But his training told him otherwise. Like a good newspaper reporter, he had always operated by confirming such a rumor on the basis of two independent sources. And so, as he sat in the subways, his face covered by the pages of the *Asahi Shinbun*, the subterranean reflections flashing past him like memories of another life, he waited until eleven-thirty before he called the two agents.

One, an English speaker, was watching CNN's transworld service. The other had already unrolled his bed mat when the phone rang. But both told him the rumor was correct, that Freeman had had large numbers of American soldiers, stationed in Japan, called to give blood for the USVUN hospital ship USS *Tampa* heading for the Gulf of Tonkin. This was normal in such war situations, but the *Tampa* had taken unusually large amounts of Rh-negative blood aboard. Chong again called the first agent, and worked the phrase "inclement weather" into his dialogue, an instruction to the agent to forward the information immediately to Pyongyang. In turn, Pyongyang sent a most secret, class one, number-for-word, onetime pad message to its embassy in Beijing.

There is no Rh-negative blood in China. If the American general was storing it up aboard *Tampa*, it could mean only one thing: he was prepared to strike deep into China proper.

North Korea secretly but immediately pledged troops to help China if this eventuality arose, knowing that China already had enough, with a professional army of over two million. The gesture from Pyongyang, however, would be greatly appreciated and might well secure what North Korea, after her forced agreements with the U.S., needed, or rather wanted, most: to have China share as much as possible nuclear technology and/or weapons with North Korea.

CHAPTER FIFTY-EIGHT

A MILE SOUTH of Ningming, the barbed-wire enclosure Mellin and the other POWs had landed near was about two hundred yards long by one hundred yards wide. Rolls of German concertina razor wire formed another, inner perimeter five feet in from the outer rectangle. There were no buildings or tents, only ten-foot-high hills of cement bricks beneath blue plastic covers about a hundred feet apart, and between them a dozen or so pallets of bamboo either lashed or nailed together—it was difficult to tell from a distance—to look like long, fifty-by-twenty-foot rafts.

"Don't like the look of this," Murphy said. "No bloody cover. What if it starts pissing rain?"

"You'll get wet," Shirley answered.

"Yeah," Murphy responded. "So will you, luv."

"Don't call me luv."

"Sorry, Shirl."

"And don't—" She stopped. Upshut was looking their way. Danny Mellin noticed that the big barbed-wire enclosure to which they were being directed had been erected on higher ground above the marsh, and he commented to no one in particular among his fellow POWs that "we're going to have to build our own accommodation. Sooner we do, sooner we'll get cover."

"I suppose now we're bloody hostages for that friggin' strip," Murphy said, nodding north toward the airfield.

"Yes," Mellin answered. "Well, let's try to get along with them, Mike. Okay?"

"You serious? Listen, mate, if you think I'm going to cooperate with this fucking—"

"Lower your voice," Mellin said sharply. The helos were taking off. He added softly, "No point in getting them riled up for nothing. B'sides, I don't see we've got much option. They've got all the guns."

"Yeah," Murphy answered. "But we don't have to bloody well kowtow to—"

"Be quiet." It was Shirley, indicating Upshut and several other guards coming their way, dividing the POWs into squads of ten prisoners each. Suddenly the sun was swallowed by cloud, and the marshlands, the higher ground, and the airfield were cast in a depressing gray metallic light that took the sheen of the long elephant grass. It made the airfield, now caught in a shower of rain, look farther away than it really was.

A dark column of three-ton, khaki-painted trucks was coming from the airfield. When it pulled up at the edge of the marsh about three hundred yards from the POWs, an officer alighted from one of the trucks with a PLA flunky a pace behind carrying what looked like a soapbox, but which in fact was a depleted ammunition box of sturdy construction.

The major waited for the flunky to put down the box, then mounted it as if he were Alexander the Great. Though somewhat dated in his phraseology, his English was near perfect. "I am Major Chen. You are prisoners of the People's Liberation Army."

"No shit!" Murphy murmured.

"You are here to work. First you will be so good as to construct your accommodation. Thirty bodies will be in each brick house. You will be pleased to build your accommodation quickly and well. Guards will direct you."

"I'll bet," one of the prisoners said.

"You will behave well," Major Chen said. He pointed northward. "After, you will assist in enlarging Ningming airfield. Anyone, man or woman, who refuses to work will be shot." He waited some seconds for the last bit to sink in. "Questions?"

Murphy had his hand up. The major pointed to him. "Speak!"

"We're not soldiers, we're civilians. We shouldn't even be prisoners."

Danny Mellin added to Murphy's comment. "Even if you do consider us prisoners of war, under the Geneva Convention you're not entitled—"

"Quiet!" Major Chen shouted. "I want nothing about Geneva. You are in China. The Geneva Convention is bourgeois propaganda."

"When will we be fed?" an Englishman asked. "We haven't eaten."

"Rice," Chen replied, thinking the Englishman had asked him *what* they would be fed. "And some fish—perhaps."

"Medical care?" another shouted.

"The same as our soldiers," Chen said.

"That means sweet fuck-all," the Aussie said. Someone told him to shut up. "Up yours," came his response.

The major said, "Troublemakers will be shot!"

None of the POWs, including Murphy, said anything. A few of them moved uneasily.

"Build well!" the major urged. "Remember the three little piggies." Despite the tension, a prisoner, unable to contain himself, burst out laughing.

The next instant the major was walking back toward the truck, his flunky trotting after him.

"What about the three fucking piggies?" Murphy asked no one in particular.

"Do you think," Shirley Fortescue said angrily, "that it's possible for you to utter one sentence without using the F word?"

Murphy screwed up his face. "Not fucking likely."

"No speaking!" one of the guards shouted, making his way toward Mellin.

"It wasn't him," Murphy said. "It was me."

"No speaking!" The guard lifted the butt of his Kalashnikov threateningly. No one moved. The guard, though still glaring at Murphy, lowered the rifle. Finally he turned to Mellin. "You boss number one squad—yes." It was half command, half question.

"All right," Danny agreed, not seeing any alternative. Then the guard, seemingly ignorant in all other respects, made a decision that, even though he couldn't have known, was as brilliant as any that King Solomon made. He designated Mike Murphy as "boss number two squad—yes."

"No," Murphy said. "I've got no bloody intention of helping you—"

The guard didn't understand all the words, but he knew refusal when he heard it in any language, and he kicked Murphy in the shin, then slammed the rifle into his chest, knocking the Australian down. "Boss number two—yes."

"Yes," Mellin said. "He'll do—"

"He say!" the guard shouted, lifting his rifle menacingly again.

"Yeah, all right," Murphy gasped, pushing himself up. "Boss number two."

The guard gave a curt nod and grunt of approval before moving on and designating eighteen more squad bosses.

"Look," someone said, nodding toward two trucks stopping at the edge of the marshy ground, steam rising from the covered rear of each truck. The first two trucks contained boiled rice for the guards, with a helping of fish paste. The prisoners received only a bowl of rice each from the last truck, and worn-looking red plastic cups of green tea.

"And about fucking time," Murphy quipped out of the guard's earshot.

Mellin moved over to Shirley Fortescue as they were lining up for the meager rice ration. "Shirley, look, I know Murphy rubs you the wrong way, but try to ignore his bad language."

"Hmm," she answered coldly, and stopped as Upshut appeared on the scene from one of the truck cabins with a twenty-six-ounce bottle of Tsing Tao beer. He was taking the top off with his teeth, and Shirley told Mellin, "It's like trying to ignore a bad smell."

"C'mon," Mellin said. "He's okay underneath. He was the only one with guts enough to help me when I was first cap—"

Upshut was now by the tailgate of the truck, arrogantly drinking his beer. It started to rain. Upshut went back to the truck's cabin and through the windscreen watched Ningming airfield turn to a watery blur.

As Murphy's turn came to receive his dollop of rice and mug of green tea, he said, "Thank you," out of habit, and returned to where the other forlorn-looking POWs were huddled in the rain.

"You're right," a fellow prisoner said to Mellin, checking that none of the guards was looking in his direction. "Sooner we lay those bricks, sooner we get out of this damned rain."

There was a low murmur of approval, except for Murphy, who commented, "Fuck the bricks. Where the hell are we? This Ning-bloody-ming—how far's it from the Chinese-Viet border?"

" 'Bout fourteen miles," another Australian said, "as the crow flies."

"Yeah," Murphy responded. "Well, I'm a fucking crow. Anybody else? Danny?"

No one answered. More guards were headed their way, shouting at them to get up and start working. "Quickly! Quickly!"

CHAPTER FIFTY-NINE

TO AN OUTSIDER, the incoming flight of Hercules helos, containing Freeman's USVUN interdiction force—made up of volunteers from the U.S. Army's Delta Force, British Special Air Services commandos, and Gurkhas—would have seemed uneventful. For some of the older men in the IFOR, however, the flight to Da Nang was a return to the old days of 'Nam, that part of their youth that was among the most hellish and intensely felt experiences of their lives. A few among the helicopter pilots who would fly them to the Laotian-Vietnamese border would be using routes they'd used before, when Nixon had authorized secret strikes into enemy sanctuaries in Cambodia and Laos during 'Nam.

Colonel A. Berry, chosen by Freeman to command IFOR, had distinguished himself behind enemy lines in the Gulf War against Iraq when Saddam Insane had invaded Kuwait. Berry was extraordinarily confident and well trained, like the men he led. He also had a prodigious memory. It was the memory of his great-grandfather schooling him in things military that came to him now, and despite the roar of the engines and the thump of the undercarriage, he could still hear the old man telling him of the French forces at Dien Bien Phu near the northern Laotian-Vietnamese border, 160 miles west of Hanoi.

The French, tired of the hit-and-run tactics of the Communist Viet Minh forces, had wanted a pitched set-piece battle, and they got it in one of the bravest and ultimately one of the most humiliating defeats in military history. The French were thrashed. Lesson one: Berry's grandfather had told him to never ever underestimate the enemy.

The planned sabotage of the thirty-five-mile Ningming–Pingxiang–Dong Dang section of the southern rail line was called off on the express order of C in C, USVUN forces, General Jorgensen. He consulted Freeman, who in an unprecedented decision, considering his military career, agreed with the C in C that not even Delta Force or SAS, the two elite Special Forces of the United States and Great Britain respectively, should be used. No one could be used. Freeman had viewed the latest KH-14 spy satellite photos, which revealed evidence of the massive manpower of the China's People's Liberation Army.

What Beijing couldn't do because it lacked the U.S. state-of-the-art technology, it did through what any economist or military strategist would call a labor-intensive operation. General Wei, drawing on reserves of the Chengdu province's Fourteenth Sichuan army, had placed a PLA soldier every fifty yards along the thirty-five-mile rail line from Ningming to the border. In all, it came to 3,696 men, each with nothing more to do on an eight-hour shift than watch his fifty yards of track, with orders to shoot anyone who even remotely looked like a trespasser.

The first sequence of digitized satfotos relayed to Jorgensen's USVUN HQ in Hanoi had picked up about twelve hundred dots which, on magnification, showed up as soldiers on rail-line sentry duty. But it was the second and third sequence of a section of track south of Pingxiang that showed up twice as many men, alerting USVUN's HQ that there were three shifts of eight hours each during every twenty-four-hour period, so that each fifty yards of track effectively had three men assigned to it. They were not any of Wei's crack front-line troops, most of them being from militia units, but they could shoot, and each man was armed with an AK-47. Rice trains came out of Dong Dang, Pingxiang, Xiash, and Ningming once a shift to feed and water the troops.

"Damn it!" Freeman complained. "I wanted that track blown up in at least three places."

"No chance of bombing it?" Major Cline asked.

"Hell, no. The fairies won't permit it. That'd be an 'in China' attack and might have 'international repercussions.' Besides, any pilot from 'Nam days or any other war'll tell you that a damn rail track is one of the most difficult targets there is. Even if the weather's good, which it isn't, and you do manage a pinpoint hit with a smart bomb, the sons of bitches'll have it fixed and taking trains the next morning."

Freeman picked up one of the satfotos and held it beneath the magnifier. "See these squares every few miles?" he asked Cline, but didn't wait for an answer. "Their maintenance shacks have T wrenches and assorted tools. Providing the train tracks aren't actually destroyed—which they aren't in most cases, only the ties are busted—then they can re-lay the track." He dropped the satfoto on the table. "Hell, with over three thousand men stationed along there, they've got the manpower to fix up a broken length of track in a few hours."

"So what can we do?" Cline asked, fully expectant that, as usual, Freeman would have an alternate plan.

"I don't know," Freeman replied. "Meanwhile, we've got the PLA coming out of their holes all over Disney, bear-hugging it to death." By "bear-hugging" Freeman meant that the PLA were pressing right up against and among his troops so that no American or other USVUN artillery could be called in against the hill without killing as many Americans as PLA, or even more. Meanwhile, the trains from Ningming kept coming, laden with troops and ammunition.

On Disney Hill the fighting was ferocious, with no quarter given by either side. Much of it was hand-to-hand, after ammunition supplies had dwindled or when the American positions on the southern side were overrun.

It was here that American technology met its Waterloo, for unlike the Chinese, who used AK-47s, most of Freeman's troops were armed with the M-16 with grenade-launcher tubes, which won't take a bayonet. This small but salient fact was in the end responsible for what looked like an impending USVUN-American defeat on the hill, for it meant that with bayonet attached, the AK-47 became an all but unstoppable lance in the hands of the Chinese.

Martinez and Doolittle were down to their last clips. D'Lupo was firing sporadically, hesitating every few seconds to double-check his targets in the flare light, and Rhin was down to his M60-E's last two link belts of fifty ball rounds each when they, along with everybody else in the dawn's early light, heard the chopping sounds of helos in the south, coming from the direction of Bien Dong. It was some Second Armored Cavalry helos heading in from as far away as Phu Lang Thuong, most of the fighter planes from the *Enterprise* now at the end of their loiter time and leaving. More fighters were coming in to take over the TACAIR support on the northern side of Disney, but there was little if anything the fighters could do to relieve the USVUN forces on the southern side, with Chinese and Americans in such close proximity.

Only the slicks, the helos, could help. Even so, as the Hueys, like so many giant gnats, descended in battle line, they were exposing themselves to terrible danger. The helos' left-side gunners tried to pour concentrated fire from their pintle-mounted M-60s at pockets of Chinese troops, the helos on occasion themselves taking fire from some PLA troops near point-blank range as each Huey slick touched to unload troops, ammunition, and water.

Colonel Melbaine, commanding USVUN forces on the hill, seeing the situation quickly degenerating into crisis, was in brief radio contact with Freeman. The general, against every tenet of his "keep moving and never retreat" philosophy, concurred with Melbaine's decision to pull the USVUN troops back down the southern side of the hill with the intention of regrouping at the fringe of the rice paddies and extricating them from the Chinese, so that U.S. artillery could pound the southern side of the hill. But Freeman, and especially Melbaine, on the spot, knew it would be one thing to give the order for his troops to withdraw and quite another to execute the maneuver.

In a microcosm of what was happening all across Freeman's front, the withdrawal was a debacle, and in the dismal gray light of a rain-streaked dawn, confusion reigned, with General Wei's PLA troops adapting more adroitly than anyone expected to the new situation. Showing no fear, their confidence surging with their successful and unexpected counterattack via the tunnels on Disney's southern side, the Chinese stuck like glue to the retreating Americans and assorted USVUN troops.

The moment a squad of U.S. Second Army's troops withdrew down the hill, the Chinese, rather than occupying and securing the vacated positions, kept pursuing the Americans and other USVUN troops. They were not only intent on driving Melbaine's troops away from the hill but equally determined to stay among them so as to keep frustrating the attempts of Freeman's artillery to scour Chinese positions on the hill. American casualties were mounting by the minute, over eighty men already killed, many more wounded.

However, through the bedlam of radio traffic at his HQ, Freeman kept his cool and, in an order that seemed eccentrically insignificant to Major Cline and others at the time, ordered more of his Vietnamese contingent's mortars flown into the paddy area south of the hill where Melbaine was trying to consolidate his troops.

"Tell those helo pilots to land well back. I don't want those mortars unloaded too close to this free-for-all on the hill. Tell them to loiter till they see a clear area from which they can pour suppressive fire."

"Trouble is, sir," Freeman's TACAIR liaison officer said, "the chinks are staying with us all the way."

"Then have the helos loiter farther back!" Freeman said in an overriding tone of exasperation.

"Yes, sir."

"And alert I Corps Airborne. I want them ready when we need them."

Things were getting worse on the hill, and D'Lupo's squad was an example of what was going wrong. Rhin, who'd been manning the M-60 machine gun, which was now so hot it was cooking off rounds without the trigger being pulled, was hit in the left leg. It was possible for him to walk, or rather limp, but he was a man down, and Martinez was already calling in a

Medevac helo. The pilot, with the exemplary courage of their breed, was coming in low while the remainder of D'Lupo's platoon stopped their retreat to quickly form a defensive perimeter around a landing zone between sheared-off trees. The firepower of the pursuing Chinese seemed to suddenly center on the Huey. The helo, the wash of its rotors kicking up dirt, leaves, and other debris, was taking hits all over, the pilot forced to take off.

In a wind shear, the helo dropped ten feet and swung sharply to the right, its rotors colliding with a broken stand of timber. The helo rose sharply, as if by some giant hand, and then fell like a grenade to the ground, its broken rotors from the main shaft and tail cartwheeling. What was left of the main rotors decapitated an American from D'Lupo's squad, chopped up a mortar squad of Chinese, and also killed a Vietnamese machine gunner. Amazingly, the pilot suffered no more than a broken arm and severe bruising, but it slowed everyone in D'Lupo's squad.

Freeman then made a tactical decision that would not endear him to the men of Second Army, or the American public if it got out. He made it because, as he would later cryptically tell Marte Price, "That's what they pay me for." He ordered squads to keep moving down the hill. He didn't want any more calls for Medevacs because every time a slick tried to come in, every American in that sector stopped moving in order to secure the LZ, and every time the retreat slowed, it meant more men were cut down and more helos destroyed. Accordingly, Freeman ordered Melbaine to tell any wounded who couldn't be moved to stay put and do the best they could for the time being.

"We'll get to them later," Freeman promised. "By Christ, I'll go in later and get those boys out myself. But damn it, right now we have to get our forces out of there or they'll *all* be chopped to pieces."

On the hill, in the cacophony of battle, the order did not go down well. Martinez was yelling to Rhin over the sound of mixed small-arms fire, the scream of other wounded men, and the steady *woomph! woomph! woomph!* of the Hueys overhead, being told to exit the area, their M-60 machine gunners risking a burst only now and then, when there was little or no chance of hitting USVUN troops, which wasn't very often.

"Don't worry, man," Martinez called out to Rhin. "Old man

says he's gonna come in himself and get you guys out later on."

"Yeah, right," Rhin said. "Tell the old man to go fuck himself." Rhin's face was a grimace, but it wasn't from pain, the morphine shot coursing through his veins. It was sheer anxiety creasing his face, Rhin wondering what in hell would happen when the morphine wore off and Chinese were closing in. Martinez grabbed a bandoleer of 7.62mm ammo for the M-60 from D'Lupo, who wasn't doing much of anything, and gave it to Rhin, who he knew would have to feed the belt himself in the absence of boxed magazine ammo.

"Aw, shit," Martinez said. "I'm staying with Rhin." Martinez dragged the M-60 toward him and set it up so that Rhin could feed in the belt.

"Hey, soldier!" a captain from Bravo Company yelled. "Move out down this hill. Now."

"But sir—"

"Do as I fucking s—" He never uttered another word, an AK-47 round bursting his head open at the base of his skull, bone splinters and blood blown out like an aerosol spray.

"Move!" a sergeant yelled to Martinez while returning fire at the closing Chinese troops.

"Go!" Rhin said. "Get outta here—go, man!"

Martinez slapped Rhin on the shoulder. "See you, man."

"Yeah."

As the remaining American and USVUN troops ran, crawled, and moved however they could down Disney Hill, Wei's PLA swarmed onto the hill, more and more coming out of the tunnels. Their losses were staggering: over four hundred casualties in firefights and rushing tactics in less than twenty minutes, and still they kept coming, many of the retreating Americans unable to fire weapons because the M-60 barrels, despite new nonferrous lining, were overheating.

The Chinese, over two thousand of them now on the hill, kept pressing the attack, which, to the delight of General Wei in his HQ just south of Pingxiang, was fast becoming one of the most humiliating routs in U.S. military history. In the southern Chinese dialect, Wei's and Wang's staff were referring to the Americans as "chicken chow mein."

The Americans, nearing the base of the hill and trying to put as much distance as possible behind them so artillery could be called in, fought desperately to consolidate their position before the entire rout became a massacre, the spearhead companies of Wei's Chengdu army moving down the hill, killing every American left behind.

Some Americans and other USVUN soldiers now out of ammunition put up their hands in surrender. One of them was Private Rhin. As he sat there, his hands up, he saw one Chinese soldier approaching him cautiously as if melting in a mirage, the heat haze caused by the red-hot barrel of his M-60, which had just jammed. His hands up higher, Rhin sought to reassure the PLA soldier, "No booby traps, man, I'm clean." Rhin knew that the Chinese soldiers, more of them nearing his position now, couldn't understand the words, but he hoped they'd understand his tone. "I'm safe, man—no booby traps."

The Chinese nearest Rhin looked down at the big American soldier as if he had never seen a black man before, then bayoneted him through the heart.

Under Wei's express orders, no prisoners were taken. Prisoners in combat were a nuisance and could cost you valuable rice rations and water.

Marte Price tried to report the battle of Disney Hill as objectively as she could, telling of Freeman's controversial order that had ended in tragedy for the men like Rhin left on the bloodied hill, but CNN was carrying the story under the news headline as FREEMAN'S FOLLY.

Pierre LaSalle didn't even pretend to be objective. His hardhitting piece for *Paris Match*, with photos, accused Freeman of ineptitude and heartlessness while at the same time implying that the men of the U.S. Second Army were cowardly and, from a strictly military point of view, had deserved to lose and be swept off Disney Hill.

CHAPTER SIXTY

AT THE NINGMING airfield's POW camp, Mike Murphy, Danny Mellin, Shirley Fortescue, and the other assorted two hundred prisoners taken either from the Spratly Island claims or oil rigs were waking up from a wet, cold night spent under badly leaking, rat-holed tarpaulins.

"In line!" came a guard's instruction.

The straggly line of worn, tired faces, bodies shuffling toward the feed trucks, looked more like a column of refugees, some who had caught cold in days and nights since they'd been captured, coughing and sneezing, unwittingly spreading their germs among their malnourished companions.

For Mellin, the problem in trying to oppose the Chinese order that they all become "construction workers"—by which the Chinese really meant construction slaves—to first build their own huts to house them, was in trying to organize his fellow prisoners. With his military background, Mellin had immediately seen that even with the simple problem of getting their rice and tea ration, what was needed was armylike organization instead of having them all moving about at random like lost sheep.

The ration this morning was the same as before: a wooden bowl of white, sticky, boiled rice and a mug of tepid water with only the faintest aroma of tea.

"Jesus," Murphy said, pulling a threadbare blanket about him as he received his ration. "Looks like they just passed the fucking tea bag over this tub of—" The cup flew from his hand, knocked away by the server's ladle, an AK-47 butt striking him hard on the head and shoulder, sending him sprawling on the wet, muddy ground, his rice bowl upturned. The guards about the rice truck burst out laughing as they watched the

Australian scrabbling in the mud to get the rice back into the bowl. He asked for another cup of "tea." He was refused.

"Bad man!" one of the guards said. Murphy had to be content with picking out the mud from the rice and using his plastic POW cup to catch some of the runoff water from the tarpaulins to drink and to clean the rice as best he could.

"He'll never learn," Shirley Fortescue told Danny Mellin as they congregated with the other prisoners under their tarpaulin.

"No," Danny agreed, his tone, unlike Fortescue's, one of compassion, which she thought was misplaced.

"Well," she said, "he asks for it, doesn't he? I mean, I don't like what these bloody Chinese are doing either but—well, what I'm trying to say—"

"Yeah!" said Murphy, who had been walking toward them in the crowd. "What *are* you trying to say, Shirl, about these *bloody* Chinese?" Despite his anger of a moment before, Murphy was now grinning like a victorious teenager, perhaps, Shirley thought, because the Australian had caught her using a swear word.

"What I'm saying, Mr. Murphy," she answered stiffly, "is that one has to get on with people."

"People," Murphy said sneeringly. "These aren't bloody people, sweetheart. They're our enemy."

"You know what I mean!"

"Yeah, I know," the Australian responded, loudly enough, Danny thought, to bring the guards down on him again if he wasn't careful. "Yeah, I know what you mean," Murphy continued, his voice growing louder. "You mean we should suck up to 'em, don't ya? Kiss their ass. Well, not me, sis."

"Hold it down," someone said. "Upshut's coming our way."

Either Upshut hadn't heard Murphy or was too busy to want to do anything about it.

"In line," he shouted. "Quick! Quick!" He laboriously informed them through the camp interpreter, Comrade Lu, that they must build the mud huts in one day. "No huts, no big covers." He meant no more tarpaulins to sleep under. "You understand?"

"Yes," Mellin said, speaking as leader for his squad of ten.

After Upshut had gone, Murphy said, albeit quietly this time, "A hut in a day. No fucking way, mate."

"Why not?" Danny said. "Twenty of us. We've got the concrete bricks. They've been kept dry under their tarpaulins. We can start now."

"Oh, can we?" Murphy answered, looking from Mellin to Shirley Fortescue. "Listen, bud, you've been listening to this sheila too much. I thought the whole idea wasn't to help the chinks, but to break out if we could. Fourteen miles to the border, mate."

"I never said anything about escaping," Danny said. "Besides, it'd be a lot longer than fourteen miles. That's in a direct line."

Murphy, his blanket still wrapped around him, glared at the American. "What the hell's the matter with you, Yank, eh? Day I helped you up, I thought I was picking up someone with guts."

"Be quiet," someone else said.

"Yes," another hissed. "You'll get us all in a jam."

"In a jam!" Murphy said loudly, his eyes bright with anger. "You fucking dodos, don't you understand? Didn't you listen to Uncle Lu? You're already *in* a fucking jam. They want you to build your own friggin' prison to lock you up in, and you're just gonna do it." The Australian's head was jerking left and right as if suddenly overtaken by a nervous tic.

"What would you do?" Shirley Fortescue asked him. "Refuse and get shot?"

"No, but—" He stopped as if he'd forgotten the question, his head again in a nervous tic, less violent than it was a minute before, but still there. "I—I wouldn't help 'em," he said. "You know, go-slow tactics."

"For Chrissake," someone said. "Lower your voice." Murphy tried, but was only partially successful, his voice rising and dropping without any warning or apparent control. "Accidents," he blurted out. "Y'know—make the mortar too wet—y'know."

People edged away from him. They all knew what they'd get for any kind of sabotage. The Australian wasn't thinking clearly.

"Listen up." It was Danny. "Before we start, I want to make a request. A guy in one of the other groups is pretty ill. Kept him on one of their ships. Hardly fed him at all. I'm asking everybody to save a spoon or two of rice per meal over the next few days. Give it to me. Okay with everybody?"

There was a murmur of assent, however reluctant they were to share their already meager rations.

"How bad is he?" Shirley asked Danny.

"What? Sorry, what was that?"

"How ill is he?" she asked.

"Well, without the extra rice, he probably won't make it."

Shirley moved off toward their brick pile, asking no more questions. Danny Mellin was glad. He'd just told them all a blatant lie, but he figured that by the time anyone found out, he'd have gotten the rice he wanted.

CHAPTER SIXTY-ONE

WITH HANOI 150 miles away to the east, and the refueling depot at Ban Lot behind them, the command helo and the three big "bananas," or Chinook troop carriers, carrying Freeman's interdiction force, two Huey gunships on the flanks, approached the Laotian–Vietnamese border in a mist that wreathed the hills and filled the valley around Dien Bien Phu.

The joint U.S.–British Ranger/SAS/Gurkha Special Forces group was under the overall command of U.S. Army Colonel Berry, with British SAS Major Anthony Leigh-Hastings and U.S. Ranger Captain Walter Roscoe, Jr., assisting. The three-platoon-sized force had been ordered by Freeman to go in four miles south-southwest of Dien Bien Phu along the valley floor to a point one mile west of the Ban Cong Deng road junction near the southern end of the valley.

Their secret mission was to interdict the road that wound eastward out of Deo Tay Chang, a small Vietnamese settlement only a mile east of the Laotian border. It was hoped the Special Force would engage and stop the infiltration of any Khmer Rouge–led enemy column before the latter could reach the Ban Cong Deng junction and have the luxury of either heading north to Dien Bien Phu, just inside Vietnam, or east, farther into Vietnam.

As the big Chinooks descended into the mist, their *woka, woka, woka* sound beating the air, curdling the mist, the thirty men in each helo gripped their weapons and their bulletproof Kevlar vests, which most of them had been sitting on against the prospect of losing their genitals from ground fire, a fear they shared with all heloborne troops.

The two M-60s on each of the two gunships opened up, pouring down what the gunners hoped would be suppressive fire in the event that, contrary to Green Beret recon team info, the Khmer-led insurgents had already reached the Ban Cong Deng junction east of the landing zone.

The moment the first helo landed, Rangers and SAS fanned out forward and aft of the Chinook to establish a fire perimeter, the rotor wash sending shivering waves of water in a nearby paddy, rice stalks bending in the fearsome wind and howl of the man-made storm. There was no return fire, and soon all three LZs were declared secure. The helos disappeared into the mist, the chopping of their rotors growing fainter. Suddenly, as the jungle swallowed up the last of the ninety commandos of the Ranger/SAS/Gurkha force, it was as if nothing had ever disturbed the stillness of this remote valley where, over four decades before, the French had met their modern Waterloo.

"Now the tricky part's over," Major Leigh-Hastings said. "The hard part begins." He meant setting up ambush in terrain where the difference between being the hunted or the hunter could be a matter of seconds, the movement of a leaf, the crack of a twig.

CHAPTER SIXTY-TWO

IT WASN'T UNTIL some of the incoming wounded—not those on Disney Hill, but from the accompanying or western left flank attacked by Wei's troops—were brought in by the

Medevac helos to the MUST that the extent of the wounds among USVUN troops became known.

In the heat of the battle, few but the medics had noticed that enemy bullets, not shrapnel, had been splitting open the Kevlar bulletproof vests. By the time the wounded were on the operating table, the vests had been taken off, revealing horrific chest and head wounds caused by just one bullet. It was almost impossible to stop the bleeding, and there were hundreds of minute, razor-sharp pieces.

The doctors at first assumed the wounds had been caused by mortar shrapnel. But it wasn't a surgeon or medic who would eventually solve the problem, it was Freeman, who had flown in via chopper from his HQ at Phu Lang Thuong after hearing about the new kinds of wounds. He'd also heard that the PLA had been firing on the Medevac choppers, using the Red Cross insignia on the nose and side as aiming points.

"That's nothing new," he said, thinking aloud. "We'll have to have a fighter escort for the most serious cases, after they've been patched up and sent on to our hospital ship in the gulf." He turned to Cline just as they were landing. "Bob, while I look at the sitreps, you get me X rays of some of our boys with those wounds everyone's talking about."

"Yes, sir."

"And Bob, bring me actual fragments."

"Yes, sir."

As Freeman exited the chopper in its dust storm, he instinctively ducked and returned a salute to a colonel of artillery whose expression told him something else had gone wrong.

"What is it, Colonel?"

"Sir, we're losing more men on the hill."

"Why? There shouldn't be any of our men left on the hill. I gave an order to withdraw."

"I know, sir, but some of the guys stayed with the wounded. They're getting cut to pieces by PLA mortars, and I don't want to send arty in on them—kill our own men."

"Colonel," Freeman said, "if we don't move those damned Chinese off the base of that hill, we'll have to withdraw farther back into those goddamned paddies, and once we get stuck in them, we'll never get out. You listen to your FAC, use H.E. and fire for effect." He meant for the colonel to listen to his forward air controller, who was up ahead in a Bird Dog 1 or Cessna, flying around at ninety miles per hour within range of PLA small-arms and triple A fire. If the colonel fired for effect, laying the high explosive down where the FAC told him, then hopefully the American arty of 105mm and 155mm would hit pockets of Chinese rather than U.S. and other USVUN troops.

Even so, both men knew some fellow Americans would get hit. But they also knew that if U.S. artillery wasn't used on the position, then the Chinese swarming down the hill would kill even more Americans in the paddies. Now the artillery colonel became the next son of a bitch that day as Americans died on the Loc Binh front, no matter that the FAC-directed arty, given the battle conditions, was as accurate as anyone could have hoped for. Freeman took full responsibility for the order, and earned the unenviable reputation of being the first American commander since World War II to call down artillery fire on his own men. Only the Chinese did that.

In just over seventeen minutes of vicious close-in fighting, when attackers and attacked both ran out of ammunition and the fighting became hand-to-hand, as it had earlier farther up the hill, the momentum of the PLA attack faltered. In those seventeen minutes, which seemed like seventeen hours to two dozen or so American and USVUN troops, Freeman's artillery stopped the Chinese advance, giving his men at the paddies' edge time to get behind the long dike and set up defensive positions as slicks, Huey helos, flew in and dropped off ammo, Baby Ruth bars, and water supply.

It began to rain then, but not before the quiet, confident tone of the forward air controller came on. "Armored column heading south approx two miles—I say again two miles—from Pingxiang."

"How many tanks?"

"Can't say. Saw five before mist closed in."

"Type?"

"T-72s."

That meant Soviet main battle tanks—top of the line—sold to the PLA after the breakup of the Soviet Union.

Freeman ordered in strikes from the carrier *Enterprise*. "This," he said, "is where we show them what American technology can do. Right, Bob?"

"Yes, sir," Cline said unenthusiastically. "If you say so."

Freeman turned on him. "What the hell's the matter with you? Can't take the heat?"

There was silence between the two men, despite the usual mind-numbing noise of artillery screaming overhead and the ceaseless babble, some of it frantic, from the remaining men trapped on Disney.

"If I hadn't called in arty," Freeman thundered, "the Chinese would be here now. We would've been pushed so far back from that hill we'd be in retreat all the way to Hanoi."

Bob Cline nodded.

"Damn it, Major—if you're not up to it, get out of the kitchen!"

It was Freeman's unapologetic tone that shocked Cline out of his uncertainty. "Yes, sir—I'll be fine."

"You bet your ass you'll be fine—a hell of a lot finer than those boys on the hill."

"Boys?" It was Marte Price, the press pool's designated hitter for the day. "Aren't there some women combat pilots, General, aboard the helos and the carriers—"

"See the front door of that tent?" Freeman snapped.

"Yes."

"Well, that gender shit stops there. I haven't time for it. You understand?"

"Yes, General." She'd never seen him so angry before, and he almost never swore in front of women.

"If you want a story," he shouted over the noise, "look at these." In his hands were tiny shards of steel that Cline had brought him earlier.

"What are they?"

"Fragments from what's called an APBR—armor-piercing Black Rhino round—made in Alabama out of carbon-based plastic. Has what they call a polymer tip. Explodes into splinters inside the body. Wounds are huge—six inches in diameter. If it hits a bulletproof vest, goes right through. Wounds are even bigger. It's banned in the States."

"Then where do the PLA get them?"

"Hong Kong probably. That's the usual source, so the CIA tell us. Who, exactly, we don't know, but we're sure as hell trying to find out."

"Is it that serious?" Marte asked naively.

"*Serious?* Hell, PLA using that ammunition is equivalent to them having an extra regiment to throw at us. And never mind the effect on morale. It's like a wildfire among the troops. Makes everyone hold back, and on top of this withdrawal—" Freeman stopped. "Withdrawal" and "retreat" weren't part of his normal vocabulary. They stuck in his throat. In that moment Marte Price discovered something about Freeman that reminded her of what she'd heard about Patton. Here was a general, a warrior whose ferocity and élan in battle were legendary, whose code of honor drew a line against this advance in technology, the use of the armor-piercing Black Rhino bullets.

"In a wound caused by a Black Rhino round," he added, "it's almost impossible to staunch the bleeding. It's horrendous."

"You're an anachronism, General," Marte said admiringly. "I thought all soldiers would use anything—"

"No," he interrupted. "Otherwise we'd be using nerve gas, another monstrosity. Besides, the need for extra blood on hand is doubled once they start using Black Rhino—tears flesh to pieces. Each fragment is like a razor, a separate wound."

"General," Marte responded. "I have pretty good contacts in Hong Kong. If you like—"

"I thought," Freeman cut in, "that you're to report on the military, not help us."

"It'd be a good story," she said.

"One good turn deserves another," Freeman responded, and they both realized they had compromised their professional integrity and that neither felt guilty.

"General." It was Major Cline, and he clearly had more than the impact of Second Army's retreat on his mind. "Could I have a word in private, sir?"

Blushing, Marte Price quickly left the HQ tent.

"What's up, Major?" Freeman asked him.

"Sir, word's got out about our Special Forces group near Dien Bien Phu, and there's hell to pay in Washington—and the rest of the country. Larry King's asked the head of the Joint Chiefs to appear on his show."

"Shit!"

"That's only half of it, sir. *The New York Times* is on to it. They're going to run an editorial on it tomorrow. They're comparing you to Nixon when he ordered the secret bombing of Cambodia and Laos during 'Nam."

"Well, they've got that right," Freeman said, unabashed. "I mightn't have agreed with everything he did, but by God he was right to hit those Commie staging areas. Bastards would slip across into 'Nam, shoot up our boys, then run back over the border."

"Trouble is, General, in Washington the Democrats and some Republicans are charging that seeing there's no big enemy troop movements out of Cambodia or Laos so far in this war—"

"That I shouldn't have sent in any Special Forces—until we were attacked. Right?"

"That's more or less it, sir. They're saying that democratic nations have an obligation not to indulge in preemptive strikes."

"Tell Israel that," Freeman said. "Goddamn it. If the Israelis had waited to be attacked en masse before they took action, there wouldn't be an Israel by now."

"We're going to have to respond, General."

"Goddamn it. It's bad enough I've had to pull Melbaine's boys back to the damn paddy fields. Now I have to fight our own press."

Cline knew all about that, but his job wasn't to agree with the general, it was to hit him "in the teeth," as Freeman had once put it, "with the bad news as well as the good." "We're going to have to respond, General," he repeated, his tone as demanding as his rank would allow.

"I know," Freeman said thoughtfully, if hastily, looking at the huge map. His steel-blue eyes followed the winding course of the Laotian-Vietnamese border around the splotch of green that marked the eleven-mile-long valley running north and south of Dien Bien Phu and Ban Cong Deng.

"Call a press conference in an hour. We won't restrict it—let in every son of a bitch in Hanoi who wants to come. I'll straighten it out."

Cline shook his head. "It's going to be tough, General. We've got every longhaired weirdo yapping on this one. We've even got the environmentalists' lobby charging that you're going to use some chemical like Agent Orange to defoliate the border areas 'round Dien Bien Phu and Ban Cong Deng. They're afraid of hurting the trees."

Freeman gave him a crooked grin. "Maybe I should let Marte Price take a photo of me hugging a goddamn bush!"

"She'd be the last one I'd give anything to."

Freeman looked puzzled. "Why not?"

"Well, we can't prove it, but our G-2 section suspects her of leaking our Laos Special Forces op. Not directly, but via that French shit, LaSalle. Scratching one another's back. Rumor mill has it that he's screwing her."

Freeman's facial muscles knotted. "Damn it, I gave her info

about the Rhino rounds. She could roast us on an open spit with that one."

"How?" Cline asked.

"I told her it affected morale. She could say—"

"Our boys are backing off," Cline cut in.

"Exactly. Damn—"

"Sir?" It was a call from the operations table. Melbaine's men, those that were off, were now all in the rice paddy, coming under mortar fire. The field was turning into a churning sea of muddy water as the PLA's 82mm mortar rounds exploded, throwing up geysers of rust-colored water, green rice stalks, and shrapnel from the mortar shells. Meanwhile, various small-arms fire, mostly AK-47s, peppered the turbulent paddy. Several bodies, two Americans and a Vietnamese, were floating bumpily in the wash.

Freeman called for arty to straddle the narrow margin of ground between the rice paddy and Disney's apron of high ground, now swarming with more PLA reinforcements coming from the tunnels. The general's request was answered in less than forty seconds with a creeping barrage of H.E. that soon covered Disney's southern slope in a dust storm of dirt and pebbles that, swept southward by the wind, fell like hail on the embattled USVUN forces on the edge of the paddy.

Anticipating the "blind pause" this would create for both sides, unless they wanted to waste ammunition by firing at nothing in particular, Freeman ordered in a brigade, three thousand men of the Third Airborne Cavalry Division, which had landed in Hanoi only a few hours before.

It was a sight that impressed even the old battle-hardened vets of both sides in 'Nam, 157 slicks dotting the gray metallic sky in an aerial armada carrying the three battalions.

"Three thousand won't be enough to stop them, General," Melbaine shouted into his cellular field phone.

"I agree," Freeman growled back, "it isn't going to stop them, it's going to push the sons of bitches back into China where they belong. You hang on, Colonel. I'm about to give you a lesson in logistics!"

"Arrogant son of a bitch," Melbaine said, collapsing the phone, slipping it into his pocket. "How the hell's he going to push 'em back? We're already running out of ammo, and the Airborne can only bring in enough for themselves, never mind us."

"He's got Hanoi fever!" a Vietnamese major nearby suggested.

"He's nuts," Melbaine's second in command said. "Crazier'n a two-bit watch."

All that Freeman had meant by a "lesson in logistics" was that the three battalions, under his express orders, were also equipped with Vietnamese 82mm mortars.

CHAPTER SIXTY-THREE

THE SPECIAL FORCES contingent that made up the interdiction force under Colonel Berry had now crossed the border into Laos, reaching the "fan stem" where two trails coming out of Laos converged. There, the IFOR contingent split up into three columns: Echo, commanded by SAS Major Leigh-Hastings; Foxtrot, U.S. Colonel Berry's men; and Delta, led by U.S. Ranger Captain Walter Roscoe.

The plan was for two columns, Echo and Foxtrot, to go farther in along the two trails that eventually spread out to make a fan, or smaller trails, and lie in ambush waiting for any enemy main force en route to Vietnam's western flank.

The remaining column of thirty men, Delta, under Roscoe, would wait back at the border in order to net any enemy survivors of an ambuscade or any smaller patrols that either Echo or Foxtrot would let pass rather than fire upon, and so betray its presence to an oncoming enemy force.

Normally, such ambushes would consist of no more than ten men, but intelligence, both from aerial pix and ground movement sensors dropped by air, indicated company-sized enemy activity, and the point of Freeman's three Special Forces interdiction columns was not simply to verify such activity and then call in air strikes, but to engage the enemy on the spot and wipe them out. However, as Echo's and Foxtrot's security teams, a pair of soldiers from each column, went uptrail and downtrail about seventy yards from the selected ambush site, the fact of their general presence in the area was already known to Salt and Pepper Two—the incursion into the fan-shaped jungle area of about thirty square miles west of the Vietnamese-Laotian border was already on page one of *Paris Match*, under the byline of Pierre LaSalle.

Immediately, General Wang ordered a six-hundred-man battalion of the elite Chengdu-based paratroop commandos south from Mengzi to Dien Bien Phu. Anticipating such a response, and despite the international uproar over his having ordered the Special Forces contingent into Laos, Freeman nevertheless asked Jorgensen in Hanoi to authorize interdiction by U.S. fighters aboard *Enterprise*. Jorgensen refused—point-blank. Now his career was on the line as well as Douglas Freeman's.

Normally a placid man, Jorgensen, with visions of a court-martial foremost in his mind, was trying to control himself. "General," he said, gripping the phone so hard his knuckles were white, "you don't seem to grasp the seriousness of the situation."

"Sir," Freeman cut in, "I understand it very well. The position of ninety of my best men has been compromised by a goddamn frog, and I want to give them air interdiction and TACAIR support."

"I don't mean the military situation," Jorgensen shot back. "I'm talking about the political fallout. Everybody in Washington and at the U.N. in New York is up in arms about you widening the war. It's the nightmare of 'Nam again. Kennedy, Nixon, LBJ—all widening the war in the belief they were going to end it."

"End it?" Freeman riposted. "By God, I'll end it easy enough. You give me an A-bomb—which I know we have on the *Enterprise*—and I'll end it in half an hour. Drop that baby on Ningming and we'll have peace talks within twenty-four hours, guaranteed. I'll turn Ningming into the world's biggest fishpond."

The moment he said it, Freeman wished he hadn't. But before he could retract it, his normally calm-spoken superior had blown a fuse. "You're mad. You're insane. I'm relieving you of command of Second Army as of now. You hear me?"

"General—"

"You hear me?"

"I hear you, sir."

The phone line went dead.

Cline had heard enough of the conversation—Jorgensen yelling—to know it was very bad news. Freeman, who had put the phone down slowly, left his aide in no doubt. "I've been relieved. By God, I—" He didn't finish the sentence.

Cline, though shocked, had pressing business at hand. But with his boss no longer in command, it was confusing all around.

"What is it?" Freeman asked.

"Sir, we've got Arty pouring fire down on Disney's south side. You want our boys to wait for the Airborne?"

"Hell, no. Soon as Arty clears a sector, I want us and the other USVUN troops to occupy it. Soon as we have high ground cleared, we take it. That way the Airborne with my mortars will have LZs for the choppers. Besides, the more dirt we can stir up with Arty, the better. Tricky for the helo jockeys, I know, but it's as good as smoke cover. Hell, our boys should be using smoke anyway."

"Wind's blowing north, General. It's taking smoke away from us. Covering the enemy."

"Well, hell, we can't have everything. Anyway, maybe it'll hide the upcoming choppers." Freeman paused. "What time you make it, Major?"

"Fifteen twenty hours, General."

"Then I suggest you record receiving my order at fifteen hundred."

Cline looked at him, nonplussed.

"*Before* I got fired," Freeman explained. "Might as well cover your ass."

"Yes, sir. But what about the press conference in Phu Lang Thuong? There must be near a hundred reporters waiting there."

"What about them?"

"Well, sir, I mean are you going to tell them you've been relieved?"

Freeman shrugged, thinking it over. He sighed, shaking his head. "Hell, no. I want to try to help my boys in those IFOR columns. I sent them in there, and now, with that prick LaSalle telling the whole world where they are, least I can do is try to help 'em—shift world opinion."

"Beg pardon, General, but how in hell are you going to do that?"

"Watch me," Freeman said.

"Yes, General, but what if Jorgensen finds out about this press conference you're about to give?"

"We tried to contact him for permission, didn't we?"

"Lines down?" Cline suggested.

"Whatever you like, Major."

It was amazing, Cline thought. Freeman had just been fired, and the son of a bitch was back on the attack.

The general noticed Cline's astonishment as the major opened the tent flap on the way to the Hummer that would take them to the press conference center in Phu Lang Thuong. As they got aboard the high-clearance Hummer, which had a bad time of it bouncing over the potholed road, the general glanced at Cline. "Bob, I want your computer boys to dig up State Department policy memos vis-à-vis 'Hot Pursuit.' "

"Across borders?" Cline asked.

"Specifically across borders," Freeman said. "Those fairies in Washington think I'm a grunt general. Well, I am—damn proud of it too—but I do my homework, Major. By God, I do. Remember what Frederick the Great said. *'L'audace, l'audace, toujours l'audace!'* " Audacity, audacity, always audacity!

Freeman knew that once he mounted the press center's improvised podium—a wooden slat tent base—he would see a phalanx of hands shoot up. One of them would belong to Marte Price, and another to Pierre La Prick Salle. Both reporters, he knew by now, were politically left. And after blowing the Special Forces contingent in Laos, La Prick Salle probably wouldn't think he'd take any questions from him.

Echo and Foxtrot column's two pairs of security teams made several listening halts along the site chosen by Major Leigh-Hastings for a possible ambush. The job of these four soldiers was to alert the rest of their columns as to the size of any enemy force coming either way. Everyone expected any enemy columns to come from deeper in Laos, to the west, but the possibility of an enemy force returning from the east, from action in Vietnam, also had to be considered.

The security teams for Foxtrot column were in position within another quarter hour, with the Echo security teams three miles south of Foxtrot. About twenty-five minutes later both Echo's and Foxtrot's leaders moved in their assault teams of twenty-five men each into their positions along each trail of the fan, setting it up for ambush. The remaining man in each of the two columns of thirty men was now free to command.

It would be these two men who, staying still for the next twenty hours, like the rest of their column, would take up the best ambush position for overall command of their respective columns. It would be their order, and theirs alone, that would unleash fire should the Khmer Rouge–led columns come their way.

Crescent-shaped, two-and-a-half-pound claymore mines, each loaded with over six hundred explosive embedded steel balls, were set up in the undergrowth of the triple canopy jungle along one side of the trail. The camouflaged twenty-five-man assault team sat behind the protective sixty-degree arcs of the mines, the assault teams making "damn sure," as Commander Berry ordered, that each convex side of each claymore embossed with FRONT, TOWARD ENEMY, was pointing away from the ambush column, each column's leader in radio link with both security teams at the two ends of the 250-yard stretch of trail.

If a man defecated, he did so by squatting over a Glad bag—no paper was to be used—and the bag would not be buried, lest it be found and dug up by wild animals, creating the possibility of revealing the column's presence. The excrement, like everything packed in, would have to be packed out, for if the hoped-for ambush did not happen for either Echo or Foxtrot, USVUN might want to return to the already scouted sites—if Freeman had his way. Because of the radio silence imposed outside their local radio link, neither Echo, Foxtrot, nor Delta columns had any information about the outside world in general, or Freeman in particular.

The men in Delta column under U.S. Captain Roscoe were waiting in the marsh area around Ban Cong Deng, six miles south-southwest of Dien Bien Phu. Without exception, every one of the thirty-man Special Forces column was covered in leeches sucking the blood out of them. With no smoking allowed, there was no way to burn them off, and the difficulty with using insect repellent was that it had an odor the Khmer Rouge guerrillas could detect amid all the other smells of the fetid swamps.

"Mr. LaSalle," Freeman said, smiling, pointing at the French correspondent.

LaSalle was caught off guard, but after an initial "Ah" and a pause to collect himself, he asked, "General, is it true that USVUN Special Forces under your command are now in action against elements of the Khmer Rouge—across the border in Laos?"

"No, Mr. LaSalle, that's not true," Freeman replied. "We've been patrolling close to the border, that's certainly true, but we're under strict orders from the U.S. State Department and the President not to engage the enemy in Laos, Cambodia, or anywhere else unless such action comes under the explicit conditions of the State Department's policy of 'Hot Pursuit.' "

"What's that, General?" yelled another correspondent, an Australian.

"Policy of hot pursuit, sir, is the policy whereby if American troops are on border patrol—which they are, to protect the USVUN left flank—and are fired upon by Khmer Rouge–led guerrillas, for example, or by anyone else, we are free to pursue the attackers until we establish what we consider a 'safety margin' at the border."

"How come we haven't heard about this before, General?"

Freeman seemed astonished by what he was clearly indicating was the naiveté of the question. "No one's asked me!" he said.

There was a smattering of laughter. Pierre LaSalle was waving his hand frantically. Freeman let him wave and took another question from a television reporter. "General, are you denying there are USVUN Special Forces in Laos?"

"Yes. But if they are there, then they've clearly crossed the border because of the increasing concern we have about Khmer Rouge–led forces violating the neutrality and environment of Laos."

The assembled correspondents knew well enough what Laotian neutrality was, but this was the first time they'd heard about U.S. military action to help the environment. Freeman answered with such audacity that it even sounded logical to Cline, who knew damn well the general was making it up as he went along.

"The environment, ladies and gentlemen, as Mr. LaSalle rightly stated in his report for *Paris Match*, is of prime concern to us all. We, meaning the U.S., committed, in my opinion, a disastrous mistake when we used Agent Orange here during that unhappy war. As well as defoliating large tracts of rain forest and jungle, it killed much other flora and fauna. Now of course we realize the acute dangers to flora and fauna all around the world. In Laos the Khmer Rouge–led guerrillas are stripping—*stripping*, ladies and gentlemen—by slash and burn the valuable and ancient teak forests to smuggle the teak across the border to sell to Chinese traders who, quite frankly, don't care how much slash and burn goes on or how much damage is done to these precious virgin forests."

The general paused. "By God, I'm proud of any American—and any USVUN member—who is prepared to do battle with these marauders who think they can plunder the rain forests of Southeast Asia. The Chinese are voracious, ladies and gentlemen, voracious in their appetite—offshore as well as inland. The Southeast Asian nations want to share ocean resources, for example, but what does Beijing want? It *demands* all the resources of the South China Sea. It wants all the resources it can lay its hands on." He paused, again taking everyone into his gaze. "And quite frankly, ladies and gentlemen, the United States, so long as I've got anything to say about it, is not going to stand idly by and let Chinese run rampant over its neighbors' environmental concerns."

There was applause. Then he hit them with what he would later describe to Cline as his "Daisy Cutter," a fifteen-thousand-pound bomb, the biggest conventional bomb in the world.

"Another thing, ladies and gentlemen. We now have proof positive that at least two of our MIAs from 'Nam are in the border areas of Laos. Thank you." And he was gone.

Within minutes CNN was beaming Freeman's press conference all over the world. Within hours MIA groups via Internet throughout the United States were clamoring for the President to authorize General Freeman to follow up all MIA information—to go into Laos, Cambodia, wherever it was necessary. And it was the first time since its inception that Greenpeace worldwide applauded and loudly supported the efforts of a member of the American military to protect the "delicate ecosystems of Southeast Asia from environmental rape!"

"Bruce," the President asked his aide, Bruce Ellman, "what's your view on Freeman?"

"Fire him, Mr. President—as General Jorgensen recommended. And make Jorgensen's relieving Freeman of command official."

"Chiefs?" The President looked around at the Joint Chiefs of Staff. It was a two-two split, Navy and Air Force tending to agree with Ellman, albeit with some reservations, "given the heat of battle." The Army and Marines, declaring their bias for the man on the ground, argued that perhaps "Douglas has acted somewhat hastily in sending a recon force on the border."

"It wasn't *on* any border," Ellman chipped in. "It was a striker force sent over the border into Laos, violating Laotian neutrality." Ellman paused. "With all due respect, gentlemen, doesn't anybody remember the uproar when Nixon secretly sent bombers into Cambodia?"

"He sent them for good reason," the Army chief said. "To destroy enemy staging areas in what's supposedly a neutral country. Douglas is doing the same thing. It's outrageous that Khmer Rouge–led brigands can carry out hit-and-run raids on USVUN's left flank and can then slip safely across the border in Laos and be untouchable."

"He's violated policy," Bruce Ellman said. "He's got to understand that Washington directs this war, not Douglas Freeman. He's just like MacArthur in Korea—he wanted to go across the Yalu and hit the PLA in their staging areas. We could've had an all-out war with China!" It was an uncomfortable choice of analogies for Ellman, as there were still people in Washington who believed the PLA's staging areas across the Yalu should have been attacked and that had MacArthur done so, he would have won the war. They believed that the U.S. would then have not had to put up with an unsatisfactory armistice—not peace—along the 38th parallel between what was now North and South Korea.

"Well," Admiral Reese commented, "at least Jorgensen's decision to relieve him has only been conveyed to Freeman. It hasn't been announced publicly yet, even though *The New York Times* and others are demanding he be fired. You can rescind Jorgensen's order, Mr. President."

"And what would that do for Jorgensen?" the President asked rhetorically. "It'd hardly be a measure of confidence in my C in C."

"I agree," Ellman said. "It's certainly not what chain of command is all about."

Up till now CIA Director David Noyer had said nothing, but Ellman's last heated comment evoked a response.

"Mr. President," Noyer began. "As of now, General Jorgensen's decision to relieve Freeman isn't public knowledge, and so if you were to rescind the order, you're not going to cause Jorgensen any great harm. Yes, his professional pride'll be ruffled a bit, but God knows everyone's suffered that from time to time. It's nothing compared to what will happen if the American people perceive that the White House is not responding to a clear and present danger to our boys in Vietnam. And I'm willing to bet that sanctimonious editorials from the *Times* and others notwithstanding, the public in all the USVUN countries will support Freeman's decision of making a preemptive strike in Laos—if it in any way gives more protection for their troops in the USVUN force."

"Mr. President!" Ellman cut in impatiently. "May I speak my mind?"

The President swiveled his chair away from his desk to face his aide. "I thought you were, Bruce."

"I mean, lay it on the line."

"Go on."

"Sir, Freeman's an insubordinate son of a bitch who needs to know, just like MacArthur did, that you're the supreme commander. Fire him like Truman fired MacArthur."

David Noyer shook his head. "Mr. Ellman, you ever seen the ticker-tape parade that MacArthur got in San Francisco and New York after Truman fired him? If it had been an election year then, as it is now, Doug MacArthur could have been elected God Almighty. Anyway, quite apart from that—" With this, Noyer turned back to the President. "—I think Freeman is right, quite apart from trying to protect his left flank. He—"

"Protect his left flank?" Ellman cut in, looking about at the Joint Chiefs. "I'm no military strategist, but the Laotian border near Dien Bien Phu seems a hell of a long way from the fighting around—" He had forgotten the name momentarily.

"Loc Binh—Disney Hill," David Noyer put in. "About 250 miles away."

"Well, there you are," Ellman replied as if the distance had put an end to any argument about an attack on the left flank.

"I suppose," the Air Force chief added, "if they carved out an airfield on the Laotian side or at Dien Bien Phu, Freeman's western forces could be in real trouble. 'Course, we have the airpower from *Enterprise*. We could rule the roost."

CIA chief Noyer tried not to sound exasperated, but it was an effort. "Gentlemen, you're thinking like good military men but—" He almost said "Doug Freeman," but sensed that would be interpreted as first-name bias. "—but Freeman is thinking like a Chinese political officer. He's not only concerned about an attack on his left flank drawing too many troops away from him later on, he knows that while Dien Bien Phu is 250 miles away from the action around Loc Binh, it's only 150 miles away from Hanoi.

"If the probes by the PLA and their bosom buddies, the Khmer Rouge, over the border are successful, go unchallenged, they could come en masse and take Hanoi—just like the Viet Cong took old Saigon. Then we'd be in deep manure. Remember, they won't come by plane, they'll march as the NVA and VC did, down the Ho Chi Minh trails and south into old Saigon. And the distance between Freeman's enemies in Laos and Hanoi is a damn sight less than it was between Hanoi and old Saigon. And no amount of U.S. air superiority will stop them, as we found out in 'Nam. If Freeman doesn't make it clear that he won't tolerate incursions from 'safe' havens across the border, we could have a Khmer-guided PLA army around Hanoi in a matter of weeks. Then we *would* have a two-front war." Noyer paused, breathed deeply. There was a long silence.

"And then," the President said, tapping the blotter thoughtfully with his letter opener, "there's the problem of the MIAs Freeman mentioned at his press conference."

"Only two of them," Ellman said.

The President nodded. "I know, but it might as well be the two thousand we have missing. Have you seen the faxes?" He meant the messages sent to the White House asking, demanding, *begging* the White House to let Freeman cross the border if that's what it took to find a single MIA.

"But sir," Ellman cut in, "from what I've heard, these two reported MIAs might have been turncoats."

"Perhaps," the President said, "but there's always the possibility that they might know about other MIAs—at least, that's a recurring theme of many of the faxes I'm getting."

"Exactly," Noyer said. "If we're seen as not doing anything about the MIAs, we look pretty hard and nasty. No matter where they are, we always try to get our people back."

"We're not talking here about one of your 'company' men," Ellman told the CIA chief. "We're talking about turncoats."

"Yes, we are talking about one of the company's men. His name is—correction, *was*—Raymond Baker, and he had his throat cut in a flea-bitten hotel in Dalat, in the central highlands, because he was trying to track down a lead to Salt and Pepper Two."

"Who the hell are—" the Marine commander began.

"Salt and Pepper," the President explained. "Apparently one's white, the other black."

"Oh . . ."

"Look," the President said, "I'm going to tell Jorgensen to sit on his order to relieve Freeman—at least for twenty-four hours—before we decide. This will give me time to weigh all the facts."

Ellman's beeper sounded. He immediately clicked it off and excused himself. Two minutes later he was back, telling the President and assembled Chiefs of Staff that Larry King's producer was on the line. "They want someone to interview about Freeman's decision to cross over into Laos."

No one volunteered.

The President gave Ellman the nod. "Tell them you'll do it, Bruce. And before you go on, make sure we've monitored public reaction, not only the MIA business, but the public's reaction to USVUN troops being in Laos, or anything else connected with this business."

Noyer was appalled—*government by Gallup poll*—but he said nothing. Hopefully, most of the public would be for it.

Ellman went to the fax office and started going through the piles of faxes with another aide. He shook his head disgustedly, commenting to the aide, " 'Course, Rush Limbaugh's for it. He'd like Freeman to invade Laos, Cambodia, and Thailand as well. Might as well throw in Singapore and Malaysia while he's at it too."

"What are you going to tell them?" another aide asked. "On the 'Larry King Show,' I mean?"

"I don't know," Ellman replied curtly. "That other pile of faxes over there—what are they about?"

"They're concerns about deforestation in Southeast Asia, applauding Freeman's concern about the natural habitat. Greenpeace faxes, most of them."

"Greenpeace!" Ellman said in a tone of disgust. "They're more worried about animals and plants than they are people." Ellman was still mumbling about Freeman and the "goddamn mess" he'd gotten them all into when more Greenpeace faxes arrived.

CHAPTER SIXTY-FOUR

ONE OF ECHO column's two-man point security team was armed with a Winchester five-round 1200 riot shotgun, while his partner was sporting a Heckler & Koch MP5K submachine gun, a weapon of choice in the Special Forces, the fully automatic gun set for three-round bursts of 9mm Parabellum.

Nothing had moved for hours as they, the twenty-five-man attack team behind them, and the rear-end security pair from Foxtrot, waited. If "Audacity, audacity, always audacity" was Freeman's motto, "Patience, patience, and more patience" would serve the three thirty-man Special Forces columns.

It had been an especially difficult lesson for some of the American and British Special Forces, who were more used to urgent rescue and fast, deadly antiterrorist actions. Even so, every man knew that a mistake, a premature move, a bush mistaken for an enemy soldier and fired upon, a fart, a cough, could cost his life and the lives of the other twenty-nine men in his column.

Approximately three miles to the south beneath the jungle canopy, Foxtrot column also lay in wait, while in the marshy area south of Dien Bien Phu, under Captain Roscoe, Delta column had taken over what high ground there was. Men's bodies, particularly the chest, were bloodied by leeches and assailed by mosquitoes.

Of the three columns, it was Delta that craved, prayed, for action, just to be able to move, to deal with the goddamn leeches, to smack a mosquito stone fucking dead.

The men of Delta were not to be disappointed, for the PLA Airborne Regiment 7885, which meant it had been formed on August 7, 1985, en route to the valley around Dien Bien Phu, were on the red light—all standing, making final checks and adjustments before the jump into the low but heavy gray overcast.

Delta column's thirty men, unlike the sixty in Echo and Foxtrot, were not strung out on one side of a trail behind a line of trip-wire claymore mines, but instead were dispersed in an oval-shaped perimeter, ten men on either side and five each at the oval's ends. In this way they could watch forces either way, in the event that the Khmer-led guerrillas or PLA decided to outflank Echo and Foxtrot, now that they'd been told by a bird-dog Cessna message drop that, courtesy of La Prick Pierre LaSalle, the whole world had been alerted to the presence of Freeman's USVUN Special Forces column in Laos.

Captain Roscoe, in charge of Delta, not wanting to break radio silence, sent four of his men ahead as runners, two for each column, to alert Echo and Foxtrot that their general, if not specific, position was known to the enemy and that they should return posthaste to Delta.

In the two pairs of runners, one man would cover while the other advanced in a tactical leapfrog until they reached their respective columns, all four messengers torn between the need for speed, quiet, and the fear of being mistaken by Echo or Foxtrot as an enemy scout sneaking up behind them.

CHAPTER SIXTY-FIVE

ONE OF LARRY King's braces was twisted. He quickly readjusted it and was on air.

"Good evening. Tonight we have Mr. Bruce Ellman, special aide to the President, and we're going to be talking about the controversy that has erupted over General Freeman's action in the Chinese–United States–Vietnamese–U.N. conflict. Specifically, Freeman sending a strike force into Laos."

"Ah, Larry," Ellman interjected politely, "it isn't a strike force. It's a long-range reconnaissance patrol."

"Yes, but it's a military force, right? That's crossed the border into Laos?"

"Well, we're not a hundred percent sure of that, Larry."

"C'mon, Bruce, Freeman's troops have either crossed the Vietnamese border into Laos or they haven't."

"No, what I mean, Larry, is that the border areas around there—"

"Around where? What part of the border?"

"Around the area west of Dien Bien Phu. Often older maps show different border lines. It reflects the various national territorial claims."

King hunched forward. "Then you're saying they're not in Laos."

"No, I just, ah—I want people to know that often cross-border incidents are not always intentional."

"But you're not saying Freeman made a mistake, are you—or are you? Are you saying the White House denies we have troops in Laos at this moment?"

"No, I'm not denying it. But it's a very complex issue, Larry."

"How so? Our boys are in Laos or they aren't, right?"

"Yes."

"Right, they're in Laos."

Ellman agreed they were, adding, "They're not all U.S. troops. Some are British."

"Does the White House support Freeman's incursion?"

"He's the man in the field and he has to call the shots as he sees them."

"So he has the President's full support?"

"Yes."

"He's certainly getting high marks from the public. I don't want to sound too cynical here, Bruce, but does the White House's support of Freeman have anything to do with the polls showing the American public is over seventy percent in favor of Freeman making a preemptive strike in Laos?"

"Well, first of all, Larry, there's been no preemptive strike as yet. As I mentioned earlier, it's basically a reconnaissance patrol. We've no reports of combat in the area. About the polls, Larry—I think you *are* being overly cynical."

King smiled. "Comes with the territory, Bruce."

Ellman smiled. "I understand, but to answer your question

about the widespread public support for Freeman. That has no bearing, quite frankly, on how the administration views General Freeman's action. This administration doesn't govern by poll. The President was elected to exercise leadership."

"Fine, but you can't deny, Bruce, that the widespread support for the President can't do any harm in an election year?"

Ellman shrugged as if the comment were irrelevant. "Perhaps, but the President supports General Freeman because he thinks the general has handled a delicate situation well."

"What's delicate about it?"

"Well, Larry, General Freeman had several options at his disposal. He could have called on the Air Force to spray defoliants on the border crossings the Khmer-led guerrillas are using."

"You mean using herbicides—something like Agent Orange—to denude the border crossings so they could be monitored, what—by satellite?"

"Exactly, Larry. It wouldn't be Agent Orange. There are other less toxic herbicides we could use, but we think General Freeman has shown both a great deal of concern for the people of Laos and great respect for the habitat. I don't know if the public's aware—"

"Wait a minute, what public are we talking about here? Laotian or the U.S.?"

"The U.S."

"Okay—sorry. Go on."

"Well, what I'm saying, Larry, is that General Freeman is extremely sensitive about the habitat. We made some awful mistakes during the Vietnam War using herbicides, and he doesn't want to repeat them. And because of the thoughtless, greedy slash-and-burn tactics practiced by those in the region, deforestation, and the loss of rare species of mammals and birds, is horrendous. In Vietnam alone more than a thousand square miles of deforestation takes place every year. On top of that, the Khmer Rouge–led guerrillas are constantly raiding Vietnamese forests for teakwood, for which there's a high demand. And all the time—"

"Got to take a break," King cut in, turning to the camera. "We'll be right back. Don't go 'way!"

After the intense barrage of commercials, King asked Bruce Ellman to take up where he'd left off on the topic of environmental protection.

"I was going to say, Larry, that it isn't just the destruction of over 240 species of mammals—deer, leopard, rhinos, et cetera—or the threat to the more than seven hundred species of birds that we're concerned about, but the fact that deforestation has a terrible side effect on the people of the region, and here I'm talking about massive erosion on hillsides, massive soil erosion, destruction of water tables, with consequent flooding and the resulting—"

"Hold on a minute, Bruce, you're losing me. You say Freeman had all this in mind when he sent in troops rather than sending in machines—bombers, et cetera—to clear the area?"

"Larry, you don't have to believe me, just read the transcript of General Freeman's press conference last night in Phu Lang Thuong."

King held up his hands in surrender. "Okay—and I ain't gonna even try to pronounce that—what was it—Phu . . . ?"

"Lang Thuong."

"If you say so," King joked, then, looking into the camera, he told his millions of viewers that after the break he'd be taking "your phone calls."

The first was from Tucson, Arizona, a young man, by the sound of him, telling Larry how much he loved the show, how he'd been trying for months and this was the first time he'd gotten through.

"What's your question?"

"Ah, it's for Mr. Ellison."

"Ellman," King corrected him.

"Yeah, Ellman. What are you gonna do about the French?"

King and Ellman looked at each other, King's lower jaw coming unstuck. "What d'you mean 'about the French'?"

"Well, it was on some news report or other. Some French guy blew the whistle—you know—"

"Oh," King interjected, "you mean the—" King snapped his fingers, trying to recall the name. "You mean the guy who broke the news about Freeman sending the Special Forces in?"

"Yeah . . ."

"LaSalle! Pierre LaSalle, right?"

"Yeah, some name like that. Well, aren't the French in this USVUN force? I mean—"

"No," Ellman cut in. "They're not."

"Well," the caller said, "that guy put our guys behind the eight ball—know what I mean? And I think we should do something about it. Teach 'em a lesson."

King shrugged. "What do you want us to do—bomb Paris?"

"It'd be a start." King switched him off. "He has a point, though, Bruce, doesn't he? I mean that was a pretty scurrilous thing to do. Putting our guys and the British in jeopardy. Now the Chinese have to know where Freeman's force is."

"We've already sent a note to the French ambassador here in Washington."

The next caller said, "What we oughta do is stop buying champagne. That'd show the sons—"

Larry switched him off, ad libbing, "We stopped buying champagne around here, the embassy circuit'd come to a dead stop, wouldn't it, Bruce?"

Ellman grinned. He was feeling great. The questioners' talking about the French news blowing the Special Forces operation was taking all the heat off the White House. He hoped it'd keep up. But the next question was from a Greenpeacer from "London, Ontario, Canada."

"I never thought I'd be congratulating the military, but I have to tell you that finally we've got a general who's using his head. Instead of blasting away with bombs and herbicides, attacking the environment, he's sending in men—I mean military personnel—to assess the situation. I've read the reports of General Freeman's press conference, and he's the only military person I know of who's concerned about the destruction of the habitat."

King pursed his lips, nodding. "He's right, isn't he, Bruce? Freeman's the only one—I mean general—concerned about the environment, I mean putting it as a policy over and above purely military considerations."

Ellman politely disagreed. "No, Norman Schwarzkopf showed the same kind of concern over the oil fires in Kuwait."

"Yeah," King said, "but I mean that happened after the Iraqi War had started. Here Freeman apparently took habitat damage into consideration before he sent in his special force. Next caller—Amsterdam. Hello."

It was a heavily accented Dutch voice. "Hello. I think it's disgraceful, Larry, that the Americans and British are making war at all. This dispute between the Chinese and Vietnamese should have been settled peacefully."

"Well, sir," King began, "that was tried in the U.N. Didn't work. So now we have a U.N. mandate for USVUN to step in and protect Vietnamese sovereignty."

The caller was adamant. "There must be a way to settle it peacefully and—"

King cut in. "So you believe everything can be settled peacefully?"

"Yes."

"I wish you were right, caller, but sometimes—however unpalatable it is—we have to get out the strap."

The last caller was a quiet-spoken woman whose phone number, showing up on the producer's console, identified her as a previous caller, a Mrs. Mellin, but the producer, recognizing her soft, hesitant voice, let it through. She said that she was as concerned as anybody about the habitat, but surely the most important considerations behind General Freeman's sending in Special Forces were to protect Americans and other USVUN members from attack from Laos and "to help free any MIAs."

Bruce Ellman saw his chance and took it. "I think the caller is absolutely correct, Larry. The MIA issue has always been important to this administration, and the President doesn't want anyone to forget it."

"But," Mrs. Mellin continued, "why is the MIA issue still not resolved? I'm the sister-in-law of an MIA—an Army nurse—and my husband has been missing since the beginning of all this."

"Ma'am," King interrupted gently, "I understand about your sister-in-law being an MIA—you've called before, right?"

"Yes."

"Point I'm making, ma'am, is your husband's not strictly speaking an MIA. Correct me if I'm wrong, but wasn't he—isn't he—one of those taken from one of the oil rigs?"

"Yes, but he's still missing and I—"

"We know that, ma'am. Sorry, we're running out of time. Bruce, administration's on to this, right? Tracking down American nationals who were snatched?"

"Yes we are, Larry."

"I mean," Mrs. Mellin said, "they say some MIAs had been—you know—turned around by the Communists over there, but we still owe them our compassion until—"

"You're right, ma'am," King cut in. "Point is, we owe every Vietnamese vet and MIA a hearing. We weren't there. They were."

"Exactly," a heartened Mrs. Mellin said.

"Gotta run. Thanks, Bruce."

"Pleasure, Larry."

"Tomorrow night—another guest. She's often nude, always

naughty, and she's a member of the Italian parliament. See you then."

The President zapped the TV, its light dying as he beamed. He looked around at the Chiefs of Staff. "Well, what's the consensus?"

Chief of Naval Operations Admiral Reese was the first to respond. "I thought Ellman handled himself very well."

"I thought he did brilliantly," the President said.

There was no disagreement in the Oval Office. "Yes," the President continued, "Freeman is riding high in the public's opinion and we were right to support him. I think General Jorgensen acted a little hastily on this one."

"You want me to speak to Jorgensen?" the Army chief asked. "Straighten out any misunderstanding between him and Douglas?"

"I'd appreciate that, General," the President answered.

"In any case," Admiral Reese added, "Douglas is going to have his hands full with this breakthrough at Disney."

"Yes," the President agreed. "I think that for Jorgensen to relieve him at the moment would be very unwise."

What they meant was that if someone had to take the heat for what all indications showed would be a disastrous defeat at Disney, it might as well be a popular public figure, at least a temporarily popular figure, like Freeman.

And if anyone on Jorgensen's HQ in Hanoi thought General Jorgensen would be offended by being overruled, albeit quietly, by the White House, they couldn't have been more mistaken. Jorgensen, who'd had time to mull over his own earlier flash of temper in response to Freeman's outburst, was in fact enormously relieved by the call from the White House. He was no fool, and also he'd seen the "Larry King Show." If Freeman was that popular all of a sudden, then let him hold on to the field command of USVUN's Second Army; let him get out of the terrible mess he was in on Disney Hill.

And it was a mess, the armada of over 350 choppers carrying the American air cavalry Freeman had called in unable, except in a few cases, to disgorge their cargoes of men and ammunition because of heavy smoke being laid down by a PLA mortar barrage, the 82mm falling all along the base of the hill blinding the helo pilots and the Huey's gunners.

* * *

The four troopers, two running to warn Echo, two for Foxtrot, were within fifteen minutes of reaching Leigh-Hastings's column and Berry's when the two most forward troopers, one running to Echo, one to Foxtrot, ran into spiked deadfalls, at different times. These were booby traps made of long, sharpened stakes protruding from a four-by-six-foot wooden box suspended high in a tree by a cord or vine whose quick-release knot end is hidden by the undergrowth near a trail. When an enemy soldier passes underneath the tree, the knot is released and the whole spiked contraption falls on him. If he's lucky, the spikes kill him outright, but in most cases the long spikes inflict terrible wounds all over the body.

The two men hit this day were badly wounded, one with a punji stick penetrating his abdomen and exiting through his genitals. Their buddies had only two choices: to finish them off or leave them. Neither could carry a wounded man out, for their mission was to warn both Echo and Foxtrot columns that their position had been blown.

One of the wounded man's buddies took out his K-bar and, hand shaking, drove it into the man's heart. He heard a noise behind him but was too late, AK-47 rounds blowing his head off, scattering its contents across the trail. Echo would not be warned unless the weather cleared and someone from high up in a tree managed to see the dots of descending Chinese paratroops over Dien Bien Phu in the far distance.

The buddy of the man hit with a deadfall on the Foxtrot trail thought quicker and fired a wide, arcing burst as he went to ground behind the man who'd been spiked. He used the dead body and the bloodied booby trap as cover while he threw two "Willie Petes," or white phosphorus grenades, into the green jungle on either side of the trail. He followed with long bursts from his Heckler & Koch, spraying twenty-five rounds of 9mm Parabellum in less than two seconds as he leapt up and kept running down the trail, his eyes trying to take in the overhead canopy as well as the trail. He rounded a bend, saw a trip wire, jumped over it, and kept running, all his senses alert for danger. He heard something moving to his right and dove to earth. A bush quivered, and he gave it a three-round burst. There was a squealing noise, the wounded boar making it halfway across the trail before he slumped dead.

Heart thumping, sweat coursing down his back, the Special Forces trooper, a U.S. Ranger, William Kaccy, looked up the trail, saw a patch of ground with less dead leaves on it, and figured it was a punji stick hole. He guessed he was about ten minutes away from Colonel Berry's Foxtrot Company. Whether or not the pair of troopers heading for Echo had gotten through, Kacey had no idea.

After five minutes of staying stock-still, letting his pulse fall, his eyes constantly looking about, Kacey decided to stay a bit longer. Something else was moving. You could sense it from the bird noises, louder than usual, as if telegraphing one another a warning.

Now Kacey heard movement coming toward him on the trail, but it was a careless sound, not the noise of someone trying to tread lightly.

The girl was probably around seven years old, and when she saw the pig, gasped with fright and stood still, holding a bamboo stick by her side, as if wondering what to do. Kacey, as yet unseen by her, was also thinking what to do. If she spotted him, could he afford to let her run back to the hamlet or wherever she'd come from? It couldn't be far away. She was standing upright, only her head bent forward as she looked down at the pig. Kacey's brain was racing. Something wasn't right. What did they say in the movies? "It's too quiet out there!" It wasn't quiet; the birds were making a racket. Was it the smell of the place? No, it was the usual damp, musty leaf odor of the forest.

It was the way she was standing, as if she had a stick up her ass, a walking booby trap, an old Viet Cong trick: turn a kid into a walking bomb. It was only now that Kacey realized her left hand was bunched up. A grenade? Right then he knew he wouldn't kill her even if she let go of a grenade or whatever—a homemade job with lots of nails and the gunpowder taken from an unexploded 'Nam bomb? But he wouldn't harm her—Jesus Christ, wasn't that what he was over here for? As part of the USVUN attempt to show China that you wouldn't put up with bullying? No, that wasn't it. She was about the same age as his daughter.

The girl moved closer to the pig and hesitantly touched its still-warm underbelly with her big toe. She did it again, then, satisfied it was dead, looked behind her for several seconds, then looking forward, stepped over the boar and stopped dead, her eyes following the short barrel of Kacey's machine gun, her body giving a start as she met his eyes, her mouth agape. She had never seen a black man before.

"Shh," Kacey whispered, putting a finger to his mouth,

then, with the same hand, gesturing for her to give whatever she was holding to him. He could see it was a grenade with the pin pulled, only her grip keeping the release lever down. She looked back along the trail again, and in that instant the Ranger was about to grab for it, but one fumble . . . He waited till she turned and looked at him again. Smiling, he very slowly extended his hand. Her tiny warm hand withdrew from him for a moment. He stopped, his dry-mouthed smile fixed, his tongue cemented to the roof of his mouth. She let him close his giant's hand around hers, and his thumb took over the pressure on the lever. Now he was in a real fix. *What do I do with the fucking thing?*

As she turned and walked away from him, stepping carefully back over the dead pig, Kacey transferred the grenade to his left hand in case he had to fire the HK single-handed, and felt for the first aid pouch around his helmet. He'd tape the grenade's lever down.

He had it done inside a minute and, first pulling the pig off the trail then moving into the mildew-smelling bush, he made his way forward at turtle speed, torn by his desire to get away and make sure Foxtrot Company was alerted to enemy presence, and the need to be absolutely quiet should the girl bring anyone back.

CHAPTER SIXTY-SIX

WITH THE WEATHER closing in, nimbostratus cloud now spreading out over the valley above Dien Bien Phu in a low, metallic-gray ceiling, the American air cavalry still had smoke to contend with. The aerial armada of helos carrying the battalion had to turn back—to the delight of Pierre LaSalle, who, from the safety of Hanoi, kept filing stories critical of the U.S. presence.

General Jorgensen called Freeman at Second Army's HQ at Phu Lang Thuong. "Douglas. Harry Jorgensen here. Washington's pressing me. They want to know if we can hold Disney Hill or whether you should pull out before casualties become unacceptable?"

"General, we have pulled back. By God, I hate to have to admit it but we have, and we're still being hit. Those bastards of Wei's are swarming out of those goddamn holes like ants. Trouble is—" There was a sizzle of static on the line. "—trouble is, we can't pull back any farther, otherwise we'll be waist high in paddy water."

"I'm not saying pull back as far as Lang Duong, but if you can get out of the paddies onto higher ground, we can maybe move some armor in."

"Negative. We're between a rock and a hard place here. We withdraw any farther, we'll have to fight waist high in mud. Turn into a goddamn turkey shoot for the Chinese. No, we're going to have to make our stand where we've dug in between the base of the hill and the rice paddies. 'Least TACAIR can hit the hillside."

"But the choppers can't see where they're going."

"General, you get me helos to bring those men in tonight, and I'll counterattack."

"What?" It was like being down twenty to zip in the Rose Bowl at halftime, Jorgensen thought, and the losing coach telling you he was going to win the game.

"Last thing they expect, General," Freeman continued. "I've got—mortars . . . I need is the men."

The static was getting worse, but whatever Freeman had said, Jorgensen told his aide in an aside that it was going to take more than mortars. Freeman's forces were already running low on ammunition, and despite some blind drops into the smoke and mist, most of the ammo crates had disappeared underwater. Anyone who had to leave his weapon and pack behind, wading out to try to retrieve them, was at especially high risk, as Chinese snipers at the edge of the smoke used the sodden parachutes as range markers.

"Douglas . . ."

"Yes, General."

"I'm sorry for my remarks—"

"My fault," Freeman cut in. "I have a penchant for sounding off when what I should do is shut up."

"You're the best field commander for Second Army, Douglas. I'll try to get you those helos."

When Jorgensen hung up, Freeman, in an uncharacteristically paranoid moment, under the stress of battle, wondered aloud to Cline what Jorgensen had meant when he said he was "the best field commander for Second Army."

"For *Second* Army?" Freeman said, hypothesizing that Jorgensen might have meant he wouldn't be the best field commander for any other U.S. Army.

"I don't think he meant that for a moment," Cline told Freeman. "He means you're the best man for the job." Cline paused. "For the situation we're in."

Freeman turned on him. "The situation we're in, Major, is a retreat. By God, is that all he thinks we're good for? I told him I was going to counterattack, and I will. Damn it," Freeman said, pacing up and down before the situation map, "I need a prayer for good weather—like Georgie Patton had at Bastogne. Get some air cover. Bob, get that senior padre of ours to see to it."

Embarrassed, Cline opined that the padre was probably pretty busy with the wounded that the "dust-offs"—or Medevac choppers—had brought back to Phu Lang Thuong's field hospital.

Freeman looked surprised. "I thought all our wounded were going straight to the *Tampa?*"

"They are, General, but there were so many wounded in Disney that there was a backup of choppers all the way off Haiphong harbor, so some came back and unloaded at Phu Lang Thuong's field hospital. As I said, the padres are pretty busy."

"What's the matter with you? Goddamn prayer only takes a minute. I want a prayer and I want to see a copy of it. Padres know the right wording."

"Yes, sir."

Reluctantly, Cline made his way toward the field hospital, feeling more embarrassed by the second until he realized that if you believed in God, Freeman's request, a symptom of "Disney"-induced stress, made perfect sense. He realized then that what really bothered him was his own angst, the persistent question he harbored at the back of his mind as to whether or not God had made man or man had made God. Freeman's order for a prayer was forcing Cline to confront his own uncertainty.

* * *

"I've already said prayers, Major," the overworked padre told him. "I'm praying for every man that's wounded on our side as well as on the Chinese."

"I don't know whether the general'd appreciate that."

"The general's not God, Major, though sometimes he acts like it."

"Look, Padre, I don't want to get in a slugfest with you. The general's ordered a prayer, a prayer for good weather so we can get proper air cover."

"To kill more Chinese?"

"No," the major said, feeling his temper rising. "To get out of this murderous trap our boys're in."

The padre said nothing. He'd just administered last rites to a man—a boy, really—whose face had been blown away by a Chinese stick grenade.

"Look, Padre," Cline told him. "Quite frankly, I don't give a hoot if you write a prayer or not—I'm not one of your flock—but if I don't have something on paper to show the boss, I'm going to get reamed out. So, what is it to be? You want to write the prayer or tell him personally that you won't?"

The padre sighed. "I'll write a prayer."

Cline resented the dog-in-the-manger tone. "Listen, Padre, last time I heard you give a sermon—which I was *required* to attend—you were going on pretty strong about defeating godless communism."

"I still am—but not men."

Cline rolled his eyes impatiently. "That's like saying you want to fight Nazism but you don't want to kill Nazis. Can't be done, Padre. Will you write it now—*please*?"

The padre took out his pen and notebook and wrote, *Dear Lord, we ask of you that you give us fair weather so that we may have time to withdraw our men from this catastrophe.*

Cline read it. "Jesus Christ, Padre—that won't do it."

"How do you know what God wants?"

"I'm talking about the general. He reads this—this 'catastrophe' and withdrawal bit, he'll go ballistic!"

Wordlessly, the padre took the note, crossed out *catastrophe*, put *danger* instead, and changed *withdrawal* to *rescue*.

"That's a bit better," Cline told him. "But it's only—I mean it's kind of short, isn't it? Can't you tart it up a bit?"

"You mean puff it up?"

"Yes," Cline said angrily. "Puff it up. *Now!*"

The padre wrote again, looking up now and then, collecting his thoughts.

Cline read it. "Okay, fine. Thanks, Padre," and he walked off.

"You're welcome. And Major?"

Cline turned around. "Yes?"

"No offense to you or the general—it's been a bad day for all of us."

Cline nodded appreciatively. "I hope your prayer works, Padre."

Freeman read the prayer aloud as he buckled on his holster. " 'Dear Lord, we most graciously beseech you to put a halt to this inclement weather so that our soldiers may more safely re-group against the attacks of the enemy and may proceed in this United Nations effort to bring peace once again to the region. Amen.' "

Freeman shook his head in disappointment. "I don't know, Bob. It's all right, I suppose. Adequate, but there's no majesty in it, no pizzazz! Almost think he was praying to the Secretary General of the U.N. We want a prayer for battle, for victory. This is a weasel prayer, not a prayer worthy of Second Army—not for warriors! Damn it!" He crushed the note. "I'll write it myself, and you can deliver it to him, and I want him to use it in the next service. By God, our boys deserve better than this." He rewrote it and read it to Cline.

"Dear God, we ask for a cessation of this inclement weather so that our men may advance against our foe, defeat them in battle, and so drive the godless hordes back to their Commu-nist enclaves. And may our victory be so decisive that the war-lords of communism will pause before committing further acts of war against those who fight in your name. Amen."

Cline said it sounded great, and delivered it to the padre. It was said that night at 1900 at the hospital. A half hour later a typhoon, "Harold," struck North Vietnam, the cloud cover de-scending even lower, the torrential downpour ruling out any possibility of TACAIR support for Freeman's beleaguered troops.

CHAPTER SIXTY-SEVEN

AT THE POW camp south of Ningming, Danny Mellin, Mike Murphy, and Shirley Fortescue were busily building the brick walls of their huts. Any reluctance the Australian had had earlier was now gone, drowned in the monsoon that had first struck the border area around Loc Binh, where Freeman's besieged troops were fighting for their lives on the narrow margin between the base of the hill and the water-swollen paddies.

Unknown to Freeman, who was now en route to the Loc Binh front, the monsoon's deluge had probably saved his troops on the margin, since the downpour coursing through the artillery-scored rust-red soil of Disney Hill was flooding many of the tunnels, whose drainage systems were clogged like leaves in a house's gutters, with the artillery-mashed vegetation strewn all over Disney.

In fact, during the flash flood more PLA troops, en route from the north via the Disney tunnels, were killed by drowning than were killed by the U.S. and other USVUN troops. The rain cleared the smoke enough for the aerial fleet of choppers to return and to go in using the margin as their landing zone, violet smoke ground flares identifying the dust-offs, the Medevac helos' LZs. Those helos whose red crosses were clearly visible on nose and sides were as usual used as aiming points by Wang's soldiers, who knew that the Americans' obsession with trying to get their wounded out would delay any counterattack. The air cavalry's gunships, however, were quick to respond, the .50s on either side of the choppers sending down a deadly rain of one-in-five tracer, the frontmost helos also firing off salvoes of 2.75-inch rockets from their dual pods of nineteen apiece.

In this ear-pounding confusion of rain-curtained battle, Freeman's air cavalry unloaded on the margin, which had more or less become a hundred-yard airfield–cum–starting point for Freeman's counterattack, because now his consultation about weaponry with the Vietnamese general, Vinh, came into play. Standard 82mm Vietnamese mortars enabled Freeman's troops once again to fire not only their own 81mm rounds, but PLA 82mm rounds as well.

In short, as the air cavalry rapidly stiffened the USVUN line on the margin—enough to push Wang's Chinese army back fifty to seventy yards on Disney's artillery-pockmarked southern face—the pyramids of mortar rounds that had to be left behind in the sudden and totally unexpected withdrawal fell into the hands of Freeman's air cavalry mortar squads. Now, they quickly fed the Chinese ammo into the 82mm mortar tubes, the mortar rounds' explosions not only an incentive for the already retreating PLA to retreat farther, but simultaneously further weakening the tunnels with a series of cave-ins from the rounds' concussion. At one point, the cave-ins sealed the fate of an entire company of 115 Chinese troops.

Yes, there were U.S. casualties caused by tunnel cave-ins that produced sudden sinkholes, which in turn swallowed USVUN troops, but the losses were minuscule compared with the Chinese losses. And now, with ample ammunition supplies to feed the gaping mouths of the mortars, the high morale of the American advance continued, elements of the U.S. cavalry reinforcements having already gained Disney's summit after unforgiving hand-to-hand combat along a deep, L-shaped trench. The same trench only a half hour before had been a tunnel filled with PLA, a tunnel that fed into the Disney complex as a conduit for those troops disembarking from the Ningming–Pingxiang–Lang Son railway's troop trains.

CHAPTER SIXTY-EIGHT

DANNY MELLIN'S POCKETS were bulging with boiled rice donated by other POWs in their belief that it was going to help one of the rig workers who had been captured first and was therefore the most malnourished POW. But the rice wasn't for any POW. Instead, Mellin, with the help of Shirley Fortescue, mixed the grains of boiled rice in the mortar used to cement the bricks together for what would be the lower center part of the wall facing the long coils of razor wire that served as the outer main wall of the prison until a proper high-wire wall could be built to replace the wire perimeter.

"So," Mellin said to Murphy and Shirley Fortescue, who were acting as his cover while he sprinkled another handful of rice in the cement, "I need you to get me a pair of wire cutters."

"Oh, right," Murphy said. "I'll order one from Sears. Just give me the catalogue. I'll fax 'em right away."

Danny ignored the Australian's sarcastic tone. "Thought you Aussies—"

He stopped as Shirley whispered, "He's coming."

Upshut was shouting at one of the POWs, an older man in the brick-passing line who had crumpled with exhaustion. The old man struggled to his feet, a bayonet prodding him sharply in the back, drawing blood. When Upshut saw the waist-high wall of Mellin's group, the highest wall so far of any of the five prisoners' huts being constructed, he nodded, adding a grunt of approval.

Mellin smiled accommodatingly, as did Shirley Fortescue, Murphy whispering, "Prick!" when Upshut was out of hearing range. Murphy turned back to Mellin. "So what was that about Aussies?"

Mellin tapped the next brick down with the handle of the trowel. "I thought you Aussies were the can-do sort. Improvise."

Mellin's fingers, like everyone else's, were raw from handling the bricks without gloves of any kind. "If you and another hut boss can lose a couple of trowels, we could make a bloody good pair of cutters."

"First thing they'd miss," Shirley said matter-of-factly.

"Shirley's right," Danny added. "Every trowel'll have to be accounted for."

"Yes," she said, passing another brick. "For God's sake, think of something practical."

"Don't be so fucking uppity," Murphy retorted. "Just a thought."

"All right, you two," Mellin said. "Knock it off! Shirley, you got any ideas? Using the rice isn't going to help us at all unless we can cut through the razor wire."

Now that they were getting near the bottom of the pile, the bricks were covered in mud kicked up by the downpour that had ceased only twenty minutes before, turning the whole compound into a red-colored slush.

"Nothing comes to mind," Shirley said. "Anybody have a good nail clipper or—"

"Gimme a break," Murphy said. "You think everyone here was doing their nails when the chinks picked 'em off the rigs?"

"I don't know," Shirley said calmly, "but I know that if they have a nail clipper . . ." She turned to Danny. "You know, some have a nail file attached."

"Oh, for Chrissake," Murphy cut in. "Yeah, great idea if we had a year or two to—"

"Just a thought," she countered, trying not to get angry. Mellin took particular note of this pointed exchange between the two because it reminded him of his sister Angela, before she'd broken up with her one and only boyfriend in the days before she had gone to 'Nam as a nurse. They used to have the same kind of bitterly sarcastic exchanges during a fight, but then it would soon be over, and though Angela never admitted it to Danny, he was sure their differences had been solved by sex. It was almost as if they had to have a row to deny the intensity of their physical attraction for one another. Danny had become convinced it was the same with Mike Murphy and Shirley. There seemed to be a strong, albeit hidden, sexual attraction between them, with no room for middle ground; it would be either sizzling hot or icy cold.

Then, as if to suddenly confirm his suspicion, Murphy conceded that a nail file, however small, might be of some use after all, not as any kind of wire cutter itself, but as something that could be used to make a cutter.

"Make one out of what?" Mellin pressed.

Mike Murphy grunted, agreeing that it posed quite a problem. "Well," he said. "There's only one way."

"Don't tell us," Shirley murmured sarcastically. "It might help us!"

"We steal a cutter," Murphy answered. Before anyone else could object, the Australian added, "Look, they must have one or more to have set up the coils of razor wire around the perimeter."

"Makes sense," Danny conceded. "But I haven't seen any of Upshut's guys carrying them about."

"Neither have I," Murphy agreed. "That's why they have to be in the trucks—glove box maybe—or tool kit in the back."

"I didn't see any toolboxes in the back of the truck that brought us in," Shirley said.

"Nor me," Danny told Murphy, "which means you're probably right. They must have cutters in the glove box."

As Murphy passed another brick for what would be their prison's wall, and its rough surface tore a small flap of skin, he cursed the lack of gloves once again, adding, "Only chance we'll have will be slop parade." He meant the five o'clock ration of rice and tea. "Somebody'll have to get under the truck and try—" They stopped talking as one of the guards ambled closer. As the guard moved farther away, Murphy said, "We'll have to get in the passenger side and have a look-see in the glove box."

Shirley nodded. "We could create some kind of diversion— get people to crowd around the truck."

Murphy frowned at the idea. "Problem is, we'd have to let more people in on our plan."

"I didn't know we had one yet," Shirley quipped.

"Well," Murphy retorted, "I take it we're going to bust out the hut wall, then cut through the wire. Don't have to be a fucking genius to figure that out. Except—" He looked now at Danny. "—you'd better be right about that fucking rice, mate, otherwise we're dead as fucking doornails."

Danny said nothing, nor Shirley, who was too disgusted with Murphy's bad language.

"I don't like your silence, mate," Murphy said as he took hold of another brick. His thumb was now bleeding. "C'mon, Danny, tell us. You ever done this before—the old rice trick?"

"No, but—"

"But nothing! Jesus Christ, Danny! Whole fucking plan depends on you and the friggin' wall, mate!"

"I know that," Danny replied tartly. "You think I—"

Upshut was coming back on his rounds, so they fell silent, Murphy still cursing under his breath about the lack of proper gloves for handling the bricks.

Gloves, or rather a glove—an asbestos one—was on the mind of the third M-60 assistant machine gunner in the Echo column west of Dien Bien Phu. He'd lost the glove—supplied so that in a firefight you could quickly change a red-hot barrel for the cool, spare one in less than three seconds. Somehow, the piece of green fishing line that he normally used to attach the glove to his kit had been severed from the pack—probably twisted in underbrush and giving way when he'd moved forward quickly after a "sit and listen."

The assistant gunner knew that if it was discovered missing by any of the other Special Forces, he would henceforth be called TOM—turd of the month. It was serious business if you couldn't change the barrel. The time lost could be responsible for a lot of men killed, causing your position to be overrun, letting the enemy inside your perimeter, from where he could wipe out the entire column, with the machine gunner's buddies having only one corridor of retreat: in front of their own "overlapping-fire" claymores.

In the jungle five miles to the south of Echo and beyond the Laotian-Vietnamese border, Kacey, the remaining Ranger of the two-man warning squad sent by Delta's Major Roscoe to warn Foxtrot, had moved well off the trail from where he'd seen the young girl. Advancing slowly, silently, on a line parallel to the trail, the Ranger could see a clearing—several huts, and now, coming down the trail, a squad of five, no six, men, Khmer Rouge, led by a brother—a black man—or was it the heavy mud camouflage?—no, he was black—and the little seven-year-old girl in front of him nudged along by the barrel of the man's AK-47.

Suddenly, the Khmer squad stopped about a hundred feet from where the Ranger had seen the little girl earlier, the Khmer patrol now using the girl as a shield. The point man inched ahead, covered by the other six Khmer. The Khmers stopped again next to where the Ranger had been hiding. They were checking out her story—probably using the girl's family as hostages back in the village, the Khmer point man wanting to see where the dead pig was and so see if anyone had been hiding by the trail. Kacey knew it would take only a few seconds for the Khmer to discover broken twigs and bruised underbrush and conclude that someone had been hiding there and had taken her grenade. The Khmer's leader gave a spread-out hand signal, and in seconds the other six men of the enemy squad had disappeared into the jungle beneath the high canopy of trees.

Kacey was caught in a dilemma: the only way for him to move fast enough to warn Foxtrot column that their general position was now known by the enemy would be to break cover and move quickly down the trail. Yet to do that would put him in danger of running smack into another enemy patrol and/or booby traps. He knew he had to risk it—the closer he got to Foxtrot, the better the chance of warning them to split in time and head back for pickup along with Echo and Delta columns.

Still moving slowly and well in from the trail, he could see the six Khmer spread out in a line about seventy yards behind him as he neared the edge of the bare ground around the village huts, working his way carefully around its perimeter. In between the huts he saw there were patches of bare ground all but devoid of the dead leaves one usually saw. He guessed that they were punji traps, the teepee-shaped bamboo stick cages that normally identified the booby traps for the village children now removed. Kacey was sweating profusely, not only because of the sticky heat, but from the growing anxiety that was creeping up on him as surely as the seven Khmer coming up behind him.

"Hey, buddy!"

It sounded like an obscenity, so unexpected was it. Kacey froze. It was definitely an American voice—not a trace of a foreign accent. It had to be the black man he'd seen. Kacey said nothing. He couldn't see the speaker, and presumably the speaker couldn't see him, otherwise Kacey knew he would now be dead.

"Hey, man," the voice called out again. "I got a deal for you." There was no echo, the disembodied voice quickly lost in the sudden hush of the jungle.

"You come out, man, or the girl gets it. You understand?"

There was nothing mysterious about it—a straightforward threat, and not even for a split second did Kacey doubt that the other black man meant exactly what he said. And not for a second did the Ranger doubt that if he didn't get to warn Foxtrot column, then thirty men would become the victims rather than the executors of a fatal ambush. It was the girl or the column.

But what if he didn't answer the black man? What if he simply kept quiet? How could the black man and the remainder of the enemy patrol be sure he was still in listening range, that he'd heard the black man's threat? For all they knew, he could have been well back on the trail by now, hightailing it in the direction he'd come from—to Delta in the marshland below Dien Bien Phu.

"You hear me, man?" came the black man's call.

Kacey, his finger on the trigger guard of his HKMP 5, said nothing. Two could play this game.

Though the tail of the monsoon had now passed over the POW camp at Ningming, the ground was muddy, and several of the weaker prisoners slipped on the way to the "slop" truck for the bowl of rice and cup of tea, the truck being mobbed as cover for Murphy to slip under the tailgate, quickly wriggling forward on the passenger side. He heard the shouting of the guards at the back, Upshut among them, and several warning shots fired. He rolled out, got up, tried the passenger door. It opened and he was inside the truck's cabin. Two things caught his eye at once: a small, battered, dirty plastic toolbox in the passenger's foot well, and a bunch of keys hanging from the ignition, the gate through the razor wire being fifty yards away. A run for it—crash through the friggin' one-arm barricade and drive like hell. He was excited, but he wasn't dumb. Probably wouldn't make it anyway. Besides, there was the minor matter of leaving everyone else behind. *Not nice.* There were no wire cutters in the toolbox. *Shit.* He grabbed a pair of pliers, a file, snatched the keys and got out of the truck.

In all it had taken less than a minute. From underneath the truck Murphy could see a thicket of legs. One of the POWs whom Danny Mellin had designated as a lookout saw Murphy under the tailgate and shouted, "C'mon, hurry up there! I'm starving!" This was immediately followed by a surge of bodies around the tailgate and Murphy scrabbling amid the legs, only to surface as the guards began pushing the line back while clubbing several POWs to the ground.

"You get wire cutters?" Mellin asked, handing the Australian his rice bowl and plastic spoon.

"No cutters," Murphy told him, "but I swiped the truck's keys. Silly bastards left 'em in the ignition."

"They're going to shoot people when they find them missing."

"You don't say," Murphy said. "But first the driver'll get shit and he'll wonder whether he left 'em in the truck or wherever. You know how it is when you've lost your keys?"

"Yeah, but when he's sure they've been stolen, they're gonna shoot people."

"Exactly," Shirley chimed in.

"All right, you two," Murphy snapped. "Cool it. Ya don't think I haven't thought that out?"

"So what are you going to do with them?" Shirley asked. "Hold out for a reward?"

"Very fucking amusing."

"All right, Mike," Danny cut in. "What's your plan?"

"Well, first we get a good impression of the key. Surely to God we've got someone in this camp who can make a duplicate—can do it from wood if you get a good impression."

"And how—" Shirley began, but the Australian didn't let her finish.

"Mud," he said. "Fucking compound's a sea of mud, if you hadn't noticed. We get a good impression—mud on a brick—anything'll do."

Shirley Fortescue conceded it was the obvious thing to do.

"Then return the keys?" Danny asked.

"Right!" Murphy said. "Only we don't have to be particular. I mean we don't need to get anyone back into the cabin. Just toss the keys outside the truck by the driver's running board. He'll figure he dropped them getting out."

"Okay," Danny agreed, "but move fast. We'll have all the POW huts up by tonight."

"Good as done," Murphy quipped, gripping the keys and disappearing into the crowd of POWs.

CHAPTER SIXTY-NINE

KACEY HAD DONE nothing, but then the black man put the AK-47's barrel against the little girl's temple. "Listen, man, you don't come out in thirty seconds I'm gonna waste the kid. Then I'm gonna start on her family. You want me to bring 'em out? We'll waste the whole fuckin' village, man—if that's what it takes. I ain't gonna let you fuck up my business, man. You dig?"

You dig, Kacey thought. It was from another era—another time, another place. And what the hell is *business*?

Kacey said nothing, his right thumb moving the catch to the full automatic position.

The black man yelled something in a language other than English, and the tail-end Charlie of the six-man Khmer squad ran back a hundred yards or so to the village. Kacey could hear nothing but the occasional faint whimper, like that from a puppy, the young girl crying. Then he heard shouting and a slap that resounded through the rain forest as the tail-end Khmer was half dragging, half pushing two elderly natives, a man and a woman—Laotians most probably—down the trail toward the black man. The young girl turned as if to run to them, but the black man cuffed her about the ears. Then behind the tail-end Khmer and the old couple there came a woman armed with the ubiquitous AK-47 and wearing one of the green lion-tamer hats so popular in the old NVA. Kacey could tell it was a woman, for despite the leafy camouflage about her head and shoulders, she couldn't hide her figure. As she came nearer, about twenty yards from where Kacey was hiding, he could see she was white.

Through the undergrowth Kacey caught glimpses of the two

elderly Laotians being driven, half tottering, up the trail, the old man tripping.

There was a shot, and a scream so loud that Kacey felt a sudden chill as he strained to see which of the old people had fallen. Neither of them. It was the young girl who'd been shot.

"You hear me, man?" came the black man's voice. "I ain't foolin' 'round here. Now you come out or we'll do the old man next. Man, we'll do the whole friggin' village if we have to. You understand? Now move your ass." The man was poking the distraught old Laotian woman with the AK-47.

Kacey stood, his hands held high. "All right!" he shouted, and made his way toward the track even as he realized it was a no-win situation. There was no doubt in his mind he'd be shot. The only question remaining was, who'd pull the trigger, Salt or Pepper?

CHAPTER SEVENTY

A GOOD MUD impression was made of the truck key stolen by Murphy, and already one of the dozens of technician POWs from the oil rigs was working on making a duplicate out of the hard base of his plastic tea mug, while another was using the file Mike Murphy had brought him to hone the edges of the pliers into a wire cutter. Murphy told Danny Mellin that he saw no reason why they couldn't bust out that night. Shirley Fortescue, glancing up at the wind-riven sky, advised against it. "Too much moonlight," she said, "now that the monsoon's passed."

Danny didn't like the suggestion of any delay. "Longer we wait, the longer Upshut and his crew have to detect something's going down. Besides, we could have an informer amongst us. Won't take long before someone starts thinking about getting extra rations of rice—a bit of meat, whatever."

"Then I say go tonight," Murphy said. "Moon or not."

"Let's see what the weather's like tonight," Danny replied. "Might cloud over later this afternoon."

"I say go!" Murphy repeated.

"Wait and see," Danny said.

"I agree," Shirley put in.

"Two to one," Danny said. "That it?"

"Women got the vote," Shirley said, looking at Murphy. "Or hadn't you heard?"

Right there and then, Murphy wanted her. Not only was she good-looking, but there was something about her standoffish manner that excited him, that begged to be tamed.

CHAPTER SEVENTY-ONE

IN HONG KONG, Breem, satiated from a smorgasbord of sex with Mi Yin and two other girls who he was sure belonged to the Chinese Secret Service, put on his royal-blue robe, wandered over to the full-length glass windows by his fax, which overlooked the harbor, and grabbed a handful of messages from all around the world. The ones that interested him most were from various hospitals requesting donor organs, and those faxes from Fukien province, a cover for Beijing transmits, requesting resupply of tractor bearings—another cover, this time "bearings" referring to bullets, "tractor" to Black Rhino, the type of bullet. Within minutes he had ordered the "tractor bearings" to be taken south to the Ningming railhead.

Breem estimated that the profit on the sale of the armor-piercing bullets alone would net him around a million U.S. dollars, and then there was the kickback from General Wei's son-in-law, who, as part of a resurging market in China, was Wei's procurement officer.

It wasn't the first time that the irony of the Chinese buying

American bullets from an American to maim and/or kill Americans struck Breem as funny. The whole business of international arms dealers reinforced Breem's conviction that in this world there were only winners and losers, and that right now the Americans were the losers. Oh sure, press reports were going out on CNN telling how the Americans were making up some lost ground in the fighting around someplace called Disney Hill, but Breem was more than confident that once the U.S.-USVUN counterattack met the fresh troops and Black Rhino armor-piercing ammunition now on their way via rail to the front from Ningming, the Chinese would soon push the Americans back. Besides, if the newspaper stories were true, then a U.S.-USVUN force sent in by Freeman to secure his left flank around Dien Bien Phu was about to be wiped out by an overwhelming number of Chinese airborne troops.

Flicking through the channels, Breem picked up another news story, this one from BBC television news claiming that as well as the Chinese airborne, a full Chinese regiment of 2,817 men had been moving down the 150 miles of secondary roads from China's Mengzi to the area around Dien Bien Phu. Whether this force had been sent by General Wang before or after Freeman's IFOR was now purely academic. What mattered was that ignoring Laotian neutrality, as Freeman had done, the Chinese now in Vietnam were closing in on the valley between Dien Bien Phu and Ban Cong Deng. And roads meant heavy artillery; not that a lack of roads would have prevented the PLA from bringing down their heavy guns. In their last war with Vietnam, they had manhandled heavy guns down piece by piece, as the Viet Minh had done against the French.

The BBC interviewer asked a military expert who would win.

"All depends on what the troops are like on the ground."

"Well," the interviewer said, "Freeman's lot around Dien Bien Phu are said to be top-drawer troops."

"We'll see," the professor said dryly. "The PLA is no pushover, and their lot are also believed to be the 'top drawer,' as you put it—and there are many more of them."

"One more question, Professor. If we—and by 'we' I mean the USVUN forces—have known about PLA intervention through Laos, why didn't the Americans bomb them?"

"Because," the professor said, looking bored, "the President of the United States has obviously made a decision—and in my view, a perfectly justified one—not to allow bombing on neutral territory. In this case, Laos."

"Yet he let Freeman in with his special force."

"Yes, but my dear chap, that was a field decision by Freeman, for which, my sources inform me, he came perilously close to losing his job."

"But he's a hero now."

The professor blinked, his forehead furrowed under the studio lights. "A hero, yes, but for how long? If he loses what must surely be an outright battle at Dien Bien Phu and at Disney Hill, he'll no longer be a hero. I can assure you of that. I might add that the eminent French reporter, Pierre LaSalle, is already predicting a humiliation for the Americans on both fronts."

CHAPTER SEVENTY-TWO

"YOU PRICK!"

"Calling me names ain't gonna get us anywhere, brother."

"I'm not your fucking brother, man."

"You black, aren't you—or that shoe polish?"

"I don't go 'round killing kids."

"Then what took you so long to make up yo' mind, man?"

"I thought you were bluffin'," Kacey said.

"Until we did her, right?" Pepper smiled, his AK-47 pointing right at Kacey's gut, his head nodding back at the two elderly sobbing Laotian hostages. "Life's cheap over here, man. Dyin' is a way of life this part o' the world."

Kacey said nothing.

"Lookit, man, all we want from you is the location of your boys settin' up ambush 'round here. We ain't interested in yo' fucking war, man. We just want safe passage."

Kacey stared blankly at him before asking, "Safe passage for what?"

"Business," Pepper said easily. By now a stream of porters were coming down the track, butter-box-sized loads suspended from poles and knapsacks on their backs. Kacey could tell they were Khmer Rouge, and when the Khmer Rouge didn't want to kill people, there was only one other reason they'd be there.

"Heroin?" Kacey asked.

"Pure." The other man smiled. "White as you inside, Oreo." He jerked his head in the direction of the woman with the good figure and the camouflaged pith helmet. "Ain't only thing I got that's white."

Kacey said nothing.

"You coming with us, buddy." Pepper said. It was a statement, not a question. "You guys put up any ambushes, you'll be the first in it, right?"

"What if I don't want—"

"Hey!" The other black man suddenly lost it, jabbing Kacey hard in the gut. "I ain't fuckin' askin', asshole. I'm tellin' you. You're comin' or grandma gets it—then grandpa, right? You dig me, Oreo?"

"Yes."

"Then off we go. You screw up, nigger, and grandma gets it. You understand?"

Kacey didn't answer, so Pepper stuck him in the back with his AK-47. "You understand, asshole?"

"Yes," Kacey said, and began to walk, knowing that up ahead, about two miles down the jungle trail, his buddies in Foxtrot were waiting, while behind him came Salt and Pepper Two with the two elderly hostages. He didn't know what to do.

Pepper suddenly stopped the column with a hand signal and gave an order softly to Salt, who led the old folks back to the village. He could hear an argument, then Salt returned with two children, a boy and a girl around ten years old. Kacey figured that Pepper had suddenly realized how the old folks might slow him down. The kids could move much faster.

They started off again, and Kacey still didn't know what to do. The only hope the Ranger could harbor was the possibility that Foxtrot's western approaches security team of two would get a good look at him, recognize he was one of their own, and let him pass before opening fire. But what about the two kids no more than ten paces behind him? To make everything worse, more confused, it was getting dark.

Like most things in war, Kacey mused, no matter how well you plan things, something always goes wrong. What kind of luck was it to be setting a trap for Khmer Rouge troops and instead run smack into a freakin' drug caravan armed to the teeth?

CHAPTER SEVENTY-THREE

DANNY MELLIN, MIKE Murphy, and Shirley Fortescue were having their own bad luck. Above the POW camp white clouds of cumulus were crossing the moon like a line of silvered galleons, at once obscuring then revealing moonlight.

The silhouette of the four PLA trucks that had been parked in a square around Upshut's guarded administrative hut were clear one moment, obscured the next, and there was no way of knowing how many guards were inside. Beyond the long coils of razor wire that made up the camp's perimeter, there were two PLA soldiers for each side, eight guards in all, constantly walking up and down the side they'd been assigned. As the camp was not yet complete, four three-ton trucks were parked at each corner of the camp, a type 67, 7.62mm machine gun mounted atop each truck's cabin. These would soon be replaced by regular guard towers. The on-again, off-again moonlight wasn't making Danny Mellin's decision any easier. If they waited a few days, the PLA would erect bamboo-supported towers, equipping each with overarching searchlights. Yet if they went now and were caught in a beam of moonlight . . .

"I say go," Mike Murphy urged, glancing around at the other POWs. "Look," he said, turning to Mellin, "pretty soon this thick cloud cover is gonna pile up, hiding the moon."

"I don't know if it will or not," Shirley said, "but I'm leaning toward Murphy. They could start on those towers tomorrow. And as you said, Danny, someone's bound to let something slip out sooner rather than later."

"All right," Danny said. "We go. Everybody know what they have to do?"

Mike answered for the others. "Yeah, two of us in the cabin, one navigator, one driver, four in the back of the truck, one man feeding the other on the machine gun."

"Right. Remember 'one'?"

"Cut the wire," Murphy answered, the tension making his throat tight.

"Two?" Danny said.

"Get the two guards nearest the truck," Shirley answered.

"Three?"

"In the trucks," one of the others said.

"Four?"

"Drive like hell—" Murphy began.

"Jesus, Mike!" Danny cut in.

"Sorry, sorry. Four—if any team has time, we hook the cut wire to the tailboard and pull the shit out of the perimeter."

"And," Shirley put in, "shoot up the four trucks inside the compound to stop them chasing us—*if* we have time."

For better security, the people that made up the two squads had all been chosen from the same hut. They had split any money they'd managed to hide on themselves upon arrest by the PLA, some preferring to carry American cigarettes to yuan. There was no survival kit, unless you included a ball of rice saved here and there—whatever was left after they'd donated enough to Mellin's wall—the wall of the hut nearest the wire, the wire looking like great rolls of silver in the intermittent moonglow.

Via biofeedback, Danny was willing his breathing to slow down, asking quietly, "Every team got their matchbox compass?" They all said yes. "Remember, the border's fourteen miles due south from here."

A voice in the darkness asked, "Mike, you got those wire cutters tied to your wrist?"

"No."

"Well, you'd better. You drop them in the dark and can't find 'em, we're up shit creek."

"Good idea," Danny said, his heart racing. Damn! he be- rated himself. Tying the cutters to the first man's wrist should have been one of the first things he'd thought of. He and the other nineteen in the two escape teams knew that the toughest part would be taking out the two-man PLA guards as they walked the couple of hundred yards or so along the wire. He and a couple of others were former 'Nam or Desert Storm types, so they knew how to kill, but none of them were anywhere near their normal strength, having subsisted on little more than a bowl of rice and the weak, lukewarm green tea. Some, like Danny Mellin, had ground up the occasional bug with a spoonful of rice and forced it down. At least it was protein.

"One more thing," Danny reminded them. "Be careful with the machine guns. I mean, when we break out, it'll make one hell of a big hole for all our fellow POWs to run through. That's good for everybody. PLA'll have to look for two hundred of us if there's a mass break, and every POW in here knows the importance of the Ningming–Dong Dang railroad."

Having said his piece, Danny now turned his attention to the sky. It had always amazed him how cloud formations change in seconds, that the patch of sky you've been watching changes completely in five minutes. It was something he'd had ample time to notice while working, like Mike Murphy and the other POWs, on the rigs in the South China Sea, something that most people in normal, everyday life didn't notice. There was such a change occurring now, the moon's face becoming obliterated as anvil-shaped cumulus piled up. Where seconds before there had been a brilliant orb, there were now only dark storm clouds. Soon it began raining. There was nothing gradual about it—it simply fell in buckets, as was its wont in the region.

Then he saw lightning, and a moment later it seemed as if God's artillery had opened up, the thunder so powerful they could feel it rumbling in the hut, rattling the locked door. Danny Mellin and three others, including Murphy, picked up the base of one of the bunks, counted in unison, "One, two," and smashed it into the wall where the rice had formed much of the mortar. Immediately they could feel that several bricks had been displaced by the shock of the bunk base, the air pockets around the grains of rice having substantially weakened the mortar between the bricks.

Waiting for the next roll of thunder, they counted and hit it again. There was choking dust, and three of the ramming squad were on the floor. Mike was stuck halfway through the hole, his knuckles badly lacerated. But he felt the rain pouring on his head and murmured, "Christ, we're through! We're fucking through!" It was a ragged hole about three feet in diameter.

"Quick," Mellin ordered. "Get to the wire." There was another flash of lightning, during which the hole was brightly illuminated. Then there was another rolling barrage of thunder as the ten of them quickly got through the hole and within seconds were at the wire.

As Murphy cut the first strand, there was a rustling sound as the tension of the wire gave way, but the noise was drowned out by the gut-churning rolls of thunder and the hiss of the rain. Soon they were halfway through the concertina wire. Murphy stopped and listened for the sentries. He couldn't see any in the rain-riven darkness, nor could he hear them, given the noise of the storm. Murphy cut more wire, stopped and listened, and all he could hear was his heart thumping. Soon, within seven minutes of reaching the razor wire, all ten of them were through, five turning left, the other five to the right.

Both teams, Murphy in charge of the first squad, Danny the second, all crouching low, moving along the outer wire, were astonished not to find any guards.

"Probably in the trucks," Shirley whispered.

"Hope to Christ they haven't locked the doors," Murphy whispered in return. "Shirley, stay with me. You too, Frank. The other three of you go around to the passenger side."

The sound of the rain was drumming on the truck's canopy, rivulets of water running down the fenders and streaming off the running boards. Suddenly, Murphy saw a red spot dancing about in the cabin, someone in the cabin smoking, nice and comfy out of the rain.

"Now!" he said in a hoarse command, wrenched open the driver's door, and pulled him out. Already three others of Murphy's crew were up in the back, while the other guard, on the passenger side, who had also been smoking, was on the sodden ground begging for mercy. Shirley hesitated, so Murphy hit him with the brick—once—as he had the driver. "Frank, you man the machine gun, Shirley, you're navigator. Let's go."

The moment Murphy felt the keys in the ignition, he couldn't contain his excitement. "Jesus loves me!" He pumped the gas pedal twice and turned the key. The truck started to life, running roughly but going.

He drove the truck halfway down the wire, his parking lights on, and saw Danny's truck, or rather its two orange eyes, approaching him. Shadowy figures jumped from both trucks and quickly hooked wire to their tailgate. But before starting northward for the secondary road west of Ningming, both trucks now swung their machine guns about and waited till the next flash of lightning, then fired at the four trucks around the administrative block.

It was about ten seconds before one of the trucks caught fire, and from then on they were easy sport for the two gunners. Another truck lurched hard to its right, tires now in shreds, the windscreens and engines of the other two shot through with full bursts of 7.62mm. The remaining two corner PLA trucks could be heard starting up, but they too were shot up in the surprise enfilade of fire from the two prisoner-commandeered vehicles.

There was pandemonium as lights came on in the administration building, only to disappear in the sound of crashing glass as Danny's and Murphy's machine guns raked the building at practically point-blank range, the temporary lights in it a perfect aiming point. Now, in the madly dancing glow of the burning trucks, Danny's and Murphy's teams could see scores of prisoners streaming out from what had been Danny's hut, using bunk beds to ram the front doors of the other huts. More prisoners came out and raced for the five-yard-wide corridor through the razor wire.

Danny and Murphy knew it was time to go, a dozen or so prisoners clambering aboard as the wire on the two trucks' tailgates was disconnected, the trucks heading off on the POW camp–Ningming road, sporadic AK-47 fire from the compound spitting into the night.

On Disney Hill, sixteen miles south, Colonel Melbaine's counterattack had regained the hill's summit by dark. The heavy rains slowed the USVUN advance in the later afternoon, but it sealed the fate of the Chinese tunnels on the north side, which were now no more than drainage conduits, their integrity gone because of the severe structural damage done to them by the heavy U.S. TACAIR and artillery fire the day before.

Even so, Melbaine knew that if General Wei could be resupplied fast enough and with enough fresh troops, of which he had many more than the USVUN, it could quickly become a stalemate again, followed by another retreat by the Americans and their allies. And though Melbaine was a toughened combat veteran whose sole job was the conduct of war, he knew as well as Freeman did the symbolic, political importance of pushing the Chinese beyond Disney Hill to the 22nd parallel, *beyond* the border, to unequivocally signal the defeat and not merely the rout of the Chinese.

But if the big question for Freeman was enemy resupply—a danger that might once again push his troops back—the pressing danger for Danny Mellin's escapees was whether anyone two miles away at the Ningming airfield had seen the explosion of the trucks in the POW compound. It was more than likely that the thunderstorm and downpour had muffled or completely drowned out the sound of their explosions, but it was just as certain that the brief firefight at the compound had been reported to the PLA guard contingent at the Ningming airfield.

The moment General Wei heard reports of an "attack" around Ningming, he immediately took it to be an Anglo-American special *ground* forces attack on his left flank behind his lines, specifically targeting the Ningming railhead, since Wei knew full well that the U.S. President had forbidden any air interdiction inside Chinese territory. From Wei's position, the enemy ground force was obviously trying what the Americans called an end run: bypassing the bulk of his PLA troops at Disney and trying to disrupt his vitally needed Ningming–Xiash–Pingxiang–Dong Dang supply line.

For half an hour all along the line, field phones were crackling, passing on the information that American saboteurs had reached Ningming. Comrade Upshut and the others at the POW camp went along with Wei's interpretation of the presence of allied troops around Ningming; otherwise, Upshut and his comrades would have to confess to the spectacular breakout in their camp, and why two of eight PLA-type BM-14 trucks were missing, and four of them destroyed, two still aflame outside the camp's administration hut. And then there was the not-so-minor point of Upshut and the others immediately calling for a head count of prisoners in the dancing firelight of what had been the administration building. It was a head count infused with fury and panic on the part of the guards.

The count showed that thirty-seven had escaped, about twenty more than in either Danny Mellin's or Mike Murphy's trucks, whose twenty had run out through the break in the wire, slipping away in the darkness even as the remaining prisoners were ordered to form up in their respective hut groups.

Another dozen or so slipped away on their way back to the huts as the fires from the trucks, now subdued by the rain, failed to illuminate the open wire beyond the huts to any of the PLA guards.

When Danny Mellin saw the egg-yolk smear of light that was the perimeter lights of Ningming airfield, he also saw stalks of searchlights reaching out like long, white fingers south of the field into the rain-slashed darkness. This wasn't how the breakout was supposed to end, with Ningming field suddenly bristling with PLA air force troops.

None of the searchlights had yet reached the two trucks, but already flares were bursting in the air beyond the airfield's perimeter, showing just how heavily it was raining, the streaks of rain illuminated like so many icicles, and here and there Mellin and Murphy could see in the distance dim rectangular shapes coming out of the airfield's perimeter: PLA trucks, no doubt full of troops.

Both Mellin and Murphy saw that it was impossible to get past the Ningming field using the Ningming secondary road, and the rain that was obscuring them at the moment was also turning the marshland around the levy road into a sea.

Mellin, about fifty yards ahead of Murphy's truck, pumped the brakes and stopped. Shirley Fortescue jumped down and ran, already soaking wet, to the dark shape of the Australian's truck, the vehicle momentarily etched in the glow of a descending para flare.

"What's up?" Murphy shouted, head leaning out the driver's side.

"Mike," Shirley told him, "Danny says we won't get past them, and if we go off the road we'll be bogged down."

"So what's he suggest? We swim?"

"More or less," she answered, her voice all but lost in the torrential downpour. "He's telling everyone to get out of the trucks and head south."

"I want to talk to them," Murphy yelled. "You get your mob out, Shirley, I'll get mine."

Within a minute there was a sodden conference on the levy leading toward Ningming, with both Danny Mellin and Murphy knowing they probably had no more than ten minutes before the PLA would arrive.

"Listen up," Murphy said. "Danny's right. We're going to have to ditch these trucks and split up. That way it's going to take them a bloody lot longer to track us all down, including the ones who got through the wire after we got through. This way we can tie up a lot of Chinese troops that might be otherwise guarding that railroad from here to the border. I suggest we pair off. Let's get going."

"Michael." It was so unexpected, it stunned him. It was Shirley.

"Yeah?"

"What are you and your number two . . ." She indicated a Vietnamese/Chinese in the truck's cabin.

"Yeah, well, young Trang and I figured we might give you a bit of a head start."

"Mike!" Danny shouted. "Don't try—"

"Upshut!" Murphy yelled, and it elicited a grim laugh. "Now go on, get lost, and try to team up with someone who speaks Cantonese."

Shadows of the escaping POWs were vanishing beyond the flickering gray circles of dying flares, and now Murphy could see six pairs of yellow-slitted headlights, like a short, fast, winding snake, no more than a mile away to the north, and another two trucks coming from the camp behind as he quickly backed up the truck that Mellin had been driving, moving it askew so as to block the road. He tossed the keys away and, uncinching the PLA-type light machine gun from its mount, ran back to his own truck and lay down by the rear right wheel.

Already the graceful arcs of light machine-gun fire were reaching toward him from the north, while behind him, Murphy could see the two remaining trucks from the POW camp now screaming along the levy. He and Trang could hear the heavy *whoomp* of mortars hitting the marsh water about them, sending spumes of water over a hundred feet into the air.

With the two opposing forces heading for one another along the levy, Murphy suddenly decided to change tactics. "C'mon, Trang," he shouted. "Let's get down the bank into the water, quick. Grab the gun from the other truck!"

And it was in that position, from the marsh, that Trang and Murphy let rip with the two 7.62mm machine guns. Soon both lead trucks on either side of the two abandoned POW trucks were afire, Trang yelling out, "Kill! Kill!" in Chinese. Further confusing the issue, the trucks behind the lead truck from Ningming field were unable to fire for fear of hitting their comrades in the front trucks.

NCOs were screaming at enlisted men to get off the trucks

and engage the enemy in the POW trucks because of the direction of fire coming from Trang and Murphy. Murphy fired a long burst, killing the driver of the first Ningming truck and setting its gas drum afire. The truck blew up, hurling bodies every which way, the PLA troops in the trucks behind now spewing out to run alongside the levy.

"Let's get out of here," Murphy yelled at Trang, and after firing the last magazine into the two camp trucks that had come up behind them, with both sets of PLA firing away at one another, Murphy and Trang dropped the LMGs into the waist-deep marsh water and, tearing out reeds for snorkels, began swimming away from a situation of utter confusion, of Chinese firing upon Chinese in the raging storm, and of escaping POWs who by now, thanks to Murphy and Trang's delaying action, had had a good twenty- to twenty-five-minute start toward the border.

But if the Chinese were confused by that night's debacle, by the following morning, though the rain was still falling in sheets, they were much better organized for the hunt. They'd already caught several of the escapees who had become disoriented and headed east in the storm instead of south. Upshut had them garroted, following strict orders not to waste valuable ammunition, particularly the expensive Black Rhino rounds, on prisoners.

Some of General Wei's staff officers initially thought that Wei was making a meal out of the escape, until Wei—and this, he informed them, was why he was being paid 675 yuan, $144, a month instead of the 21 yuan of a private—drew his staff officer's attention to the fact that most of the escapees, if they had any brains at all, would stay in sight of the Ningming–Dong Dang rail line, traveling parallel with it until they reached the border and the country around Disney Hill. Wei also advised his subordinates that if any of the escapees, most of them technicians from oil rigs, decided to try to sabotage the line and were successful, even in delaying the heavy artillery-mounted supply train to the front for a few hours, it could prove decisive in the battle against Freeman's mounting thrust against Disney Hill and environs.

"But Comrade General," an eager young division commander pointed out, "we—you have already posted a man along every fifty yards of track."

"Yes, yes, I know this, but anyone who is innovative

enough to mix his rice with brick mortar—to engineer such an escape out of practically nothing—he is a dangerous man, comrades, and so we must not only try to capture as many of the escapees as possible, but we must be particularly vigilant along the thirty miles of rail from here to the border. I want all rail-section commanders to emphasize this to their troops."

Among themselves, Wei's senior officers were convinced that Wei was overreacting. In their view—and they were correct—most of the escapees from the POW camp would have only one thing on their mind: to get back through enemy lines to safety, and to hell with messing around with Wei's railway. Oh yes, there might be the odd fanatic who would try something like the genius who pulled the rice trick, but with a PLA soldier every fifty yards—what chance did he have?

Nevertheless, Wei was not to be dissuaded from taking extra precautions, and so onlookers saw the strange sight of a regiment of mounted Chinese troops—an anachronism in modern war—heading out in marshland south of the Ningming-Pingxiang line, able to go where armor or any other vehicle could not. And they were protected from U.S. TACAIR by both the foul weather—God's response to Freeman's prayer—and by the President of the United States, who, like Truman forbidding MacArthur to take action beyond the Chinese-Korean border, had ordered Freeman not to launch air strikes over the Sino-Vietnamese border.

CHAPTER SEVENTY-FOUR

SHORTLY BEFORE PIERRE LaSalle returned to her tent, Marte Price had found her asbestos-lined film box had been opened. She'd put a hair between the lid and sides before closing it, and now the hair wasn't there. While she was no military strategist, she believed that in matters of sex and blackmail, a good defense was the best offense. In this instance, her offense took the form of insisting that Pierre wear a condom.

"You're the only one, *chérie*," he said.

"And I'm Marilyn Monroe."

"No, truly," he told her. "You are the only one."

"Not counting your wife, you mean."

"Of course. But this is the *grande affaire*, no?"

"It's good sex," she said. "If that's what you mean."

"Surely it's more than that."

"If you say so."

"You are a hard woman."

"You're the one that's hard. I still have some illusions."

"About what?"

"Oh, I don't know—about honesty among friends, loyalty."

"I hope you are not talking about me!" He sounded offended.

"No," she lied. "Just in general."

He slid his hand between her thighs. "I love the smell of you. . . ."

She said nothing for a moment, then suddenly mellowing from her public persona of tough, hard-bitten war correspondent, having shown she could mix it with the boys, she was now the vulnerable, soft lover Pierre wanted her to be. She gently stroked him, and as he grew hard, she touched a freckle near the base of his penis, all but hidden by his pubic hair. "You always had that?"

"Yes," he said. "A little birthmark, I guess."

"It's cute," she said, stroking him. "Pierre?"

"Oui?"

"Do you love your wife?"

He shrugged. "You know how it is. We've been married—"

"You don't love her?"

"No, not really. She's more of a—how do you say, friend, confidante."

"Then she wouldn't mind you making love to me."

He gently pushed her down on the army cot. "I think she would mind," he said with studied understatement. He laughed. "She would mind it very much, *chérie*."

She moaned softly as he entered her.

After, when they had parted, Marte went to the media pool office and told the officer in charge that if they were ever asked to send a pix of General Freeman "in action," she hesitated, "with the wounded," she would appreciate them telling her.

"May I ask why, miss?"

"Yes," she said bluntly. "It's my fucking picture and anyone who tries to send it is stealing it. And rest assured I'll have the general on my side."

"Yes, ma'am."

She put a hundred-dollar bill on the table. "So you won't forget."

"Yes, *ma'am*."

CHAPTER SEVENTY-FIVE

KACEY, NOW FORCED at gunpoint to lead the Khmer Rouge column away from the Foxtrot ambuscade out toward the valley of Dien Bien Phu, could hear the pat-pat-pat sound of the children walking behind him. He knew there was nothing he could do about the little girl who lay dead and discarded by Pepper by the trail, as if she were nothing more than refuse to be consumed by some carnivore during the night. In all his years in the Army, he'd never seen anything so wantonly cruel. But now he tried to put it out of his mind, knowing he had to stay alert.

Kacey had no way of knowing that radio silence had been broken and Foxtrot ordered to withdraw to boost the defense of Dien Bien Phu. But he did know that even if the prearranged signal spot on the trail told him the column had been ordered to withdraw, soon Pepper's column would be leaving the jungle canopy and entering Delta's fire zone in the valley. And, being the first man in the column, he had no desire to be the first blue on blue in Operation Homecoming.

Then they heard the faint rattle of machine guns and the louder *whoomp* of mortars.

It meant that Delta and the PLA paratroops were already at it.

"Hey, Ranger!"—from the side of the trail. It was a scout from Delta. Pepper unleashed a burst. The scout dropped to the ground, and Kacey dived off the trail, the scout returning fire at Pepper. Kacey moved fast and low—fuck the bamboo, fuck the brambles, fuck the thorns, just run, man, run—as Pepper and the Delta scout continued the duel, the terrified children flat on the trail, Salt at the rear telling them to stay put or she'd do them. Somebody—Pepper maybe, or the Delta scout?—ran out of ammo, only one man firing, then the two were at it again. Jesus, could they even see one another, or was it all bullshit fire?

Then Kacey was yelling to his fellow Delta buddy, "Delta, he's a turncoat! They're Salt and Pepper Two— our MIAs both gone bad! Heroin!"

The jungle reeked of cordite and decay. The Delta scout didn't care who the fuck they were—Salt and Pepper, Oil and Vinegar—all he knew was that some fucker was trying to kill him.

"Back off!" Kacey yelled to his fellow Ranger. "We can pick 'em up later."

No one was moving now—no birds, nothing—except in the distance they could hear the *thump!* and *thwack!* of mortar rounds in the timber around the Delta perimeter.

Kacey knew it had to be the PLA paratroopers harassing the Delta perimeter till they had time to set up heavy arty in the hills around the valley. The mist was thicker now, and ten minutes—an eternity—passed, and who was heading where? Kacey kept heading east, glancing at his watch compass in the gloom. Only once did he see the trail, a rust-red strip about a hundred feet off to his right, while to his front, a half mile off perhaps, he could hear the chatter of small-arms fire. Through it all he felt that something or someone was marking him, either his compadre from Delta or Pepper, who would now be eager to meet up with the PLA troopers.

"Jesus Christ!" Kacey stopped. He could be walking into his own—Delta Force's—ambuscade. They were bound to have rigged one up as soon as he'd gone forward to try to warn Foxtrot. Shit a brick, it was getting all screwed up, as usual. Didn't matter what plans you made, something always went—

He froze. A drop of moisture on the trip wire, that's all it was. He was in the middle of a claymore alley. "If anyone can hear me," he said in funereal tones, "get me outta here!"

" 'Bout time, you fucker. We were gonna see how far you'd go!"

"Very funny."

"Turn right, my man, and go straight ahead."

In three minutes he was out on the trail. God, it felt good! "Where're all the chinks?" he asked.

"Just north of us, Ranger man." It was the Delta scout who'd been keeping parallel with him.

"How far north?" Kacey asked, his breathing short and fast.

"Not far enough," the scout said as he passed his canteen to Kacey, "but they're just probing now. Won't do any major stuff till they get arty in around us—which they're doing now."

"Where's our TACAIR?" Kacey asked.

"In this pea soup? Home, where you'd be. Back in Hanoi, waiting for it to lift. Only do so much with infrared, man."

"Scout tells me," said Delta's C.O., Roscoe, "that you ran into Salt and Pepper."

"Yeah," Kacey said.

"They're probably headed north of us for PLA sanctuary. You get a good look at them?"

"Pepper, but not her."

"A *woman*?"

"Yeah," Kacey said. "Made a real nice couple. Moving dope."

"A *woman*!" Roscoe repeated, as if it were an offense against nature. "All right," he said. "I want you and Jonson to stay here on the perimeter where the trail exits the canopy—make a damn nuisance of yourselves against any chinks who try setting up mortar positions or whatever—'specially since you know, Kacey, what this Salt and Pepper look like. They might just come our way. I'll send a squad out here with you and—"

Suddenly there was a horrendous rattle of machine-gun fire, both M-60 and Chinese-type 67 LMGs. Then more mortar rounds, but for the experienced men of Delta like Kacey, Roscoe, and Jonson, it all had the sound and feel of probing, no one really sure yet of exactly where the other side was.

"Wish we could get out of this fucking marsh," Jonson said.

"I agree," Roscoe said. "Trouble is, if we do that, we no longer have an LZ when the choppers arrive."

"They're not going to come in this weather," Jonson said.

"They'll come in any weather. But clear weather'd help."

Jonson shrugged mischievously. "Then maybe we *should* get the old man to pray for a typhoon!"

"Yeah—incoming!"

They hit the marshy ground as a PLA 82mm mortar exploded twenty-five yards away, earth and water erupting in a high, dirty column. For Delta's Roscoe there was something wrong—he felt it in his bones. Something peculiarly disconcerting about the almost laissez-faire way in which the PLA mortar squads were lobbing their mortar rounds, an almost lackadaisical attack, filling in time. But for what, to sucker Delta's British and American forces into wasting precious ammunition in return fire? But return fire where?

Roscoe concluded it could mean only one thing—that the PLA paratroopers, having landed farther north near Dien Bien Phu, had not yet connected up with the PLA ground troops on the way to the valley. Once they connected, they'd no doubt ring the whole valley, sealing the Americans and their allies in the marsh, where they could cut them up piecemeal as Giap had done to the French in the very same valley in '54.

In fact it wasn't as organized as that. Few battle plans are, the hand of chance always in play. Due to the unusually heavy rains, the PLA infantry columns—over a thousand strong—had found it much more difficult, much more time-consuming in the wet, to manhandle the bits and pieces of their heavy artillery south from Mengzi to Dien Bien Phu.

It was now 0230 hours, and the day before, Wang had ordered the elimination of Echo, Foxtrot, and Delta forces. But the weather and the apparent failure of Echo and Foxtrot to yet join Delta had fouled up the timetable. Colonel Cheng, the PLA military officer in charge of the destruction of Freeman's Special Forces, had wanted to attack at 0230 hours, while Delta Force was still only thirty strong. The political officer, however, argued forcefully that it would be better to wait till all three Echo, Foxtrot, and Delta columns had rendezvoused in the valley, so that they might be wiped out to a man. Such a victory, he argued—the annihilation of an entire U.S.-led force—would be infinitely better from a political and international point of view than a piecemeal attack on only one section of it.

In fact, the new battle of Dien Bien Phu would not begin

with all of Freeman's Special Forces in an LZ position and the Chinese in position around the valley, but would start in earnest around 1630 with the sixty Echo and Foxtrot troops making their way back to Delta, and the Chinese having only half their artillery set up. In short, the situation was what Echo's Leigh-Hastings would refer to as your usual run-of-the-mill cockup.

Two hundred fifty miles to the northeast, the winding summit of Disney Hill was still in American hands, due to the bravery of Vinh's USVUN contingent. In hand-to-hand fighting they had finished off many of the Chinese troops forced to vacate their warrens because of flash flooding. It wasn't that the Americans were backward in going forward with a bayonet, but most were equipped with the 203 rifle with grenade launcher tube underneath the barrel to which a bayonet could not be attached.

Though it was a battle where each side was looking for a knockout blow, both knew it would be a seesaw fight, depending as much on the reliability of supplies to the men at the front as on fighting ability. The mist had only partially cleared, and hung low in the valleys, stretching back north into China, where a two-engine train over a mile long could be seen, safe from U.S. TACAIR, bringing guns, food, and ammunition to the PLA battalions in the smaller hills and revetments cloistered about the base of Disney.

Now, more U.S. air cavalry troops and supplies were being unloaded at the southern base of Disney. It wouldn't make up for the awesome tonnage being hauled by what Doolittle, Martinez, and D'Lupo were already calling Von Wei's Express, but Freeman was trying to get "bananas"—Chinook choppers with slings—to ferry 105mm howitzers, made lighter than the usual field 105mms because of aluminum parts—in behind the southern side of the hill, in order to try knocking out the PLA storage areas beyond Disney. But all there was behind Disney now was an inland sea, following Freeman's prayer for good weather, a prayer he was asked about at a quick but intensive news conference later that evening.

"Weather prayer?" he said, face perplexed, feigning ignorance. "I don't petition the good Lord for good weather to kill my fellow man! The United States Army—" Cline whispered in his ear. "—ah," began the general again, "the USVUN forces do battle no matter what the weather."

After the conference it was Cline's turn to be perplexed. "Ah, sir, General?"

"Yes."

"Man-to-man, General."

"All right, man-to-man."

"Sir, why did you—lie about the weather prayer?"

"Well, in the interests of press accuracy, the padre gave the prayer. I merely requested it."

There was a long pause as they walked back to the operations room. "You're right, Bob. I lied. Tell you the truth, I don't know why. Guess I've been getting some pretty lousy press lately, and I thought—well, hell, I shouldnt've done it. I'm sorry. I'll correct it in my memoirs if I don't get killed here. By God, how do they expect me to fight without TACAIR over Chinese territory?"

"Chinese haven't got TACAIR over us, General."

"No, because our boys'd knock 'em out of the sky, that's why."

"Well," Cline said, "at least we can go in over Dien Bien Phu with TACAIR."

"When this foul weather clears—if it ever does. Thing I'm most worried about is that damn no-stop supply train Wei has at his service. Like having a damn Wal-Mart at his beck and call."

"We can't send troops across the line, General."

"No, damn it, but we can try pushing their butts past it."

Near Dien Bien Phu, Colonel Berry's men were making their way back toward Delta when they ran into a squad of PLA hauling a wheel for an artillery piece. Both sides instantly disappeared, except for the man with the wheel, and he was dead in seconds, his body having literally disintegrated on the trail.

Both sides went quickly into defensive positions and froze. It looked like it was going to stay that way for quite a while, until another PLA squad came across the first, took their cue from the one downed wheel, and evaporated into the mist-shrouded jungle, each side knowing that come nightfall the other side would be laying trip wires and mines.

The Chinese had the best of this situation, because Foxtrot

had to get past them before they reached the Dien Bien Phu valley.

On the far side of the valley, five to six miles away and high above the valley floor, elements of Wang's Chengdu army had already installed several AA batteries of SU-23-2 twin 23mm guns, each twin capable of firing two thousand rounds a minute, should any American aircraft be foolhardy enough to come down into the mist-roofed valley. Along with the SU-23mm, there were banks of M1938 12.7mm dual-purpose machine guns set in the antiaircraft configuration, threatening any chopper that came within three thousand feet with six hundred rounds of flak a minute.

The Chinese paras had brought the dual-purpose 12.7mm guns, but the much heavier four-crew 23mm AA guns, whose wheels collapsed in the firing position, had been hauled by vehicle as far south as possible from Mengzi in China, then manhandled by the infantry over torrential rain-swollen rivers and poor secondary roads to Dien Bien Phu. But for the Chinese, the "pièce de la resistance," as Pierre LaSalle reported gleefully, was the Chinese 122mm self-propelled howitzer, whose range, over 22,000 meters, meant they could "pummel," as LaSalle put it in *Le Monde*, any American-USVUN position in the valley. It was also mounted on a PT-76 tank chassis with an in-water speed of ten kilometers. And these were only the guns that Delta's Ranger scouts had pinpointed.

There was no doubt in Freeman's mind that the Chinese did not merely want to defeat Freeman's Special Forces at Dien Bien Phu, but were intent on humiliating the Americans as the Viet Minh had the French almost fifty years ago. Whoever won Dien Bien Phu would eclipse the famous General Giap, would defeat the white man again. For the French, an American defeat would not only exonerate France for the loss in '54, but would, as Pierre LaSalle put it, "cut the Americans down to size." The only hope the Americans might have, Freeman knew, was TACAIR support, and even then it would be touch and go, so long as the valley was locked in by foul weather.

"Goddamn it!" Freeman said, venting his frustration. "On my northern front at Disney I've got clearing conditions, though it's still raining, but I can't send U.S. aircraft across the parallel. On my western flank, where I'm allowed to use TACAIR, I have foul weather, locking in our flyboys and our ground forces. Life isn't fair, Major."

"No, sir. But there is another alternative."

"You suggest it," Freeman said, "and I'll cut you off at the waist!" Before Cline could say anything, Freeman said it for him. "I know there are only about nine thousand of our boys, and maybe ten, twenty times that many Chinese around us, but the international political situation we'd create if we were to surrender, to give up without a fight, would be—" He paused. "—catastrophic! The world's superpower beaten by chinks. Good God, if that happened, we might as well give up on any oil claim anywhere in the world's oceans, and not just in the South China Sea. No one would take us seriously. Might as well say, 'Take the Spratlys, take the Paracels—take any damn thing you like!' No one could rely on us."

His fist slammed against the map and caused a six on the Richter scale from Dien Bien Phu to Ningming. "No, Bob, whatever happens, we have to hold at Dien Bien Phu, and we have to push the bastards back at Disney. There're only two points of battle along the whole line—I realize that—but they are the two plays the whole world is watching. If we win them, we win them all. They're the two hard-ass cases. Besides, if you hadn't noticed, we haven't yet rescued one single MIA!"

The general walked back and forth, pausing every now and then to thwack his jodhpurs with a riding crop. It was an affectation he took from Patton, as Patton had taken his from others. Abruptly, he turned to Cline. "Heard some damned sitrep last night saying some of our boys atop Disney could see horses—through the big binoculars."

"Horses?" Cline said.

"Horses!" Freeman repeated. "Don't know what that frog reporter'll make of it. That kind of Frenchman would love to see us lose. Probably say all we have against us is Chinese cavalry."

It was Chinese cavalry, used largely as packhorses nowadays to subdue minorities, such as the Tibetans, in hard-to-get places. But this day they were hunting the POWs from what official communiqués to the Zhongnanhai HQ in Beijing were calling the breakout at Ningming. Upshut was told bluntly by the Ningming divisional commander that he would be executed for gross negligence of duty unless all forty-two—the morning count had found another five missing—POWs were recovered, dead or alive.

Already he had caught seventeen—women and mostly older

men, Americans, Australians, and Brits, ex–rig foremen, beer bellies, out of condition, and nothing but boiled rice and swill since their captivity.

"Seventeen," Upshut repeated proudly if nervously to the divisional commander.

"Good, comrade. That only leaves *twenty-five* unaccounted for."

The horses and riders were getting tired, but Upshut kept them at it. Any man who failed to catch a prisoner would be executed.

Of the remaining twenty-five, most of them, including Mike Murphy, Trang, Shirley Fortescue, and Danny Mellin, were nearest the railway, shivering, chilled, and hungry. But at least the cavalry were not paying the area near the tracks much attention, leaving it instead to the guards, one posted by Wei every fifty yards along the length of the rail line.

Danny Mellin and Shirley Fortescue were ahead of Murphy and Trang, wading in the paddies adjacent to the Ningming-Xiash road, the rain still falling. It brought with it a mist that, with the turbulence in the paddies caused by the rain, would hide them from view unless they were to get too close to the flooded road.

Despite the chill and the slimy leeches they could feel sucking blood from every part of their bodies, they did not let up. Mellin and Shirley were now closer to the road than Murphy and Trang, Mellin whispering to Shirley that he was going out to get them.

"Why? Aren't they safer the farther out they are?"

"This paddy is giving way to flooded fields where there'll be more cover as—"

"You mean we have to wade for fourteen miles to the border?"

"No. Sooner we can get onto the unflooded part of the road between Ningming and Xiash, the better, but I might need Mike's help."

"Doing what?"

"I'll explain later," Mellin said, and nodded to one of the many tree islands, about a quarter mile from a long section of road that, unlike the elevated rail line above it, was well underwater, several trucks bogged down. "Wait over there for us. Rest up a bit. Won't be long."

Dragging herself to the base of the tree island, up through

tall, slimy elephant grass, Shirley hoped none of the specks she could see, which were guards on the rail line, was using binoculars.

It was something she needn't have worried about, for even given the vital role the railway was playing in the battle of Disney, the People's Liberation Army—or any other army in the world, for that matter—wasn't flush enough to provide each soldier with a pair of ten-power field glasses. Though the day wasn't cold, she was shivering from having been so long in the water. As the sun climbed higher, the entire countryside steamed with moisture evaporating, so thick in parts that, as if in a mirage, some of the Chinese cavalry seemed disembodied from their mounts.

The elephant grass gave way to a patch of brown grass where a deadly black and yellow krait was curled up, basking in the early sun. It struck out. She dodged, letting out a yell. The snake vanished. A cavalryman heard her. So did Mellin and others. Almost immediately she heard the sloshing of water against her tiny island. She could hear Danny Mellin's voice but couldn't see him, though he'd barely left her before she'd seen the snake.

"Shirley, one of them's seen you. Make out you've hurt your leg. Can't move."

"I'm sorry, Danny, I—"

"No matter—just stay where you are."

Within a few minutes a mounted PLA trooper, his horse making a loud, sloshing noise, looked down at her imperiously, his right hand waving a revolver at her to get up. She made a pathetic-sounding plea. "My leg." She pointed. "It's hurt. I can't—"

A stick of wood as thick as a man's arm and about four feet long shot up from the mist and bashed the trooper's head. He slumped on the frightened horse's neck.

"Didn't you hear her, you bastard? She's fallen and she can't get up!"

"Mike—what are you—I thought Danny—"

"I'm here too," Danny told her, coming around from the blind side of the tree island.

Shirley nodded at Trang, who had the horse by the bridle, talking soothingly to the animal in Cantonese.

"Maybe he only understands Mandarin," Mike joked.

"He understands love," Trang said.

"Well, keep him on this side," Mike said, "where they can't see much from the railway. Trang, I hope you can ride."

"Of course."

"Swap clothes with him," Mike said. "No, I don't mean the bloody horse!" They all laughed, all on the edge of that hysteria that comes in the wake of near disaster, a sense of overwhelming relief that Danny Mellin knew he had to get on top of lest it make them foolhardy.

Trang changed into the mounted trooper's uniform and, using the coiled rope on the saddle's pommel, Danny, Shirley, and Murphy tied themselves into a line of three prisoners.

"Trang!" Danny called. "Take it slow. Parallel to the rail line, but don't go in close till you see a culvert. And Trang . . ."

The Asian looked down at the American. "Yes?"

"Make sure you can get that Kalashnikov and sling off in a hurry."

"I will. Who has the Malenkov?" He meant the Soviet-made handgun.

"I do," Murphy said. "Hope it fires after it's been wet."

"I hope we don't have to use it," Danny said.

"So do I," Shirley echoed. "But what happens if another rider sees us?"

"Then," Murphy said nonchalantly, "I'll hit *him* with the fucking stick!"

Trang spotted a culvert then, about a quarter mile west of them. It was difficult to tell exactly, but Mellin figured the culvert itself looked about a quarter mile long. For his plan to work, a culvert was better than open track. "Keep a watch out for the maintenance sheds along the track," he told the others. "There should be one every couple of miles."

" 'Bout the size of a dunny," Murphy explained. "An outhouse!"

Despite her fatigue, Shirley found the Australian's buoyant mood infectious, and she began giggling uncontrollably, as one sometimes does when physically and nervously exhausted.

"Trang," Danny said, "give me his knife."

Shirley suddenly stopped laughing as she realized what had happened to the luckless cavalryman—that Murphy's blow had killed him, that they were at war with the Chinese.

Soon they were passing more islands on the flooded plain. At one point another PLA cavalryman waved and Trang waved back, his three prisoners strung out behind him. "My God," Murphy said. "*I* almost waved to him."

"C'mon," Mellin said sternly. "I know we're all dog-tired, but let's stay with it. If we can—"

A horn beeped. Soldiers by a bogged truck were waving for Trang to come on and bring the prisoners in.

"Shit!" Murphy said. "If Trang doesn't take us in, they'll suspect something."

"We've got no choice," Danny said. "Now listen, here's what we do. Go in close. Wave, Trang, but tell them you have to take your POWs to the culvert."

There was more horn blowing. Shirley was more frightened than she'd been the day she was taken from her rig. She knew why the soldiers wanted them to come in—they had seen her soaking wet—and Danny Mellin knew too. Everybody did. But there was no option.

CHAPTER SEVENTY-SIX

THE BATTLE OF Disney Hill was swinging back in favor of the Chinese, whose supply trains kept bringing up ammunition and more soldiers. But once they moved below the 22nd parallel and into USVUN territory, they came under devastating TACAIR support. It was provided by one of the oldest aircraft in the U.S. inventory, the Skyraider, capable of carrying more ordnance than its own weight, and with a loiter time that made it the sentimental favorite by far of those downed pilots who—while waiting for rescue pickup from the relatively slow Skyraider—would hang around and shoot up anything that tried to get near them before they could be rescued by chopper.

It was a paradoxical military situation, since the more territory Freeman's army gained—by pushing farther north—the less it could depend on TACAIR, because of the Washingtondecreed inviolability of Chinese airspace beyond the Chinese-Vietnamese border. In Washington the "Yalu" complex was alive and well in the State Department from the days of the deep-seated American fear of an all-out nuclear battle between the United States and China.

But for D'Lupo, Doolittle, Martinez, and all the others in the seesaw battle of Disney Hill, politics was a bullshit land where men in three-piece suits talked diplomatese over café latte while the men on the line were dying for yards.

And it was now that General Freeman gave another controversial order: that Melbaine's battalion was not to seek any ground farther than the ridgeline of Disney Hill, for at least that way if Wei's forces crossed the 22nd parallel in force, they would be open to unrestricted TACAIR as well as artillery bombardment.

"Fine!" Doolittle growled. "Why don't we just pull back into the rice paddies and let 'em have the whole fucking lousy hill?"

"You don' understand, man," Martinez said, adopting a tone of mock condescension. "You just a dirt farmer. Don't you know how important this hill is to the negotiations? Testing our will, man. Here and at Dien Bien Phu. Ain't you ever hearda Pork Chop Hill?"

"Stick it up your ass," Doolittle replied. "And rotate, mate."

"Wish to Christ we had more ammo," D'Lupo said. "Half of that last drop is in the fucking drink. All on account of that prayer of his. Meanwhile, the chinks are getting resupplied by the fucking Ningming express, which we can't fucking bomb because it's in fucking Chinese territory. And they're using Black Rhinos."

"How do you know that?" Martinez asked.

"You blind or somethin', Martinez? Last guy we Medevacked outta here was hit in the thigh, man. You could put your fist through it. He'll die 'a just plain shock, man!"

"All right, knock it off, you guys," a sergeant cautioned. "Chinks are gonna have another run at us."

"Oh nice," Doolittle said. "Ain't that fucking lovely. Low on ammo and we're on for another inning."

"Can it, Doolittle."

There was the high screech of incoming, and reply fire from the few air cavalry 105mms that had been dropped onto the narrow margin between the paddies and the south side of

Disney, everyone save the U.S. Arty gunners crouching low as they could in the sloppy, mud-filled foxholes.

As the afternoon wore on, mist and low cloud now mingling in a diaphanous veil over the flooded fields along the Ningming-Xiash line, another dozen or so POWs had been caught. Trang led the trio of Murphy, Shirley, and Danny Mellin closer to the bogged truck, but told the soldiers he was under orders to take them to the culvert.

"What if there isn't a maintenance shack inside the culvert?" Trang asked Mellin.

"There will be," Danny assured him. "I've been watching the spacing between them—one every couple of miles. Besides, with a culvert, you always have the danger of slides—have to have something nearby to mend a track. All you have to do, Trang, is take us along the track. Tell the guards—if they bother to ask—that you've been ordered to take prisoners to the culvert and check the tracks, help fix 'em with your prisoners if need be. Everyone knows how uptight General Wei and his boys have been about this supply line to the border, especially now that the rain's washed away parts of the road. Only supply line they have is the railway."

"Yeah," Mike Murphy said, with more bravado than he felt. "They'll expect the recaptured prisoners to be used as coolie labor."

Shirley said nothing. The lack of sleep and food and the long, tense day in the flooded fields were taking their toll, but she didn't want to let on, particularly in front of Murphy. Then, as if he'd been reading her thoughts as they sloshed their way through the waist-high water and mist toward the rail line, Murphy said, "Hey, Trang, let's stop awhile. I'm feeling a bit whacked!" Murphy looked at her as he said it and winked. Weary as she was, she smiled at Murphy. "Thanks."

Suddenly they heard shots and people screaming, somewhere a hundred yards or so east, behind them. This was followed by shouting.

"Sounds like Upshut," Murphy said. They all stood still in the water, Shirley frozen in fear. Something had slithered across her foot in the muddy ooze that squelched beneath her toes. For a moment she was paralyzed with fear. She wanted to scream. Murphy sensed it and put his hand on hers. "We're almost at the rail line," he said by way of encouragement.

"Tracks are elevated. We'll be on dry ground—well, as dry as it gets 'round here."

He could feel her gripping his hand. She was shaking—cold and fearful.

"Got the Jim-whimmies myself," he said softly.

Trang had turned in toward the rail line as the light began to fade, making it particularly dark in the culvert, whose appearance now took on the aspect of a long, dark tunnel.

There was a shout from a PLA guard a hundred yards off, and Trang, "without," as Murphy would have said, "batting an eyelid," answered loudly, his voice carrying across the water as if through an amplifier. His tone, even to Mellin, Shirley, and Murphy, who didn't understand Chinese, was so pregnant with authority that it gave them a surge of confidence. As his horse took the incline up to the railway lines, Shirley slipped, Trang turning on her with a stream of invective, waving her impatiently up the embankment.

The guard they saw in the dying light looked as miserable, Danny thought, as he himself felt, it being no joke standing out all day in the rain with only one meal of hot, or rather, warm, rice and fish sauce delivered by the short food train that preceded the one big supply train a day, which Wei sent through to the Disney front every night.

They were on the standard four-foot-eight-and-a-half-inch-wide track now, walking alongside the wooden sleepers that had been laid in a bed of stones, each segment of rail fixed to its tie by a screw bolt and a steel wedge between the rail and the bolt. Danny had told Trang to pretend to be inspecting the ties for any maintenance that might be needed.

CHAPTER SEVENTY-SEVEN

THE PRESIDENT OF the United States was holding an emergency conference in the White House, not in the War Room, but in the Oval Office, and the significance of that was not lost on Chief of Naval Operations Admiral Reese and the other Joint Chiefs of Staff. The President wanted a political assessment of the situation, and he was sure—not only from the CIA's reports from agents in Beijing, but from his own gut feeling as a politician going into an election year—that Chairman Li Peng was calling a similar meeting in the Zhongnanhai Compound on Changan Avenue before he would give his request to the delegates in the Great Hall of the People.

The President and chairman both knew that the military conflict at Disney Hill on the Chinese-Vietnamese border, and at Dien Bien Phu near the Laotian border, were chess pieces in a game of political will, ostensibly between China and the U.N., but in reality between China and the United States of America.

The President told the assembled Chiefs of Staff and adviser Ellman that his position was very much like Truman's situation in the Korean War. There, it had been Pork Chop Hill over which the U.S.-led U.N. force and China had to battle it out while both sides were negotiating at Panmunjon.

"As far as I'm concerned," the President announced, "once the Chinese agree to withdraw all their forces to their side of the Vietnamese-Chinese border, it's over. The whole reason this started is because they thought they could invade other people's territory and claim it as their own. But—" He raised a hand to stifle any immediate objection. "—I realize that Dien Bien Phu is another matter. The Chinese are farther away from their border there."

"Yes," the Army Chief of Staff said. "And they've chosen

Dien Bien Phu on purpose because it was there that France—
the West—was defeated."

"Humiliated," Ellman said.

"Yes," the Army Chief of Staff agreed. "That's a better
word for it."

"Just as we were humiliated," Admiral Reese said, "in Saigon in 'seventy-five. Two things Americans remember vividly:
where they were when JFK was shot, and the photo of the last
helicopter on the roof of the American embassy—panic-
stricken people trying to get the last ride out of town and people being pushed off." He paused, sure that he had everyone's
attention. "Mr. President, if we allow that to happen again—if
we just pull out—nobody in Asia will trust us ever again. I
know a lot of our 'Nam veterans feel like that."

"Ironic, isn't it," the President said, "that we're discussing
how best to make our point in Vietnam that we'll stand up to
bullies—the very country we fought?"

"History's full of irony, Mr. President. We once fought the
British, and now they're at our side at Dien Bien Phu."

The President nodded, picked up the silver letter opener, and
began tapping on the desk blotter. "Well, now that Jorgensen
has got us in Dien Bien Phu, how does he propose to get us
out?"

The Army Chief of Staff spoke. "Matter of fact, sir, you
might recall it wasn't General Jorgensen's idea. It was Douglas
Freeman who got us in there with rumors about U.S. MIA
sightings—although to tell you the truth, I think he was probably looking for a way to protect his left flank. The Dien Bien
Phu valley is a good staging area for the Chinese."

"And it's surrounded by mountains," Admiral Reese put in.

The President put down the letter opener. "Can't we just
pull the USVUN Special Forces out of there?"

"Not now," Ellman said. "Number one, the U.S. public have
expectations of possible MIA discoveries. Second, and most
importantly from the political angle, Dien Bien Phu is crucial.
Whether we like it or not, it's become a litmus test. The world
media is fixated on both Disney and Dien Bien Phu. But
thanks to press creeps like Frenchman LaSalle, the whole
world is seeing Dien Bien Phu in particular as a test of U.S.
will. Third, SATINT shows us that the PLA must have been
building up supplies there for at least a month. We all thought
it started with the PLA paratroop drop, but they were probably

among the last Chinese to enter the area. They're all around us."

The President sat bolt upright. "Are you telling me we've been set up there?"

"Yes," Ellman said. "Started with some cock-and-bull story about one of our officials in Ho Chi Minh City—" Ellman realized it was difficult for the President to recognize Ho Chi Minh City as anything but old Saigon. "Anyway, Jorgensen's HQ apparently got some story from Freeman about MIAs in the area—one or a hundred, I don't know. I would've thought most of them would be dead by now."

CIA chief Noyer interjected. He didn't like Ellman's tone when the aide talked about "some cock-and-bull story." Noyer had had a friend who'd gone missing. Only people who had lost someone could understand. "Far as I know, Mr. Ellman, it was no 'cock-and-bull story,' as you, I think, ineptly put it. One of our people, a Major—" Noyer couldn't recall the man's name now. "—Barker? Baker? But anyway, he'd followed what he believed was a genuine lead up to Dalat."

"Where's that?" the President asked.

"In the central highlands."

The President nodded, not much the wiser. "Well, it doesn't matter now whether he was set up with a false lead to get us involved in a vulnerable area or not. The fact is, now we've got ninety Special Forces with the enemy ringed all about them. The question is, what is it going to take to help them out?"

"To win," Admiral Reese said, "Douglas Freeman has to resupply his Special Forces trapped in there and drive the PLA out from around them. There can't be any half measures here, Mr. President, or we'll have nothing at the bargaining table. We're barely hanging on to Disney Hill. They're both Freeman's call."

"Think he can do it, gentlemen?"

There was silence in the room.

CHAPTER SEVENTY-EIGHT

IN ADDITION TO the battalion of seven hundred PLA paratroopers who had arrived in and around Dien Bien Phu village days before and had seized the small airstrip immediately north of the village, now four companies, over four hundred men, of the PLA's Chengdu Twelfth Army attacked Delta's perimeter, some PLA rushing on the surface but most—over three hundred Chinese—coming in via the old tunnels used by the Viet Minh Communists against the French, the tunnels brought back to basic maintenance level not by the North Vietnamese, but by Chinese and local Laotian hill tribes who had infiltrated the area. The enemy tunnel rats were popping up like jackrabbits all over the place to fire off a burst and throw a few grenades before the American and British defenders had time to get a bead on them.

But most damaging was the sustained fire of the enemy's mortars, many of which, like the bigger artillery guns, were firing from dugouts so deep in the mountainside that their camouflage nets were at ground level, the dugouts themselves shored up with logs. The fighting had already reached the wire at places where firefights were breaking out even as the mortar rounds tore into the ground inside the perimeter, throwing up clouds of dust that drifted ghostlike over the wire, which was littered with over thirty PLA dead and wounded.

For PLA commander Colonel Cheng it had merely been a test of the American and British firepower. The defenders' firepower, or rather their accuracy, was much better than that of average field troops. Colonel Cheng had expected as much, for his own intelligence section had already advised him of the allies' Special Forces training regimen, carrying over 250-pound loads, and the required ability to burst into a room of hostages, identify the hostage-taker, and take him out with one shot. The final test for the U.S. Navy SEALs was to go six days with only four hours' sleep. These were crack troops. It would take more than a few forays at the wire to unnerve them.

Both sides realized the airstrip would be unusable by the planes of either side, and in any event it had been potholed by the Chinese using concrete-splitting mines, and all supply roads—mule trails into Dien Bien Phu within a fifty-mile radius from north to Ban Pa Haute in the northeast to Bang Beng in the southeast—had been severed and/or were covered by ambuscades of PLA infantry. In short, Dien Bien Phu had been cut off. The weather was now clearing in the valley, but not enough for accurate supply drops, and even when, or if, the weather cleared, Freeman knew that any drop zone would immediately be pummeled by what was now recognized as a formidable ring of Chinese field artillery and triple A dug into the sites of the PLA's mountainous redoubts.

At his Phu Lang Thuong HQ, Freeman was pacing like a caged lion. "Well, by God!" Freeman proclaimed to Major Cline. "I'm not doing another Navarre."

"I don't follow," Cline said.

"Navarre," Freeman grumbled, "French C in C in 'fifty-four—sent in a swashbuckler—Colonel Christian de Castries. Like General Navarre, Castries was a cavalryman—a damn fine one too, but when the enemy is all around you—with arty—you can't fight it like a cavalryman. Can't do a George Patton when you're in a bull ring and the stands are thick with guns. No . . ."

Freeman, both hands on the map table, was staring down at Dien Bien Phu. Cline could hear the heavy rumble of PLA howitzers beyond Disney as the sky lit up in flashes. Cline admired Freeman's ability to focus—as if mesmerized—on another battle while a different battle was raging so close at hand.

"No, Bob," the general said. "When you've got this situation, the only way is to dig in—hold your position until the cavalry can come in."

"Is there a chance of them making a fighting withdrawal?" the major asked.

The general was slowly shaking his head. "Ninety men? Even if Echo and Foxtrot can reach Delta, my guesstimate is we'd be lucky to get out one or two. But there's another reason why we can't try a fighting withdrawal." With that, he thrust his HQ's copy of the order from the Pentagon, adding, "It went direct to Jorgensen's HQ south in Hanoi." The message read:

NEGOTIATIONS FOR CEASE-FIRE MAKE IT IMPERATIVE YOU HOLD POSITION. HOLD UNTIL RELIEVED.

"Pawns," Cline said disgustedly, throwing down the message. "They're not here. They don't care about our men."

Then Freeman, the acerbic critic of the U.S. State Department, stunned Cline. "No, they're right, Bob. We try to run out of this at Disney or Dien Bien Phu or show Wang a white flag, we're finished in this part of the world. We haven't got nearly the size of force here the French had, and they lost. But we have to hold. Our will is being tried here—just as it was for France in 'fifty-four. If the enemy busts our balls here like they did the French, that's it for the American century in Asia. China'll rule the roost, including Japan and everybody else. But—" The general took in a long breath of air. "—we have a cavalry the French didn't have."

"Planes?"

"Oh, the French had aircraft—not enough, but they had 'em. Now Giap, that clever little history teacher, made sure that as well as cutting all the trails into Dien Bien Phu, he also hit the big airfields to destroy the French air force on the ground. But one thing the French didn't have was—"

Freeman was interrupted by a signals officer handing him the news that all major USVUN airfields within striking distance of Dien Bien Phu were under Chinese sabotage attack. Over half the aircraft—most of them helos—had already been destroyed.

"What?" Cline said. "What didn't the French have?"

"A big boat," Freeman replied, "called the *Enterprise*."

Freeman knew not to call a ship a boat in military parlance, but Cline realized that Douglas Freeman had a Churchillian sense of history and was conscious that if his Special Forces could take a pounding at Dien Bien Phu and could hold, then Freeman's words to him this night would enter military legend.

"We don't have to win, Major," Freeman added, as if reading the other's mind. "All we have to do is hold."

"Yes, I know," Cline said somberly. "Until relieved. I've heard that somewhere before."

"I think," Freeman said, focusing on Dien Bien Phu, and in

what struck Cline as a peculiarly jocular tone, given the odds, "we'll do some gardening—a little clear cutting.

"Now, Bob, I want you to have signals flash an order to our boys in Dien Bien Phu not to radiate out in patrols to engage the enemy. We already know where the enemy is—all around us. What Berry, Leigh-Hastings, and Roscoe have to do is dig in—interconnecting trenches with zigzags—and have the trenches reinforced with whatever they can find. I want them to dig deep—keep the trenches narrow, behind razor wire, and machine-gun strong points and claymore mines around the whole perimeter. And to be ready to cannibalize enemy mortar ammo. We can't get heavy artillery to them yet, but now that all columns—Delta, Echo, and Foxtrot—are in Dien Bien Phu on the Vietnamese side of the Laotian-Vietnamese border, we can use TACAIR. That's going to be our artillery. We'll drop them the razor wire ASAP."

"How about the weather?" Cline asked.

"We'll go in with infrared fighters and bombers. We're going to lose some if they go in as low as I have to, but without them our boys won't be able to hold."

Cline doubted if Delta, Echo, and Foxtrot could hold, even with TACAIR, but he recalled Freeman's earlier point that there was an enormous difference politically between being wiped out and surrendering. Quite bluntly, being wiped out meant military defeat but not a breaking of will, a difference that was critical for Washington at the negotiating table. Of course, there was always the possibility that Wang's buildup in the high ground above Dien Bien Phu was much less than anyone thought, and that the memory of the stunning French defeat at Dien Bien Phu was coloring USVUN intelligence reports. The writers of these reports might have recalled how, before Giap's siege of 1953–54, French intelligence had performed so badly, assuring Navarre that the enemy buildup, because of the rugged limestone cliff terrain, could not be so substantial as to defeat the French garrison.

Echo, Foxtrot, and Delta were now busy digging in the complex of interconnecting trenches leading to and from machine-gun strong points in front of which they had cleared fields of interlocking fire in the shape of a triangle. Later that evening, fifty-pound spools of razor wire were successfully dropped before the plane was shot down, exploding on impact. The most optimistic situation report sent to Hanoi and Phu

Lang Thuong by Colonel Berry was that he estimated, from interdiction of PLA radio traffic, that his ninety-man Special Forces were outnumbered by at least twenty to one, when everyone knew full well that, all other things being equal, such as artillery, the optimum number of men needed for an attacking force to be victorious over a dug-in force was a five-to-one advantage.

Based on this rule of thumb, the situation for the Americans and British in Dien Bien Phu, in Pierre LaSalle's latest report to CNN, was "hopeless."

"How long do you think they can hold, Pierre?" the CNN anchor inquired.

LaSalle gave his usual Gallic shrug. "Twenty-four, perhaps forty-eight hours at most."

"Thank you, Pierre."

Fortunately for Colonel Berry, Major Leigh-Hastings, and Captain Roscoe, CNN reports were not considered the voice of God, and when Berry heard the CNN report off satellite feed, it inspired rather than depressed him. He immediately requested reinforcements, although he knew that this, depending on what Freeman was willing to send him, might make it necessary to fight for a drop zone north of the marshes at the old airstrip immediately north of Dien Bien Phu village.

While he was waiting for Freeman's reply, Berry conferred with Leigh-Hastings and Roscoe, drawing up a plan to do something that he thought the PLA would not expect from the dug-in Special Forces—an attack to take the airstrip, utilizing the fact that the Nam Yum River formed the left flank of his triangle.

Freeman pored over the three-dimensional computer mock-up of Dien Bien Phu. There was no doubt that Berry had to be given reinforcements—whatever it took to hold the garrison until the negotiations reached a more favorable stage. The question was how and what to give him, and how for maximum defensive effect. For Freeman to think in the defensive mode was difficult, for he still clung to the axiom that mobility was the best form of defense, though in reality he knew such tactics could degenerate, as they did for Navarre, into merely feeding men to the enemy's guns. Any fool could say, "Charge!"

"When will our planes from the *Enterprise* reach Dien Bien Phu?" Freeman asked.

"Seventeen hundred hours, sir. Fifteen minutes."

"Dropping their bombs either side of the valley."

"Yes sir. Weather report—mist lifting."

"Beautiful," Freeman said sarcastically. "We wait for the valley to clear, and when it does, we'll be flying into night."

Cline reminded him that with infrared and terrain matching radar, the planes should still be able to put the smart bombs just where they wanted.

"Well, let's hope so. Wang's bound to have planted the high ground either side of that airstrip with triple A—turn the whole valley into a shooting gallery." He picked up the weather report. "No moon. Well, that's something."

No moon meant not enough light for the PLA to attack, and brought back memories to Freeman of the Viet Cong moons years before.

If the brilliant use of camouflage nets by Giap had fooled French reconnaissance in '54, then the pilots flying the fighter-bombers from *Enterprise* were fully confident their infrared radar would pick out the enemy's hot spots even if, as Giap had done, the guns were buried in deep, shored-up earth revetments from which they could be pulled and fired as needed.

As the F-14 Tomcats and F-18 Hornets peeled off and came into the valley heading north, the infrared images were popping up all over, whether from the residual heat of weapons having been fired earlier in the day, or from collective body heat, it didn't matter. And the hot spots on the hills told the pilots where to place their five-hundred-pound laser-guided bombs.

Soon the valley erupted in strings of earth-shaking explosions and an intensity of crisscross tracer triple A of a density not seen by veteran pilots since the attacks on Baghdad in '91. The pilot of an F-18 had just slid a thousand-pound LGB down the beam when his cockpit began rattling violently. Everything from his caution lights through his backup gauges, digital display, and heads-up display was shot to pieces, and his control stick wasn't responding. He pulled the eject straps over, elbowed in, pulled, heard the bang of the explosive bolt, and he was in a swirling, cold, wet, pitch-dark sky, illuminated by long, gentle arcs of triple A multicolored tracer and by the blossoms of orange light below, where bombs had hit. He felt the shock waves. Several minutes later he made a remarkably light landing in a marshy area, and had just released his harness and chute when he heard, "Don't move!" It was a distinctly British voice and the pilot didn't move.

"Get to you in a jiff, old boy!"

It was Leigh-Hastings, aware that the American pilot had just landed in a trip-wire claymore minefield off strongpoint Echo.

Overhead, Phantoms roared in, firing salvoes of 2.75-inch-diameter rockets and bursts from three 20mm machine-gun pods, strafing the jungle at the rate of six thousand rounds a minute. Then came Skyraiders firing their four 20mm guns, each Skyraider carrying over eight thousand pounds of ordnance. It was all very impressive-looking, the multiple explosions lighting up the valley at moments like a string of Chinese firecrackers in a long alley. It was good for the morale of Freeman's trapped men, but they found via a short but ferocious enemy artillery barrage on the triangle later in the morning mist that few, if any, of Cheng's heavy guns had been silenced.

"Jesus," one Englishman opined. "I thought they walloped them last night."

"So did I," Kacey replied. "Sounded like the Fourth of July arou—" A cluster of four 105mm hit the triangle, throwing wet mud and dust into the air before the barrage ceased.

The depressing truth—that the raid from the *Enterprise* had not destroyed the enemy's dug-in arty—came via Freeman's message that morning to the garrison at Dien Bien Phu. He said he would reinforce Dien Bien Phu with a battalion of Airborne as soon as the reduction in enemy firepower was sufficient to give him confidence to send in troop-carrying helos. His message explained how aerial recon had shown HQ that what the *Enterprise* pilots had seen as hot spots on the infrared were bogus revetments. They were bombing a lot of warm holes—hurricane lamps, paraffin stove tins, anything that'd show up on the infrared.

In his headquarters two hundred miles to the east at Phu Lang Thuong, Freeman was feeling far less confident than he had the night before. He was unusually tense and, for him, extraordinarily racked by conscience, torn between his overall obligation as field commander and his sense of obligation toward the men he'd sent in to Dien Bien Phu.

It hadn't been a popular decision in either Washington—

with the President, his Commander in Chief—or with Jorgensen in Hanoi. And now instead of the hard-hitting Special Forces preemptive strike he'd envisioned, the ninety men—or however many were left—were cut off deep in northwest Vietnam.

What had he told Bob Cline? *"L'audace! L'audace! Toujours l'audace!"* and now he was sitting on his bum in Phu Lang Thuong with an impending disaster both northward at Disney and west at Dien Bien Phu.

"Bob, I'm going in."

"Where?"

"Dien Bien Phu. I ought to be there. Damn it, it's my responsibility."

"Begging the general's pardon," an alarmed Cline cut in, "but your responsibility is with Disney as well as Dien Bien Phu. You'd be robbing Paul to pay Peter."

"Look," a clearly agitated Freeman responded, "I'm personally responsible for sending these guys into Dien Bien Phu. From first to last it was my idea."

"Maybe so, General, but I don't think it's a good idea. If you go into Dien Bien Phu, you're as much as announcing you've no faith in your commanders there. That can't be any good for morale—to relegate Berry, Leigh-Hastings, and Roscoe subordinate to your command."

"Not if I go in as commander of the Airborne."

"Then, sir, you'll undercut the commanding officer of the Airborne." Cline paused. "General, sir. No one doubts your courage, if that's what's at issue here. You've been awarded a string of medals as long as your arm."

"You're right, Bob." He paused. "All right, then let's draw up the reinforcement plans. First we have to do some—"

"Deforestation?"

"Yes."

"Sir, are you going to use any herbicide?"

"Only if I have to. Why?"

"I'm thinking about the press. If they got on to that—I mean the herbicide you have in mind—how's it compare with Agent Orange?"

Freeman was already drawing up attack plans against the enemy's lines of communication beyond the Dien Bien Phu valley. Already totally immersed in the details of his TACAIR plan, code-named "Zebra," and walking about a sand table mock-up of the Echo, Foxtrot, Delta triangle like a pool player lining up his shot, he quietly responded to Cline's question about the herbicide. "Compared to the herbicides we have now, Major, you could use Agent Orange as a douche!"

"Christ!"

"Don't worry, I won't use it if I don't have to."

As Trang approached the culvert, the rain-sodden guard forty yards away stepped out from a lean-to made of a ground sheet and a collapsible teepee frame of three bamboo sticks and gave him a desultory wave. Trang waved back and asked when the next supply train was due. The guard answered, "In about a half hour."

"Where's the nearest maintenance shed?" Trang asked. "I've got orders to check the tracks—make sure everything's secure after the rain."

"Another hundred yards or so into the culvert," the guard said uninterestedly, watching Shirley walk by, her figure in sharp relief under her sodden clothes. The guard looked up at Trang. "I'd like to check out her track, eh?"

Trang gave an appropriate grunt of agreement and, his horse's head drooping with fatigue, led his three exhausted-looking prisoners on. Trang couldn't see the next guard even after going into the culvert for another thirty yards, the drizzle of rain no doubt helping to obscure the view. Soon Shirley whispered to Mike Murphy to tell Trang she could smell tobacco smoke. "You sure?" Murphy whispered.

"Are you kidding?" Shirley said. "I'm allergic to it. I can smell a cig—"

"Be quiet," Mellin whispered behind them.

Murphy was about to pass on the information to Trang, who told them quietly that he could see the red glow of a cigarette bobbing about. Looking back, Trang could no longer see the guard they'd passed.

By now they were well over a hundred yards into the culvert, and Trang could just barely make out the outhouselike shape of a maintenance shack, and now, with a surge of relief, he realized why Shirley couldn't see the red glow of the cigarette although she'd smelled it downwind. The guard was inside the shed having a quiet smoke, the bobbing glow of his cigarette visible only now and then through the slit of the open door.

"Comrade!" Trang called out. The cigarette disappeared.

"Yes, comrade," came a gruff, accommodating voice.

"I've got a few prisoners here—we're to use them to help

check the tracks. We need a few tools—a rail is loose back there."

"Oh, all right, comrade. Authorization."

"Yes," Trang said, reaching in his top left tunic pocket, the guard unslinging his rifle, the better to see the authorization.

"You have a flashlight, comrade?" he asked.

"Got everything," Trang said, who out of the darkness brought the Makarov 9mm crashing against the other's temple. The guard dropped with a thud, his head bumping the door as he fell.

The next second Murphy had slit his throat. "C'mon," he said to Shirley. "He's about your size. C'mon, c'mon, the rain'll wash the blood away. Quickly, in the shed." Murphy undressed the man, handing the clothes into the shack, where Shirley, despite her five feet, three inches, could hardly stand upright. But she was done in a few anxious minutes and Murphy gave her the Chinese T-56, an AK-47 look-alike. "It's got a full mag in and the safety button's on—feel it?" His warm hands touched hers.

"Yes."

"Goes off this way—got it?"

"Yes . . . I think."

"No thinking. Have you got it?"

"Yes."

"If you haven't got time to pass it to Danny or me, just tuck the butt under your right arm, hold it tight, and fire like you're aiming a hose. It'll jump high on you, but don't let it frighten—"

"Quiet!" It was Danny. There was a noise like a faucet turned full on. The horse was urinating on the track.

"For Chrissake," Murphy cussed. "Rude bastard! Nearly crapped myself."

"Trang," Danny said, "you move up ahead about twenty-five yards. Shirley back the other—" They heard the distant whistle of a train, and it reminded Mellin just how far they were from the border, given that the PLA engineer on the train could still sound his whistle without announcing it to the enemy soldiers on the border thirteen miles away. "If we succeed, each goes his own way, but get away from the line fast! Remember to head south."

"What if it isn't a supply train?" Murphy asked as he took the Makarov pistol, and Trang and Shirley, now on foot, walked in opposite directions down the track. No one had answered him, each intent on his or her task.

Danny Mellin handed Murphy a two-foot-tall T-socket wrench, the top of the T being the handles, the bottom of it a socket that fitted over the screw bolt that held down the tie and bracket up against the rail. When a screw bolt was taken out, the tight steel wedge between the tie bracket and the rail could be knocked out with a sledgehammer.

"We won't use the hammer till we've taken all six screw bolts out," Mellin explained. "That way we make all the noise as the train gets closer—use its noise to cover our noise."

"Bit bloody dicey, isn't it, Dan?"

"You got any better suggestions?"

"Yeah, blow the fucker up. Y'know, like the movies. A pack of TNT and the little plunger box." They heard the whistle coming closer.

"Keep working on those screw bolts. Three to go. Hurry!"

As Danny hit the first wedge and knocked it out, it sounded as if it'd be heard for miles.

"Christ!" Murphy said.

There was the sudden chatter of a submachine gun. Danny hit another wedge.

"Christ!"

"Shut up, damn it!" Danny said, and hit the wedge again before it came out.

The whistle sounded shriller now and they could see a shape coming at them. There was a woman's voice. Shirley.

"What the—" Murphy began.

"The— A guard back there was coming up the track! I shot him."

"Good girl!" Murphy said.

Danny was hitting the fifth wedge, not even looking up. "Mike, throw those bolts to hell and gone." As Murphy did so, Danny hit another wedge and it shot out. They heard firing from Trang's direction farther on but knew—or prayed—it wouldn't be heard over the mounting rumble of the train about a half mile off now. They heard Trang—they assumed it was Trang—firing again.

Danny hit the last wedge and it wouldn't budge. He was exhausted. They could hear the train coming up the straightaway before the bend that was the culvert. Mike grabbed the sledgehammer and hit the sixth wedge and it was out.

"Run!" Danny gasped. "Run!"

Somebody, perhaps the engineer or fireman, might have seen something wrong up ahead, but the yellow slit-eyed headlight showed only the shape of Trang's horse as it took off down the culvert between the tracks. As Shirley, Danny, and Murphy clawed their way frantically up one side of the embankment they could hear the pained metallic squeal of brakes being applied and see rushes of bright, golden sparks. But by now the locomotive's wheels had reached the loose rail and immediately plowed off the track into the stones, the headlight slamming into one side of the culvert even as the locomotive's wheels were frantically reversing in a futile effort to stop the train. The locomotive was now at a more acute angle to the track, the long string of boxcars and wagons telescoping into one another and climbing higher and higher on one another so that the great pile of wrecked cars formed a logjam, as it were, from one side of the culvert to the other. Already several cars were alight from the spilled fire of the locomotive.

The flitting shadows of guards could be seen, some approaching the enormous rubble of overturned cars, and once they realized the train's cargo was about to cook off, turning and running down the culvert as fast as possible.

There was an enormous orange-red, fireworks-like display as Kalyusha and 90mm rockets went off, followed by a sustained roar made up of tens of thousands of Black Rhino going off, the culvert, because of its tunnel-like shape, a natural conduit for the force of the multiple explosions. Trang disintegrated in a hail of Black Rhino splinters, his blood vaporized to a fine mist, and amid all the noise, screams, and chaos of PLA bodies and supplies toppling out, the only thing Danny Mellin could hear and didn't want to was the distraught neighing of the horse cut down by shrapnel and lying helplessly somewhere on the track. If he could have, he would've gone down to finish it off, but by now the area in the culvert was swarming with dazed troops, their officers yelling, adding to the confusion of the wreckage.

A parachute flare shot out of the burning culvert, and now the full extent of the derailing could be seen to have surpassed Mellin's wildest expectations. It would take the PLA days, at least, to get a rail crane up from Ningming, and even with the number of troops Wei had at his disposal, it would take days to clear the culvert, let alone get another train through.

* * *

As Danny Mellin, Shirley, and Murphy headed south through the sodden fields, they were exhausted, their adrenaline used up in stopping the train, and weakened by the effort. They stopped for a while to rest, and Shirley searched her baggy, sodden PLA uniform for any rations, but found only a mush of wet tobacco and rice paper.

"Don't worry," Danny advised them. "Dehydration's the problem, and we sure aren't going to die from thirst."

"You can eat the eucalyptus leaves," Murphy said.

"You sure?" It was Shirley, feeling a lot calmer now in her mind but very shaky, and suffering from a stunner of a headache from lack of food.

"Eucalyptus leaves?" Murphy said. "Sure I'm sure. Koala bears live on 'em."

"Koala bears look pretty dopey," she said good-naturedly, then suddenly fell quiet. "I hope he didn't feel much."

"No," Murphy said. "I mean, he wouldn't have felt a whole car of ammo going off like that."

"C'mon," Danny said, "let's try to make as much mileage as we can tonight. There'll be Chinese swarming around here tomorrow once they figure out the line was sabotaged."

"How far south, Danny? As the crow flies."

"Ten, eleven miles."

"Christ!" Murphy said. "Didn't figure we were that close."

"Much longer if we kept to the rail tracks."

"We're practically home, mate."

"That's just the border," Danny informed him. "Then we'll have to work through to our lines, wherever they are."

"Oh ye of little faith!" Murphy joked. Despite his fatigue, he was still high on the rush of stopping the train.

"Pipe down," Danny cautioned.

"Right," Murphy said, carrying the PLA rifle, giving the Makarov to Shirley. Now they could see a saffron glow, blurred by the rain, hanging suspended like an enormous upturned bowl of flames over the culvert.

CHAPTER SEVENTY-NINE

THE SATPIX RELAYED to Freeman wasn't of the best quality, but it told him exactly what had happened—a massive train wreck on the PLA's main line of communication. He didn't hesitate, and like a juggler in midact, shifted all his attention from one problem, Dien Bien Phu, to the other, ordering all elements of Second Army in the Disney area to press home a dawn attack preceded by a creeping barrage from the 105mms and 155mms on the margin between the southern base of the hill and the flooded paddies.

Even as his artillery began to pulverize the PLA positions on the north side of Disney, Freeman, like a good political cadre, was making "damn sure," as he put it to his senior commanders, that every man in the USVUN force on Disney would know that the PLA's logistics line had been severed and that this was the best chance they had.

As a gray dawn stole upon the hill, the USVUN troops—over ten thousand of them—moved from Disney's ridgeline to the northern slope. It was touch and go for six and a half hours of close combat, but like one grain at a time in an hourglass, the ratio of mortars between the USVUN and the PLA moved from 1:1 to 2:1 to 3:1 in the allies' favor.

Wei's commanders had to give ground, not much at first—a hundred yards or so—but by 0115 the USVUN had pushed off Wei's best troops. Running low on everything because of the train wreck, particularly ammunition, the PLA had to give more ground until it was a rout and Freeman's forces owned the hill. This also allowed the U.S. air cavalry to put down its helos without being fired upon from Disney's crest.

CHAPTER EIGHTY

AT DIEN BIEN Phu things were not nearly as upbeat. The ninety men of the Special Forces weren't so much depressed by the sense of siege as by the lack of action. Though they had been well-trained in defensive maneuvers, their natural disposition was to go on the offense. They also knew that if they went on the offensive now, they would be quickly pounded and eaten up by the vastly larger enemy force.

The big enemy guns the experts had told Navarre couldn't be brought through such terrain were there and in fine shape. Though firing sporadically, they forced the men of Echo, Foxtrot, and Delta—who had turned the first initial of their designations around to form "DEF" and defiantly hoisted a makeshift flag above the triangle of deep, interlocking trenches and firing bays—to scurry for cover.

DEF was equipped with 82mm mortars, but overall there was no heavy ordnance.

Freeman knew that his first *Enterprise* raid was a failure, and that if he was to avoid a second Dien Bien Phu defeat of the kind meted out to the French in '54, he would have to order in the three companies of Airborne to help, enemy artillery or not. To avoid, or at least minimize, the massacre that could result because of enemy triple A on both sides of the valley, Freeman ordered that the Airborne go in that night. And here American technology in the form of the infrared goggles—which led to ferocious headaches after several hours of wear—allowed the slick pilots, with a fully night-equipped M53J Pave Low helo acting as pathfinder, to ferry in the nine hundred men.

* * *

The thousands of PLA troops could hear the choppers landing, and opened fire with their artillery, but however good their gunners were during the daylight, using open sight down-the-barrel direct fire, at night it was a different story. Even with the help of para flares turning night to flickering daylight, they were less effective because of the inferior computer guidance targeting necessary for the kind of deadly, vectored, indirect fire of the kind provided now by the American Airborne gunners. The 105mms and 155mms were ferried in by the huge, dragonfly-shaped CH-54 Tarhe helos to positions behind the ring of hills that surrounded the valley and were fired without their crews ever seeing the enemy, but with devastating results.

In short, the more sophisticated computer-fire-directed American guns could shoot from beyond the hills, out of sight of the enemy, with the Chinese guns unable to silence them.

It meant that while U.S. artillery could fire at any enemy gun position whose flash gave away its position, the PLA could not fire back with any accuracy worth talking about. Nevertheless the PLA, with their hidden dug-in guns and their mortars, did their best, pounding what they *could* see below on DEF's triangle, the bombardment resulting in over a hundred American Airborne casualties during the hectic unloading phase. As soon as the Hueys unloaded their cargo of men and supplies for the DEF garrison, they began loading up with dead and wounded.

A PLA 105mm round hit a fully loaded Huey, and in the ghostly flickering of flare light and gas tank explosions, unidentifiable body parts could be seen dangling and dripping with blood from the nearby bushes and trees—one of the legless torsos belonging to a soldier who had apparently remembered his drill sergeant's advice at Fort Bragg, for the media found his set of dog tags in his boots.

While this disembarkation was taking place at Dien Bien Phu, hundreds of miles eastward in the South China Sea Elizabeth Franks, her "grape" refueler jacket barely visible on the rain-slashed flight deck of the USS *Enterprise*, fought to keep her footing as the giant carrier came about, heading into the wind.

As soon as Gunner's Mate Albright Stevens, stamping his feet to keep them warm, got off his watch, he and Elizabeth would find some warm, hidden place, and there all the stress and strain of the flight deck would be released. For a split second Elizabeth Franks was nearly blown overboard as the blast from a Phantom, its engine moving onto full afterburner, was not fully deflected by the water-cooled shield. Someone, a yellow shirt, grabbed her barely in time.

The Phantoms were punishing the PLA at several locations in the Spratly Islands where Wang's troops had defiantly and bravely—or stupidly, depending on your point of view—raised the Chinese flag. In addition, *Enterprise* was also standing by to launch "Operation Landfill," drawn up by the commander of the Second Army, General Freeman, as an alternative strike force now that so many Air Force bases east of Dien Bien Phu had been struck by PLA hit-and-run saboteur squads.

The DEF triangle now had an extra thousand men in and around it, where a circle a quarter mile in diameter ringed the dug-in garrison's timber- and sandbag-reinforced command and hospital bunkers. The initial disorganization that besets most Airborne for the first few minutes after touchdown provided an opportunity for Wang to attack, but the mist-shrouded valley dissuaded both the PLA and DEF from moving too far from base positions. Though the Chinese still outnumbered the garrison's defenders more than ten to one, Wang was waiting for when he could best use his dug-in artillery.

Flare light had allowed his gunners to get a few deadly salvos by direct fire down at the garrison, but the flashes of his guns would also show their positions to Freeman's forces. Wang wanted to wait for daylight to make maximum use of his guns.

"Son of a bitch'll attack at dawn," Freeman opined to Colonel Berry over the secure scrambler phone. "So all you can do, Al, is dig. Dig like a bastard because the only way they can get that piece of real estate is to take it by hand-to-hand. Their artillery'll be pounding you, and we'll be pounding them, but in the end they have to take the friggin' wire like they did with the frogs."

Berry didn't need a history lesson. He needed more time to inspect and to exhort his men to shore up their positions against what he was sure would be the coming massive bombardment from the PLA-owned hills.

Along with the reinforcements Freeman had sent in were dozens of the latest Heckler & Koch 40mm automatic grenade launchers, the lightest on the market, and constructed so their thirty-two-round belt could be fed from either the right or left.

Instead of firing machine-gun bullets, with the HK40 they'd be firing machine-gun grenades.

"I don't fuckin' care!" Doolittle said, thoroughly pissed at being relieved on Disney only to find himself and his colleagues reassigned as support troops for the Airborne. Freeman had apparently predicted that there might be a lot of massed assaults on the wire and that men already blooded in this kind of combat should be airlifted into either DEF's triangle or the outer defensive circle.

"I don't fuckin' care!" Doolittle repeated as they were digging in. "I mean, we've done our bit, haven't we? Time for a bit of friggin' S and S."

"What's that?" D'Lupo asked, not really caring.

"Sex and sex!" Doolittle said. "I wanted to say something to the captain 'fore they carted us off from Disney—wanted you to back me up, eh? And what 'appens? D'Lupo can't find his tongue and Martinez—well, you're a great fucking disappointment, you are, Martinez. 'Yes, sir, no, sir, three fucking bags full, sir. We'd love to go to Dien Bien Fuck.' "

"Well, you're here now, Doolittle, so make the best of it. B'sides, it's pretty important."

"That's right," D'Lupo echoed.

"Yeah, 'course," Doolittle said. "They're all bloody important, especially when you might buy it!"

"The French lost here," Martinez said.

"Oh," Doolittle said. "I get the picture. Wherever the frogs get beat we 'ave to go in an' put it right. That the story?"

"Nah," Martinez answered. "You know, I mean—it's important politically."

"Oh," Doolittle said, taking a rest from digging a shooting bay. "I see. Now we've got Henry fucking Kissinger here. Since when did you give a shit about politicians, Marty?"

"I dunno. I thought about runnin' for Congress sometime."

"Oh, Gawd protect us—Congressman Marty!"

"Doolittle," D'Lupo said, "why don't you shut up and dig?"

"All right, all right." He started filling sandbags again. " 'Course, y'know—Christ, there's a lot of noise going on 'round here."

"It's called artillery, Doolittle. Our guys and their guys, remember?"

"Yeah, well, you know where they're gonna hit us? Across

the fuckin' river—on our left flank. All this rain—everybody figures they won't try to cross."

D'Lupo tossed up another bag as flashes of artillery outlined his arm like a broken tree. "They'll hit us from all directions at once."

"Of course, everyone knows that. I know where I'd hit 'em."

"Where?" Martinez asked.

"Behind their latrines."

"Bullshit—"

"Nope—that's the truth, mate. PLA never post enough guards near their latrines."

"No wonder," D'Lupo said, "if they smell bad as you."

"Oh, very droll," Doolittle commented.

"You guys want some coffee?" It was a young Airborne corporal.

"I'd kill for coffee," Doolittle said.

"Well, you might have to if those gooks have a crack at us in the morning."

They took the coffee quietly and gratefully. The mist was still heavy in the valley, and they knew, as did everyone in the thousand-man defense force spread out from the DEF's inner triangle to the outer gun ports of the half-mile-wide circle, that as dawn approached, when it was most difficult to distinguish the shape of a man from the shape of a tree, an attack must surely come. General Wang was no doubt just as determined that Dien Bien Phu should fall as was Freeman that it should not.

When the first salvo of Chinese 105mm and 155mm artillery hit the circle, the earth shook violently and a machine-gun emplacement was gone, two men dead and several more injured as everyone hit the deck, hugging the dirt in the trenches. The din was earsplitting. Within fifty seconds American 105s were answering the flashes, and soon the artillery bombardment fell off.

Within thirty seconds Wang's first wave of sappers hit the wire with everything from explosive charges strapped to their waists to satchel charges ready to penetrate the perimeter's defenses and wipe out command bunkers and strongpoints. There were explosions, fountains of red earth, screaming all around, and shadows to the west coming through the mist, rubber boats full of PLA on the river, the boats now in a hail of mortar fire, with one direct hit flinging bodies skyward before they fell back and were swept away, some clinging to the boats' remains. Mortars still rained down, giant spumes of water erupting amid the multiple spouts caused by the Americans pouring in M-60 fire as well.

The initial shock of the sappers' wave was now over, and though many more explosions were heard along the wire, the sappers were paying a terrible price for their initial attack. Their bodies and bits of them were strewn all along the wire, the holes they'd opened already being breached by the second assault, this one by PLA *tujidui*—storm troopers—heavily armed and moving fast to enter the bunkers and trench system that was the outer circle. These were met by a curtain of M-60 machine-gun fire and from the DEF triangle by mortar fire of such concentration that only a handful made it into the circle trench ring, followed by earth-shattering explosions and the screams of some of the dozen or so Airborne troops torn to pieces by the C4 exploding in such narrow confines. Over thirty PLA storm troopers were inside the circle for about a minute before the Airborne cut them down. A bugle blared, and as suddenly as it had begun, the Chinese attack ceased.

"Beat the bastards!" one of the Airborne proudly announced. "There must be forty, fifty dead chinks out there!"

"Terrific," Martinez said. "That only leaves 'bout five thousand!"

In fact, Wang's forces, including porters and underground engineers, were twice that number, and what had depressed Martinez, Doolittle, and D'Lupo, as well as Berry's Special Forces contingent, was the enemy's morale. There had been absolutely no hesitation at the wire. Even from DEF's triangle it had been at once impressive—at least from a strictly military point of view—and frightening to see how many of the sapper wave were suicidal.

Berry was anxious for the mist to lift so a striker force of fighter-bombers from *Enterprise* could hit the hillsides east and west of Dien Bien Phu and suppress Wang's triple A. Then the air drops could be made within the half-mile-wide circle without too much interference.

"Wang has a measure of us now," Leigh-Hastings commented from his bunker at the northern tip of the DEF triangle. He had punched in the numbers on his PRC-77 so the message couldn't be intercepted.

"Of our outer ring," Berry replied, "but they're not 'our

boys.' I don't mean any disrespect toward the Airborne, they're doing a great job, but—"

Leigh-Hastings cut in. "But our chaps are best at offensive operations."

"You think I should be using them now?" Berry asked.

"Not necessarily. I understand your strategy of the strong control defense, but each of our DEF chaps has a starlight scope, and the met report from Freeman's HQ is that the mist and low fog will abate later today. Tonight it'll be a VC moon—just enough light for Wang to attack by, but not enough for us to see them." Leigh-Hastings also pointed out that starlight scopes, which Freeman's G-2 had confirmed the PLA did not have, at least not in any substantial numbers, would allow the Special Forces troopers to play havoc with the PLA in the dark.

"I'll take your suggestion under advisement," Berry responded. "I'll request more starlight scopes—for the Airborne."

"Good show. I think—"

"Incoming!" Berry shouted, and the next moment Leigh-Hastings was thrown to the floor of his bunker, his radio flying out of his hands and hitting one of the wooden cross beams. He heard the high whistle of more artillery.

"They're at the wire!" someone shouted, and the outer circle defenders opened up with everything they had. At least thirty to forty PLA were inside the outer wire, some of them having played dead outside the wire from the first attack. It was chaotic, a satchel charge detonating midair, killing more PLA than Americans; a screaming bayonet charge by PLA into one of the trenches, American and British fighting PLA hand-to-hand in the trenches.

An M-60 jammed, its quick-charge barrel glove lost and both machine gunner and assistant killed within seconds. But the HK automatic grenade launcher was proving its worth as Airborne gunners sprayed the breakthrough points with three- to five-round bursts, creating in effect a wall of small-arms artillery, the fragmentation grenades cutting the Chinese down as narrow breakthrough points forced them to cluster at the openings in the wire, running over their dead and dying comrades.

Another artillery duel erupted, the PLA issuing direct fire inside the circle, willing to kill their own as Freeman had done on Disney to gain ground by forcing the enemy back into the network of trenches. Had it not been for the Z turns built in the trenches, there would have been many more American and British casualties. The Z turns, like a traffic island, were plonked into the middle of a trench, where one man could hold off a whole squad. Martinez's M-60, overheating, jammed, and had it not been for Doolittle cutting down two Chinese with his M-16, Martinez would have been dead. D'Lupo, out of ammunition, threw his rifle at a Chinese soldier, who ducked and bayoneted the American before being chopped to pieces by an M-60 burst at near point-blank range.

"Medic!" Doolittle yelled, firing his last grenade from his M-16 launcher at the wire. A medic was already at D'Lupo's side, stanching the blood flow and yelling for a stretcher. The next moment the medic was dead from a burst from a Chinese T56-1 RPD, a gaping bloody hole where his chest had been. It seemed like minutes to D'Lupo, but in reality it was only a matter of seconds before a stretcher arrived and he was taken away to a hospital bunker inside the triangle.

As D'Lupo, hemorrhaging profusely, was being prepped for surgery, a Chinese who miraculously had made it all the way from the outer wire circle into the DEF triangle without a scratch, leapt into the trench, through the curtain—an artillery round shaking the overhead light violently—and began firing. He killed two nurses before the surgeon whipped his scalpel across the man's throat, immediately returning to his patient while calling for orderlies to take out the dead nurses and telling a whey-faced medic to get a Special Forces type from DEF "down here right now. Tell him to stand outside the prep room."

"Yes, sir."

D'Lupo was dead.

Kacey, the Ranger who had run into Salt and Pepper, arrived a minute later with a Winchester 1200 shotgun whose hardened lead slug was guaranteed to stop a train and whose flechette rounds, or darts—thirty of them—were lethal up to three hundred meters.

"Any fucker jumps down here," Kacey proclaimed to no one in particular, "his fuckin' head'll end up in Laos!"

A man did jump down, but Kacey held his fire. The soldier, one of those who, like Doolittle, had been flown in from Disney, had his right hand missing, was covered in blood, and was staring disbelievingly at something he was carrying in his left hand. It was his other hand, having been sheared off at the wrist.

"Jesus!" Kacey yelled. "Medic—on the double!"

The bugle sounded again, and the Chinese, most of whom had failed to make it more than fifty yards into the circle, began to withdraw. This time the Airborne raked the bodies with machine-gun fire to make sure that no live ones were left waiting for the next attack.

In the two attacks so far, over forty Airborne and two of Berry's men had been killed, and over 220 PLA "hard hats." The "hard hats," or "piss pots," as the Americans called them, were steel khaki helmets, a sign that Wang was using only strictly professional troops from Chengdu's Fourteenth Army, that no militia units were being used, that Beijing was determined to win the battle for Dien Bien Phu.

Direct-fire artillery opened up again, and by now even the dimmest soldier on the battlefield could tell what Wang's tactics consisted of—to shell the hell out of the allied force now under the thousand-man mark, and, once their position in the circle had been pulverized enough, turning dirt to sand, and their heads ringing and nerves stretched to the limit, send in another wave of sappers and storm troopers. The old Chinese water torture method, only instead of a drip at a time, you wore down the enemy by attack after attack. After all, as Wang had told the party chairman himself, the Americans weren't going anywhere.

And though the Americans' artillery of six-gun batteries was responding with careful forward-observer-directed fire, it wasn't effective. Whereas the Americans had dug in within a half-mile-diameter circle whose now treeless moonscape offered an easily seen target for the PLA gunners, the PLA targets, their guns and suspected troop concentrations, were spread all over the hills about Dien Bien Phu. This amounted to a huge ambuscade around the Americans in an area so big that by the time one PLA gun was spotted, it would be retracted, often on wooden rails, deep into the cliffside and on a downgrade. Even if an American 155mm hit a target zone dead on either side of the valley, there would be little if any damage to the Chinese wagon. One or two PLA gunners might die if shrapnel sliced through the camouflaged nets down into the man-made cave or revetment, but there were plenty of PLA soldiers to replace them.

The mist had still not risen by noon, and the joke passed

around between enemy salvos whistling then thundering in was that Freeman must have been praying again.

In fact, Freeman had now decided to place his faith in what he had briefly referred to as "essential deforestation," or, as his HQ staff were soon calling it, "clear cutting." The men in the trenches of Dien Bien Phu called it "fuck the forest." There was nothing strikingly new about it, as Freeman had seen it used in 'Nam before, but he did go about the preparations for it with a zest that later appalled Greenpeace and other conservation groups throughout the world. Freeman, avoiding passion, going for reason instead, would tell a hastily convened press conference that "when it comes to preserving the habitat or saving American lives, there is no contest."

Bob Cline did whisper to him that he should have mentioned the British and other USVUN contingents, but before he could rectify the omission, LaSalle and others were pillorying him for it.

Freeman had told the combat information center aboard *Enterprise* precisely what he wanted, and when the mists finally rose and disappeared at 1420, the three-component strike force from the carrier was on its way. Entering "flak alley" between the hills of Dien Bien Phu, the first wave, guided in by forward air controllers, dropped fuel air explosive bombs. Unlike napalm, the FAE consisted of dropping a huge blanket of vaporized fuel over the target and detonating it all at one instant. This burnt much of the vegetation off in one enormous blanket of intense fire, consuming any troops directly beneath it.

The second wave of fighter-bombers then streaked in, dropping five-hundred-pound Snakeye bombs, which denuded the target area of any trees still standing. The third wave then swept in and, with the hillside devoid of vegetation, looking from the air like huge patches of mange, the fighter-bombers dropped laser-guided and high-angled two-thousand-pound bombs directly into the gaping holes that were, or rather had been, the revetments for the Chinese guns. This, as Leigh-Hastings put it, "upset" the Chinese gunners inside, and made a mess of their guns as well, which the USVUN forces in the circle and DEF triangle greatly appreciated.

There was a problem, however, and to his credit, Freeman, playing devil's advocate to his own strategy, realized it before anyone else at Dien Bien Phu. The problem was that this awesome attack upon the hillsides meant that if Wang was not to lose any more men in such clear-weather attacks, it had either better rain or Wang had to speed up his artillery and massed-attacks combination tactic to overwhelm the Dien Bien Phu garrison before the "gangster arsonist," Freeman, burnt him out—driving him out of the hills.

Accordingly, Freeman, his G2 section telling him of suddenly increased enemy radio traffic after the *Enterprise* attack, ordered his DEF commanders and Airborne to prepare for massive *tujidui* thrusts later that day, probably beginning at sundown and possibly going on all night. Air interdiction would be maintained by the *Enterprise* fliers, but the closer the PLA got to the Dien Bien Phu garrison before they attacked, the less help the garrison could expect, as once the Chinese began "bear-hugging," closing with the Dien Bien Phu defenders, U.S. artillery and airpower would have to cease because of the danger of decimating their own troops. Then not even "Spooky," the awesome AC-47 festooned with heavy-caliber machine guns, infrared scopes, TV cameras, and a 105mm howitzer, could be used, for fear of killing the Dien Bien Phu defenders as well as the attacking Chinese.

Despite this danger, and as a further countermeasure to what Freeman believed would be Wang's biggest massed attack so far, Freeman, after conferring with Berry, Leigh-Hastings, Roscoe, and with the Airborne commander, decided that starlight scope patrols would be sent out before sunset and position themselves in the thick vegetation around the half-mile-diameter circle. Their job would be to "sniper" anything that moved, in hopes of first breaking up Chinese concentrations massing for attack, and second, locating and identifying, by radio and red flare, enemy concentrations, which Skyraiders— the old faithfuls, with a loiter time of up to eight and a half hours—could then bomb and strafe, in addition to the indirect fire from the American batteries behind the hills of Dien Bien Phu.

But if the present fine weather had given Freeman a break and allowed him to launch the deforestation attacks, the lack of mist also meant that the American 105mm and 155mm batteries' positions could be seen by PLA patrols, and by 1630 hours, out of ten USVUN batteries south, behind Dien Bien Phu, seven had been overrun by PLA storm troopers. Both sides had paid a price, Wang having lost over four hundred men in Freeman's FAE/Snakeye and laser-guided bomb attacks, and the garrison's defenders losing over forty-two gunners, one small consolation being that all but one of the seven American guns overrun had been spiked before being taken and so were of no use to the PLA.

Each commander had now forced the other's hand. Any further delay by one would mean the other would have time to plug the gaps so recently opened.

At 1630 six starlight patrols began edging out from the perimeter east and west of Nam Yum River. Immediately there was trouble, as over half were engaged by PLA snipers, some of whom had come right up to the tree line of the perimeter, forcing the USVUN snipers back into the circle around DEF's triangle.

"Maybe we can try later when it's dark," Leigh-Hastings opined.

"We've got no choice," Berry answered. "Trouble is, they've still got a lot of vegetation on the valley floor, while their artillery has done a real job on ours. We've got nothing but a few dead trees and bare earthworks."

"All the better to see 'em when they rush us, Colonel," Leigh-Hastings said.

"You think they'll rush us?" he asked the Englishman, feigning surprise.

"Mad if they don't, old boy."

There was a screech of incoming, and they instinctively ducked even though they were in the HQ bunkers.

Roscoe came in through the burlap bag flap. "Colonel?"

"What is it?" Berry asked.

"Some of those reinforcements Freeman has sent in—some of Vinh's boys among them—are worried about old tunnels. Some of them are saying their kinfolk fought here against the French, and they think—"

"Jesus!" Berry said. "They think the PLA are using them?"

"Some of 'em, at least, Colonel. That's why there're so many all at once when they come at us from the trees. No movement in the trees during the day—zilch—but come nightfall—"

"Right," Berry said. "Send out probe teams, bayonets, any damn thing you can find."

Ten minutes passed, a long time with barely an hour of daylight left, before squads ventured out from the trenches to probe the earth about the perimeter.

Almost immediately there was the screech of incoming, only this time the bombardment increased, the vibration of the

H.E. shells shaking the earth so violently that streams of dirt were falling from the roof of Berry's bunker. "Some bastard's watching us!" Doolittle said in one of the trenches.

"You don't say," an SAS trooper said.

"I do fucking say, and anybody who shows his scalp'll fucking well lose it!"

"Shut up!" yelled Martinez, still in shock over D'Lupo's death.

In Colonel Berry's bunker the consensus was that the bombardment would not cease till nightfall.

"You think we can stop them?" someone asked Roscoe.

"I don't know. I need to get through to Freeman for TACAIR."

CHAPTER EIGHTY-ONE

AN ARMY IN retreat is never a pretty sight, but with the flooding of the plains north of Disney and the mangled rail line of the culvert in their way, Wang's soldiers were in no mood to be merciful to any escaping POW they found, and eleven escapees from the camp near Ningming were summarily butchered with bayonets, their heads and the remainder of their bodies floating aimlessly in the waist-deep flood fields south of Xiash.

With only five miles in a direct line to go to the border, Shirley Fortescue in PLA uniform, Danny Mellin, and Murphy purposely lengthened their route by heading due east instead of south. It was harder going, but Mellin needed no argument to make his case that it was safer, after the three of them had seen bloodless torsos and heads float by, eyes picked clean.

"Why in hell don't they send in Tomahawks?" Martinez asked, wondering why the *Enterprise* had not weighed in with the wizardry of the terrain-contour-matching guided cruise missiles, the wonder weapons of the Iraqi War. "The carrier too far out?"

Doolittle was about to answer when instead he ducked down in the trench as more incoming slammed into the circle outside DEF's triangle. "No," Doolittle said, "the carrier's close enough in—few hundred miles is no trouble for a Tomahawk—but it's got to have a particular target programmed into it. In Baghdad you had specific buildings, but here all there is is fucking jungle."

"Well," Martinez responded, brushing off mud and dirt from around his neck, "I wish to hell they'd drop a big blue." He meant the 12,500-pound gelled slurry of ammonium nitrate, aluminum powder, and polyethylene soap.

"Gotta be careful with that one," another SAS trooper said. "Drop it too close to us, it'll suck the air right out of *our* lungs, matey, as well as the chinks'."

The tempo of the shelling abruptly increased as the Chinese fired "time on target," the worst form of artillery for the victims, as it is concentrated and coordinated so every round hits simultaneously, saturating the target, in this case the DEF triangle, with high explosive. It was bad news all around, for it meant that in order to mount such a time on target offensive, the Chinese must have restored communications between various gun positions in the hills, despite the earlier *Enterprise* strikes.

Berry ordered no flares be sent up, that starlight-scoped M-16s take the front foxholes on the perimeter. He'd no sooner given the order than he heard, "At the wire!" and the battle of small arms erupted, the USVUN defenders outnumbered four to one in the first wave. The enfilade of fire was deafening, the fighting at the outer perimeter already hand-to-hand, sacrificial Chinese sappers with charges strapped to them hurling themselves at the razor wire, blowing up themselves and gaps through the rolls of wire. The starlights' green, blurry images were shot down with impunity, but the numbers of attacks seemingly never ended, as for every dead man, another rose in his place.

The most effective "hole pluggers" on the USVUN side were the Heckler & Koch automatic grenade launchers throwing a curtain of hot steel at the invaders in three- and five-round bursts from their thirty-two-round ammo box, the only problem being that a number of AGLs were picked off because of the HK AGL's lack of a flash hider. Some of the gunners fixed the problem with improvised fluted flash extinguishers made from meals ready to eat foil-taped to the end of the barrel.

"At the wire, at the wire! Two o'clock! Through the wire! They're through the wire!"

Reports of Chinese breaching the wire were streaming into Berry's bunker in surges of static, audible despite the cacophony of the firefights going on all around the perimeter.

Now the company of Gurkhas among the USVUN forces, having no grenade launchers on their rifles, showed their stuff with bayonet and Gurkha Kukri knife, heads literally rolling down in the mud, grotesque Dantelike figures—torsos that kept running, spurting blood like a gusher before they fell, their blood and mud a greasy mix for all but the surest-footed.

"Second line!" yelled NCOs and officers. "Second line," as the PLA now owned the wire, forcing the allies back to the second line of trenches. Chinese para flares were now descending slowly, turning night to flickering day, illuminating the masses of men—over two thousand—fighting and dying, advancing, withdrawing, at point-blank range.

"Jesus!" came one voice out of all the rest streaming into Berry's bunker. "They're inside the wire! Inside the fucking—"

The voice stopped short, and for a split second Berry didn't understand the full import of the message. Of course he knew they were inside the perimeter wire, but—

Then another voice explained they were "coming up from inside!" They had tunneled *under* the wire and were now coming up well within the circle as well as breaching the wire.

Martinez fired the last of his clip, went to reload, saw the long, stilettolike bayonet of an AK-47 coming at him, then a shot so close to him it left his ears ringing, the Vietnamese soldier having shot the Chinese at point-blank range.

"Thanks," Martinez said, the two of them advancing momentarily until driven back by the grenade concussion. But in that moment, when the Vietnamese had saved his life, for Martinez and for all the other Americans fighting side by side with Vietnamese, 'Nam was now not forgotten, but was in some strange way resolved, and, as is often the case, the old ferocity between the two onetime enemies now underwent that strange metamorphosis in which old enemies join in an equally close friendship as only men who have been under fire can understand and feel.

The Gurkhas in particular put a stop to what Leigh-Hastings described as "this tunnel nonsense!" by not only slitting throats at the tunnels' exits, but going down and creating the only mass panic of the whole Chinese attack: one man in a tunnel a formidable force, effectively blocking the way of the long line of Chinese troops in the tunnel who, in the near pitch-dark, couldn't shoot forward without killing their own. Not one of seven Gurkhas who went down came up, but what they cost the Chinese by comparison was huge, for the pile of mostly headless bodies jammed the tunnels' exits, and now a fifteen-year-old with a .45 could have kept anyone from coming out.

The outer perimeter, however, had collapsed, and the three IFOR columns and the USVUN reserves were stretched in a tight perimeter around the DEF triangle, their concentrated fire hitting the Chinese with a veritable curtain of lead that for a full five minutes was a roar like some great waterfall cascading hundreds of feet over a precipice. The Chinese were driven back, only two or three actually reaching the trench leading to Berry's command bunker, outside of which Kacey fired the Winchester shotgun twice, the sixty darts felling the three would-be intruders.

The Chinese began to withdraw. The defenders surged after them in a final enfilade of fire that filled the valley with sound.

"What d'you think?" Berry asked Leigh-Hastings and Roscoe over the telephone. "They'll hit us again tonight?"

A voice from Leigh-Hastings's bunker at Echo informed Colonel Berry that the major was dead—a stomach wound from a Black Rhino bullet had all but blown him apart, his entrails covering his men nearby and the bunker wall. It was the same kind of story coming in from DEF all over the perimeter—wounds that should not have been critical were of a kind never seen by the two Airborne surgeons at DEF's hospital bunker. Men with shoulder and thigh wounds, normally candidates for recovery, were dead because of the enormous blood loss from the wounds.

"Colonel Berry, sir." It was a sergeant who had just entered the bunker.

"Yes?"

"Sir, we took a few prisoners. The Vietnamese are seeing if they can get some info. Ah, their methods—I mean, they don't seem to like the Chinese very much."

"Can't say I do either," Berry replied, "but limit the rough stuff. Just keep pumping them separately. See if we can get a pattern."

"Yes, sir. Ah, sir, we've got a surprise. I don't think you're gonna like it." With that, the sergeant pulled in a prisoner, a black prisoner in tiger-pattern fatigues, different from the Chinese greens but wearing a PLA helmet. What infuriated Berry wasn't so much that this was probably the MIA gone bad—what had Kacey called him, Pepper?—but the sneering attitude of the man.

"You fools are all dead! You know that?"

"What's your name?" Berry asked.

"Fuck you, man!"

Berry fumed but held his temper, saying only, "Take him away. POW cage."

"You all fucking dead, man!" Pepper yelled. "You all—"

It was only now that Kacey, posted outside, realized that the black man was Pepper. "Well, well, big shot! Whaddya know?"

"You dead too, you motherfucker Oreo!"

"Where's the woman?" Kacey inquired.

"Fuck you, man. Fuckin' Oreo!"

Kacey wished he could escort Pepper to the cage personally, but he had three dead PLA to drag out of his trench.

Roscoe told Berry that he didn't think the Chinese would attack until predawn, "but when they do—" He didn't get to finish his sentence for the PLA artillery started up, and to make matters worse, fog started to roll in. Roscoe called from his bunker and reported the capture of a white woman—no ID tags.

"Huh," Berry said. "So the Chinese gave each one of them a rifle, and they gave up first chance they could. PLA won't like that. We've got Pepper here. No ID tags on him. Yours?"

"Same here. What are we going to do with 'em?" Roscoe asked.

"Same as we do with all the other prisoners. Take 'em back with us, if we ever get out of here. But right now I don't give a damn about those two. What I want is some in-depth defense. I'm going to get a few Skyraiders in here."

"In this fog?"

"We'll use purple smoke. At dawn."

"If they wait."

Meanwhile everyone was ordered to dig deeper around the

DEF triangle, the last line of defense, every man knowing the Chinese now had the circle.

At dawn three of the old warriors of 'Nam—prop-driven Skyraiders—came in to answer Berry's call for jelly. It was not something he wanted to do, because of the terrible danger to his own troops, but he could see no other way—not just of defense, but of survival.

Two miles from the border, in the early-morning moonlight, where flooded paddies gave way to higher ground, Mellin, Murphy, and Shirley Fortescue tried to move cautiously, but it was difficult, their excitement in anticipation of crossing the border, of outlandish dreams of fantastic things such as warmth, soap, clean clothes, good food, perhaps even coffee, dancing in their heads, at odds with their reason, which told them that being in the area where Chinese troops were most concentrated was inherently dangerous. They had no way of knowing the PLA had suffered a major defeat at Disney. They did not even know the hill called Disney was only four miles southwest of them. All they knew for certain was that earlier that day they had seen thousands of PLA troops to the west, trudging northward, following the rail line they had sabotaged. Perhaps the Chinese had won and front-line troops were being recalled? Whatever the situation, they had every intention of avoiding them after the grisly and unspeakable horrors they'd seen around noon, in particular the sight of a severed head having collected flotsam and grass about it in a slimy halo.

Murphy suddenly stopped. Shirley grabbed his arm.

"Danny," Murphy said in a hushed tone. "You hear that?"

"Yeah." It sounded like linoleum tearing, a machine gun in the distance. But whose?

"Let's stay put for a while!" Danny said.

"Good idea," Murphy said. They were near a grove of trees. "I'll take the first watch."

Shirley eased herself to the sodden muddy ground and felt dizzy from fatigue and hunger. After the explosion at the railway, Trang being killed, the horse, she'd had no appetite, but now she was ravenous and reached into the pockets of her PLA uniform and remembered that what few rice balls she'd managed to save were back at the railway in her jeans pockets. She had taken them off and put on the PLA uniform, forgetting in her hurry about the rice. Her sigh of disappointment was audible to Murphy.

"What's up, Shirley?" She told him. He gave her his last ration, but she refused. He insisted, saying if she didn't take it, he'd start swearing again.

Despite her exhaustion, she couldn't help a smile, which he could barely make out in the moonlight. "In that case," she told him, "I'll eat it." When he gave it to her, he folded her fingers over it and kissed them. She was astounded. As far as she knew, Australians only did that kind of thing when they were blind drunk. Maybe it was the concussion of the rail wreck.

The point man on one of Freeman's unofficial border patrols had them in the green circle of his starlight scope, especially the one—a woman, he thought, from the blur that looked like shoulder-length hair—who was wearing a PLA helmet. One of the men had an AK-47, at least that's what it looked like in the moonlight. What to do?

The Skyraiders, six of them now, among the last of their kind, were swallowed by ominous soon-to-be-storm clouds seventy miles west of Hanoi. They went to instrument flying and radio silence. They knew the drill: go in as low as you could, drop the jelly without fuses—so that it wouldn't explode—then leave.

Colonel Berry had thought about requesting a flare ship, a plane with a two-million-candlelight power beam, but to illuminate the area for the drop would also have lit it up for the PLA, enough to encourage them for another rush at the triangle. Berry called Roscoe about the tactical beacon.

"Tacbe on?" Berry inquired.

"Sending out its signal now, sir."

"Soon as we hear them, I want you to have a squad with purple smoke, but don't throw it until I give you the word. I don't want any chink throwin' it back at us. When you throw, make sure you've got it right."

"Affirmative."

Berry passed the word to listen for the planes, but suddenly became alarmed by the fact that all he could hear was a persistent, high-toned ringing in his ears, drowning all other sounds. "Kacey?"

"Sir."

"How's your hearing?"

"Okay, sir."

"Moment you hear those Skyraiders, let me know."

"Yessir."

"And Kacey, what was that between you and the brother?"

"He ain't no brother, sir. He's an asshole."

Berry nodded and walked down through the foggy darkness past Kacey, along the trenches of the DEF triangle. "Anyone here from Foxtrot column?"

"Yo," came the response, but the two men lying in the trench beside him were dead. The other men from Foxtrot, who were piling up bodies on the trench lip for extra cover, hadn't yet reached them.

Berry spoke softly but without alarm. He patted the man who'd answered him and said, "Take their dog tags, son. Medics mightn't get 'round to it."

"Yessir," the soldier replied, but he knew that what Berry was really telling him was that if the Chinese made another attack en masse, there wouldn't be time to take out the dead, no time even for body bags, maybe not even enough time to withdraw to the designated LZ south of Dien Bien Phu in what would be a terrible humiliation for the U.S. No matter that such a defeat would be assigned to USVUN, everyone knew the force majeure was the United States. The soldier, as others were doing all down the line, took off the dead men's tags.

There was sporadic fire in the gloomy fog from both sides, but Berry advised Roscoe and the NCOs to conserve ammo and the men to fire only when they had a definite target. "Men here from Echo?"

"Yessir." He went about bolstering morale in what was now the almost uncanny quiet of the battlefield, the PLA waiting for dawn, Berry waiting for the Skyraiders. He shook hands with Vietnamese NCOs and other troops, a smile here and there for the Airborne as well, and a bracing, "You'll be all right, son," where needed, Berry for a moment like Freeman's double, as he was conscious of doing exactly what Freeman had done in the Battle of Skovorodino. It was a battle Freeman had lost.

The unfused jelly was also one of Freeman's little-known tricks. Hopefully it would work.

At 0530 hours an SAS trooper heard the distant hum of prop-driven planes. The relative slowness of the old faithfuls, the Skyraiders, would allow greater accuracy for the jelly drop, but it would also expose them to much greater danger from any of the PLA's radar-guided triple A flak.

The fog began to lift, but only enough to glimpse enemy positions through the starlight scopes. "Shit, they're everywhere!" Kacey opined. "Like bats in the belfry." He checked his Winchester 1200 for the sixth time in as many minutes, and he could feel the fog's dampness seeping into the marrow of his bones.

It wasn't yet dawn, but over Disney Hill and the surrounding countryside the air had been cleansed by the rain, and the predawn light allowed the point man of Freeman's patrol to discern that it was a Caucasian woman in the PLA uniform, and that the other two were both males, dressed in nondescript clothes—light-colored shirts, one of them in what looked like jeans, the other in baggy shorts. The point man, by hand signal only, ordered the other ten members of the patrol to stay down, for it looked as if the three were headed up the knoll toward them. The point man didn't want to spook the guy with the AK-47. But who in hell were they? They couldn't possibly be some kind of Chinese resistance movement. Or were they?

The six Skyraiders came in V formation and were now peeling off and coming in on the beacon, but Kacey had already heard them and alerted Berry, who in turn told Roscoe and the C.O. of the Airborne.

"Show 'em purple!" Berry ordered, and from all around the DEF triangle violet smoke canisters were fired into the outer perimeter's breached wire, parts of the wire hidden from view, so dense was the outpouring of the smoke. Firing broke out, mainly from the Chinese side, Berry trying to limit the response. Within thirty seconds of the purple smoke canisters, a dozen or so, being thrown to form a rough circle a hundred yards or so from DEF's triangle of trenches, at least three were picked up by PLA and flung back toward the triangle.

Without hesitation Berry rushed out. Four or five men, including a Vietnamese, immediately followed him into the open where, despite the fog, PLA gunners could see them. Berry was cut down in the first burst, as were an SAS and a Delta trooper. Now the triangle opened up in covering fire as the Vietnamese trooper and Doolittle grabbed the flares and flung them back into the mess of outer razor wire before making their way back to the trenches.

The first Skyraider, radio silence now broken, guiding the others, swooped down out of the cloud to no more than two hundred feet above the ground, like some enormous bird of prey in the dawn's early light, and dropped the silvery tanks of napalm just beyond the purple flares. It banked hard left and dropped another tank, and like all the others, it burst in midair into a giant hoselike spray.

Chinese triple A was filling the air with hot metal and tracer, slicing the early-morning mist. The question Roscoe was asking himself was, Would the Chinese go for the trap? Would they attack in the hope of "bear-hugging" the USVUN troops, getting so close in among the Americans that the two remaining big guns beyond Dien Bien Phu would not fire for fear of hitting the DEF triangle, killing more Americans than Chinese?

Another Skyraider swooped by, dropping his "jelly beans" around the violet-smoking perimeter, the plane then suddenly going out of control, the pilot slumping in the seat, a dull bubble of light in the distant fog as it slammed into the eastern sides of the valley.

Suddenly, bugles sounded from beyond the perimeter and the attack en masse began.

"Grenades!" Roscoe shouted, his order repeated on the three sides of the DEF triangle, and the grenades falling mainly from the AGL gunners. The first Chinese had reached the wire when the first grenades exploded among the jelly, and suddenly, like scores of Christmas-tree lights coming alight—only there the similarity ended—the burning fuel air explosive ran like a wildfire through the masses of Chinese troops where the jelly tanks had burst, releasing an aerosoled fuel air explosive like a fine but dense spray all over the perimeter and the troops around it. They were afire. To make doubly sure that all the jelly spray was afire, the five remaining Skyraiders came in with rockets, a tongue of flame licking so close to Foxtrot's position in the DEF triangle that three Americans and two Vietnamese caught fire and burned to death.

Anyone touching the victims suffered the same terrible fate because of the mixture's sticky adhesive quality. Dozens of Chinese with either extraordinary bravery or madness kept running toward the DEF lines, only to be cut down by the concentrated cones of fire that issued forth from Freeman's Special

Forces, Gurkhas, and Airborne. So as not to waste ammunition, each sector of DEF's three lines had been assigned its own cone or field of fire for which each force alone would be responsible. Now the five Skyraiders came in, strafing the wire perimeter to sow further chaos among the PLA troops, another Skyraider downed in the process.

The sheer volume of fire from M-16s, M-60s, AK-47s, AK-74s, type 56s, AGLs, and the rest was of a kind Roscoe had never even imagined possible. The Chinese, most of them burning to some degree, were cut down as though some great arc of scythe had cut through a field of grain. The losses were now so high that neither Wei nor Wang, the latter already dispirited by the defeat at Disney, wanted to persist. And as if to underscore their decision, the forty-three remaining from Echo, Foxtrot, and Delta led a running counterattack charge. The Chinese lines broke and withdrew, their sudden panic not something the victors despised them for, but rather understood as fellow warriors. The combination of U.S. TACAIR and the elite corps of commandos had simply held beyond the point the PLA had thought possible. Only now did Beijing decide to talk—not promise, but talk—about an armistice, a cease-fire to go into effect at noon.

Two hundred fifty miles eastward, where the early-morning light suffused the trees and tall grass in a golden hue, the point man now saw that all three were Caucasian. Not that this made them automatically risk-free, but everyone had heard about the PLA having taken a large number of oil rig workers and the like prisoner. "Freeze!" he shouted.

Within a few hours Mellin, Murphy, and Shirley Fortescue were the center of attention at a press conference, better described as a media feeding frenzy, that was making them famous via CNN. Had they arrived an hour later, the rushed news story of their heroism in breaking the PLA's supply line would have been drowned or at least temporarily shunted aside by the reports coming out of the recently besieged but now victorious garrison at Dien Bien Phu. Among the reports of heavy losses on both sides there was a rumor of two American MIAs from 'Nam having been found by either Captain Roscoe's men and/or by the U.S. Airborne battalion. It was difficult to get any more information, and an exultant yet sober Freeman, the press, and Danny Mellin would have to wait until the victors of Dien Bien Phu returned to either Freeman's HQ at Phu Lang Thuong or Jorgensen's HQ in Hanoi.

As the choppers came in to pick up the body bags of the USVUN force—most of its dead being American and Vietnamese—Kacey was assigned by Roscoe to look after the partially burned and now dead white woman, the one they'd called Salt, and the big-mouth MIA, now POW, the black man called Pepper, his hands now locked behind his back with the serrated plastic zap straps that had replaced regular handcuffs in the Army.

Kacey was surprised by Pepper's postdefeat mood. He thought that the death of the white woman would have plunged Pepper into the depths of despair. On the contrary, Pepper was elated, with the tremendous sense of release that surges through the body after the narrowest of escapes, the law of averages dictating that he should have perished with the rest of his PLA colleagues, as Salt had.

"I guess," Kacey said, "you were right up front of the charge, huh?"

Pepper spat contemptuously.

"Nah," Kacey continued, "you're a shit bag. You were in the rear, right? I mean, some Charlie sticking a bayonet up your ass to keep you moving, otherwise you'd be back with your dope, right?"

Pepper smiled malevolently. "What were you doin', motherfucker? Jerkin' yourself off in a trench?" He spat again.

Kacey could still see the terrified look on the little girl with the grenade, her lying there like some discarded rag doll. "Get on the fuckin' slick, man," he ordered Pepper. But the chopper was so full of wounded, there was no room and they had to wait another half hour until there was a chopper with space for them.

The more Kacey thought about the girl, the more he felt like shooting Pepper right then and there—"accidental discharge." The money and time they'd waste on this son of a bitch didn't bear thinking about.

Finally there was a chopper free and Kacey, dumping Salt's body bag in first, ordered Pepper into the chopper. He made him sit on the floor, gave the pilot the thumbs-up, and they were off the ground, quickly gaining altitude till they reached a thousand feet. Pepper was whining loudly about not being able to sit on a seat.

"Here!" Kacey yelled. "Turn around, you prick. I'll undo the cord and you can sit up."

Pepper turned his back to Kacey, who took his knife, cut the plastic cord, and kicked Pepper out. Prisoner trying to escape. *Fuck 'im.*

When the chopper landed, Kacey saw a white guy coming over to him. "I hear you've got a—" He stopped and looked at the body bag. The rotors had not stopped turning. "A white woman," he called out, "an MIA."

Kacey nodded at the body bag.

"Can I—" Danny Mellin began, and Kacey zipped open the bag.

"Pretty badly burned . . ."

The khaki shirt looked as if it had melted into her—she smelled like burnt chicken—but there was enough of her face visible that, with his heart pounding, he knew it wasn't her. "Oh Jesus!" he said, and walked away, tears in his eyes.

In another piece of identification in Hong Kong, there was considerably more difficulty because, while the people's police were sure that the victim was the rich and powerful owner of the penthouse—Mr. Jonas Breem, head of Chical Enterprises and South Asia Industries—the killer, whoever he or she was, had used some new kind of bullet. The victim was shot shortly after he'd ejaculated, and his face had been obliterated, so it was doubtful that a positive ID could be made by dental records.

There was no problem, however, in Phu Lang Thuong for Pierre LaSalle in identifying his own voice and that of Marte Price on the tape that she told him she would send his wife if he ever used the pix of General Freeman putting one of his badly wounded men out of his misery.

Lee Chow, the representative of the People's Republic of China at the U.N., in New York, said that Beijing was willing to discuss the multinational exploitation of all islands, including the Spratlys, in the South China Sea.

WWIII:
RAGE OF BATTLE

From beneath the North Atlantic to across the Korean peninsula, thousands of troops are massing, protected by the most stunning armaments ever seen on any battlefield. The war that once seemed impossible is raging everywhere: Every nation, every individual, is both hunter and prey.

WWIII:
WORLD IN FLAMES

NATO armored divisions have escaped near-certain defeat in the Soviet-ringed North German Plain. Russian MiG-25s and Sukhoi-15s are unable to maintain air superiority over the western Aleutians....On every front the once impossible war blazes its now inevitable path of worldwide destruction.

WWIII:
ARCTIC FRONT

In the worst Siberian winter in twenty years, blizzards are wreaking havoc with U.S. air cover, and the Siberians are ahead. Their forebears had destroyed the Wehrmacht at Stalingrad. Now they would do the same to the Americans—unless the highly unorthodox U.S. General Freeman could devise a breakout.

WWIII:
WARSHOT

General Cheng is massing his divisions on the Manchurian border. To the west, Siberia's Marshal Yesov is readying his army. Their aim: To drive the American-led U.N. force back to the sea.

The counterstrike: Unleash the brilliant American General Douglas Freeman. If this eagle can't whip the bear and the dragon, no one can....

WWIII:
ASIAN FRONT

At Manzhouli, near the border of China, Siberia, and Mongolia, the Chinese launch their charge into the woods. There is the roar of fire—and from the other side, a response of explosives. Suddenly the sky is aglow with phosphorous flares like shooting stars as the ChiComs' four missiles streak toward the B-52s. It's all-out war.

WWIII:
FORCE OF ARMS

Three Chinese armies swarm across the trace, with T-59s providing cover. The Chinese armor, T-60 tanks, 85mm guns, and 90,000 PLA regulars rush in. Four sleek, eighteen-foot-long Tomahawk cruise missiles are headed for Beijing. It is Armageddon in Asia.

The World War III series
by Ian Slater
Published by Fawcett Books.
Available in bookstores everywhere.